*It's the nigl

Tessa and Richie
In a moment, they will both be shot!
Imagine how everyone's life might have changed if
Tessa had survived.

He's coming for me, Duncan!

Duncan threw his arms around Tessa – the woman he loved more than his own life – as if by this act and his force of will alone he could somehow halt the impending nightmare which was unfolding around them.

She released him and, reaching up, threaded her fingers through her Highlander's hair which had fallen to his shoulders.

"I finally understand what you have felt all these centuries – what it feels like to have another human being trailing you for your head. But now it's my fate that's coming to a head and I must act. You can't sense his presence, and there is nothing you can do to stop this."

Highlander *Imagine*: For Love's Sake

An **RK Books** production
www.RK-books.com

ISBN: 978-0-977-7110-5-5   ISBN: 0-977-7110-5-6

Highlander *Imagine* Series

RK Books and **RK Productions, LLC**
are owned by **Royal Knight, Incorporated**

This edition was printed for on-demand distribution
By **Lightning Source** in the USA.

First edition
First printing: May, 2015
Second printing: November, 2015

Cover photograph from Davis-Panzer Productions Inc.
Back cover photo provided by Mariel Bordoni

Highlander *Imagine*: For Love's Sake

A NOVEL BY

WENDY LOU JONES
&
LILIANA BORDONI

RK BOOKS

Chapter One

The quiet beeping of an infusion pump by her bed roused Tessa once again and she opened an eye. Surgery had ended hours ago. The anesthesia had worn off in recovery. A sterile, monotonous, dove-pastel wallpapered room, with white curtains that were partially pulled on the off side of her bed, greeted her sense of sight once again.

Did you really expect to see something different this time? This is the room the attendants brought you to after your surgery. You're supposed to be resting not critiquing the décor, her subconscious mind replied a bit snarky.

Something is different this time, her conscious mind thought back in counterpoint. *Light—reflecting from somewhere.* Turning her head brought an unexpected ache to her side and she winced. *The window –it was dark before. There is light now—it's finally morning.*

The flood of light that greeted her eye was painful and she shut her eye tightly against the photonic assault. *Even light hurts now—why can't it be gentle?* She needed something gentle by her side – not the infusion pump which beeped intermittently, not the IV lines which she was tethered to—she needed Duncan's touch.

Sleep—try to sleep, the subconscious echo droned once again. *Sleep will make it all go away.*

"No—I don't want to go there again—not again." She moaned, almost a whisper, as she began drifting off once again.

An explosion—then another! Two shots rang out in rapid succession, the space between them measured in a fraction of a heartbeat—her heartbeat. Over and over again the scene replayed with crystal clarity—like some macabre clip from an internal horror movie she could not shut out. But this wasn't a movie. It was her life, and it had just about ended. The shooting, only hours old, was happening once again.

The boy, scarcely a teenager, shaking and uncertain, shouting, demanding their money—anything!

"*What? Is this it?*" she heard herself speaking to herself in her thoughts. "*A holdup going bad—he's terrified—there's death in his outstretched trembling hand.*"

*Tessa, you have always had a comeback to what life throws at you. Why didn't you just—*a half-dozen shoulda coulda woulda's surfaced, then a hundred more. *Throw something—hit the ground—attack him –I could've done so many things.*

"No you couldn't—there wasn't time. There never is. There wasn't time—time is your enemy. It always will be."

No, wait!

A flash of light from the barrel—the explosion! *Richie was closer to him than I was. He must have seen his finger tighten on the trigger.* His arm had suddenly been in the way of a bullet that had already been fired—suddenly reaching out to knock her to the ground, and suddenly pierced. The bullet, aimed squarely at her chest, had struck the outstretched arm. That first shot had hit his arm, shattering the thinner ulna bone, and was deflected before it had struck the right side of her chest and arm. The second shot had hit Richie in mid-motion, catching him squarely in the chest. Richie had collapsed against her, throwing them both to the ground.

An explosion! This time, it wasn't the gun but her world. *My world is exploding around me.* Blood spattered her face and her clothing. Stunned, only half-hearing and half seeing as the teenager ran, she felt the slick wet sensation of blood covering her arm and hand.

Am I bleeding? Was I hit? There was pain in her chest, her side, and in her arm as she struggled in vain to sit up.

"Richie?" Her voice was just a thin whimper. *Had she felt him gasp?*

Richie was partially draped across her—blood running from the gaping wound in his chest and arm was mingling with hers.

Her shock benumbed brain fought through the pain and she propped partially up on her uninjured arm as Richie's head slid to her lap. She heard him draw his last mortal breath.

"Time is your enemy," she heard another half of her submerged self-chide. *"It can never be your friend—you are mortal—you are dying."*

No, Richie was there, he saved my life! I'm alive, here and now. Whoever you are, you can't take that from me. I'm alive I say!

In another room and in another place, Duncan sat with his face in his hands. His mind was also rewinding the horror of what had happened only hours ago.

Duncan wiped his face once then flipped the computer on. *This was too close,* he thought. Close enough for all his fears to surface again. A 400 year-old pain was arising from deep inside his heart with the force of an iceberg finally freed after centuries of being hidden below the frozen water. But that was Tessa. The same Tessa that made him feel young every time he looked at her, every time he touched her.

She is going home with me now, he reassured himself. A timid smile crossed his worried face for a microsecond at the thought of what was to come. *Better focus on what you have to do here and now.*

'Access denied,' the computer returned once again.

How he hated those two words! *What password could a lunatic like this man have used? Come on—Tessa will be waiting by the car. I want to get her as far away from this place as I can—focus, Duncan, focus.* He typed in another combination then hit the return. *This will happen again and again,* his mind replayed an all too familiar phrase he'd told her before all of this had begun.

"I know," had been her simple acceptance of a life she could only be a temporary guest to.

Then, why can't I accept it now? he reminded himself. He knew why. This time, it had been too close. This time, he had admitted to himself that it was not a question of *if* I lose her, but merely *when* I lose her. And he was too tired. Maybe the loss of Darius was just making him feel nostalgic. *Tessa is waiting—focus—you are wasting precious time.*

An explosion, then another! Two shots rang out in rapid succession, the space between them measured in a fraction of a heartbeat—Duncan's heartbeat. An icy chill shot down his spine. *Run, move, do something,* his mind had prodded.

Hands, Tessa thought as she lay in her hospital bed. Her inner vision shifted. *Hands, reassuring hands are here. Hands reaching out to touch me, to heal my spirit, to make my world whole.* Warm thoughts flooded her mind once again. *Her Highlander was by her side – Duncan MacLeod.* Carefully lifting Richie from across her, he was laying him beside her.

"Duncan, he's dead. It all happened so fast. Richie—"

His hands were moving swiftly to examine her. She saw the worry clouding his features.

"Shh, please don't try to move or speak, Tess. I'll get you to a hospital as fast as I can," he said. As carefully as he could, he was scooping her into his strong grasp.

"But Richie—"

"I'll get him in a moment. Let me get you settled in." With the utmost care, he lowered her into the seat and secured her, then popped the trunk and fetched Richie.

"What are you doing with him, Duncan?"

Closing the hatch, he quickly swung into the car. "Richie will become an Immortal now. We all knew he was destined for this someday—just not this way—and not so soon." Duncan shook his head. "He'll come back eventually, and he can't be seen like this at the hospital. You need help now—we can't wait for him."

Because you won't come back, the unspoken words were mirrored in her thoughts. This added a silent period to the end of her cold fear.

"Time," the voice chimed in her thoughts, erasing the image only hours old.

Leave me alone, she snapped to her unseen mental specter. *Duncan is here, with me. My world and my time. I have time with him now.*

"You are mortal".

"Get out!" she moaned audibly.

"Are you in pain?" The male voice queried quietly.

She opened her eyes to slits. She was in pain, but not the kind an injection could ever make go away. The center of her world had been fractured by a bullet this night, one whose lethal trajectory had been deflected by a soon-to-be Immortal; one that had threatened to forever separate her from her Highlander, her unswerving gentleman, her patient immortal lover. No one could ever understand that kind of trust, intimacy, and the secret he had shared with her – the one she too now had the burden of guarding so ardently with him. Her pain was for an Immortal. *Oh God, Duncan, where are you? I need you so much right now.*

Looking up to the young male nurse she forced a wan smile. "Yes," she replied weakly. "I do ache. I could use something to help me rest more comfortably."

He obliged her with an injection into her IV line.

Maybe I can get some uninterrupted sleep, at least for a while.

"Time," the faint echo sounded.

But the voice was too late to catch her as the drug took effect.

Chapter Two

Sergeant Richard Berry's pencil paused in mid mark. He flipped the heavily noted pages back and forth, adjusted his glasses, and then exhaled. Tapping the well-worn eraser against his furrowed brow, he looked up to Richie once again.

"I know you're giving me all you've got, but it's still not a lot to go on." He flipped back to the beginning of the report. "Let's see if I got it. The two of you and Miss Noel went out for a moonlight drive. You picked a nice spot under some trees on a quiet street to run short on gas." He glanced up and over the rim of his heavy glasses to Duncan and Richie.

"Two guys and one woman—uh-huh."

Duncan gave him a blissful smile. "It's the 90s, Sergeant."

Clearing his throat, he returned to his report. "You take a walk – ostensibly to locate a gas station. As soon as you're away, a Caucasian male, maybe sixteen to eighteen-years, comes out of nowhere with his cap pulled down so only his face showed in the streetlight. He asks Mr. Ryan for a ride—a distraction—then he pulls a gun."

"A few curls stuck out on one side—I think they were a reddish color. And then there's the jacket. I couldn't miss that it had a large Indian head on it. The hair—" he paused and gestured down the middle of his head, "it was right down the middle."

"A Mohawk," Duncan supplied once again, casting a frustrated glance around the Spartan walls of the cramped office.

They had already been over the entire story more times than he cared to remember, and still this conversation was only going in circles. *Why are we still sitting here? You have an eyewitness. Why aren't we doing something to find the man that almost killed my Tessa?* Duncan thought as he ran a hand over his face and silently told himself to calm down. They had been here for hours, the night was almost over and he was very tired; more than just tired, he was emotionally exhausted.

"OK, OK. I've got the jacket already. So the jacket is the only really unique thing about this attacker." Leaning back, his chair groaned as the dry wood shifted ever so slightly. "Son, if I was that attacker and I knew that this was the only thing that could identify me, I would lose that jacket as fast as possible in the fire."

Richie rubbed his tired temple—his half-zipped jacket gaped slightly. Bouncing to his feet, he gestured wide with an arm. "That's all I've got, man. It happened so fast, and he was gone just as fast."

The back of MacLeod's hand bumped purposefully against Richie's side and he sat down once again.

"You're lucky to be alive, Richie." He pulled off his glasses and cleaned a smudge. "When someone with a gun panics, they usually don't stop with one shot. I want the name of that guardian angel who must have been standing next to you. You've given me all you can now. I'll get a statement from Miss Noel when she's able. She may have seen a little more."

"Yeah," Richie snorted absently. *A lot more,* he thought, rolling his eyes. *She saw me die. I doubt if anything could top that.*

Duncan shot him a sideways knowing glance. *Keep a lid on it. You're lucky his glasses are off and he's just as tired as we are.*

Richie rubbed his eyes with the palms of both hands then exhaled, exasperated.

"Where do we go from here, Sergeant?" Duncan leaned forward. "He's out there somewhere right now. He may try to kill someone else. You must have a patrol in that area. They could be searching."

"More than one." He put his glasses back on. "Before this gets any older I'm going to put out an APB for this guy. People who are this freaked out make mistakes. Just maybe one of my people will get lucky and spot this guy on the street. It would help if I had the name of your guardian angel." He managed a half smile then rose, shaking his head. "If they see anyone fitting this description—even in general, we can invite them in to clear their name, as we like to say it."

As he started toward the door, Duncan and Richie rose to follow. "You two just wait here. I'm going to get our sketch artist in here. That way my people will at least have something visual to go on." "Officer," he called to a young tall man, as he leaned out the open door. "Go grab our sketch artist. I saw him down the hall a couple hours ago, third door – left," he waved him in the direction with the report still in his hand.

"And bring something hot—a coffee—whatever is down there, anything for these people. They can use it."

Duncan and Richie settled back into their still-warm chairs.

"Is this ever going to end, Mac? I mean, he could be in Timbuktu by now."

"Not unless he can swim the ocean, then trek through the West African nation of Mali," he quipped trying to make light of the exhaustion he felt and the absurdity of the matter. "Then there's always that pesky Sahara desert in your way." He sent a good natured slap to Richie's shoulder.

A nondescript man poked his head in and identified himself as the artist. A loud voice halted him, and he apologetically said he would be back with a pad in a few minutes then disappeared.

A moment later, the young officer appeared with two cups of piping hot coffee in his hands. His name bar said 'K. Kilgore'

"Here you go. Got it fresh out of the machine." Handing them the Styrofoam cups, he quickly reached into his uniform pocket for the creamer and sugar he had hastily grabbed from the cafeteria condiment cart.

Richie took a short sip as the steam rose.

"Someone is awake at this time of night," Duncan said, looking at the crisply starched uniform which lacked so much as a wrinkle.

The young officer straightened, squared his tie and smiled.

"Just came on duty about half-an-hour ago. When you're new, it pays to be wide awake and spit-polished at three o'clock in the morning." He took a few steps to the side of his Sergeant's desk, glancing at the few scribbled notes on several random sheets which remained on top. His position afforded him a view of Richie's arm.

"Is it that early already?" Duncan asked, taking a sip of his hot coffee.

"Yup," he said not glancing to Duncan. His eyes were on Richie's bloody sleeve, the gaping entrance and exit holes visible. *Your sleeve is shot through,* he mentally made a note as his line of sight flashed between the half-open jacket and the sleeve. A red-stained shirt, though fairly concealed, was still partially visible.

"Were you wounded as well?" he asked, concern coloring his voice, as he reached for Richie's arm. "Everyone on the floor has already heard you were in a shooting. I can get you some help?"

Duncan gave Richie a discrete but deliberate elbow in the side.

"Ah, me—no," he withdrew his arm as casually as he could make it seem. Glancing to Duncan, he saw him eyeing his open jacket and quickly zipped it up.

"No, Tessa was bleeding—I was trying to help her—she was on the ground and my jacket—" He shrugged. *A smooth line and a smile, don't fail me now,* Richie thought as he tried to palm it all off as if all this young, eager-beaver officer had seen was a threadbare piece of cloth.

A fortunate turn of fate bailed him out. The sketch artist returned, and hastily seating himself in the Sergeant's chair, opened his pad. Nodding a polite dismissal to the young officer, he took out his pencil and eraser block.

"I hope you catch him soon," Kevin Kilgore said as he reached for Richie's empty cup.

"I'm sure the police will," Duncan said absently then added, "Thanks for the coffee."

"I'll be around if you need anything else this morning." He left for his desk in the corner. *There was a bullet hole straight through that sleeve—the front of his shirt was stained red.* He replayed the observations over and over in his mind. Tossing the cups in the waste basket, he reached into the inner pocket of his jacket, which was hung over his chair, and retrieved a small palm notebook. Glancing at the time, he opened it and began making notes. The small button on his sleeve pinched his left wrist—*it is still a little sore,* he thought as he undid the button momentarily to carefully rub the spot. The Watcher's tattoo was still new.

Chapter Three

Corporal Jacob Sandowski, 'Sandy' as he preferred to be called, quickly unscrewed the thermos and poured himself a second cup.

"Do you want another cup, or are you good?" His peripheral vision caught sight of his partner's hand waving him off. He had taken advantage of a red light to pour himself a cup. *Oh well, it's just after three a.m.—no one is in a hurry behind us.* He recapped the thermos jug in no particular hurry then drove on.

A soft-spoken career man in his early forties, almost 6 foot tall with a slender build and light brown hair, that was pie-balding right on schedule, Sandy had been with the police force for most of his working life.

"This is the kind of night I like, Duke—absolutely nothing happening."

Sergeant Duke Maxim gave a noncommittal "Uh-huh." In stark contrast to Sandy's modest muscular features, 'Duke' as he preferred to be called around the police force, was built like a bull. For all his five-and-one-half foot height, his heavy muscular neck and shoulders, along with his rock solid abs, made him very formidable in hand-to-hand combat. He never lost a match at the police force proving grounds.

The squad car's computer blinked its annoying green-screen message alert cursor, and Duke pulled the screen around to read what was coming across.

"So much for your absolutely nothing night. We've got an APB coming through."

"Oh, that's just great. What's happened and where?"

"Some teenage scumbag just shot a woman a couple of miles from our position then ran. His description is pretty so-so. More details about the jacket than the kid. He'll probably lose that thing in the first trashcan he passes. It's just after three a.m. now. Let's see what we can shake out of the bushes in that area. By this time, any self-respecting drunk is either passed out in the park or on their couch at home. So anyone – male of any description that we find still kicking around the streets, we're going to stop and question." Pausing, he passed a finger over several lines of text then added. "If we do stop someone, you let me take the walk. Dispatcher thinks the shooter was either freaked out or a psycho."

"I'm wearing my Kevlar vest," Sandy replied. "I could take the walk."

"Yeah, and I've got my Fruit-of-the-Loom underwear on too," he retorted in a good-natured, but sarcastic tone. "That isn't going stop a bullet to the head. You let me take the walk if we run into anyone. The last thing I need is for you to get your brains shot out by a nut-case."

Duke and Sandy had been a virtually inseparable team on the police force for years. Like brothers, they watched each other's backs, when they took a call they were by each other's sides–and in those rare times, when there was real danger, they went in with guns drawn together. Though Duke always pushed Sandy behind himself when he could, Duke knew he could count on Sandy whenever he needed him.

Sandy fell silent then shrugged an '*OK*'. The willingness of his partner to persistently place himself in front of mortal danger never once escaped Sandy's grateful notice. He knew that this late 30-ish looking man, with distinct Roman features, was a very special partner indeed. Duke Maxim, an Americanized version of his real given name–Ducanus Marcus Maximinus, had been the Captain of the elite recruitment of Roman citizens—the Praetorian Guard. Millenniums old beyond his appearance, he was an Immortal.

Flashback – Rome, 25 AD/CE:

Ducanus Marcus Maximinus stamped the dust from his sandals as he entered the garrison building in Rome. The streets were dusty, dry, and a hot wind had been blowing all day long—too hot for a *Martius* (March) day. The thermal bath was calling. Thermal springs were warm and soothing and his tired muscles could use it. He would be able to lose the street dust there for another evening. Leaning his spear against a column he clapped his hands.

"Something to drink," he shouted in the direction of a loose knot of men near the far column. A young man darted out of the group dressed modestly in the garb of a slave. Bowing briefly as he approached, he handed Ducanus a pewter cup filled with liquid. He drank then indicated he wanted more. The slave obliged him. While drinking was not allowed on duty, or in the garrison, a low-grade wine was permitted in the Praetorian Guard's quarters. He'd get something a lot better later. Sending the slave on his way, he unstrapped his helmet.

"Captain," an unfamiliar voice called from the door. "My master, Senator Taren, is outside. He sends for you."

Securing his helmet once again, Ducanus followed the slave to the waiting man.

"Hail Caesar," the Senator said blandly as Ducanus approached.

Ducanus gave a casual salute—fist to his breastplate but remained silent.

The Senator casually glanced to the few on the street beyond the garrison. "I'm hosting a private celebration this evening and will require your, as well as four or five of your most trustworthy soldier's, presence for—ah—guest control. This gathering is strictly by invitation only."

"All of my men are trustworthy, Senator."

"Of course—I misspoke. I should have said, *discrete.* My wife is about her usual trip to the oracle in Delphi."

Ducanus stifled a knowing grin. He had served as guest control for the Senator on such previous occasions when his wife was away—the best time for a self-affirmed, dignified Senator to host a private Bacchanal.

The festival of Bacchus, the Roman god of wine and drunken orgies, was generally acknowledged around mid-Martius. However, its public celebration had been outlawed for almost 200 years in Rome because of the degree to which depravities had been carried out in the past. *No matter*, thought Ducanus, *he always pays well for discretion.*

The sun had set when Ducanus and his men took their post at the Senator's party. Some of the guests were already inside and more were arriving. The Senator met one particular group at the door and personally ushered them in.

Suddenly Ducanus sensed the presence of another Immortal. Casually, he looked about—his hand perched on the pommel of his sword. The street before him was almost empty—only the occasional mortal man passed by.

Whoever it is must be inside, he thought. Ducanus and his men were expected to stand their posts unless summoned. He wanted to know who this was so he waited a long moment before nodding to the nearest soldier. He then slipped quietly inside as the guard took up his Captain's former post.

Ducanus took up a discrete position just inside the house. All around, on dais and lounge, were examples of the Senator's *social elite* engaged in debauchery. Their carnal pastimes sparked no interest in him. He had no taste for such crude self-indulgences. *Where is that Immortal?* His immortal sense of presence told him another Immortal was near – somewhere close by. But, he dare not investigate further unless he was summoned.

A loud female voice rose from a group of guests in the next room. The voice, astonished at first, quickly took on an angry tone. A moment later, a slave hurried from the room toward the door. Seeing Ducanus, he quickly motioned for him to come. This was the break he needed and he took it.

Near the far corner of the room, there stood Methos–fully clothed in a perfectly wrapped toga, blithely sipping his wine; before him was a woman–dressed in the gaudiest, revealing attire imaginable and having an utter meltdown!

"All I said, my dear *plucked* flower of Rome (prostitute), is that stimulation, or should I say its *art*, comes in many forms – all of which have long abandoned you," he finished with poetic flare and the driest of sarcasm. He popped another grape into his mouth.

Utterly furious at the insult to her and the profession, she shouted at this party guest who obviously had the eyesight and desires of an aging eunuch.

"Well! I have never been so insulted! I'm one of the most desirable, highest paid free whore in all of Rome!"

"And I don't doubt you are," Methos continued, downing another hand full of grapes and cheese. "Probably sing stories as well while you work–though I fear most are off-key and of only one crude flavor. All in all, too strong for a man of my delicate stomach."

In a fit of rage, the woman grabbed a half filled tray and flung it at him.

Methos easily dodged the culinary projectile, but not the irate woman's temper. She was about to lunge at him when Ducanus stepped in between them.

"What's the problem here? Oh, hello Methos," he added with a look of mock surprise.

"Well, well, if it isn't Captain Ducanus Maximinus of the Praetorian Guard. What a surprise to see you here," he replied with a deceptively innocent smile.

"Not really," he shot back in an equally smooth tone. "The good Senator insists his guests follow house *etiquette* at all his social gatherings. My men are here to remind everyone that they are in a dignified home."

Out of the corner of his eye, Methos saw the irate woman seize the host and appear to be giving him an ear-full of complaints. The host, summoned the head house slave, spoke briefly to him then quickly slid out of the room with the woman. The slave approached.

"I'm sorry, but the Senator has insisted that you leave at once."

"Why am I being evicted?"

"Indecency."

"In an orgy? Is that even possible?" Methos replied and looked about, a very real wide-eyed expression on his face. He didn't have to look far before it was obvious that this was a trumped-up charge. "I never once touched that woman, or any other for that matter."

"That's the problem."

"And you're still fully clothed. Come on, you're leaving," Ducanus added with a wide toothy grin. Grabbing Methos' arm he propelled him toward the door.

Methos considered a hundred snappy replies to that comeback but decided in favor of silence for the moment—at least while he was being strong-armed out of the house.

Once outside, Ducanus' hand dropped firmly and purposefully to the pommel of his sword.

Methos caught the motion out of the corner of his eye and froze. Staring questioningly into the face of this immortal Roman, his mind went into overdrive.

Will he play by the rules of immortal combat—discreet confrontation away from the eyes of his mortal men—one-on-one, swords in both combatants' hands? Or, would he try to take advantage of this situation with his men sworn to silence? He hoped he knew Ducanus to be a better Immortal than this. He was being held in an awkward, poorly defendable position. *He could run me through without a moment's notice. I could die in his hands right here,* thought Methos. *And, it's a short drag to the next street ending with my head and my Quickening.* His mind juggled options.

"I believe you're still on duty," he said in a quiet probing voice.

Ducanus discretely looked around. His men were unmoved from their posts. Glancing back to Methos, he quietly released him then spoke formally.

"The Senator has requested that you leave his gathering this evening," he said loudly enough for his immediate men to hear then he returned to stand his post.

Methos breathed a sigh of relief and walked away. Though he was a skilled swordsman, he didn't want to have to face a fully armored Praetorian Guard.

Chapter Four

The precinct hallways were becoming busier as Duncan and Richie wended their way through the building to the car park.

"They're never going to find this kid. He's probably crawled down some crack in the earth and is hold up by now."

"Richie, we just spent over two hours in there. You've given them quite a bit to go on. Give the police a chance, will you?"

Richie gave a frustrated shake of his head and, stepping in front of Duncan, continued walking backwards instep without missing a beat. "Mac, the moment that kid thinks the coast is clear he'll blow town and no one will ever see him again. We should go after him now."

People were coming down the hallway with more frequency as they neared the car park, and Richie was getting a bit loud. His last line had turned a few heads.

"Keep your voice down." Duncan took a deep breath and stopped, looked about quickly then moved purposefully to a row of doors along the corridor. The second knob he tried turned. Patting Richie's jacket sleeve, they went in and closed the door.

"The last thing you want to do in a police station is give people the idea you're about to blow out of here on a vendetta. You're an Immortal now—you just can't start killing mortals."

"That guy? Why the hell not? He almost killed Tessa—and for what? Mac, if I hadn't been standing right where I was, she'd be on a slab right now."

Duncan reached quickly and purposefully to Richie, wrapped his arms around him, then looked briefly to the ceiling—to nothing in particular—as his eyes misted over with unspoken emotions welling up in his heart. The manly embrace, ending in a backslapping, lasted only an instant, but spoke volumes as to the depth of the *thank you* in Duncan's heart for the life of his precious love he had saved. Duncan's eyes were wet when Richie's met them, and they both glanced briefly away. Duncan passed a hand over his tired face, pushing the loose hair back, clearing his eyes momentarily.

"Richie, I can't even begin to find the words to express how I'm feeling right now. How do I say thank you to someone who just gave up their only chance at a relatively safe, mortal existence to save a mortal woman so I can continue to love her for another couple of decades? That's far from a fair exchange for you."

Richie shuffled uncomfortably. "Mac, you don't have to say it."

"Yes, I do. I have to say it, or the feeling in here will rip its way out. I love Tessa – more than I have loved any woman in centuries since I left my home. She has become a part of me – my soul – more so than I had ever realized until she was kidnapped. The thought of her dying on that cold concrete last night – I don't think I could bear to go on. If it were at all possible right now, I would gladly give her whatever part of my life makes me an Immortal so she didn't have to suffer, and I would take her place in that hospital." He smoothed his hair again, exhaustion taking its toll.

"Look, I was there—it was happening—it was an instinctive reaction because Tessa mean a lot too—"

"Thank you," Duncan said quietly and turned to face Richie. "Thank you for giving up so much for a woman who means more to me than life. You are one of us now, and that means you're part of the Game, and in immortal danger of losing your head. You just can't go running off untrained. I just can't—". His voice faded out betraying his thoughts and feelings. *I just can't bear the thought of losing you either, my son.*

Richie broke the silence. "Look," he began softly, "I haven't lived even a fraction of the time you've been alive. But there's one thing I know how to do and that's run when I have to. I'm sure you'll have me armed and dangerous soon enough. Until you do, I'm not going to stand there and let some Immortal hack my head off. Don't worry."

"There is more you need to know about all of this than just fighting. You need to know the immortal Rules. I just don't want you to go off on your own right now."

Richie tucked a hand in his jacket pocket and turned briefly away toward a stack of empty boxes lining a wall. "I understand what you're saying, but he's out there – and if I find that bastard, I'm going to kill him."

"Don't," Duncan said very quietly, with painful wisdom in his deep brown eyes. "Don't start then you won't have to stop yourself—the way I did."

"Is that what this is all about, Mac? About something you regretted doing in one of those wars you fought in centuries ago? He shot me too you know – he deserves it."

"You're an Immortal."

"He didn't know that—and had I not been, I'd be lying on a slab myself right now. Look, I'm not planning on leaving a trail of bodies in my wake every time I leave the house for a loaf of bread. But that guy—no way."

"Richie, he thinks you're dead. As an Immortal, one of our Rules is if you are killed in public you must leave the area for a generation, about fifty to one-hundred years. You cannot appear to people who know you've died. To do so, you risk revealing you are an Immortal. None of us can risk that."

"He didn't stick around to take my pulse. Besides, when I find him, he's not going to be around to talk about it."

Duncan hung his head. "I'm exhausted. I can't stop you. All I'm asking is for you to come home with me, get into something that isn't bloody and shot up, then get some sleep. We both need it. We need to be thinking with clear heads – that's all I'm asking now."

He looked at his watch. His eyes focused with difficulty.

"It's almost five a.m. We have to get cleaned up and get a little rest. Tessa will be awake soon and I don't want her to see me this exhausted."

Richie reluctantly nodded. Leaving their confessional room, they made their way to Duncan's car.

Chapter Five

The squad car turned slowly onto the next block as Sandy updated their position with dispatch. They had been joined in the manhunt by two other vehicles – no one had seen anything in the past two hours. It was early dawn and traffic was starting to pick up as people began heading out for the early shift. A jogger and a biker presented Duke and Sandy with momentary adrenalin surges until they realized they were looking at the wrong gender.

"I could have sworn that last one was a man – or at least a boy, Duke."

"You don't get out enough," Duke replied dryly as his eyes continued to scan the bush-lined properties and porches of the homes. "We're almost a mile from the original shooting site," he added. "If we don't see something soon, let's double back."

"What makes you think he's near the scene yet?"

"The woman's companion said he was on foot – running down the street. They didn't say he hopped a bike or got into a car."

"He could have later – as soon as he was out of sight."

Duke shook his head. "It's possible that he was parked out of sight, but I don't think so. Something about all of this doesn't sound like he planned much of a getaway. He may not live far from where he shot the woman or, there could be someone else involved."

"Interesting theory. No one mentioned a gang."

"No, not a gang – just not alone. Just a feeling." Duke scanned the computer monitor. "There is a new report in here," his finger moved down the field. "Suspicious circumstances at a Tudor house very near where the shooting occurred were just reported. Door was found open – someone is investigating now. The owner apparently wasn't at home. I wonder if this isn't somehow connected to the shooting."

"Usually is when it's that close. Anything further in the report?"

"No, not yet."

Duke's eye caught movement in the next block up ahead and he motioned for Sandy to speed up a bit and kill the headlights. The movement was a bit erratic. Whoever it was, was hugging the bushes as they walked along.

Sandy took his foot off the accelerator, letting the car roll toward the pedestrian. Suddenly he stiffened.

"Nothing wrong with my eyes, Duke. Take a look at that jacket."

"I've got him." Duke switched on the side flood light and called. "Police! Sir, stop a moment! We'd like to speak to –,"

The boy bolted like a rabbit!

Duke threw the squad car's door open before Sandy could stop and gave chase. Sandy called into dispatch and followed as far as he could go – down the block and through an empty lot and finally into a residential construction zone.

With Duke about half-a-block behind, the boy dashed into a partially constructed home then disappeared from sight as he went silently from room to room.

Switching the car lights on full, Sandy was out of the car and after Duke with his gun drawn.

Slowly Duke drew his service revolver. "I'm Officer Maxim. We just want to talk to you about where you've been tonight, that's all." He heard footsteps and nodded an acknowledgment to Sandy as he entered the building. Silently he motioned him into the next room. "Listen to me, son, there won't be any trouble if you come out with your hands where I can see them. We just want to ask you a couple of questions."

The floor creaked near the entrance of the doorway to the next room and Duke readied himself to tackle. His muscles tensed and he leaned into the anticipated motion. At the last moment, he drew himself up and back as Sandy appeared in the open archway. He shook his head.

"Come on now," he said into the seemingly empty building. "You're making this all unnecessarily hard on yourself." He motioned for Sandy to hold perfectly still as he slowly scanned the room with his ears for the sound of rapid breathing.

Sandy pointed toward the kitchen and started toward the opening, but Duke cut him off with a quick wave of his hand and instead pointed toward what was to become the dining room. As he approached the kitchen, Duke thought he heard the sound of someone move around the corner by the wall. He lunged around the corner to find – *a cat*!

Startled, Duke lurched back as the frightened animal leaped from the counter, sending bits of construction debris flying. The sound of a second squad car skidding to a stop on the building's threshold caused Duke to glance instinctively back toward the door. A motion, caught in the corner of his eye, returned his attention to the room he was in – but not soon enough. Before he could refocus his attention fully, he felt two slugs hit his chest, heard two shots reverberate in the empty room, saw his attacker, who was standing rock-still when he fired, run. Duke gasped then forced himself to take a deep breath as he felt his heart stop and life drain rapidly from him.

An instant later, Sandy bolted past him and fired through the open section of the building. Realizing he hadn't connected, he turned in time to see his partner drop to his knees. He was at Duke's side in an instant.

Through the opening in the building, both heard the outside officer's radio call.

"Shots being fired, requesting backup immediately."

Holding himself together as best he could, Duke looked up to his partner and with his last breath said, "Get me out of here – now," then collapsed into Sandy's strong grasp and died.

Sandy dragged his lifeless partner through the building just as a young officer was entering from the other side. "He ran out that way," Sandy shouted, motioning energetically into a direction that was opposite their position. The young officer darted off before he noticed Duke and Sandy finished dragging his partner out to the living room portion of the building and behind several construction boxes. "Come on Duke," Sandy said quietly and urgently, placing an expert hand on his partner's carotid artery and feeling for a pulse – any sign of life. "Come back to me before anything else happens – come on, boy."

Duke lay lifeless on the floor. His shirt bathed red in the blood brought forth from those two shots that had struck him dead-center in the chest, penetrating his heart. With solemn reverence, Sandy considered what he was witnessing for a moment. *That could just as well have been me – only no one would be expecting me to 'come back'. I would have just cashed in my chips.* He listened carefully, not wanting to hear footsteps. *Come on Duke, you've been dead long enough. The clock's running on this one. Say goodbye to Saint Peter up there and get your immortal spirit back into your immortal body! There's an eager-beaver buck of an officer out there somewhere and I don't know when he's coming through this building again.*

Helpless, Sandy could do nothing to bring Duke back to life. He could only kneel by his dead friend – a silent vigil as the Immortal healed – hopefully able to keep him away from mortal eyes who knew nothing of Immortals. To Sandy, the seconds crawled like minutes.

Duke suddenly gasped, then coughed. An instant later he clutched his chest, rolled to his side and groaned loudly.

"Come on Duke," he urged and grabbed an arm. "You have to get to your feet. I have to get you in the squad car. There's another officer here – somewhere."

Reluctantly, Duke rose with Sandy's strong-arm help. Looping an arm across Sandy's back, they started toward the car – Duke half walking and half staggering. Before they reached the car, the young officer rounded the corner of the building at a dead run. Seeing the pair, he skidded to a halt. The front of Duke's blood soaked shirt was partially visible.

"Oh my God – you've been hit!" the young man exclaimed.

"Just a flesh wound – I'll call it in and–"

Before Sandy could finish his statement, the young officer had engaged his uniform's two-way.

"Officer has been hit, requesting an ambulance immediately!" he shouted into the com.

"I'll take him in – cancel the call – it is minor."

Duke suddenly straightened, un-looped his arm and pulled his shirt straight.

"Bullet caught the edge of my badge and winged me," he said none too convincingly. Then he walked purposefully in a not so straight line to the squad car, just as the sound of an ambulance siren was heard. "Come on Sandy. Take me in so I can get a Band-Aid for this flesh wound."

"Its OK boys," Sandy waved to the ambulance paramedics as the van pulled to a halt. "Just a flesh wound – I'm taking him in now."

Duke could not completely conceal his shirt from the paramedics either as he got into the car. Their reaction was instantaneous.

Advancing rapidly toward Duke's side of the car, the woman called, "You don't have to. We're here for that. We'll get him on the stretcher."

Reaching in, through the open window, Sandy hit the siren. The blaring sound caused the paramedics to move away, holding their ears against the shrieking sound.

"Sorry," Sandy yelled back over the din. "We just got another call – no time to wait." Jumping into the car, he put it in motion. Gravel went flying in every direction as Sandy floored it leaving the construction site. Once he turned the corner he slowed to a more sensible speed.

"That was no scared kid, Sandy. He planned to kill me. Just the way he took me tells me he was practiced. I wonder what he is all about. I was right about what I said earlier – the feeling I had. There is something else here that's going down." Reaching to the side, Duke grabbed the thermos. "You want a cup?" he asked as he finished pouring himself a lukewarm cup of coffee.

"Not now. I'll get a fresh one at the hospital."

"You're kidding me – you're not actually taking me in?"

"Afraid so, Duke. Two people saw part of your blood stained shirt, and one heard the shots."

Duke leaned back against the headrest and rolled his eyes upward. "No one saw me dead, did they?"

"No, I sent that young officer off in another direction while you were dead."

Duke thought for a moment. "That young man could have gotten killed going after him alone."

Sandy shook his head, '*No*'. "That guy was long gone before he arrived."

"I just got a brief look at his face. Did you get a look before he ran?"

"Only for a second."

"Could you recognize him again if you saw him?"

Sandy nodded slowly. "I believe so."

Duke swore quietly. Had he not been distracted by the sound of that squad car, he would have likely heard the shooter leap from the side pantry and dodged his aim.

"Sorry, it wasn't the brightest in there, and the look went pretty fast."

Duke pulled the front of his shirt up to get a better look at it then shook his head. "He knew what he was going to do before he did it. Those two shots are almost on top of one another. He had a rock-solid lock on me. Nothing frightened about this kid. He's done this before – somewhere. If you had gone in ahead of me, you wouldn't have been with me anymore, Sandy. Who's on duty where you're taking me that knows about Immortals?"

"Dr. Grace Chandel."

Duke heaved a sigh of relief. The immortal physician had been working at the hospital for less than a year, but her presence had come in handy on more than one occasion.

Sandy picked up the com and put a call through, requesting to speak with Dr. Chandel, then explained the situation.

"So how long am I *in for* this time?"

"Gauging by the expression on the faces of that young officer and the paramedic, I would say a minimum of three to four days."

Duke groaned. "I can't handle the get-well cards and the flowers. Bandages make me itch."

Sandy smiled. "If your act is good enough, maybe we can sweet-talk Grace into signing your medical leave for a week's rest at home. You can go fishing."

"At home – and let you go out on a manhunt by yourself – no way.

You know there isn't a scratch on me by now."

"I know, but the rest of the world doesn't. So when you're ready to break the news to the department – that they have been decorating an Immortal for mortal-bravery – above-and-beyond all these years, let me know. Probably take away your medals for heroism if they knew your, uh – *immortal* status," Sandy finished with a large knowing grin. "Don't worry. I think Grace will agree I twisted my back during the pursuit. I will need a couple of days at home to rest – and go fishing with you, of course." His eyes twinkled with a smile.

Duke grimaced. "Tell her to use cloth tape – and don't press it down so hard. That way it won't rip all my chest hairs off when it's pulled. By Zeus, I hate pulling tape there."

Chapter Six

Duncan awoke with a start and looked around. It took him a moment to orient himself. His mind rewound the last things he remembered. *You returned home about 5:00 this morning and began multitasking. Grabbed something from the fridge and wolfed it down, tossed your clothes on the floor and jumped into the shower, tripped over your clothes leaving the shower, new clothes on, car keys in hand, headed for the car, passed the couch, just going to sit down for a moment—.*

And that was the end of his mental check-list. It was 6:30 now. His exhausted mind had switched off enforcing a desperately needed hour of sleep. The sun was rising and he so wanted to be by Tessa's side when she awoke, but he had been so exhausted he knew he couldn't have even seen the road straight to drive. Crashing his car on the way to the hospital, then *coming back* in front of however many witnesses was not on his list of things to do today.

Flowers came to mind and he made a mental note to stop on the way to her room and get a bouquet of white roses—a symbol of his pure love and sincerity to a woman he felt so deeply for.

The brief but deep sleep had rejuvenated him.

"Richie," he called as he opened the door. "I'm on my way to the hospital." There was no answer. He went back to the kitchen and scratched a brief note, then tossed it in the middle of the table. '*Me, Hospital – 6:30 – going now*'. There was no real need to wake Richie. He knew he had been on an emotional high, even more so than himself. He had just become an Immortal less than twenty-four hours ago. *Let him sleep today—it will clear his mind—it's better this way,* he thought. He headed for the door once again when the presence of another Immortal, in the immediate area, lit up his senses. He halted before the door.

"Knock, knock," came the lyrical voice of Amanda as she peered around the door at Duncan with a beaming big smile and school-girl charm in her eyes.

Duncan exhaled, relaxing. "Hello, Amanda and goodbye, Amanda. I'm in a rather big hurry and I don't have time for whatever is on your mind."

Amanda spooled around Duncan's body like a feline in need of some quality petting. "I thought we could all sit down for a talk. The last time you and I ran into each other you were with—ah—Tessa, and, well—it didn't quite come off the way I had hoped. I thought I might smooth things over between us." Her hands slowly found their way up the front of Duncan's neatly pressed shirt to his neck, encircling it. "Where is she?"

Reaching around his neck, Duncan gently peeled Amanda's arms off of his warm flesh then held her hands in his. "She's in the hospital—which is where I'm going to go right now. She was shot last night and nearly killed. If it weren't for Richie—" his voice faded out. He closed his eyes, shaking his head.

"That's awful," Amanda replied, recoiling. "Do you know who and why?"

"By a psycho kid. That pretty much sums up what Richie gave for the situation that went down. We were at the police station most of the night. He was looking for drug money. A couple of dollars was all Richie had. He almost killed Tessa for nothing."

"What happened to Richie?" In the next moment, Amanda felt the presence of another Immortal approaching. "Who else is here, Duncan?"

Richie entered the living room yawning, his hair tousled. "Mac, I thought I heard your voice then suddenly I felt this *presence* in my head. I was up like a shot then I heard Amanda's voice."

"Well look at you," she said leaving Duncan and walking to Richie. Her eyes passed up and down his form as if she were trying to somehow see a physical transformation connected with his immortal one. "All brand new. Has Duncan helped you pick out a sword yet?"

"No, it just happened yesterday evening. Tessa was shot. I was killed saving her. He hit me first and I deflected the bullet."

"Ouch," Amanda grimaced. "So now what?"

"He stays right here until Tessa and I get back and I can start his training."

"Mac," Richie began.

"I've got to go. I want to be there when she wakes up. Why don't you help me out here, Amanda? You can start with the immortal Rules."

"Like that's going to take more than three minutes to recite."

"Amanda, would you humor me, please. Richie needs to get started on the ground work. The Rules and the Game are the groundwork every Immortal must learn."

"Look, Duncan, I can easily do that," she replied, hands gesturing to no place in particular. "I can spend some quality time with Richie today if that's what you really want me to do, but that's not why I came."

"I have a hunch why you came."

"I came because I really wanted to smooth things between Tessa and—well—you know—all of us."

"Tessa is fine with Richie and me," he replied sidestepping the obvious indication.

"That's not what I meant, and you know it, Duncan MacLeod of the Clan MacLeod," she said in a stern tone with a direct stare, all hint of cool coy disappearing from her voice.

Duncan turned to face her eye-to-eye. Before she could speak, he spoke. "I've asked Tessa to marry me and she has said yes."

Amanda took a deep breath and stepped back, away from the man with whom she had shared her body over the centuries. "I'm happy for you," she said in a dead monotone voice. "Look, you have made Tessa a part of our immortal world, and like it or not, she is going to have to interact with other Immortals—me for one." Turning she went back to Richie and grasping his shoulder led him wordlessly into the kitchen.

Duncan shook his head then left.

Passing a mirror in the hospital's flower shop, he stopped to check his appearance once again. Something about his reflection made him linger. He gazed unmoving at the immortal man who was staring back at him. *Are you as troubled as I am on the other side of that looking glass? Is your world filled with the joys, the pain, and the uncertainty of more than 400 years of living the way mine has been on this side? Would you object if I, like Alice in Wonderland, stepped through the looking glass and tasted your existence for just a brief moment? Maybe I could understand my world just a little better.*

So deeply lost in thought was he that he did not notice the infatuated look in the nurse's eyes behind him, which was reflected in the mirror's corner.

What a handsome man, the tired nurse thought as she relaxed into the cafeteria chair with a hot cup of coffee. Her shift had been long and this attractive stranger was a pleasant sight to rest her eyes on for a moment.

Movement in the corner of the mirror caught Duncan's eye for a brief instant. He saw the look she was giving him. It barely registered in his thoughts, as if he could have ever cared how much she, or any other nurse, may have wanted to flirt with him. He moved on.

The shower had erased some of the tension in his muscles and the nap made him look more relaxed, but now all the emotional turmoil he had trapped in himself was draining him of the little energy he had left. With a finger, he brushed the hair from under the lapel and checked the rest of his outfit. If she was awake, he had to look his best.

Impatience was beginning to grow within him, tracing a clear path from his toes to his eyebrows, back and forth. The elevator door crept shut. *Why is this elevator so slow?* Each step to her room made the adrenaline in his body play with his senses. *What if I open the door only to find an empty bed? What if, for all my frantic rushing, she has died and I wasn't here with her?*

His mind thought back to the memories of Linda Plager—the *young, vibrantly passionate photographer. Her desire for photographic perfection drove her to a career away from me, and away from my love—until the final day of her life.* He had almost been too late when he went to see her. *To tell her what she and her work had meant to me—and how proud I was of her for pursuing her passion.*

Suddenly he felt a slight burning feeling in his hand. For a microsecond, he instinctively moved his wrist as if he were holding his katana. *That couldn't be—could it? Of course not!* The white roses he had bought for her were not appreciating his rough grasp and the thorns had left clear puncture marks, which were rapidly healing. *Calm down!* He ordered himself to let the tension flow from himself and focus on room numbers, 233, 234, 235. *What if I open the door and she is not there?* His mind prodded again. *How many more times can I go through this?*

His immortal senses lit up as he felt the immediate presence of another Immortal. Slowly he looked around. People, mortal people, were coming and going—staff, visitors, patients. Suddenly the elevator door opened in the next hall block just ahead. An orderly, a police officer, and a man on the gurney were coming toward him. Duncan did a double-take—the Immortal was on the gurney. *What's he doing with life-support equipment by his side?* The orderly turned into a room a few numbers up from Tessa's door. The police officer followed. Duncan's instinctive curiosity about what he had just seen propelled him several steps past Tessa's room. He stopped. He had no reason to enter another room. Hesitant, he turned back to Tessa's door and opened it.

The room was dimly lit with only the sunshine reflecting off the adjacent building. Its stark décor coldness upset him. This was no place for Tessa and the roses he had brought would make no difference in here. She looked asleep but restless. He had seen that expression many times before, when he arrived home late after a challenge and she had not managed to stay awake. He would go to her, hold her in his arms, reassure her that everything was fine, and they would make love to heal each other's pain. *Not this time. Your pain for her will have to heal itself. She can't respond to you now.* Softly, he walked closer and noticed how pale she looked. *Fragile, almost sickly.* He felt the urge to touch her soft skin but did not want to wake her. *Besides, what if she feels cold?* He knew he was going to the darker places in his mind and tried to concentrate on finding something for the roses. He saw a glass on the table and went to the bathroom for some water. *Another damn mirror. What is it with people and their own reflections?* He placed the roses on the table and brought a chair as close to her as he could, yet he still did not dare touch her. He could not help but see the resemblance between Tessa and the roses. They were on this earth only to bring beauty and happiness without asking for much in return—a little sunshine, and a gentle rain here and there. They could stand strong winds, lose a few petals, survive the winter chill, but they would inevitably bloom with a little warmth. Yes, Tessa reminded him of the wild roses in the Highlands of Scotland. It brought images of his clan, his family, his home back to him. *But what happens if people cut them? Was it a sin?* He now realized the roses had been a mistake. She had told him several times not to bring cut flowers to the house because they made her sad.

"*They are dead already,*" she used to say. "*The only thing I can do is watch their agony. The only things that are living have roots so they can be nurtured and grow. Separate them from their life blood and they can only die*".

That memory and the thought of her mortal life chilled him to the bone, making his blood run cold.

"Duncan?" It was an almost inaudible whisper.

They are dead already. It is just the agony of contemplating their decay.

"Duncan?" Her voiced led him back to reality. His eyes lit up.

"Hey sweetheart, here I am. Everything is fine, you are going to be OK," he said, not aware of the tear that was rolling slowly down his cheek.

She managed to lift her hand and lovingly caress him, wiping his tear with her gentle touch. "What's wrong, then?"

He smiled sheepishly. "Nothing, it's just that when you called my name I suddenly remembered a couple of poems I read once—they were beautiful love poems."

When did I stop being a fierce warrior to become a silly romantic movie star? Is this some kind of middle-age crisis for immortals?

"Tell me," she softly said.

"Oh well, I'm not sure I could say it just the right way." He feigned ignorance.

"Tell me—make it up as you go," she pleaded with her usual, *I know I am going to get what I want,* look in her eyes.

He finally found the courage to run his fingers through the strands of hair which had fallen across her lovely cheeks. His eyes followed his touch—fingers gently caressing her cheeks, her neck, her lips. He exhaled, and complied.

"Feeling your love for me was the first time I felt I could go on loving forever. From the very moment you whispered my name on that boat."

His voice suddenly faltered. There was something deeply moving in those words. Trying to speak them once again, he found he had no voice. Collecting himself, he spoke their meaning from his immortal heart.

"I knew from that first moment, your eyes had seen my soul – yet you dared to love me fearlessly, knowing what I am. With you I have no need to hide; your strength is my refuge from the cold I've felt so often outside."

"That's absolutely beautiful," Tessa whispered, then slowly, ever so carefully, pulled him into her loving embrace.

Sandy walked past the flower shop on his way to the main lobby. Around the corner, and down the far end of the wall, away from the many people who were coming and going, he picked up a courtesy phone.

"Officer Sandowski—I'm calling for Joe Dawson." Sandy glanced around then propped himself against the wall where he had a clear view of who might be near. "Joe—it's Sandy. Listen, I think we might have a problem. The kid that shot Miss. Noel also took Duke out tonight like a pro. I think it was Mark Roszca—yeah—one of James Horton's protégés. I don't think Pallin Wolf was working alone."

Chapter Seven

Richie followed Amanda as she helped herself to a look around the house.

"I'd really like to get my hands on this guy for what he did."

"You don't like being an Immortal already?" Slowly she eyed the kitchen then moved to the next room.

"No, that's not what I mean. I really haven't been an Immortal long enough to know anything about it."

The living room is—well—quaint, she thought. "It's living, Richie, just living. Besides, you don't even know where this kid went, do you?" *Let's see what the bedroom has to offer.*

Richie shook his head. "I haven't a clue. He just split." He waved his hands in the air. "So you've been an Immortal a very long time – over 1,100 years I understand?"

"And counting." She stopped by the door and grasped the handle.

"I think this is something Mac and Tessa would like to keep private," he said, with a grin and leaned against the door, closing it.

Amanda slipped an arm around his neck and drew him towards herself – away from the door. "You know, revenge isn't all it's made out to be." Her other hand slipped past his side. Her finger slowly pried the bedroom door open, just a crack, so she could see inside. "You know if I had gone after every mortal that did me wrong, I don't think I would be standing here talking to you now."

"Why not?"

"I would have been arrested so many times that I would likely still be killing myself in order to escape from all the jails I would have ended up in. Look, every mortal simply isn't worth your time.

Hum—quite a lovely little nest they have in there, she mused silently as she peered past Richie through the open crack into the bedroom.

Richie sensed what was happening. "Right – you're good." With a chuckle, he leaned hard against the door. Amanda got her fingers out of the way just in time. Her tongue brushed the tip of her lip and she lowered her head and smiled. Staring into his eyes, she said nothing. Releasing him, she moved on.

"Actually I was thinking of what he did to Tessa—not really me—when I said I wanted his ass. I mean look at the situation. He saw she didn't have a purse or anything on her. So where was she going to pull the cash from? Then what did he do? He fired, just at the instant my arm happened to be reaching to shove her out of the way. His next shot was for me—it hit me square in the chest. If this had happened to

Tessa, she would have been dead right then and there." He looked briefly to the floor—to nowhere in particular. "Amanda, I can't even begin to imagine how bad Mac would have reacted to losing her—it would have changed his whole life."

Throughout Richie's monolog, Amanda continued her way toward Tessa's workshop. She stopped to look at some of Tessa's unfinished works. "My, my—I see art comes in many forms."

"Tessa is quite good. She has gotten a couple of good reviews from her shows. Well, not that I'm an art critic, mind you, but this stuff is interesting."

"OK," Amanda said. *If you say so. I prefer the sparkly round, faceted kind usually found in expensive necklaces or tiaras*, her mind finished, as she passed a finger down and around the curved surface of a piece of artwork that was still blackened by the torch. "Look, Richie, being an Immortal doesn't make you feel any different. I wouldn't have expected you to come back after your first death saying, *"Thanks for shooting me—I'm immortal now, everything is just dandy."* You just live longer—hopefully. And speaking of which – ah-ha, this will do nicely," Amanda said suddenly, carefully thumbing through a bunch of Tessa's welding rods. Most were about a meter in length and all were at least one-half-inch thick. She picked two out. "Here," and handed one to him. "You know the immortal Rules, let's do something practical about keeping you alive—come on."

Rod in hand, Richie and Amanda went out into the living room and moved the furniture to the walls. Amanda motioned, indicating what they were about to do and Richie followed her lead. "A rod isn't a sword. It doesn't have a handle and it doesn't swing like one, but for an hour or so, we can pretend. Besides, we can't do much damage with a blunt rod in a house, can we? Now follow my lead."

Duncan spooned up another helping of mash potatoes and delivered it into Tessa's waiting mouth. Then setting the spoon aside he reached and folded a hospital napkin then gently dabbed the corners of her mouth. She smiled back. This was fun. It was well past noon, but Tessa was not in a hurry to finish her meal. Adjusting her position on her large pillow, she pushed aside the hair that had tumbled across her cheek.

"Your little bird is still hungry," she said with a coy smile as she accepted another serving of the cold vegetable. Anything served up to her at the end of Duncan's spoon went down much better anyway. Her eyes were beginning to sparkle once again. She was really beginning to enjoy being fed by her rugged Highlander, now turned soft hearted poet.

Duncan was happy to oblige her. This feeding exercise was becoming just as much fun for him as it obviously was for her. *Anything to see her smile,* his heart whispered. *She's looking positively glowing with each spoon full. If that's what it takes, I'll feed her the whole kitchen. I have got to get her out of here – I want her home – safe at home with me.* His conscious mind reminded himself sternly, *she's mortal – she will need care to heal – this takes time. Mortals aren't all healed up ten minutes after the act.* He exhaled, trying not to show his tiredness and outright depression at the situation he knew she would have to endure for several more days.

A knock at the door was followed by a male voice. "Knock, knock – I'm Dr. Andrews, one of the residents here. Can I check your surgical site?" Placing his clipboard down on a side table, he pulled on a pair of gloves.

Duncan scooted off of the bed so Tessa could roll over. The bandages covered an area the size of a softball on the lower outer right edge of her ribcage.

"OK, looks good – everything is dry. We'll leave this in place until tomorrow." He wrote a few notes.

"Is it too soon to ask when I can take her home?"

"And you are?"

"Duncan MacLeod. We're getting married soon. I just want to get her home as soon as possible – as soon as it's safe."

"Congratulations," the physician said, smiling to Tessa then turning to Duncan. "I was going to ask if she had a support system at home, but I see that isn't an issue. No, it is not too early to ask about going home. Let's talk about going home sometime after I see you tomorrow."

"That soon?" Tessa asked, her voice a mixture of hope and apprehension. Duncan brightened considerably.

"You're not going home tomorrow, but tomorrow will tell me how soon you are going home," he finished. "We don't keep people any longer than we have to. Open heart surgery is usually only four to five days. A transplant is usually six to ten days, depending on many factors. Your situation is a lot less serious."

"Really," Duncan said, taken a bit aback by the statement. "She was shot – there was a lot of blood."

"That was an immediate problem which was resolved once we got the bleeding stopped, the bullet out, and corrected for volume loss. Oh, that reminds me." He reached into his lab coat and took out a small plastic bag. "I have a souvenir for the police. I thought you might like to see what sent you here." He handed the bag to Tessa. It was the bullet. Tessa turned the bag over in her hand and grimaced, but said nothing.

Dr. Andrews pushed out a place on the edge of the bed and sat down beside her. "There's something interesting about all of this," he began. "I served as a medic toward the beginning of the Gulf War. I have seen a lot of bullet wounds. Yours was, to my eye, definitely different."

"How so," asked Duncan, taking the small plastic bag and turning it over in his hand.

"You were shot at close range with a small-caliber weapon. At that distance this should have passed straight through you, at the angle you were hit. But, the inside of your rib stopped it cold. Either you've got concrete for bones, or something slowed this down before it reached you."

Tessa tried her best to look blank. *Richie was that something. I wouldn't even be talking to you now except for Richie. He became an Immortal because of me. Had things gone just a little differently – even a fraction of a second, I would have become immortal – in a spiritual sense. Oh God, I hate deceiving you, but you can't ever know what really happened.*

Duncan handed the bag back to the physician.

Another knock sounded, this time followed by a tall, slender woman in a business suit with a badge clipped to her belt. "I am Inspector Barns," she said in a pleasant, but official tone. "Are you the doctor?"

"Andrews," he supplied as he got up from the bed.

"Is there any reason Miss Noel can't answer a few questions?"

He shook his head '*No*', and then added. "Surgery was a little over eight hours ago. I do recommend that you only stay until she says she is tired." He left the room.

The police inspector approached. "I have a couple of questions, Miss Noel. Would you mind?" Tessa shook her head and the woman brought a chair up to the bed.

Duncan exhaled, a bit annoyed and thought, *you know that Richie and I just spent four or five hours at the station. What more is there to be said? Can't you leave this poor woman alone?*

"I know it all probably happened pretty fast for you, but I need to know if you can add anything to the information we already have."

"I'll try."

The woman handed her the sketch the artist drew from Richie's description. "Is this the man who shot you?"

"Yes."

"Is there anything else you can add to what you see here?"

Tessa looked closely at the sketch. To her, his sketch appeared more two-dimensional than what one would expect to see in a photograph, but the details captured were frighteningly accurate.

"No, this is the kid. He came out of nowhere. All I remember was he was yelling at me – at Richie – to give him whatever we had. Then he shot me." She closed her eyes and put a hand to her forehead.

Duncan swooped in protectively on the other side of the bed. "Are you getting tired, sweetheart? Do you want to stop?"

"Mr. MacLeod, if we could continue uninterrupted."

"Inspector, this woman – soon to be my wife – has been put through a traumatic event. She just got out of surgery early this morning. Besides, Richie has been at the police station for over four hours giving a detailed description."

"I know this, and I understand that you want to protect her now, but if there are any more details she could possibly give, we need them." Then looking to Tessa she asked, "Can we continue?"

Tessa nodded. "I am afraid I don't have any more details about him. It really did happen fast."

"You just happened to be in the wrong place at the wrong time. What happened to Richie in all of this? Did he just shoot you then run? Did your – uh – companion try to attack him? Follow him? Anything? It seems a bit odd that with two people standing there he would only shoot one – the woman at that. It would make more sense if he had shot your companion. He would have been more of a threat to him. But he did nothing to him? Did the attacker know you? An old acquaintance with a grudge, perhaps?"

I can't tell you what I know Inspector, she thought. *I can't tell you that he died to save me – then he came back to life, now an Immortal. I know none of this is adding up, but that is the way I am going to have to leave it. You just can't ever know what really happened.* Tessa shook her head. "I never saw him before last night. After he shot me I must have blacked out. I really can't tell you anymore."

The Inspector heaved a sigh. "I understand. I do wish you had more information for me." She folded her notepad. "From everyone's description so far, his profile would appear to be that of a teenage-junky looking for drug money – on the surface that is."

"What are you saying, Inspector?" Duncan asked.

"I'm saying appearances can sometimes be deceiving. Coincidentally, around the same time as your shooting, a half-dozen or so houses up from where your companion said you were parked, there was a break-in at a Tudor home. Something went down there, but we haven't pieced it together yet."

Duncan felt a cold shiver run down his spine. He had killed the man who kidnapped Tessa less than 30 minutes before the shooting. He had done it none too neatly either – *a katana can leave a bloody mess! I never even thought to close the door – I just ran to Tessa. What did the police find?* He braced himself for the revelation.

"What did you find?" Duncan asked, holding his breath.

"An early morning jogger called in as suspicious circumstances. The house door was wide open. Apparently the intruder gained access without forced entry."

That's right – Tessa's kidnapper left it open for me – he wanted me to come after him. I never did learn his name or what this was really all about.

"If I may," Duncan began again, very carefully. "Who owns the house?"

She paused and weighed whether or not she wanted to give him that information. Finally, she shrugged. He could easily find that much out from the courthouse registry, or the Internet – everything seemed to be ending up on the Internet sooner or later. "The house is registered to a Walter and Ema Wolf."

"Were the owners at home during the break-in?"

"The officer found no one at home when he got to the door. The family is probably traveling. He flipped the locked and closed the door."

You'll find one of them dead in that room upstairs—as soon as someone bothers to look, Duncan thought. *I'm going to do a little background checking on this Walter and Ema Wolf when I leave the hospital.*

She took a deep breath then nibbled her lip thoughtfully. "Miss Noel, your attacker also shot a police officer a few hours later."

"Oh how terrible. Is he still alive?"

"Yes, he was lucky as well. His partner brought him in here. Seems to be everyone's night for luck, except me."

"When I got here this morning, I saw a police officer get off the elevator and walk beside a gurney to a room – he went in, just down the hall, a couple of rooms away."

"Was he tall and slender?"

"Yes."

"That was probably Officer Sandowski. His partner was shot early this morning."

The Immortal. I have to find out what is going on – what can I use as an excuse? He looked to Tessa. "Sweetheart, would you object if I left you for a few moments to see how that officer is doing?" He fidgeted a bit, his left hand rubbed the side of his face – his temple – his hair. "After all that has happened, I just feel I should give him – his partner at least – a few words of encouragement about you." He knew that was a very lame excuse, but he hoped that he was coming off as a bit of a nervous wreck – convincing enough not to raise any suspicion.

"It's OK, Duncan," Tessa began gently. "You go and see how that poor man is doing. I will be fine. There is nothing more I can add to what Richie has probably given the police already. As I said, I must have blacked out."

The inspector got up and moved her chair away. "If you think of anything else, give me a call." She handed Tessa her card. Tessa nodded her '*OK*' and the woman left.

Duncan waited by the door until he saw her enter the first set of elevators before he left Tessa. Slowly, Duncan walked down the corridor until he felt an Immortal's presence – that indescribable singular sensation in his head of another Immortal nearby. *I'm sensing two Immortals?* He stopped by the door. *What will my reception be?* He knew the other Immortals sensed his presence as well; however, there should be no cause for alarm. Not only was a hospital a public place, this was also a *religious* affiliated hospital and the grounds had been consecrated. No Immortal would ever fight on *Holy Ground,* or in a public place. Never-the-less, he was still uneasy about meeting a new Immortal without his katana near. He knocked gently then entered slowly. I'm Duncan Mac–" he began then halted.

Dr. Grace Chandel was bending over the bed. She stopped what she was doing and looked up at him with a bright smile. "Hello, Duncan. What brings you here?"

He carefully closed the door as Sandy got up from the chair beside the bed. "I'm Officer Sandowski. And you are?"

"MacLeod – Duncan MacLeod," he finished. *There are four people in this room – three of us are Immortals. What does the fourth one know of us – if anything? What can I say in here?* He gestured down the hall. "Tessa Noel, my fiancée, was shot on the street last night by some junky looking for drug money. I just learned that a police officer, who came in here earlier today, was shot by the same kid."

Grace gasped. "Someone shot Tessa. Oh, Duncan, I am so sorry to hear this. I'll go and see her when I'm finished here."

Duke pushed back the covers and sat up interrupting Grace. "You're more than finished here, Grace. I'm Ducanus Maximinus – Duke Maxim nowadays—and this is my partner, Sandy. He knows what I am – about Immortals. Is Miss Noel going to survive?"

Duncan nodded. "She is awake and just had something to eat. She is looking better. Can you tell me anything about the shooter?"

"He was no strung out junkie looking for drug money. That is certain."

"What do you mean?"

"He took me out tonight—two slugs right through the chest," he motioned to the area. "One almost right on top of the other – rock-steady lock on me and a practiced hand. He fired then moved out of Sandy's way very fast. He wasn't strung out on anything. He knew exactly what to do and how to do it. He was a pro."

"I don't get any of this," Duncan said looking from Sandy to Duke.

"Neither do I," Sandy spoke up. "He dropped Duke like a shot at close range. Miss Noel was also shot at close range I understand. She is one incredibly lucky woman to have survived."

Duncan bowed his head momentarily, then taking a deep breath, looked Sandy in the eye. "There is a bit more to it than that. But this has to be off the record, Officer."

Sandy glanced back to Duke then to Duncan. "Alright," he said slowly, nodding.

"Richie was killed saving Tessa. The bullet that hit her had already passed through his arm. This was his first death. He came back an Immortal."

"He gave up his mortal life to save Tessa," she said, sadness in her eyes, but with a strong feeling of pride in her heart for Richie's actions. "Did he know he was going to be an Immortal? This happened a lot sooner than I would have wanted it to for him."

"I agree, too soon," Duncan said, a sad kind of wisdom reflected in his eyes. "Yes, I mentioned it briefly to him shortly after we met – the reason I knew he was in the shop – the first Quickening he saw, but I never brought it up after that. I felt Richie was too impulsive to handle the whole immortal discussion. At the time we talked, I felt if he would have seriously acknowledged it, he would have taken reckless chances without any thought for self-preservation. I wanted him to mature a bit before he became an Immortal. A bit is all he got."

Sandy listened, then looked to Duke, but did not comment for a long moment. "Did Miss Noel know the attacker?"

Duncan shook his head. "No. This whole thing is making less and less sense to me as we're talking. What you're suggesting is there is a kid with paramilitary training working as an assassin in our city. What does this have to do with Tessa or Richie?" Duncan finished looking first to Sandy then Duke. "If you know something about this person, please tell me. I have to protect Tessa."

"Sandy and I both got a brief look at him as well. We'll check for priors, in the meantime, Mr. MacLeod, if none of you have ever seen this person before, I don't see any reason why you should feel your fiancée is in any particular danger now from him. This may simply have been a case of her being in the wrong place at the wrong time. There is still a puzzle here though that has to be pieced together. He may have been involved in a break-in around the same time as his attack on Miss Noel."

"The Tudor house?"

Sandy's expression shifted noticeably to a combination of surprise and alertness, but he remained silent.

"The inspector who just stopped in to see Tessa mentioned it," Duncan finished. He saw Sandy's expression change and noted it. *What does he know that he's not saying?* Duncan set the thought aside as *'police business'* which he knew they wouldn't reveal. *Odd, Duke's expression never changed. Either he is very good at playing poker, or he doesn't know what his partner does*, he thought.

Duke looked to Sandy then back to Duncan. "Would you mind if I spoke with Miss Noel now?" Duncan shook his head *'No'*, and Duke reached for the side of the bed, to get leverage. The IV tether got in his way.

"Grace, would you get this stuff out of me and away." He reached to pull the IV line when Grace stopped him. "Get rid of this – give it to someone who needs it."

"Duke, this isn't going to hurt you or anyone else, mortal or immortal. It's just physiological saline." She started dismantling the lines that went to Duke's veins. "Besides, you know the rules."

"Yeah," he said in an exasperated tone, though not nearly as annoyed as he was letting on. "Seen getting shot—go straight to the hospital—don't pass *'Go'*."

"What is an Immortal doing in here as a patient in the first place?"

"I was shot in the field. A couple of others – police and paramedics both saw part of my bloody shirt."

"They didn't see you die then *come back*, did they?" Duncan asked, concern in his voice. "When we die in public we are required to leave the area for at least fifty-years if not longer."

Duke huffed. "No and not a chance. I'm not leaving the police force and Sandy, here alone, to get killed." He made a general sweeping motion with his arm. "I know the rules here. I get shot and Sandy covers for me. I come in here, I have to endure a couple of days flat on my back, hospital food, get-well cards, flowers, balloons, a few worried faces from the Police force, and I'm out of here for a few days at home – convalescing while I go fishing. I've been paraded through this hospital already with all this stuff connected to me. Everyone has seen me so I've served my time. That's Sandy's job, to keep me from dying in public."

"And it isn't always easy," Sandy said with a grin.

"Does Miss Noel know about Immortals?"

"Yes. We had that discussion early on in our relationship. She has seen me fight and the Quickening. It doesn't bother her. She has been one strong woman. But after last night," Duncan paused not really knowing himself how to put the next sentence into words. "I get the feeling her world has become destabilized. I can't really describe what it is."

"She's mortal, Duncan. She only has one time in this life. I think I might know what's happened – maybe with you too, after going through this experience with Tessa because you love her so much. Be patient and loving, Duncan. I'll talk to her." She finished unhooking Duke's IV "Fast or slow, Duke?" she asked.

"Fast or slow what—**Ouch**!" he exclaimed loudly as Grace ripped the empty IV cover off his arm, taking a couple dozen of his manly hairs with it.

"All done." She smiled sheepishly as she packed everything into a Biohazard container.

"That hurt worse than being shot," he grumbled as he reached for a handhold and scooted off the bed. A light knock on the door halted him and he sailed back under the covers.

"Come in," Sandy called.

A young lady walked in with an enormous bunch of flowers and a small heart-shaped balloon in the center.

"Please say he's going to live," the young girl begged in a small voice, her green eyes welling up with tears.

"He will be as good as new," Grace assured the teenager, knowingly. "It really wasn't that serious and his partner brought him in quickly."

"Oh, thank God," the girl replied and sighing, set the flowers on the tiny nightstand. The massive bouquet swallowed it up. "I don't think I could go on if anything happened to Officer Maxim." She bubbled, glowingly and headed for his bedside.

Duke slowly pulled the covers up over his nose until only his eyes showed. Then he began to moan softly.

"This isn't the best time to visit, though," Grace said stepping between her and Duke's bed. "He needs to recover from his wounds. He's not feeling the best."

"I know he was so brave out there," she beamed as Grace turned her to the door and nodded her assurances.

Sandy whispered after they passed. "Work-study student from the high school. She's got a real bad crush on Duke."

Duncan grinned as Grace closed the door behind the young lady, all the while assuring her that her very handsome police officer would live to return to work.

"By the gods, is she gone," Duke whispered, opening an eye.

"Your admirer has left," Duncan affirmed with a smile.

Duke looked at the roses and shook his head. "Maybe you could take these to your fiancée. I'm not a rose man."

"Actually I was thinking of bringing you some extras. She isn't really a rose woman either."

Chapter Eight

Sandy reached into his uniform shirt pocket and took out two small plastic bags, each with bullets inside, and tossed them on Joe Dawson's desk.

"We need to talk. Tell me what you know about this Mark Roszca. Is he a Watcher?"

Joe looked at the two bags lying on his desk then to Sandy, his expression a mixture of conflicting emotions.

"What's all this," he said, slowly glancing up to Sandy and gesturing to the bags before him.

"This is the bullet they took out of Miss Noel."

"And the other?"

"This one came out of the body of Michelle – former mortal companion of the now also deceased Immortal, James Fly. On a hunch, I ran the ballistics on this bullet. They match."

Joe grimaced and shook his head. "I was afraid of that after Tessa was shot so close to the house. I was hoping it was just a junky looking for money – a random shooting. I see that it wasn't."

"What's been happening there that I better know about?"

Joe propped against his desk in his private conference room. The large room, in the back of '*Joe's*' bar – a building the Watcher's Council helped him set up, was being organized as a local Watcher's central. Joe had recently been promoted. This bar was to become a headquarters for Watchers in the area.

He knew an already bad situation had just become much worse. "Pallin Wolf was one of James Horton's renegades. We only recently made that discovery after MacLeod confronted James for killing Darius in the church he served. Mark Roszca, on the other hand, was contacted by James. James used our standard protocol for making *introductory* contact with someone to determine if they could become a Watcher. Mark never went through with it, and from what I recently learned, James never broke off contact with him after that."

"I heard something about a Watcher killing an Immortal. It's something I could hardly believe, Joe. That's not what we're here for."

"Observe and record but never interfere." Joe nodded. "James was one sick man and we never knew." Joe looked away – he was ashamed for James. "James apparently formed a special group of renegade Watchers – '*Hunters*' they called themselves – on a crusade to wipe out an *immortal cancer*. Besides Darius, several other Immortals and their Watchers went missing recently. The Council never made the connection. To tell you the truth Sandy, I wouldn't have believed it either if MacLeod hadn't confronted me with what James had done. He killed James in the factory." Joe fell silent and glanced away.

It would truly have been better for everybody if MacLeod had actually killed him in that factory and if I hadn't hauled James' near-dead carcass to the hospital. Guilt was biting his backside at that moment. *But that's a secret I can never share – not even with you, Sandy.* He exhaled his mind churning. *James swore to me that for saving his life he would stay in that sleepy little island retirement town.*

"I just want to leave the country and live very quietly," were his parting words.

I hope he keeps that promise. He's a dead man if he ever lets his existence be known to anyone outside. I've finished him with the Watchers, that's for certain.

Finally glancing back to Sandy, he finished his statement.

"When the Watcher's Tribunal learned that he and his warped group had broken one of our cardinal rules – to never interfere and especially to never harm an Immortal – the Tribunal placed him and his group under a death sentence. They all went underground after that and it has simply been hell trying to find the last of those who were involved. We didn't piece together the Pallin connection until Immortal James Fly disappeared then suddenly his Watcher couldn't be found either. The Tribunal was sending a security *sweeper team* to bring Pallin in to be executed. I'm going to tell them they don't have to bother. MacLeod did the service for them."

"When – where?"

Joe shook his head again then sat down and pulled up MacLeod's file on his computer. "I don't understand what happened. MacLeod is not one to kill mortals. Yet he apparently killed Pallin in his house. The question is why?"

"Who's his Watcher?"

"I am, Sandy. But I was sick with the flu for about a week. The *bug* was hitting this area and several of my Watchers were down with it too. I just got back to work today. There were a couple of days no one was watching him. I put that new Watcher graduate, Kevin Kilgore – to work finding out what MacLeod was doing the day he arrived. Ha – I can just imagine his shock at having to hit the ground running on his first night out. And what happens? He finally locates MacLeod's car after cruising nearly the whole city; he catches sight of it, coincidentally near Pallin's house. It was leaving the curb as if it were on fire! The door to the house was wide open and, fortunately, he stopped to investigate. He found Pallin's body upstairs. We sent a *cleanup* Watcher's crew to retrieve it before it became public knowledge. I don't know why Duncan went there in the first place and what the hell Pallin was doing with a sword trying to fight an Immortal."

"Joe, this is a very complex puzzle and we don't know all the pieces yet. I do know both these bullets were fired by the same gun, and Mark Roszca was holding it in his hand in at least two cases. My bet is he killed Michelle as well. But what's the motive? Is he simply going after Immortals like James and Pallin did? What about their companions? Is that what Tessa's shooting was about? If so, he wasn't prepared for Duke—he shot him. I didn't see a blade on him which tells me he wasn't prepared to kill an Immortal. He mustn't have known Duke is an Immortal."

Joe could only shake his head. "I wish I knew the answers to all those questions, too. I wish I hadn't been sick this past week. Why was Duncan in that area with Tessa and Richie that night? It doesn't make any sense that they would have simply all gone over to Wolf's house to watch Duncan kill a man because he killed another Immortal – one that Duncan never even had contact with in his entire life. It is completely out of character for MacLeod." He threw up his hands. "This is what happens when mortal Watchers get sick – time and events stand still for no man." Joe leaned on an elbow, turning over a few sceneries out loud.

"Sandy, is it possible that Mark was working as a bodyguard for Pallin – he saw everyone leaving the house, figured MacLeod must have got Pallin and confronted them?"

"Except that doesn't wash with the story Richie Ryan gave at the station," Sandy continued.

"I doubt seriously that all three were out cruising for a romantic moonlight spot so two guys could make love to Tessa. That is really not MacLeod. No, something else happened."

"If MacLeod had been with Richie and Tessa when Mark shot her, either everyone would have been shot, or one of those guys would have gotten Mark. Nothing else could have happened," Sandy interjected.

"We just found out Mark shot and killed Richie. He became an Immortal that night. But you are right about Duncan. He could not have been with them when Mark attacked. That doesn't add up either." Another set of wheels began turning in Joe's head. He was barely on speaking terms with this Immortal – something that was also a Watcher's cardinal *no-no*, and could possibly earn him a death sentence if he wasn't quiet about it. If he really wanted to know what Mac was doing there, he was going to have to ask him.

During Joe's pensive silence, Sandy retrieved the plastic bags. "I didn't get involved with the Watchers to see Immortals being slaughtered by psychotic renegades in Watcher's guise. Duke is the best partner I could ever ask for, Joe. I won't simply remain silent if he becomes a target."

"You're a Watcher – remember?" Joe said quietly but never met Sandy's eyes.

"I'm a police officer first. Partners protect one another. There is a killer on the loose in our city. He's already shot four people and killed three – fortunately, two of those were Immortals. If I see this guy on the street – anywhere – I'm taking him down. He's a dead man."

Chapter Nine

Grace placed a gentle hand on Duncan's shoulder, rousing him from sleep. He woke with a start. His senses immediately registering the presence of another Immortal and his instinct for self-preservation fought to orient him in a split second.

"It's just me," she said quietly so as not to wake Tessa who was sleeping soundly in her hospital bed. "You've been here all day – you were exhausted. I am glad you caught a nap."

Duncan straightened in the poorly padded hospital chair. He winced just a bit – his muscles were stiff from sitting in one position. "How long have I been here?"

She glanced at her watch as she reached for the window shade pull chain. "You've been sleeping in that chair for about an hour or so, but you've been here all day. It's time for you to go home."

He pushed his hair back and re-clipped it. "I don't want to leave Tessa, Grace. She has had a very traumatic experience. Her words – the feeling I got when I held her in that bed. I don't want to go. I can't be apart from her now. She needs me."

"She needs to heal and so do you. Your experience was just as traumatic as Tessa's." She sat down beside him. "I am so sorry for the both of you," she said, then hugged him close. "She came within a heartbeat of losing her mortal life – the only life she will ever have. And you came within that same heartbeat of losing Tessa, right after asking her to marry you. Someone almost took that out of your control – took her away from you."

Duncan rested his face in his hands. His gaze focused on the nondescript pattern the floor tiles made. *Am I that kind of a man*, he pondered. *In the 400 plus years that I have existed, I have loved so many.*

"It is our immortal way – we live so long that it's natural not to get that close. It's best not to get mortals too involved because of the Game."

These are the lines I've been handing out to those I've loved – and for what reason? To protect them, or me? What have I been running from? Immortals have been taking mortal mates as long as we have existed. So what's my problem? Duncan's mind drifted back.

Flashback – Gypsy camp, 1848:
Her flesh was warm, her scent that of the field and the rich earth. Carmen caressed his cheeks with the softness of her lips, and he responded in kind.

He had known her, loved her, and traveled with them in their wagon these many months. He could not think of life beyond her, beyond her family, their futures together. When their passions cooled, she lay with her long, dark wavy hair draped across his lap and read his palm, tracing the lines in his flesh very carefully. Her expression changed and she rose—he followed. She kissed him, then slapped him hard across the face.

"You bastard!" she screamed. Her voice was raw and it grated on his nerves like a knife. "I have loved you with my whole heart, and you have only used me as a plaything." Grabbing her knife she went for his throat. He wrestled the blade from her.

"What are you talking about, Carmen?"

Without responding to him further she ran from the wagon shouting for her brother. Standing within the circle, surrounded by her family, she had told them that he was destined to never marry, but to bury many women in his wake.

"You will always be alone," were Carmen's parting words.

Present time:

The Gipsy curse? Was Tessa meant to be one of those women I would bury, but never have a chance to marry? His mind refused to go any further. He looked up to Grace, unconsciously pleading for an answer.

Grace read volumes from the expression in his eyes. "You both need to heal," she said again, very gently. "But now, it's time for you to go. You have a life—be kind to it."

Duncan rose, smiling at Grace for her quiet wisdom. "I'll be back before she wakes tomorrow and—"

Grace cut him off with a finger placed purposely on his lips. "No, you won't. Tomorrow you'll sleep in. I am going to have a long talk with Tessa. I may even have a private therapy session with her later tomorrow. This is something she has to work through herself. Trust me, Duncan. Whatever the issues are she has to bring them out in the open and look them in the eye before she can resolve them. You can't start a marriage with this kind of bad baggage."

So many Immortals have been married, his mind reminded him. *Rebecca Horne, Amanda's teacher, was happily married to Walter, and–* "Amanda," he said suddenly, remembering. "I have to get home."

As MacLeod's car pulled up next to the building his immortal senses lit up. *Two Immortals,* his mind told him. *Richie and Amanda were both here. This I expected*, he told himself. Opening the car door the sound of metal striking hard on another rang in his ears – this was not what he expected to hear. He grabbed his katana, and reaching the door, flung it open. He stopped and stared.

There was Amanda and Richie sparring in the living room. Amanda perched on top of their overturned, overstuffed chair and Richie on the coffee table.

"What have you two been doing?" he exclaimed as he glanced around the room and beyond. "The living room looks like a bomb hit it."

"Hi, Duncan," Amanda began sheepishly as she climbed off her perch. "I was just teaching Richie some of the moves he'll need to use when he gets a sword." She looked around, the guilt of what they had been doing clearly visible on her face. "Ah—we moved everything to the walls, then—well—I guess we sort of spared our way to the walls—you know. Swordplay is an active sport, not something you practice sitting down—usually."

Duncan groaned, placing a hand to his temple. "In the house? It looks like a war zone, people! What were you both thinking?" he looked from Richie to Amanda. "What have you been using to spar with? Tell me that isn't a—"

"Mac, it's OK. Tessa has tons of these rods she won't miss a few bent ones. Besides, she fires them anyway until they melt," he said with an equally sheepish grin.

"You've been in Tessa's workshop? What were you doing in there and—"

"I was doing just what you asked me to do. I was giving Richie his first instructions."

"In the Rules of conduct – not sword fighting in the living room."

"Mac will you chill for a moment. I know the Rules. Besides, it took Amanda three whole minutes to recite them to me so I could check them off my list. This was way more practical." Amanda added her glowing smile to Richie's energetic hand gesturing.

Duncan wordlessly gestured around the room as Richie jumped off the coffee table. "Sparring is permanently ended in this house. From now on, as far as both of you are concerned, this is *Holy Ground.* No one—and I do mean no one—draws a sword or a welding rod in here to spar ever again. Is that clear? The two of you are going to put this house in order—**now**!" The way Duncan said 'now' told both combatants that their heads might be forfeited if they didn't comply at once. Richie headed for the broom closet as Amanda began righting furniture.

"Look, I'm going to take a shower then I have to get to bed. By the time I get out of the shower, I want to see this place as I left it this morning."

"Duncan, do you need someone to scrub your back," Amanda called after him, wistfully.

"Don't even think it, Amanda," he replied as he shut the door.

Chapter Ten

When Tessa awoke the next morning and Duncan wasn't by her side, she called the house. Richie answered. After assuring him, as quickly as she could, that she was healing OK, she asked for Duncan.

"He's not here right now, Tessa. He said something about meeting an art broker downtown this morning. Acquiring the rest of a private collection he had bid on earlier this year. No, he didn't say when he'd be back. If you need something I can be over there on my bike in about fifteen-minutes. Hey, Tess—I can't wait for you to come back to us. It really isn't the same here with just Mac." Richie hung up the phone.

Tessa sounded really down. If he had to lie in a hospital bed, instead of being home with people who were family, he would be down too. His thoughts of when he was confined to his bed with a bad cold, a couple of times when he was in the orphanage, were not happy times for him either. He could relate to Tessa's situation. He shook it off.

I'm in the hospital, Tessa grumbled to herself as she hung up the phone. *There are more important things here for him than acquiring more art. What was he bidding on?* Her mind rewound the weeks until she reached the day he brought home a large, padded package. He had fussed over it to the point of annoyance. *You never have been one to be patient,* she had reminded herself. After all, it was just a package.

Almost a year ago:
"Duncan—I'm dying to see what's in there. How can you be so slow?"

"I am not slow, Tess, I am being careful. This single piece is part of a larger collection. Together, they were created approximately five centuries ago. If this little figurine survived that long, I am not the one who is going to break it."

Tessa slipped her fingers around and passed Duncan's. "I know, but it's just taking ages. If you just untied this little knot here—"

"Don't touch it like that. I want to get into it slowly. There might be something else going on here I don't know about. If the protective cushion falls away too quickly—"

She released his fingers and threw up her hand. "OK, OK I understand."

"*La paciencia es una virtud, amor.*" (Patience is a virtue, love)

She cocked her head. "Are you talking to me, Duncan MacLeod?"

"Be patient, sweetheart." He chuckled playfully. "How about a little Spanish language lesson? The language of any people is an important expression of who and what they were or are."

A pouty expression formed on her face. "I am patient – for the right occasions."

Duncan raised an eyebrow and chuckled once again. "Oh no, you are not. *Patients* is not your middle name."

"Yes, I am," she exclaimed, a little peeved at this Scott.

"No, you are not," he finished quietly, determined to get the last word in. "Why don't you make us some coffee?"

"Oh, so you want me to leave you alone?"

He stopped unwrapping and put his hands squarely on his thighs. "Tess, you are driving me crazy—just give me a few more minutes and I'll have it open."

"OK, Coffee it is. I'll be back to check on your progress – snail."

"I know, I know," he replied, ignoring the nip at the end of her sentence. Duncan continued working with the wrappings as if he were disarming an atom bomb—full concentration. Tessa's incessant questions were enough to make anyone's finger slip and hit the trigger.

Tessa had gotten over her tiff when coffee came to him after a welcomed fifteen-minute reprieve from her nattering.

Taking a seat beside him, she looked at the single, tiny, gold figurine on the table. "So, tell me. What is this piece about?"

The gold statue looked like a stylized kind of llama. *It is truly a work of art,* Tessa pondered. *There is strength in those lines. The body is perfectly designed, showing elegance, grace, and strength.* She began peering at it from different angles. There was something different here. *The eyes—they're full of expression, so is the mouth and ears. Not two-dimensional in their gaze; they seemed to be alert, watching for possible hunters. No matter which way I look at it, it is always looking at you. I wonder if this is how the living animal really looks from the observer's perspective.* As an artist herself, she could sit back and praise whoever created this work. *Whoever did this with rudimentary tools and materials was a real artist. He or she gets my respect as a fellow artist.*

"You said this was part of a larger collection? Where is the rest of it?"

"Like so many cultural finds, this one was taken from its cultural location. The person who was mining those treasures never bothered or cared about the people he was taking them from. In this case, I intervened—somewhat." Duncan shrugged a bit, his eyes betraying a secret he was not willing to speak of just yet. "It is a part of a group. There have been several other sets of llama statues unearthed in Chile and near the area around Mount Llullaillaco in Salta, Argentina. The dig sites have been entering parts of history—exposing cultures which existed in the region anywhere from 500 to 800 years ago. It is mind boggling all the things that have been found up and down South America over the last one-hundred years or so. This, and the many other archeological finds of art in the area, were all made by craftsmen before I was born."

Present time:
"Incan art," she sighed.

A light knock sounded on the door. A moment later, Grace entered dressed in her medical attire.

"Good morning, Tessa." Her voice was pleasant, warm, and vibrant. "You are looking worlds better than when I looked in on you earlier. You seem to be healing almost as fast as an Immortal," she added by way of a light joke.

She helped Tessa adjust the angle of her bed then she reached for a chair and brought it beside her. "I thought we should have a chat today about what happened to you and other things on your mind."

A concerned look crossed her brow. "Am I OK? Is something wrong with my wound?"

Grace reached out and took her hand warmly, easing her anxiousness and reassuring her. "No there isn't. I looked at your chart early this morning. Your blood values are fine and you are healing very well. It won't be long before you're out of here. No one wants you to overstay your welcome." She smiled then averted her eyes for a moment before releasing her hand.

"That's not what I am here to talk to you about. I want to talk about what happened to you that night and how it left you feeling."

"What? How it left me feeling?" *I beg your pardon,* Tessa thought. "I was shot by a teenage-junky looking for drug money. I could have been killed. It happened so fast. How am I supposed to feel?"

"Scared, threatened, violated, angry – and a dozen other feelings you are entitled to. I would just like to talk with you."

Tessa braced in her bed just a bit. "Are you a psychiatrist, too? Do you think I need help – that I might be going crazy?" Her tone was testy. "Did Duncan say something to you? I don't know why he decided to run his little errand this morning. He would usually be here now."

Grace didn't respond for a long second. When she did, she chose her words very carefully. "I asked him to give us today – alone. I'm not a psychiatrist – just a friend – your friend, Tessa."

"You did what? Why? I need him – I want him."

"You're in pain inside. Duncan feels it too. He's exhausted. Whatever led up to it, and the shooting, has drained him emotionally."

Duncan has asked me not to reveal the events that led up to the shooting – not until he is able to find out more about the situation. I am not about to share this with you no matter how you choose to play 'therapist' with me, Tessa thought.

"It would be better for everyone to find an emotional release. I would like you to share whatever feelings you can put into words with me. Sharing always makes things a little better." She shifted gears in her approach.

"Being shot is physical agony. I know, I have been in the line of fire myself a couple of times during various nameless skirmishes. Whatever you choose to call them, over the centuries I've lived, I've been there. When you're staring down that barrel, someone else is rolling the dice for you. You never win; the question is simply, how much are you going to lose?"

A tear quietly rolled down Tessa's cheek, and Grace had to steel herself from reaching out to comfort her. She had hit a raw nerve. *Will Tessa open the door to her psyche for me just a crack?*

Tessa bit her lower lip but remained silent for a long moment. When she spoke her tone was almost accusing.

"You are an Immortal, Grace. What could you possibly know about the kind of loss that comes this way? You have all the time in the world to enjoy life, desires, and love."

Sadly, Grace slowly shook her head. "We don't age, or succumb to illness, but Immortals haven't all the time in the world, Tessa. The stroke of a sword can end a millennium of living, desires for loving and to comfort those who love you so much, all over in a millisecond. Then for us, time's up too. Oh yes, Tessa, I do know about the emptiness, the helpless, the desperation that wells up inside. I've loved so deeply, and lost so completely at the point of a gun and a sword."

Tessa backed her feistiness down just a bit. *Could Immortal Grace actually be a kindred spirit to me in pain?* "I can't even put into words what I truly feel." She looked briefly to the ceiling. "I see that face and think, *"How dare you steal from me."* Not my rings—not any money, which I didn't have, but *time*—my time, Grace. He was taking time—he was reaching into my possible future self and like some god-damned superior being who was above us all—gazing into his crystal ball. He was saying to me, *"Your life is mine – I decide how much you're going to live, to love—your time is mine to take!"* Her face was flushed, and she took a deep breath before continuing. "You don't think much about death at my age." She paused to collect herself. "It's not the act of suddenly dying that bothers me, it's just, well, every time I replay what happened, I am so angry, frustrated, hurt, and scared of what I am *really* losing. I hate myself, Grace—for what I am not—and I don't even know why."

As she spoke, Tessa began wading the blanket that covered her lap, into her hands in a strangle hold. Grace noted the emotional turmoil building.

"I'm lying there dead," she continued, choking back a sob. "And another Immortal steps smoothly in to take my place—into what should be our bed—Duncan and mine's—our future, our time together! What should have been my life with him is gone in a second. I have replayed an alternate reality of what happened that night—I see myself lying there, Duncan holding me—begging me to come back to him, the immortal pain in his breast for me and I can't respond to him because I am not an Immortal too." She squeezed her eyes closed to hold the tears back. "In the end, I have given my entire body and being—everything that I have and am—to him. Yet I'm nothing more than a brief moment in his life – and a bullet sweeps me aside for someone else—like so much dust in the wind. Oh God, Grace, I love him more than my own life, yet right now all I want to do is shake the stuffing out of Duncan when he comes near me."

How dare you be immortal before me? Is that it Tessa? Her subconsciousness prodded her conscious mind. "You asked him to 'grow old' with you once—did you want him to die with you too? Better dead than in the arms of another Immortal? Take a long look at your reflection—do you like what you are seeing? Are you a lady, or a vicious tiger?

"I hope that substitute, faceless Immortal in the back of your mind, waiting for your demise, isn't me," she said gently.

Tessa averted her eyes and shook her head once but did not respond. Finally, after a long moment, she glanced up to Grace out of the corners of her eye. "How well did you know Duncan?" she asked, quietly.

OK, now we're digging down a little to the root of the issue, Grace thought. She wet her lips. "I met Duncan the day I thought he came to take my head."

Tessa opened her eyes wide and stared at the immortal physician. "Duncan wouldn't do something like that to a woman."

She raised her eyebrows and stared back. *You really know nothing about Immortals, do you?* "No, Duncan didn't take my head, but there are many Immortals that would. I was just lucky it was him. I was in the middle of birthing a child—it was a hard labor and the woman screamed in pain toward the end. I think that her scream is what attracted his attention at first. The main road was too far away for him to have sensed me as he was riding. We can only sense one another a couple dozen or so yards away. The baby was coming when he charged through the door with his sword drawn."

"What did Duncan do?" she asked, trying to picture the man she had lived with, and loved so tenderly, with a sword in his hand – heading toward a defenseless midwife.

"He put up his sword and helped me birth the child. When I finally got the baby and the woman cleaned up, I nodded to him, we walked outside and I closed the door."

The inflection of Tessa's voice shifted. "What did the two of you do in the countryside then?"

Grace caught the hint of, *'Did the two of you go off somewhere quiet and make love?'* She warmed up for a punch of a reply. "You don't understand. It's our Rules of Combat. I understood that he was likely *calling me out* as it were to fight to the death in private. The transfer of our immortal Quickening is intimate, not a spectacle for mortal eyes. I asked Duncan, when he burst through the door, to wait till I was finished. He acknowledged that request and did not take me away from bringing a mortal life into the world. But when two Immortals meet—with a sword drawn—a challenge is being given. He behaved in a dignified manner in that vulnerable woman's presence. When I closed the door behind me, I told him to get it over with, just leave the infant and the mother. I was too tired to run, and I knew I could not outfight him. Yes, Tessa, I was staring down that proverbial *Immortal's gun barrel.* He just chose not to pull the trigger on me."

Astonishment flashed across Tessa's face and she looked away to the wall.

"Duncan is my lifeblood and yet I can only hope to enjoy a fraction of his life with him. In the end, someone else is going to swoop in and steal from me." She began to cry softly. "Grace, right now I am so torn up inside with conflicting feelings I can't get my hands on any of it to put it in order. What is really wrong with me?"

She reached out placing a consoling hand on Tessa's shoulder then kissed her forehead gently. "I think I know. And I think I know how we can find out." She pushed back the covers. "Let's take a walk."

Grace knocked once then opened the door to the private conference room. It was empty. It was late in the afternoon—unlikely anyone would need it now. She helped Tessa to the couch. Tessa settled herself, pulling her lap blanket around her. Grace disappeared for several long minutes. When she finally reappeared, she locked the door and lowered the lights. Tessa looked around, a bit apprehensive.

"OK—what are we going to do in here? Are you going to hypnotize me?"

"No. I don't know how to do that. I'm going to help you through guided imagery. It's not the same. You're not going to be a zombie—don't worry."

"Is this supposed to cure me?"

"I can't cure your soul. But you can. Let's see if you can get to where you really want to go this way." Grace lowered the lights further until it was comfortably dusk. She began with breathing, instructing Tessa to relax and focus on a small, almost insignificant, part of the middle of her body.

"Watch it start to glow, then expand that *glow* until it becomes the entire *you*." Grace's voice droned softly as she listened to Tessa's breathing slow down. "You are now the *glow*—the *driver*. Your body is surrounding you—it is just your *'vehicle'*." She felt Tessa relax completely into the couch cushions. "I'm going to place objects into your hand. I want you to take from it what you need to go where you want to be." She slipped a round metallic disk into Tessa's almost limp hand and asked softly, "What is this?"

Tessa's fingers fondled the object, her sense of touch probing the intricate design on its metallic face—interwoven creases—spaces with holes. *A hair clasp,* her mind registered.

Grace watched her expressions carefully in the dim light of the room. "Now take yourself to wherever this leads you and don't be afraid."

Tessa smiled as an image formed in the front of her mind. She saw herself moving to become a part of it.

His hair was still moist—toweling had sopped up the endless torrent of water the rain had poured onto his head, but it had left him with the rich smell of earth and grass from their earlier romp in the meadow. She was soaked to the skin—steam rose ever so lightly through her loosely-woven pullover—from her warm body now excited by the odor that was Duncan. She reached with both hands into his dark highland-mane and tousled it, pulling the clasp from the back of his hair. She plunged her face into the tangle and inhaled. "I love you," she heard herself repeat softly, and a part of her knew she had whispered those words aloud as well. *"I want to eat you up, I love you so."*

Grace waited until Tessa's expression returned to neutral, until she had lived that scene out in her mind, then she gently exchanged an ornate button for the clasp in her hand.

Tessa's fingers probed this new object. *It is a button, but not from anything he is wearing now? Where did it come from?*

Grace let her wrestle with the puzzle awhile before she spoke softly.

"It's 1815—a button from the uniform of a Highland Rifler. Duncan fought with them at Waterloo. He's there now." Grace fell silent and waited, watching as a storm of confusion clouded Tessa's expression. She worked her way through various stages as the storm inside of her became a crescendo.

He's in a time and place before you were born. What are you willing to do to reach him? she thought.

"I can't," she whispered softly, to the darkness, to her inner voice.

But you can – you must, her desires fought back her rational thoughts.

You know the way, another voice from within called. Images, rendered only by Duncan's words in the retelling of his meeting of Darius, on a field of slaughter, were the roadmap that gave her spirit impetus to travel.

Flashback – 1815:

Duncan walked, stumbled, then catching himself, walked on, carrying his wounded comrade across his back. All about in the snow lay the dead and dying. The pain of Napoleon's war around him was etched in his brow.

She reached out to those thoughts, which he had instilled by his words. With her desire to be with him, and comfort him, she moved toward him and instead touched a 'glass' in her mind, through which she could not pass.

"Let me pass!" Her rational, mortal consciousness fought her irrational desire to escape time—the space she was locked into—time that ticked away her fleeting existence in the here and now. On the other side of that dark glass was forever in the form of Duncan MacLeod. She saw him reach for his sword.

"I am Duncan MacLeod of the clan MacLeod."

"I am Darius," came the gentle voice from beneath the tired, worn, snow-covered hood. "You won't need that."

The image began to fade and she fought to hold it, to reach through the impenetrable glass of mortal reality.

Unnoticed by her conscience senses, the button was slowly slipped from her grasp and replaced by a smooth metal cylinder. Carefully her fingers inched along its length, probing for any clues to its identity. It was smooth and seamless.

Her sense of hearing grew keen as she waited in the stillness of that darkened room for a sound, any sound that would lead her to Duncan. In the stillness a tick sounded then another and—*what is that?*

Tick, tick, tick. The sound was relentless – growing steadily louder.

Tessa's creative imagination 'flipped' through the pages of her memory like sheets of her art portfolio until she reached a space and time with no name.

Null:

A dull brown, lifeless, surreal landscape lay before her, broken only by a flat mirror calm sea that seemed to fight for space on the canvas of her imagination. A crisp cliff was rising out of the pool of nothingness.

Tick, tick, tick. That sound?

Clocks!

As far as her minds-eye could see they were there—hanging from branches and draped over geometric shapes, dripping from rocks, floating on the water—clocks.

"They're ticking away time—my time!"

"There is nowhere to run," her mind heard the words, but she knew not from whence they came. Were they from '*outside*'? *Where was this outside?* This world which threatened to envelop her was a surrealistic, frightening, hallucination. Her mind fought to make any sense of what she was seeing. Out of the confusion, a rational thought surfaced among the branches hung with limp clocks. *Salvador Dali's painting, Persistence of Memory.*

"Face time and defeat it." The words she heard were from *outside,* but they were as meaningless as the landscape.

How? She queried the unseen speaker with her mind. *Time is eternal.*

Don't you mean, immortal, her subconscious self-responded.

That ticking? It's coming from one clock. Where is it?

Defeat immortality and you stop the clock.

I don't understand?

Before her, draped across the sand dune, was a clock with no numbers, only one strangely shaped hand.

"Strike!" Her subconscious voice prodded.

There was something in her hand, it was heavy and smooth. She felt anger toward the clock.

You thief! she mentally shouted and angrily slammed the object in her hand down on that clock's face.

The hand slipped from its shattered face—it was Duncan's katana!

Reality:

Tessa's eyes snapped open and she gasped, startled. Shocked by the sudden transition, her mind and reflexes fought to identify the weight that was unexpectedly still in her hand. Bringing her hands up toward her eyes, she focused. Grace's sword was in her hands!

"My God, No!" she gasped, dropping it with a 'clang' as if it were red hot. Anger filled her eyes—the same anger she had held for that surreal clock, ticking away her time—was now directed at the Immortal beside her.

"What have you been doing with me? Are you some kind of sick Immortal?" She tried to jump to her feet and found herself fighting the pain in her side.

Grace reached out to steady her. "Tessa, who and what were you fighting? Please say it – for yourself and your peace of mind, say it."

"What have you been doing to me – inside me?" She looked down at the sword as if she were reviling a serpent. "You put a sword in my hand," her voice rose, furious. "What did you want from me? I could never kill," *like your kind,* she mentally finished.

And you could never hope to be an Immortal for him either, her mind responded. *Your enemy is time.*

Tessa froze for a long moment, a cold shiver passed through her soul as she heard that final word. She looked back to Grace. "I'm checking out." Tessa fought through the pain and rose, steady. Grace blocked her path but did not try to touch her.

"It is late and you're not going anywhere this evening," she said in an official, but gentle tone of voice. "If it is medically advisable, I will try to get you discharged in the morning. Please, Tessa – whoever or whatever you were fighting – say it!" Grace exclaimed forcefully.

"How dare you presume to understand mortal feelings—you intruder! My feelings are *mine*!" Tessa shouted.

"Tessa, please, I'm not your enemy. The man that shot you brought something to a head. For you to move forward with Duncan, as the wife of an Immortal, you must either make peace with this fear or defeat it. If you don't, it will defeat you."

"We're done here," she said with a tone of absolute finality.

Chapter Eleven

Richie fastened his helmet on his head and turned the key in the ignition. The bike's engine roared to life. A fleeting thought crossed his mind; *I should leave a note for Mac?* He was already on his bike—he'd do it next time for sure. Mac said he had gotten a call from Tessa and was heading to the hospital to pick her up. He planned to be away for a while.

This was the third day after the shooting and that killer was still out there—somewhere, he had reminded himself. *OK, I came back to life, but if I hadn't been an Immortal I'd still be dead, so I can legitimately call him a 'killer'. Besides, if that bullet had connected with Tessa the way it did with me, she would have been dead.* Not that he had really expected that the police would have found the kid by now. Mac always wants things to be handled in an official manner. *Not to worry, Mac, if I find this kid, I will officially kill him – save the taxpayer a little money on the cost of court.* He thought a long moment before sliding back onto the seat and cranking the accelerator.

Amanda said it. It wasn't really about him dying and coming back an Immortal. It was really about the way Tessa sounded on the phone to him the other day. It wasn't what she had said, but the way she had said it – there was fear in her voice coming from her 'core' now – something he couldn't ever remember hearing in the voice of this strong-willed Tessa. He could only assume that it was a fear of walking somewhere, sometime and meeting that shooter once again. *And the next time, neither Mac nor myself, would be there to save her.*

He had no idea where to begin looking so, like so many comic books he remembered reading, he returned to the scene of the crime.

It was Saturday mid-morning and life in this nice upscale neighborhood was on a slow roll, *walk the dog, polish the car, kids with their bikes, a hot jogger on the sidewalk*, his mind acknowledged. The well-groomed lawns and large picture perfect homes all made what happened at this spot, three nights ago, seem impossible in Richie's mind. *Unless one of these nice well-off families has a real hit-man in their household closet, this doesn't make sense.* He shook his head and moved on.

The scenery changed very little as he cruised the streets – traffic was light, occasionally he passed a group of people with and without dogs – nothing. He had looped around the streets – spiraling out from ground '0' covering miles without seeing anything. The initial inner fire that had gotten him out the door and on his bike earlier was all but gone.

I could do this all day. Mac and Tessa are probably home by now wondering where I am. OK – so I'm not the greatest Sherlock Holmes in the world. One spin around that large park, or whatever, and I'm out of here. There was almost no one around the park in the morning as he rode – *wait a moment!* He slowed. Up ahead a block or so, walking beside the row of bushes lining the street-side of the park, was someone in a baggy, blue-gray jacket; the hair was partially concealed by a baseball-looking cap. He stopped and focused – *a dark image on the back of that jacket – could it be an Indian head?* The first person met another, who seemed to materialize out of the bushes, and then the two slipped between the bushes and disappeared.

Richie hit the accelerator and tore through the first opening in the hedge he could find. An instant later he overtook them. Skidding to a halt in front of them, he sent dirt and grass flying in a dozen different directions.

An astonished cry escaped both girls as they leaped back against the bushes to avoid Richie's bike as it skidded to a halt just a few feet away.

"What the hell? Like the road is that way!" a girl's voice snapped.

Richie shoved his visor up, an equally astonished look on his face. He tried to bail himself out in front of two girls who were obviously still in high school.

"I'm sorry ladies—uh—girls. Thought I saw a couple of *hot numbers* a block away and—well—I guess I couldn't help myself. Just checking it out."

The younger girl giggled and began making ogle eyes at Richie.

"Hot? You must have x-ray vision back there," she said. "All the good stuff is up front," she finished as coyly as a grammar student could muster up a sexy voice and began tugging on the front of her baggy, but totally flat, tee-shirt.

"I don't know so much about this one," the other girl said, looking Richie over as if he were a used library book. "Kind of a lame pick-up line if you ask me," she snipped, pretending to ignore him, whilst attempting to flirt in his direction with her butt.

The image he had seen on the back of her well-worn jacket was a faded peace symbol from a bygone era. Richie seriously considered that this jacket was old enough to collect social security. He beamed a pained smile back in their general direction. *I am so out of here!* he thought and slipping back on the bike, rode away. *No more parks for me.*

He knew he wasn't supposed to be on the bike trail with his motorbike through the park, but this park was huge and he hadn't met anyone else riding in the area so he continued.

Suddenly *that feeling* hit him. That empathic immortal sense of another's presence; he was nearly shocked off his bike. He hit the break, quickly removed his helmet, and looked around for the source. He had *felt* the presence of Duncan and Amanda after he became an Immortal. These people he expected to find in certain places – this was unexpected.

"Axel Whittaker," the voice behind him announced, taking him by surprise. "And you are," he asked when Richie didn't immediately respond.

"Richie Ryan," he replied haltingly, uncertain what to say.

"Well, well, if it isn't little Richie all grown up and just look at you, a new Immortal. Will wonders never cease." Axel slowed his pace, carefully glancing around then back to Richie.

"I don't think we've met before," Richie said cautiously dismounting.

Axel shook his head once. "Doesn't matter, I know who you are. You were kind of a punk little kid—always wanting candy from old Mr. Stubbs candy shop," A small chuckle escaped his devious grin. "I remember when old Mr. Stubbs was young Mr. Stubbs. I stole candy out of his jars the day he opened that store – my, my how time flies when you're an Immortal."

A very uneasy feeling began working its way from the pit of Richie's stomach up to his jaw. The feeling was growing stronger by the moments. "Nice chatting, let's do it again in another life."

"Not so fast, my young Immortal," he began and quickly drew his sword from his oversized jacket. "I'm here to welcome you to the Game." He swung at Richie!

Before he realized what was happening, Axel's blade had sliced through the shoulder and sleeve of his jacket. Richie yelped in pain and jumped to the side as Axel swung again, this time for Richie's head. Turning to run, he stumbled briefly. Axel bore down on his position, driving the point of the blade into the ground just a fraction of an instant behind Richie's reflexive lunge. Richie was five frantic steps ahead of Axel and heading into the woods. His hands found a loose branch and he released it, slapping his pursuer, buying himself a precious few extra seconds to flee. The next branch he grabbed was loose and he swung at Axel with it. The wood was no match for a steel sword and it snapped on contact, Axel raked Richie's side on the return swing.

There's never a good welding-rod when you need one, he thought frantically. He spun with the sword stroke against his side, lessening the impact it had on his flesh, then threw the branch stub at Axel and jumped him. Against an experienced sword-wielding Immortal, Richie knew he had no chance to survive, but in a fistfight, they were fairly equal. Knocking him to the ground they went back and forth, both Axel and Richie connecting with their punches. At one point, Richie thought his fist had stunned Axel and he reached across his body for his sword. But the Immortal caught him in a leg-scissor and flipped him on his back, then reached himself. His hand found his sword and he arced it high up and over to the other side of his body – where his mind had placed Richie's last move.

The moment Richie had landed on his back he had rolled quickly to his knees and sprang just as Axel's sword came down. He ran, as fast as he could, back to his bike, grabbed his crash helmet and shoved it on his head, then jumped on his bike and turned the key in the ignition. A split second later he felt the force of Axel's blow against his crash helmet as the sword connected – he had swung for Richie's neck. The force of Axel's swing tore the helmet off his head and he was thrown off balance. Overturning his bike on top of his leg as he fell, Richie was pinned.

Axel stepped toward the overturned bike then raised his sword above his head with both hands for a killing blow.

Grabbing the handlebars, Richie turned the front wheel hard-over against Axel's leg.

Axel was caught off balance and sidestepped against the rear wheel. Richie gunned the engine and Axel was spun to the ground by the force.

Squirming out from under the bike, he ran with Axel trailing. *A public place – I have to get somewhere where there are people,* he thought frantically, trying to remember if this park had a play area, sidewalk cafes, or something, somewhere in it. Topping the knoll, he saw a group of small park-cafes near a large fountain in the distance. *Only one car – please let there be a crowd inside.* Richie didn't spare a second to look behind himself to see how close Axel was – he could hear him. *Please – let me be out of the reach of his sword! I've been an Immortal for only three days and my head is already on the chopping block. Mac, if I survive this I promise to stay home like you told me to until I am trained.* Suddenly, in the middle of his fleeing steps, he felt the presence of a second Immortal. *Oh no—now they're coming out of the woodwork after me!* His heart was pounding in his throat and he frantically thought, *I'd have had a heart attack and died by now – if I weren't an Immortal – little good that is going to do me if he catches me.* Richie didn't know which way to run anymore. As he swerved toward a row of dense trees, Amanda stepped from behind the second one, sword in hand. Axel slowed. Richie continued to the farther tree then bent over, a hand on his knee for support. Gasping for breath he looked back at his pursuer.

Axel halted well out of the reach of Amanda's sword. "You can't interfere," Axel said pointing to Richie. "The battle is joined."

Amanda gave Richie a quick sideways glance then refocused on Axel. "Oh really? Don't see a sword in his hand. Did Richie challenge you with his bike?"

"Doesn't matter," and Axel began slowly maneuvering around Amanda toward Richie. "He's an Immortal—same as we are. He's part of the Game now."

Amanda deliberately stepped in front of Axel. "Usually it is acknowledged that they are trained by one of us first before they meet their first challenge." She eyed him with an expression reserved for smelly trash. "What happened to your last sweet, very young, girlfriend. I don't see her around you anymore. Didn't lose something important—like her head, did she?" She raised her sword and Axel backed up a step. "I've heard you like to rob the cradle as it were. Your first death came over a fourteen-year old girl you—uh— seduced. Her father, a minister I believe, put a bullet in you. For the last almost 400 years you just keep coming back for younger and younger girls. I guess old habits never change, except this time they're alone and immortal. The trouble is I never seem to see the same one with you for very long. I suggest you take a walk unless you want to try and take me."

Axel glanced to Richie then back to Amanda. He played with the idea of going for her head for a long moment before *immortal sanity* kicked in. *There is no way I am going to take Amanda down, not under these conditions—maybe someday.* He smiled then made a short bow and walked away.

Richie finally took a deep breath, the first one since he encountered Axel. "Thank you, Amanda. I was beginning to think my life as an Immortal was about to become a whole lot shorter than anything I could ever expect to have as a mortal."

Amanda ran an experienced hand over Richie's slashed and blood-stained jacket. She shook her head briefly then put a friendly hand on his shoulder. "OK, Richie, what are you doing out of the house without Duncan? You know what we both told you – there are

Immortals out here," she made a wide sweeping gesture. "Most of us – well – some of us, respectfully walk away from a new Immortal – we can sense a new one."

"How?"

"Sort of the way the *energy* feels when we first meet them. And if they don't have a sword in their hand, the better Immortals will leave them alone – at least the first time they meet."

"And I take it Axel isn't one of the 'good guys'?"

Amanda wrinkled up her brow and shook her head once. "Not even close. So where's your bike?"

"I stopped when I sensed an Immortal – he kind of took me by surprise. It's over that raise – up there, by the bike trail. I was just getting used to sensing Mac and you – and well this is only the third day." He shook his head. "I should have just kept going and not stopped. This is all just too new yet." He ran a hand through his damp hair and looked around absently. Do you know it's only been about seventy-two hours since I woke up immortal in the trunk of Mac's car? Mac was coming out of the hospital emergency exit when I popped the top. I didn't even get to get out. He came up and told me to stay put and slammed the lid on me again! What a way to begin an immortal life."

"He couldn't have you jumping out of the car, by a hospital emergency entrance, looking like something out of the graveyard." She patted his shoulder. "Still didn't answer my question. What are you doing out here?"

"That guy is still out here somewhere."

"The shooter? I thought you were going to let it go?"

"Not for me, Amanda – for Tessa. Look, I got what you said to me the other day – I'm an Immortal now. I don't know – he probably did me a favor – maybe I should thank him. But the police haven't found him or they would have called me in to make a positive ID. He's still out there and Tessa is scared. She didn't say it, I heard it in her voice when she called the house. She's only going to go around once in this life, Amanda, and she doesn't want to be looking over her shoulder every time she steps out of the house. I don't know what that guy was all about. He could see she didn't really have anything on her that would be worth killing for. Mac's T-bird isn't exactly a Rolls-Royce either." They started walking toward where he left his bike.

"The police thought it was some junky looking for money – that's what you said, right? So he's probably long gone from here by now. The street you said it happened on isn't exactly a slum."

"You can say that again. I rode by that spot and through that neighborhood this morning. I can't believe anyone would litter let alone shoot someone there. They must scrub those houses with bath brushes every other weekend." He shook his head. Reaching his bike, he stood it up on its kickstand then picked clumps of grass-roots out from under the fender and chasse while Amanda retrieved his helmet.

"It's nice to know your helmet can handle a sword stroke. Looks like that's the only thing that saved your neck." She pointed to the long deep abrasive streak at the base of the helmet near what would have been his collar.

Richie stopped cleaning his bike and took the helmet. There was a very somber look of realization in his eye. "I had just shoved that helmet on when I felt his blade hit it and catch the edge right here. It felt like a cannonball hit the back of my head then the helmet was ripped off. My head would have been off already if it weren't for this."

Amanda looked away briefly. Her eyes were getting moist. *Must be the sea air,* she told herself, then coughed and changed the subject. "How is Tessa healing?"

"Good, I guess. She called early this morning—she is being discharged already. Mac is picking her up now. He said he would be late coming back—probably wants to take her somewhere private as sort of a welcome home thing."

Amanda looked down to the ground and away from Richie. "That's great," she said very quietly. "I'm glad she's doing better." She fell silent.

Richie watched Amanda for a long moment then got to his feet. Setting the helmet on his bike, he walked over and slipped a friendly arm around her waist. "Look," he began a bit hesitantly. "Tessa and Mac – they had been together a number of years before I came along. They sort of took me into their lives before I became Immortal and well, we've sort of been a family, Amanda. I don't know what's going to happen with me down the road, when Tessa finally becomes Mrs. MacLeod, I mean, but this is the way Mac wants it for now. You're an Immortal, Amanda. Could you let it be Tessa's turn for a little while with Mac?"

Amanda finally looked back to Richie, her big eyes meeting his and gave a non-committal nod then sighed. "You've got me there, kid. I've never been good at sharing anything. Guess when you grow up a starving street girl in a plague-infested city you learn to 'take' and not give. I've never been good at waiting behind someone to take 'my turn'."

Richie turned her to face him. "It's not my fault officer, it's my bad childhood," and he gave her a knowing experienced expression. "I used that line myself, more times than I can count. I guess we both have one way or the other – except it wouldn't be the truth, would it? I had a couple of good people before and when I was in the orphanage. One family even let me stay with them on and off for a couple of years – they were really good. Not that I didn't have good people now and again, I just chose not to listen sometimes and things really went wrong. Of course Mac and Tess have been like a real family to me. I heard you had a pretty good mentor yourself – Rebecca Horne."

"Yeah," Amanda sighed. "I was killed stealing a loaf of bread from a plague house in the early part of the 8th century. She took me out of that cart full of our city's dead, taught me everything I needed to survive as an Immortal, gave me a lot more than just an education. A real princess to me—a pauper. I was street trash."

"You were just a starving girl. I can't imagine that I would have done any different if I would have lived then. But this isn't 'back then' Amanda."

She stared into his eyes, a bit puzzled. "Are you sure you haven't been around a lot longer than you look?" She put her arms around his neck.

Richie followed suit and pulled her close. Then glanced as far down as his eyes could on her body before meeting her warm flesh. "You're really *hot*, Amanda. The first time I saw you on Mac's barge I could have – well, you know. But now that I'm an Immortal and – well – you've sort of been here for me, helping me keep my head on my shoulders like today with Axel. I feel if I did anything with you— more than what we're doing right now—that is—it would be like I was doing it to my big *sister*. I hope you take that as a compliment because that's the way I meant it."

Amanda pulled back, her jaw dropped open—for the first time in her life, she was utterly speechless. *What?* she thought. *You think of me, Amanda, as your big sister?* It took her a very long moment to recover from that shock. "Thank you, I think," she finally said haltingly and released her feminine grip on his neck and shoulders. "Well then—brother, shouldn't we both go and see how Tessa is doing?"

Richie gave her a varying knowing expression. *OK, you mink. Haven't we been over this share thing? Come on, I might not be 1,100 years, old but I'm not dumb.*

"Look—the truth, Richie. When Tessa, Duncan, and I met the last time, things didn't go as good as they should have. We Immortals need each other—our immortal friends, that is—and I just want to try and smooth things over with Tessa since she is obviously going to be a part of Duncan's life for a while however long that is. Duncan has already made up his mind to marry her, Richie. He and his 'boy scout rules' about honor, loyalty, and monogamous devotion – that's Duncan all over and he's not going to change for anyone. He makes people like me better for knowing him. We're all going to be in and out of each other's lives from time to time and Duncan knows it too. We've done a lot of things for each other—getting out of tough spots over the centuries and it would be better for everyone if Tessa accepted this before something comes up." *It would be better too if she understood that 'mortal' means very temporary in Duncan's mind also,* Amanda thought privately. Then glancing back to where Richie was walking, *Sister – hum? You learn something new every millennium.* In a way, she was starting to like the sound of that.

"Sir," a young male voice called. "There are no motorcycles allowed in the park."

Richie turned to see a bicycle officer approaching. *Crap!* He thought. *OK, a smooth line should bail me out of this one.* "Sorry officer, I was just—haven't we met somewhere before? The station?"

Officer Kilgore removed his helmet. "Mr. Ryan? Yes, at the station. What are you doing in the park with your motorcycle?"

"Look, I was on the street when I saw a couple of cute numbers, or so I thought they were. Turns out they weren't as hot as I thought and they started hitting on me, so I split."

"Through the park?"

"Look, it was anywhere away from them—I didn't think, OK? Then my bike broke down suddenly and I just found a—mechanic here." He looked to Amanda.

Amanda nodded vigorously. "I'm very good with my hands," she added, giving him a totally innocent smile, sort of like the one a cat would give whilst trying to deny swallowing the canary.

"OK. Just run it over to the road by the coffee shop—that way," he motioned in the direction they had just come.

"Thanks, I will. Say, did the police catch that guy—the one who shot Tessa, yet?"

"I haven't heard anything. But then again, I don't work in investigations yet. I'm on park patrol now, later I'll be doing something else. Are you looking for him now?"

Richie tried his best to play the question down, but he knew his expression had already given his intent away. "Well, if I did, I mean, it would help you people—right?" It was a lousy line delivered very unconvincingly. He walked his bike a ways before mounting. Amanda got on behind—her long, light jacket draped carefully around her on the seat. Richie ran the motor as quietly as he could.

Officer Kilgore stared fixated after them. *That was the Amanda – Wow! And they say a junior Watcher doesn't get to meet the legendary Immortals. Wonder what heist she's in town for? I hope to see her in action. I'm going to check the Cultural column when I get back to the station. Maybe the art galleries–*

A Frisbee landed near his feet breaking his stare. A jogger switched off the trail to retrieve it.

"Being a little too obvious aren't you?" The female voice said quietly. The jogger reached for the Frisbee, exposing her Watcher's tattoo. "Amanda's covered—focus on your Immortal," she finished and jogged off in the direction of the receding pair.

He sighed. There was nothing like Amanda's Watcher to throw a wet blanket on his fun. He took out his recorder and logged a few notes about Richie. *He's after that guy alright, but if he doesn't get a sword soon he won't have his head on his shoulders with Axel around. A pity, I'll get reassigned. I was hoping that I could keep this Immortal. He knows Duncan MacLeod. That's one Immortal I want to see fight. In the Watcher's Academy they said his sword work is legendary.*

Chapter Twelve

Duncan helped Tessa out of the car. He had stopped just a few feet from the door so she wouldn't have far to walk. He would re-park it later. Reaching quickly, he turned the key in the door then went to aid Tessa. Tessa was at the door before he could offer her his hand. She pushed it open as fast as she could then slid around the wall as if this familiar place was her refuge from the nightmare experiences of the last three days.

Duncan followed a moment later with the hospital bag which held the blood stained clothes she was wearing when she was shot. His foot had just crossed the threshold when she grabbed him wrapping her arms around him, holding him—her lifeline to protection.

"I'll just close—" he reached back to close the door. Tessa never loosened her grip; instead, she pulled him closer.

"The door can wait – I can't." She buried her head in his neck, his hair, his collar – anything that could hide – would hide her from the world outside, from which she had just escaped. "Oh God, Duncan, I'm home – really home. I never thought I'd see this place again." She kissed him again and again.

Not with the warmth and deep feeling of love, the passion he knew was Tessa, but *with the feeling of desperation – a gratitude for my rescuing her? From what? The hospital? From Grace?* Duncan was confused, but he didn't refuse her kisses. She was frightened by *something* and Grace had made that clear during their 'extended' check out time by admissions.

"She's frightened, Duncan. Very frightened," Grace had said quietly as she pulled him aside while Tessa started on a rather extended discharge protocol with her young assistant. "She's fighting with someone or something *inside* herself. She won't speak to me about it."

"Considering what she's been through, it's understandable." He paused, glanced about, then back to Tessa. "There is a lot more to all of this than what has been said."

Grace gave him a quizzical look. "What do you mean? What else happened to her?" Tessa was working her way through the last form. She glanced around to Duncan.

"I don't want to talk about it right now. Later, Grace."

"Just hold me, Duncan – never let me go again. I never want to leave this sanctuary. Too much precious time has been lost already."

Duncan smiled then he pulled her back, away from his body so she could see his face. "Sweetheart, you're safe here with me. What happened was the work of a maniac. I never had a chance to find out who he was or what this was all about. What happened in those few days just makes no sense to me. Did he say anything to you? Did anything happen to you while you were being held prisoner that might give me a clue?"

Tessa shook her hair back then pulled him to the couch. Her wound was still a bit sore and she was physically tired. *Why can't I heal like an Immortal? Pain is such a waste of time,* She thought.

"I don't really know what he was about either. I was kept blindfolded until I was led into that room upstairs. He kept me chained – I escaped once, but he recaptured me. Duncan, he was obsessed with a sword, he always carried it. The only thing he kept saying was, *"He'll come, just wait and see. They always do."*

"They always do," Duncan repeated then thought for a long moment. His mind rewound the events of the past week. "He called and left the address with Richie. He was expecting me. He was wearing some kind of infrared night vision when I found him in there. He switched off the lights." He paused and thought. *He had a sword – not a gun. Was he a psycho? Or was he expecting an Immortal? What did he mean by, 'He'll come ... they always do?'* "Tessa, did he say anything else – anything at all that would suggest he had a vendetta against me or anyone who was an Immortal?"

Tessa hugged a lap blanket to herself and slowly shook her head.

"That's all he kept saying. He was like a parrot, repeating himself constantly." She looked into his eyes. "He wasn't an Immortal? I assumed he was. He came after you with a sword—not a gun?" An awful feeling began to creep into her soul. "He kept parading around with that sword. Oh God, what was he? He must have done this before."

Duncan's mind riveted itself on one name – *Horton. Was this man one of those Watcher-hunters too?* He took a deep breath but did not share his thoughts with Tessa. "I'm going to check the computer. I need to know a little more about who owns that house."

"Why should we care? He's dead in there anyway. It's over, isn't it?" she added when she saw the look in his eyes. "Oh, please Duncan, say it is. I don't want to think about it anymore—that it could possibly—"

He hugged her to his breast. "Shh. You're safe here." Slowly, he brought her back, his reassuring hands on her trembling shoulders. *Tessa,* he thought, *there is a dead man lying in that house. I haven't heard a word about it the entire time you have been in the hospital—well, not that I have been listening to the news 24/7, but a find like that would come to everybody's attention one way or the other. Wait a minute, Officer Maxim mentioned they thought there was a break-in at that house that night. Someone from the police department has already been to the house and must have checked. Either the police are keeping the death a secret or—*

He smiled back, gently. "I need answers, sweetheart, that's all." *I think I know who might be able to confirm my suspicion, if I can get him to talk—Joe Dawson.*

"Why don't you lie down for a while sweetheart?"

She shook her head. "That's all I've been doing and I don't feel any better for it – in fact I feel worse." She pushed away from Duncan and rose. "I'm going to try and do some work today. Maybe it will make me feel better." She took a step in the direction of her workshop, then stopped and slowly looked around the room. Her keen artistic eye suddenly registered the subtle differences in the room's arrangement and décor. *This room has all been rearranged and this thing has appeared since my kidnapping.*

Duncan rose with her and seeing her looking about, tried to follow her gaze. "What is it?"

"You've rearranged all the furniture and over there, added a new cloth wall-hanging—by that sconce. I see now why you were too busy."

"Busy for what? A new wall-hanging? Where?" Duncan looked around the room. *Everything is clean and looks normal to me. What is Tessa seeing?*

Tessa waved her hands in a large sweeping motion indicating the room. "Look around, Duncan. The furniture—nothing is where it was before." She walked to the wall and stared at the long, tightly knitted cloth which hung haphazardly in a relaxed form from the sconce. Tessa folded her arms. "Hum—it looks a bit gaudy and out of place given the print hanging next to it. Where did you get this?"

Oh no, for the love of—, he thought, placing a hand on his forehead. "I didn't rearrange the furniture, Tess. Richie and Amanda did that."

"What!" She exclaimed and whirled on Duncan. Grabbing her side as a twinge of pain shot through her, she took a deep breath. "What in hell was Amanda doing in here rearranging our furniture?"

"Tessa, would you just calm down," Duncan began, his outstretched hands motioning for her to tone it down as he saw the *volcano* in her threatening to explode. But Tessa was just getting warmed up.

"What do you mean, *wait a moment calm down.* Duncan, this hanging thing looks like a—"

"It's Amanda's scarf, she must have tossed it up," he began as he reached to pick the scarf off the sconce.

Tessa beat him to it. Furious, she grabbed it, ripping it and the sconce off the wall. "Wait? For what?" *Me to be gone or dead*? she thought. "Before Amanda, the clean-up vamp, sweeps in and starts changing the house, what was once my life – our lives – what?"

"Calm down, Tessa! Richie and Amanda were sparring in the house and—"

Wadding the scarf angrily in her hands, she threw it on the floor and stamped on it. "Oh now our home is a training ground for Immortals?" She swept an arm in the direction of the couch and chair as she walked around the room—a room she now viewed as foreign. "And I suppose they were sword fighting on top of our couch, chairs, and table—though the refrigerator would have been a bit too high to scale without a ladder," she continued, sarcastically. "But didn't you tell me Amanda is an accomplished cat burglar. Why she could have swung up there from the chandelier—if we had one in the kitchen!"

Duncan grimaced. "I wasn't here Tessa. I was at the hospital with you when it happened. They moved all the furniture to the walls so it wouldn't be in the way."

A large footprint shaped mark on the top-back part of the overstuffed chair caught her attention. "I see someone must have fought their way up the side of the *castle* on this. I'm actually amazed nothing has been demolished in this arena. There are no sword slashes on anything."

Duncan cringed as he followed her angry pacing in the direction of her workshop. "They weren't using swords, they were using—"

Tessa stopped by a large, tall vase at the end of the living room near the door to her workshop. There among the corkscrew willows, reeds, and other decorative dried plants, were four bent, twisted, and generally deformed metal welding rods, *her* welding rods from *her* art workshop. Slowly she picked them out of the vase.

"Oh, I see. So after she finished rearranging the furniture in our home, Amanda found her way into my private, and very personal, art room and began randomly picking through my things and re-arranging whatever. Is that what happened? So now I should go into *her* space and see what artistic creation *she* has managed while I was out."

Duncan squeezed his eyes shut and taking a very deep breath, exhaled loudly. "Tessa," he exclaimed, his voice elevated, "That's not what happened. It's not what you think."

Turning, she waved a hand full of welding rods in his direction forcing him to jump aside. "Then what *did* just happen here? What should I think, Duncan?" she shouted.

Suddenly Duncan's immortal, empathic senses lit up—there was another Immortal near. Tessa, in the midst of her meltdown, didn't catch his subtle acknowledgment. *Wait a minute, not one, but two Immortals—oh, that's just great!*

"Why don't we go into the bedroom now, sweetheart?"

"Not a chance. I'm in the mood for war, not love."

"Knock knock, Duncan," Amanda called as Richie opened the door. "Did you miss us?" She slid smoothly past Richie.

"Amanda!" Duncan growled.

"Mac, you won't believe what happened to us in the park."

"Oh, I could believe just about anything," Tessa replied, her tongue razor sharp. "Why don't you enlighten us on your *romp*?"

Amanda froze at the tone. Her hands nervously straightened her shirt as if she were preparing for an interview – or a police grilling. "How are you feeling, Tessa?" she began carefully. "I'm glad you're out of the hospital and back home." She took a cautious step forward, toward her. "I was hoping you would be here – I wanted to talk with you a little while."

"About rearranging the furniture to your taste perhaps?" She motioned in a broad sweep around the room. Stabbing the scarf on the floor, she lofted it into her hand. "Or you're idea of artistic décor on our sconce – I must say it certainly wasn't 'la epitimy de syle artistique' (the epitome of artistic style). And while we're on the subject of art, I was just on my way to my private art studio to critique your latest creations. You must have been quite busy in there pawing around in my personal things during my absence, judging by this," she thrust her angry fist full of bent welding rods in her direction. A mock startled expression formed over Tessa's furious one. "Or maybe I should go to the bedroom, that is where you wanted me to go earlier, isn't it Duncan? On second thought, why don't we all go and see what surprises Amanda has in store for me in our bedroom, or do you already know, Duncan? "

"That's enough – stop it, Tessa!" Duncan all but shouted at her.

"Chill Tessa!" Richie said as carefully as he could over MacLeod's irritated din. "It's not what you think—nothing's been happening here. Amanda just—"

"Amanda is *everything*! She's Wonder Woman, is that it?"

"She saved my head today," Richie exclaimed, turning so his

slashed, blood-stained jacket was visible.

Tessa hardly noticed. Her eyes were riveted on Amanda. "That's just wonderful Richie, it's nice to have at least one of them on your shoulders."

"Look, Tess," Richie began apologetically waving his hands, "Amanda was just showing me how to fight. We shouldn't have done it in here, Mac gave us hell for that; and we shouldn't have taken your welding rods without asking. I'm sorry—we're sorry, but please chill. The world isn't coming to an end over four bent rods. You fire those things anyway."

"Look, Richie," Tessa began and took several steps towards Amanda. "This isn't about you, so why don't you chill! This is about her, that immortal Mata Hari, slinking into my private world, my bedroom—"

"I haven't been in there—I haven't done anything," Amanda replied, shaking her head, alarmed, and began shrinking against the wall under Tessa's vicious stare.

"Into my life," Tessa continued, pointing at Amanda with the welding rods as if they were lightning bolts in her hand. "You can't even wait one-half of one normal, mortal lifetime before you want to sink your female claws into Duncan. Well, here's a news flash – I'm not dead yet! So, why don't you step out for a coffee break for the next twenty-five years? That's nothing for an Immortal, I hear. When you get back, you can start *playing house* by sweeping the dust of my bones off this floor. Until that day, take your horrible taste in art, clothing, and yourself, and get out of my life and leave us alone!" She flung the wadded up scarf at Amanda, hitting her square in the face. Amanda collected herself and quietly, quickly left.

Duncan was furious. "Richie would you excuse us, please— outside." Reaching out he grabbed Tessa, pulled the welding rods from her hand and threw them on the floor, then marched her into their bedroom. His grip on her arm was rough, rougher than he had planned, and he silently cursed himself for his temper with a woman who had just gotten out of the hospital.

Tessa felt his anger directed at her, something completely new. Since the first day of their relationship, he had never once shown her an angry side. For a brief moment, she felt fear. *Duncan is angry at me – is this how those he fought met him? An angry Highlander, sword in hand? Only the bravest could have wheeled a sword against him, his anger alone would have caused all others to flee. But not me! Sword or no sword, Duncan MacLeod of the Clan MacLeod, I will not shrink from you!*

The bedroom door was slammed shut behind them. Duncan released Tessa near the bed, backing up a couple of steps, closed and rubbed his eyes then took a deep breath. He needed to calm down and focus. This was not the Tessa he knew a week ago. "Tessa, it would really help both of us right now if you could explain what is going on between you and Amanda."

"Nothing is going on; she doesn't have to do anything, you know, except wait."

"Wait? What are you talking about?" he said, his hands trying to massage the tension from his temples. *Encourage her to speak, Grace said. She is at war with someone inside.*

"And surprise," she continued sardonically. "She doesn't even have to wait until I am stone cold dead, either. A few more years and I will be old enough to be your mother. She's had more than one look at our bedroom, no doubt getting ideas on how to change the décor to match her awful taste in colors!"

"Tessa, you're just plain mad. You're not saying what's really on your mind either."

"Oh, are you going to try to psychoanalyze me too? Is that what this is all about? Are you going to play *Grace* with me?"

"You know this is getting us nowhere. Nothing has happened between Amanda and me in your lifetime. I am an Immortal and that is all any mortal can ask. Let's stop right now before either of us says something we'll regret for the rest of our lives."

"You are going to regret it much longer than I ever will," she replied, bluntly.

That remark really hurt Duncan, and he had no intention of hiding how he felt. *Tessa had always been totally understanding since the very beginning. She has never had time to assimilate how her life had been turned on its ear, changed upside down. She is just venting her fears and frustrations,* he told himself.

"Look, Tessa, I have no idea what you are so angry about right now. Amanda is my friend—just a friend, and nothing else. Immortals need other Immortals as friends. No one knows what is going to happen as we near the time of the Gathering. I have never really explained it to you—I'm not sure I totally understand it all myself. I will say it again—Amanda is just a friend, and you know it. She was standing out there just now trying her best to start a conversation with you—smooth things over. She is not the most eloquent of people when it comes to this sort of thing."

Tessa placed both hands on her hips. "Really? I thought that Immortal was French—and has been all over France, the capital of etiquette. Oh, come on Duncan, you know what she really wants."

"Enlighten me."

Tessa turned away and fumed silently. *I won't dignify that with an answer!* she fumed.

"Tessa, sweetheart," he began, with all the control he could muster. "I have asked you to marry me. Marriage is about commitment and trust. And if you feel you truly can't trust me or don't trust me," he paused and took a deep breath, "then you can't marry me either."

Tessa whirled, and looked him straight in the eye, giving him a piercing stare.

"I'm going to step out for a while now. I don't know how long. We both need some time to think things over, cool down and decide what we want to really do between us. If you don't feel you can talk to me and tell me the truth about what's really bothering you now, this isn't going to work with us anymore. You decide."

Chapter Thirteen

Duncan turned and walked purposefully out of the bedroom. He scooped up the bent welding rods as he passed through the living room without breaking his stride, and out the door he walked. Tossing the rods in the back seat of his T-bird, he thought for an instant then turned back to the house door. *No matter how angry I am with her, or hurt I am feeling now, Tessa is going to be kept safe inside.* Reaching in, he flipped the lock then closed the door. He looked up the alley. Richie and Amanda were waiting near the far corner of the building. He joined them. "Richie, I'd like to know why you left the house when I asked you to stay inside." He gave the slashed jacket a cursory examination. "You could have lost your head. Just seventy-two hours after becoming immortal you would have been gone – permanently."

"Yeah, I know," he said as he held up his helmet. The large mark near the base gave Duncan pause. "Axel Whittaker—he took my helmet off with his sword, literally."

"You haven't answered my question."

"One-word answer—Tessa. That killer is still out there."

"Tessa's alive."

"*Hello*! – I died," he exclaimed.

"You're an Immortal."

"I wasn't." Richie lowered his head, looked to the ground, then back, up to Duncan. "Look Mac, this isn't about me. Amanda and I have been over this already. It's about Tessa. That outburst—what I just heard in there wasn't the Tessa I know. Not by a long shot. She's scared to death because he's still out there. I would be too if I were still mortal."

"Tessa is my responsibility, Richie. I'll take care of her."

Richie slowly shook his head. "You're not Super Man, Mac. There are too many things coming and going with you with what happened. You need to let more people in on this."

"In on what?" Amanda asked, peering around Richie's shoulder and into his eyes.

Richie exhaled loudly, a bit exasperated. "Mac, I've been back by there where it happened and all through that neighborhood. Unless there's a *Jekyll-and-Hyde* in one of those expensive homes, this had to be connected to what happened to Tessa."

"Connected to what? Duncan, what's this all about?"

Without waiting for approval from Duncan, Richie spoke up. "Tessa and I weren't simply walking down the street together when we were shot. Tessa was kidnapped by some guy apparently to lure

Mac to his house where he tried to kill him."

"What? Which one of us was it?"

"It wasn't. He was mortal. He's dead now. I killed him. I never got any information about him. Tessa and Richie were both shot shortly after they left the house. I wasn't with them or I would have gotten him before he shot," Duncan finished.

"So you think," Richie chimed in.

Amanda gave her head a confused shake. "So someone had something against you. He came up with an elaborate plot to get you in his house to shoot you? Why didn't he just come here, wait outside, and shoot you when you left the house—or anyplace?"

"He came at me with a sword, not a gun, and it's more complicated than that." He motioned to Richie. "You fill her in – you might as well anyway." Retrieving his car keys, he turned back to the pair. "Look—what happened in there just now—I'm sorry. This wasn't the Tessa I knew a week ago. Be that as it may, Richie, I would give her some personal space for a while. And as for you, Amanda –"

She threw up her hands in a mock, *I surrender* gesture. "I'm taking a coffee break for the next twenty-five years—remember?" Duncan gave her a serious scowl.

"You don't have to worry about protecting my head for a couple of days," Richie said as he looked to Amanda. "I think I'll *hang* with Amanda for a while."

Duncan favored both of them with a very surprised stare.

His expression elicited a big grin from Amanda, who was clearly amused by the surprise. "Come on, *brother*," she said with a wink in Richie's direction.

Richie shook his hands in a gesture which said '*it's not what you think*'. "I'll explain later," he said turning to follow her to her car.

Leaning back against the T-bird, Duncan exhaled and bending over, placed both hands on his knees for support and tried to stretch his upper back. He couldn't remember the last time he ached like this. His shoulder muscles were stressed—his head ached from trying to deal with an emotional situation with which he had little to no real experience. As he stood completely motionless, the shadow cast by his shoe toe slowly slipped over a nearby pebble with nothing new happening in his life, he noted. *If I stand perfectly still, will the rest of the world stop with me,* his sub-conscious mind queried. "Huh?" he murmured to himself.

It's almost 'Time', the strange inner voice continued.

"What?" he whispered.

Time is ending—time is almost up, his sub-consciousness replied in a matter-of-fact tone.

"Where did that thought come from," he whispered once again to himself. Had he been thinking of the Gathering? Duncan straightened and shook his head once, then paused. Was he sensing something now? The sounds of the traffic in the street beyond the buildings were barely heard. A breeze was moving lightly through the branches of a nearby tree—the sound of the day was a faint whisper on the wind. There was no 'sense' of anything pressing. He shook it off. His katana lay sheathed in its scabbard in the back seat. He opened the trunk, then the back door. Absently he reached for the handle of his sword. His hand gripped—

Feathers!

He withdrew his hand in a lightning fast reflex action. Then stopped and stared at the handle of his oriental weapon—*nothing*. He leaned in the door and peered closely at it. Had he just seen something there? Had a bird flown in the open window? Had it just been sitting on the handle of his sword? His hand gripped the handle and he withdrew it from the car. There was nothing unusual now. He blinked. *Is this what stress does to people. It plays tricks with their eyes.* Placing the sword in the trunk, he closed the lid. An instant later his immortal empathic senses were on alert. He turned searching for the source. Then he sniffed, puzzled. *I have always known I can sense another Immortal, but can I now also smell them?* Whoever it was, they were on fire—no—his mind corrected him, *not on fire, smoldering.*

"Well, thought I'd find you back here, laddie," came the bright, exuberant voice of Hugh Fitzcairn. "Tried the front shop door – blasted thing was locked up tighter than the Crown Jewels. Don't know how you think you're in business if you keep your bleed'en business door locked when it's this beautiful out." He waved his pipe in the wind to further reinforce his affirmation of the 'glorious day' then took a puff. "Customers running all over themselves shopping on a day like this."

"Fitz, I am very glad to see you." Duncan gripped his arm and smiled briefly. "When did you get in Stateside?"

"Less than a fortnight ago—oh, two-weeks in the American language," he chuckled. His timeless complexion, blond curly-wavy hair cut to above his collar in length, sparkled in the late morning sun. "Any rate, I've come round to see you and that lovely Tessa of yours."

"Bad timing I'm afraid, Fitz."

Taking the pipe out from between his teeth a worried look crossed his brow. "Oh, she's not sick now, is she?"

"Afraid it's worse than that. Tessa was shot."

Fitz took hold of his friend's shoulder "She's still alive, isn't she? What's this world coming to when people go about shooting beautiful women like Tessa? Do you know who did it?"

Duncan nodded. "Yes, I have a name. She just got back from the hospital this morning. I left her in the bedroom."

"What!" he replied, his expression mirroring his statement of astonishment. "What did you leave her in there alone for, man?" And he started toward the door. "I'd better go in and comfort her." Duncan tightened his grip on Fitz's arm, halting his amorous intentions. "Well, laddie – one of us better go in to the poor woman," he replied motioning to the door.

Duncan released his arm. "Maybe I should let you go. That would likely be the end of your amorous career. I'm telling you, she is ready to take someone's head, Fitz."

"Not Tessa, not that sweet young thing. She worships the ground you walk on."

"Fitz, believe me when I say she wants to put me under it today. She verbally slaughtered Amanda."

Fitz rolled his eyes and waved his pipe in Duncan's direction, much to Duncan's disdain of the smell. "Oh, Amanda. That vixen is trouble with a capital 'T'. I thought you knew better than that, old boy? You can't go around threatening Tessa by bringing Amanda in on her turf, especially if she's wounded as it were. I'd have had your head off already if it were me. She needs to know that she has a safety zone – her *Holy Ground* as it were."

"I haven't a clue what you're talking about, as usual, Fitz. I didn't bring Amanda she—well—brought herself with Richie. He became an Immortal trying to protect Tessa from the shooter."

Fitz folded his arms, his pipe perched against his left sleeve, all trace of jocularity gone. He gave Duncan a calculating stare. "What's been going on here recently, Duncan?"

Duncan looked to the ground then away. "It's complicated, Fitz. I'm not sure I have assimilated everything that's happened over the past week and then some—not yet."

"You look like a man with too much on his mind. It's time to share. Come on," And he motioned to the car. "If Tessa's safe inside, you're going to drive us somewhere, where we can talk this out. Two heads think clearly, a clouded one does not."

Duncan nodded and they took off. Fitz insisted on a quiet café by the water—anywhere. Water was relaxing.

"That's all I know, Amanda," Richie said between bites of his shortbread bar outside the café. "Officer Maxim said the kid gunned him down like a pro. That was no junky and no coincidence that he was in the area either, I bet."

Amanda thought for a long moment. "So where are you going with this? What's the answer you're looking for?"

"Was that guy working for the kidnapper? And if so, what does he have to do with Mac?"

Amanda shook her head. "Other than he might have been working for him. but he had a gun. You didn't see a blade on him when he attacked you—of course you weren't an Immortal then, and he wasn't an Immortal or that police officer would have said something to Duncan. This is a twisted plot. I guess what I'm asking is, what do you think is going to happen next—to any of you?"

"I don't know, Amanda, but I've got a bad feeling down deep, and that usually means no good."

Across the street from a vantage point in front of the café, Officer Kevin Kilgore stopped to check a parked car. Slowly he strolled around the back side and casually looked at the license plate then to the pair of Immortals across the street engaged in conversation. Removing his pad he noted the time and made a few notes. As he did, his peripheral vision caught movement by the parking meter. A coin was dropped in, barely registering in his brain.

"You're not needed here," the female voice said quietly and placed a hand on the lock of the car trunk exposing her Watcher's tattoo. "I've got this covered."

Kevin looked up at the woman who was standing with her side toward him. She looked away as he glanced up, assuring he did not see her face. Kevin noted she was a little taller than him, wearing a light-tan, summer-weight jacket—wrist length sleeves and matching slacks; a smart looking dove-colored tam was perched on her head at a forty-five-degree angle. "My Immortal is here also," he said, his eyes returning to his notes.

She ambled to the store window and gazed absently. "He is with Amanda—my Immortal. It will all be in my report to Joe. You aren't needed here, rookie. I can handle this alone."

Kevin thought for a moment. *I'm not letting this Watcher intimidate me again. She isn't my supervisor, at least I hope not.* He straightened and walked casually beside her then placed a purposeful hand on her arm.

She turned her head slightly and glared at him out of the corner of her eye, but remained silent.

Kevin pulled his jacket back, exposing his police badge. "I have a reason to be here, what's your excuse? Now, to my eye, you're just loitering. That's my Immortal over there and I don't care if you don't think this street is big enough for the both of us to watch. Give me an excuse, and I'll cite you for loitering."

"I beg your pardon!" her voice rose as her one-eyed stare hardened.

"And if you give me any trouble here, I'll run you in to the station on resisting arrest." Kevin's smile broadened. "Explain that to Joe Dawson," he finished with a smug tone in his voice.

Slowly she peeled her arm out from under his hand. *If looks could kill Sony, you'd be dead right now,* she thought but said nothing. "Make sure your report is up to standard and complete," she said quietly. Turning away from him, she walked slowly on toward the next store window.

Kevin smiled to himself. He was not going to let some fellow Watcher tell him what he could do where his Immortal was concerned. Kevin considered, *Maybe I should be sure I've crossed all my 'Ts' and dotted all my 'Is' in my report. I may be up for a performance review faster that I can imagine.*

Chapter Fourteen

The wind played softly through his blond locks as Fitz looked casually out across the water. The gentle waves lapped against the café's dockside veranda as he absently took another sip of his coffee. Fitz listened, without comment, as Duncan revealed the events of the past week to ten days. The shop, an upcoming art show, Tessa's projects, his art contact, the attack on Richie in the store, Tessa's kidnapping, the strange *hide and seek* game played by her kidnapper, the mystic message that led him to find the house, the cryptic messages Tessa's kidnapper had parroted to her, the man's death, the shooting.

"That's everything up till now, Fitz. Where do I go with it from here, if anywhere? Is this where it ends? And if not, then why not?"

"What do you think, Duncan?" He set the cup down and scrutinized his friend. "It wasn't that long ago we both had a rather nasty run-in with a Watcher named Horton and his goons. Don't you find it a bit odd that something like this should be happening? Tessa did say the chap was going on about, '…*they always come*...,' and the like. That should tell you at least this old boy has done this before with other Immortals—and they lost their heads. You did say he was mortal?"

Duncan sighed. "I was afraid you were going to say something like that. I didn't have time to get any information about him before the shooting."

"Didn't you tell me you had made a friendly contact within the Watcher's ranks?"

Duncan nodded. "We're on friendly speaking terms. I'm not sure how much to trust the man yet, though he wants to speak with me. Something about a Watcher's code of secrecy. How did he say it – '*We observe and record but never interfere*'."

Fitz raised both eyebrows. "I'd say if this man was a Watcher he was doing a whole lot more than just casually interfering. But right now we don't know what he was and we need to. All we know for certain is that he's dead."

"Yeah, and there hasn't been a word about it in any of the media outlets." Duncan thought for a long moment. *Ms. Randi McFarland, that eager-beaver TV reporter would have been all over this story if she had ever gotten wind of it. There is no way she would have or could have been kept quiet about it.*

"I am almost one-hundred-percent certain that no one knows about the dead man in that house or, the police do, and they are keeping very quiet about it for some reason." He shook his head. "Something doesn't add up, Fitz. I met the immortal police officer who was shot several hours after Tessa was. He is certain the guy was a professional."

"Who is he – the policeman?"

"Ducanus Marcus Maximinus – Duke Maxim he's calling himself now."

"He's legitimate, Duncan. I will stake money on his reputation."

Duncan put up his hands in a, *'you got me – now what'* gesture. "This still all seems disjointed to me. How do I make any sense out of it all?"

"I think you need to get yourself in good graces with that friendly Watcher and find out if that dead man was a Watcher, and more importantly, if he had a companion – your mysterious shooter." He pulled his pipe out of his pocket and put the mouthpiece between his teeth, unlit. "There's a remote possibility that the two events were separate –"

"I wouldn't bet my life on it now," Duncan replied and picked up his cup for a sip.

"Oh, if our guess is wrong – dead wrong, it isn't your life, laddie you'd be betting – it's Tessa's."

Duncan stopped in mid motion and set the cup back down.

"It's more than a fair bet that Tessa was a deliberate target – it's Richie that was the random element. We need to find that shooter, Duncan – and fast. Tessa's life is still on the line."

Tessa stood in stunned silence. She could hear Duncan walking angrily away from her—through the house and out the door, slamming it in his wake. Her legs failed her and she sat down on the edge of the bed. *What have I done? What is wrong with me?* A small voice inside spoke up. *"You're defending your right to exist in this space, this time. Amanda is an intruder, an immortal intruder."*

"***Enough!***" she exclaimed out loud in the stillness of the room. "Whoever—whatever—part of me is acting out, I am sick of hearing about *time.* I am here now and this is my time with Duncan. Now stop it, Tessa! Do you hear me?"

She placed a worried hand to her lips, her cheek then caught a strand of her hair and wrapped it around her finger nervously. "Tessa, you're a lot smarter and stronger than you're giving yourself credit for," she continued her stern self-reprimand, unabated. She knew time was her enemy, but she had no way of fighting it – the battle was already lost, and inside she knew it.

"You don't have to shout and throw things at people to make your wishes known." *You're mortal,* her rational mind affirmed in the stillness. *You were born knowing you would die one day. Duncan's life will go on without you. He is an Immortal and you have accepted him into your life as he is. You can't change either of those facts—do you really want to change him? He will not die with you—would you really want him to? You aren't that petty.* She paused to study her reflection in their small bedroom mirror. *I can't believe this entire outburst today has been simply about accepting my eventual death and an immortal replacement for me.* But was it actually death, or growing old by Duncan's side that was still an unresolved issue? *Will there come a time when making love to him will no longer be an option?* "You're being ridiculous, Tessa—of course not," she spoke and wrapped her arms tightly about herself, holding herself like a strong security blanket. "People make love until the day they die." *What if I died in his arms at the height of my ecstasy? Complete release—my body and my soul—to him in one act of love?*

Her consciousness paused her train of thought. *You don't have a Quickening to transfer to him and no Immortal can take your soul. This is not within their power—they are not God.* She sat back against the bed and closed her eyes. *You would just die—being in his arms at that moment may be a comfort to you, but you would not become a part of him. You're mortal.*

"I can't go on living like today," she whispered. "Go crazy with jealousy every time I see Amanda near him, and what about Grace? Am I condemning myself to spending hours, for the rest of my life, pacing up and down the store like a caged wild animal, wondering which Immortal's arms he has been in every time he comes home late? And what about Ceirdwyn? How many times did she lie in his arms, feel his warm embrace? Through how many centuries did he make love to her? That woman has existed since around the time when Christ and the Apostles actually walked this earth." A sardonic chuckle escaped her lips. "I should be grateful, not reproachful. If I asked nicely they may be willing to share what they've seen and experienced in this life with me—not dusty dry history from a book— living history, willingly shared, if I would just ask." *If I make a scene like today every time he arrives home, he'll soon get tired of these scenes and end up hating me and eventually leaving me.* Since the kidnapping, she had somehow felt especially vulnerable. Duncan's presence felt strange to her; and, of course, there was Amanda. *Why do I keep coming back to her? Duncan has said time and time again, "You're not in competition with her – I've made my decision – stop worrying so much." Can I ever finally accept that Amanda and the other immortal women, would always be part of his life.* "He needs immortal friends, I have no right to try and change that." She exhaled. *"Good,"* her rational mind replied. She felt herself reaching a stable level of emotional and psychological control within herself. She was finally beginning to think like the Tessa she knew she always was strong. A distant conversation—from more than a year ago and shortly after she had seen him behead another Immortal, replayed in her mind.

"Hey, Sweetheart," Duncan called. He had been watching her from his office for several minutes, not knowing whether to interrupt her or not.

"Where are you?" Her head came up and she peered around the smooth metal sculpture.

"Over here," he mused playfully. "Second star on your right and straight on to morning," he chuckled, repeating the words from a modern rendition of Peter Pan.

"OK, well then I'm just over here—a few light-years ahead of where you're thinking."

"Tess, I didn't mean—"

"I know Duncan, I know. It just takes me a little time to accept all of what an Immortal really is. When I think I am ready to graduate as it were, new things turn up and I just need to readjust my focus."

Duncan folded his arms and leaned on the table. "You are an extraordinary woman, Tess."

"Thanks, but I wish I could be stronger. Sometimes I feel you must be getting tired of all my insecurities."

Duncan rose, crossed the distance between them then pulled her to her couch, as she had lately claimed it. Gently, he took one of her hands in his and looked lovingly into her eyes.

"That is never going to happen and you know it. Besides, I am the one who should be afraid of you getting tired of the kind of life I have. It is not something I am proud of, you know? I do feel tired and sometimes short tempered with all of mortal life's quirks from time to time."

She rotated and leaned into him. He made a place in his arms for her. "I know, but I just see how Grace and Amanda can handle themselves better in situations when I would probably fall apart. Those women have had to swing a sword to stay alive – I can't ever see myself doing anything like that. They're the really brave ones. I can't help but think sometimes that you might be safer and more comfortable with one of them at your side."

Duncan laughed then stroked her cheek gently. "Tessa, you make me want to come home whenever I have to face a challenge. It is you waiting for me here, in our home. That's what I think about. Besides, you are much stronger than they are."

"Why do you say that?"

"Because they are Immortals. They can't choose what life they want to live; they either challenge other Immortals or accept their challenges and fight for their lives or die. There is no other way for them but to go on with the flow. You chose this and you are therefore faced with this because you are strong enough to fight for our love. You have the power to choose if you want to stay in this strange Immortal's world. You can leave and have a happy *normal* married life with a man who is going to grow old with you, have children with you and who would certainly not leave the house with a sword in the middle of the night to behead another Immortal. In my book, you are the strongest woman I have ever met."

She sat up straight with a new sense of renewed spirit. When had she stopped remembering that conversation? She smiled to herself. "I'm going to be OK," she whispered. "All will be OK now." Placing her hands on the bed cover, she pushed herself up to her feet. "Duncan," she called, "Duncan, wait a moment," and started toward the bedroom door.

Suddenly, a violent rush of emotion seized her—*anger, hate, despair, dread.*

"***The end of time!***"

She heard those last four words as if they had been shouted in her ear. Grabbing her head and ears as if it were a blast of sound that had hit her like a freight train, a shriek escaped her lips.

Like a flood bursting forth from a weakened dam, images and emotions poured into her mind, torturing her body and soul with their razor-sharp, barbed, dark sensations. She collapsed to her knees as the onslaught continued filling her with a foreign, internal rage and frustration beyond anything she ever believed she was capable of enduring.

Let it out! her soul cried silently, *or it will overwhelm and kill you!*

"***Time is almost up!***"

She heard the voice shouting, as if it were beside her, once again.

The alien palpable emotion seized her throat and shook her until she gasped for breath.

"*Speak me out,*" it demanded, a physical voice in her head.

But she could not. Try as she might she could not utter a single sound. *Something wicked,* her subconscious mind retorted as she recoiled, overwhelmed with panic. *You're an artist, you speak through your hands, let it out that way,* her subconscious mind coaxed. Crawling to a small bedroom night stand, she reached up and pulled her sketch pad from it to the floor. *Light, I need light for my hands to speak,* her inner voice pleaded with the alien emotion to give her leave to reach the bed. Taking a deep breath, she lunged against the covers, threw the sketch pad on the bed then hoisted herself up and onto the soft covers. Her artist sketch pen was clipped to the side of the pad. The fingers of her right hand ripped it off and flipped the book open to the first page.

A lovingly rendered full face sketch of Duncan, gazing benevolently off the page, met her eyes. Unexpectedly her left hand grabbed the center of the page, clawing the paper together and ripping it from the book. Then she began to draw – not with slow, tentative, creative strokes that an artist uses to start a work; but with frantic, hard strokes – as if the pencil were a knife in her hand and she was trying to *cut* a picture out of the page. Her hand moved relentlessly fast. A half an hour of constant, near maddening, stabbing, stroking, scraping sounds followed.

Is it ever going to stop? She thought. *I'd rather be working in the middle of the JFK's runway without ear protection than this—having to listen to this pencil scratching, stabbing and cutting at this paper.* Something—no, some *presence* had taken possession of her hand. It would not let her go.

Lines formed and intersected on the page, hard, deep, black lines— a shape a human form a face was emerging—Duncan's face. It was hard, stark, distant, unshaven, tired, worn and a hundred other things she had never seen him as at any time he had ever been with her. This was another Duncan, from another time. *What is he wearing—a blanket? Something with an odd checkered pattern formed over his worn body. Old, he looked so old, but that cannot be – he's an Immortal! What in hell, or from Hell, is my hand drawing?*

Or carving, her second inner voice replied entreating the question from her other-half. Each stroke of the pencil on the paper was now like a stab. "Who am I stabbing*?*" she said out loud. "Duncan? What is this thing forming in the background?"

"A sword, you need a sword," the violent emotion-loaded voice prodded her conscious mind painfully.

"*No!*" she screamed, the sound which had escaped her throat was one of pure desperation. With all the swords in the shop, she was not going to put one in her right hand—not now—not with the violence in those pencil strokes.

What was her hand drawing now? A human silhouette – her silhouette was forming on the very edge of the page – an animal took shape by her side – *what is it? A small camel? No, a llama.*

"A sword," the emotional inner voice demanded once again.

Her left hand dropped the pad to her lap and gripped the bed covers. *No one and nothing is going to make me get up and get a sword,* she thought fiercely. Shoving her back against the bedstead, she willed herself not to move from that spot; all the while, her right hand continued to draw, stab, cut, slash, and mark on that piece of paper.

"Stop," she pleaded hoarsely. "Please stop!" But there was no stopping it – the motion was relentless. She felt trapped by her hand – trapped in some 'B' grade horror film. With all her strength, her left hand reached and wrestled the pencil from her right hand, then threw it on the bed. No sooner had it landed then the fingers of her right hand cramped and groped back toward the pencil, finally grabbing it.

The pain was agony! She slammed the point into the paper breaking it off. *Finally,* she thought, *this will end this drawing.*

But it didn't. Her hand now moved across the page in straight geometric lines – the paint on the pencil itself became the led, flaking off and smudging into the paper with each forceful stroke. Unconsciously, she bore down heavily on the page with a wide stroke – the skin covering the small joint of her guide-finger skinned itself raw across the paper, adding her blood to the image of the sword that was evolving independently of her own will.

Duncan's katana, a fitting place for the color red, she thought.

Now, what's coming? What is that thing in the sky? A dragon? A snake? It has feathers. Why is it in the sky? Her crippled pencil and bloody finger circled round. *Symbols, hieroglyphs, letters – what is my hand drawing now?* Something in her distant memory half-recognized the strange symbols as writing.

Her hand suddenly shifted to another part of the page. *Oh no – not another damn clock!* she thought, cringing. She fought to stop, fought for control – and lost. Instinctively she knew it was a clock that was forming on the page, but this wasn't any clock she had ever seen. There were only symbols around its perimeter, no hands. These strange symbols spiraled into the center, to a face. Fiery eyes stared out at her – eyes that had seen the beginning and end of many *times,* cycles without end. She didn't understand, she was not sure she wanted to. This clock was more fearful to her than all the rest she had ever seen in her mind.

"Time is almost up!" it shouted from the page back into her face.
With the last symbol on its ponderous face, the malevolent feeling
finally spat the last of its fire out onto the paper – the bloody pencil
dropped freely from her hand. She drew a deep breath – the deepest
one she had taken since this entire ordeal began.

Marked with colors of gray, yellow, and red – the pad lay in her
lap. Exhaling, she looked upon a foreign image – one she certainly
had not, by her conscious will, wrought. Exhausted, she collapsed
back onto the pillow and closed her eyes. There was nothing left
inside herself to give.

Chapter Fifteen

Slowly and very carefully, Duncan lifted the sketch pad that lay across Tessa then retrieved the remnant of the art pencil. He turned it over briefly in his hand. The art pencil and the paper bore the distinct marks of blood on the page. Quickly he set them down in a nearby chair then peered all around Tessa, without touching her, to see what had been bleeding.

Her hand – no – a finger. She scraped her finger working at this, whatever it is. His mind registered a minor injury and he decided not to touch her to care for it. *Let her sleep – it's the best medicine for her now.* Carefully folding the soft, thick bed cover over her, he slowly pulled it up to her chin and tucked it in. Gathering the sketch pad and crumpled piece of paper, he sat down to ponder them.

Without fully opening the crumpled piece, Duncan knew it to be his portrait done in the studio evening light. Tessa had been working on it a week or so before the kidnapping.

She must have been very angry with me to have destroyed it. She's never done anything like this before. Tess has always said when you create something with your hands, the moment it 'becomes', you have breathed life into lifelessness. Duncan pondered what she was feeling that would have made her wish to destroy the life she had given that page. Placing the paper on the side of the nearby nightstand, he focused on the pad.

He wasn't a sensitive artist like Tessa, however even he couldn't ignore the sheer starkness and raw violence of the strokes that had made this. *What was she trying to depict on this page?* He knew Tessa to be a very accomplished artist, something he admired her for so deeply. But this style of art was something completely different for Tessa. It was a type of abstractness he had never known her to do. Turning the page around several times he settled on one viewing angle and began studying it. The things she had drawn in the picture were reasonably distinct in and of themselves, but the picture was a montage of sorts.

A massive roughly shaped pyramid, a sort of building fills the background. It is built into a mountain. A wheel with a face inside – it's an Aztec calendar. Something black, it looks like a human form near that man. His eyes focused on the man. *It's me. She has drawn me, but she's never seen me like this. She's drawn me wearing a tilmatli. The last time I was wearing a tilmatli was in–*

Flashback – 1830:

Duncan and his guide, Paco, had been trekking into the unexplored back areas of the Peruvian jungle, looking for undiscovered ruins, when they had been captured by a people his guide insisted, "…should not be in this area." They had been taken to their 'god', Gavriel Larca, a Portuguese Immortal from the early fifteenth-century. Larca, raving mad with the desire for power, had offered the mortal Paco as a sacrifice to appease the 'evil spirits' causing the jungle fever that was ravaging the tribe. Failing to halt the fever with this sacrifice, Larca attempted to take Duncan's head, only to be shot with a curare dart by one of his disillusioned followers. He was entombed by the tribe.

Duncan had escaped but *died* briefly from jungle fever. Without food or water, he tried to make his way back to civilization. Disoriented in the dense jungle, he walked on for weeks, living on meager plants, small reptiles and insects he managed to catch, until he finally walked out of the dense growth and into a rocky landscape with relatively sparse vegetation near the Inca ruins of Ollantaytambo.

The well-trodden path in the Peruvian foothills was dusty and dry. The April winds, cascading out of those hills, were strong. All about his legs, with each step he took, fine rust colored grit swirled then disappeared into the wind. It was coming into winter in the South American hemisphere and the nights, at the altitude he knew he must be, were cold for a man wearing tropical clothing and a tilmatli—a simple blanket/cloak made of cactus fiber. After weeks of no one in sight, his only interest was in finding another human being.

It was evening when he saw the first signs of civilization on the road in front of him, a man and woman with a donkey cart. *Yes, they spoke Spanish*—the wheel had slipped off the axle. *Slide it back on – hammer a chunk of wood into the axle to hold it – fixed for now.* The couple was very grateful for his help. *Where were they going? Could he travel with them?*

They were returning to their home near Ollantaytambo with supplies.

Well, he thought, *at least I haven't walked clear out of Peru.* Duncan stayed with the family, sharing their hospitality for several days until he met an Englishman in the area with a sketch pad.

"We're miles from a seaport and a respectable cup of tea," Duncan said lightheartedly, as he walked up to the man who was sporting

British field attire. The gentleman turned from his work and folded his pad.

"Duncan MacLeod," he said, pushing his brown-rust colored tilmatli aside for the handshake.

"Hayward Lawrence," the young man replied and quickly shook Duncan's hand.

"Are you an artist? You're a long way from the fashion center of the world." Duncan said.

"An artist – yes, and this is the fashion center, so to speak. It's where I belong." He flipped open his sketch pad revealing page after page of crisply rendered drawings of various ruin sketches. "Until that blasted contraption called a camera is perfected, they still need people in the graphic arts – like me. I'm out here to capture what it really looks like before it gets carved up and carted away by some university."

Duncan shifted his position so he could see the sketch. Putting a hand over his brow to shade his eyes, he looked up the steeply stepped embankment into the ruins beyond. The drawing on that page matched the ruins perfectly. He nodded. "I heard of the camera." He motioned back to the pad. "That's very good work – don't think this camera invention will ever replace people like you. There is real talent here. There will always be a need for art and artists. It's what comes from the soul." He thought a long moment. "What did you mean by, '…*before it gets carved up and carted away…*' ? These are ruins of a civilization, not a tree trunk."

Hayward grinned. "So you'd think – and it would seem to be impervious to even time itself, but not so. It has stood since the late fifteenth-century, withstood the onslaught of wind and weather and war. Yet, if men like him," and he motioned to a small knot of people in the distance, "are let to do as they please, this will all be lifted up stone by stone and carted off to a museum in another country."

Duncan shook his head. "Who is he? And what's his business with these ruins?"

"His name is Kawill Redford. Educated in Oxford, I believe. He's a broker of antiquity. Travels up and down this side of the continent looking for anything old and of value. Not really interested in gold, I hear tell. It's the art of antiquity that gets his pulse racing, if you take my meaning."

Duncan shrugged. *I think I'll see what art from this area has his interest.* He left Hayward and started toward the group in the distance.

Hayward folded his sketch pad and placed it in its large leather pouch, then he retrieved a leather bound notebook and un-strapped it. He watched Duncan approach the group and made a few notes before re-buckling the binding strap across its cover—a cover with the deep imprint of the Watcher's symbol.

As Duncan approached the group, all of a sudden his immortal sense of *presence* told him he was drawing close to another of his kind. He slowed as he approached the knot of people. *Which one was it? There had to be at least twenty people in that group—a number of them had machetes tied to their belts.* As he stood by, waiting as the group slowly dispersed until one man remained. He walked purposefully up to Duncan.

"I am Kawill – Kawill Redford these days."

"Duncan MacLeod of the Clan MacLeod."

Kawill looked him over. "That's a Scotsman's name. You're a long ways off from your home and clan. Did you travel all this distance to come for my head?"

"No, I haven't come for anybody. I'm here to view the ruins. I hear tell you deal in antique art?" Kawill shifted his stance as Duncan scrutinized him.

Here was a man in about the mid five-foot tall range—an olive complexion—straight brown hair, braided neatly into a single braid down his back, whiskerless, smooth oval face and piercing brown eyes. His physical features could fit anyone of a dozen different ethnic groups from Mexico, through most parts of South America. He was virtually timeless. His clothes were native—hand stitched local fabrics in earth tones, a shirt, a pullover, trousers that were knee-length with leg wrappings and moccasin shoes. A semi bowler-shaped hat, walking stick, two-handed machete, and dark rust-colored tilmatli completed his outfit.

"Indeed I do," and he looked to the ruins. "There is much cultural art here, a king's ransom many times over if you know where to look. I'm scouting around for a few good men to help me retrieve some of it before the rest of the world discovers its hiding places."

"Selling off your own culture," Duncan said with noticeable disdain in his voice. "Your culture and the treasures thereof belong to the children's children, many generations down from those who created it. It should remain with them."

Kawill grinned and chuckled once, then shook his head. "I've heard that line before—purest sentiments. Leave nature where it's found. Only that doesn't put gold in your pocket or you in a palace." He motioned in the general directions of North and South. "I lived during the time when civilizations, all up and down this continent, rose from the dust of the ground—laid each of these stones one upon the next – wrestled gold and gems from the earth, then fought over them and died. I know what they created, where they hid it, and how to get to it. So now that there's real interest in owning it, I'll retrieve it or take hunters to it for a price. These European and North American treasure hunters only trample themselves looking for it. Besides, it's not my culture—we're all 'cousins', so to speak."

"Where are you originally from?"

"It was a city—a city on an island which no longer exists. It was off the coast of what is now called Chile. I am a descendant of the Olmecs."

Chapter Sixteen

The Present:
Duncan blinked, his mind returning to the here and now. He refocused his eyes on the drawing. Tessa had drawn him and his clothing with inexplicable and impossible accuracy. This was during a time period when she could not have known how he dressed in South America in 1830.

But that's impossible! his mind corrected him. *There is absolutely no way Tessa could have ever seen this then—my clothing down to the buckle on that pouch attached to my belt. It's perfect, but how? I kept nothing from this period or place.* His eyes followed the lines of the structure behind him in that scene. *She's also drawn a type of roughly shaped pyramid.* He took a deep breath and allowed his rational mind to organize and bring his imagination under control. *She could have seen this temple, or whatever it really is, somewhere in an art gallery, on TV, on the computer, in a book – somewhere. At least this much of it could make sense.*

The fainter outline of the circular calendar, which Duncan could identify as Aztec in origin, was superimposed over the pyramid. A bizarre flying snake-like creature was above the pyramid in one part, swooping down toward him in another.

A silhouette, he recognized as Tessa, was barely perceivable, hiding in amongst the many dark lines on that page.

But what is this? A dark, faceless, humanoid-shaped figure with what appeared to be a raised blade in its outstretched limbs, stood behind a severed stone head of a statue. The head crisply resembled Kukulkan – the Mayan deity. *This dark figure is also behind me!* A small shiver shot down his spine as his eyes traced the line of sight between that faceless specter and the drawing of him. *Is he after me, or what is being pictured here? Has she drawn my death? What's in my hands?* The object, which should have been his sword, looked only vaguely familiar as a sword, except for the handle. *It has red and yellow feathers – I'm gripping a feathered sword?* Tessa's blood streaked across the image at that spot added an all too real touch of life – *Or death? But for whom? What is this picture really saying? Three people—one is me—a pyramid or a temple—a beheaded statue—the stone calendar—a black moon with symbols etched across the sky—so much darkness on this page—dark lines and rips everywhere—Tessa's blood across this sword.* He shook his head 'No', as he considered the poignant symbolism—*her blood is on my sword!*

Duncan sat up straight in the chair. This picture had become far too weird and unnerving for his taste. This—this mental imagery—whatever it was, wasn't Tessa—it couldn't be. Slowly he rose, walked quietly from the bedroom, closing the door behind him. He picked up the phone in their living room and dialed the hospital—Dr. Grace Chandel.

It's time I shared everything with her about what happened that night—and she with me about what happened with Tessa when the two of them were alone.

And as she slept, Tessa began to dream:

Something—an unfamiliar sensation roused Tessa from sleep. At first she resisted opening her eyes. She reached to pull her plush bed cover closer to herself, like a kitten kneading – her hand felt beyond the cover—she touched cold stone. Her eyes snapped open at the touch and she glanced around.

I'm no longer in my bedroom or on my bed. The surface beyond the cover was unexpectedly hard. She sat up, then pulled the bed cover back and stared.

The strange clock—I'm lying on its face. She got to her feet and looked back behind herself.

I see my bed, my bedroom, my world—it's just through that opening. Am I in the next room? Something told her she wasn't—she hadn't left her bedroom—she had left her *reality.*

If I reach out I can touch our bed? She put out her hand only to touch a barrier. There was something over that opening. She felt around the strange gray film.

This barrier has holes—no—rips! I'm on the other side of my drawing, inside the paper! Something was drawing her back into this world of graphite, paint and blood – *my blood seals the door.*

Before her stood a massive, roughly pyramid shaped stone building built into the side of a mountain. Up one side of this building – at regular intervals—snake-like statues stood on their tails. They formed a line down the center of the rough-hewn steps.

As she watched, a humanoid-shaped featureless figure descended the stone stairs. As it neared the bottom of the staircase it paused.

Glancing casually to her left side, she saw Duncan beside her. She watched as he walked purposefully to the base of the stairs to stand by one of the statues. Her right hand casually touched a soft wooly creature and she turned her head to see what it was. The small golden llama pressed its body next to hers and looked up at her with gentle eyes.

Tessa saw the dark humanoid, on the steps, raise the object in its hands and advance toward Duncan. He didn't move. The dark figure swung, striking the head of one of the statues—beheading it.

The stone head rolled to a stop by Duncan's feet, yet he still did not move.

The sky and surroundings grew ominously dark—the moon turned red and bled. Lightning sprang from the top of the building—a feathered snake-like reptile launched itself skyward from between the bolts.

A deep rumble arose from within the depths of the pyramid, fire erupted from the building and the scene around her began to crumble.

This is Holy Ground, an offense has been committed here. Duncan will not fight him. No! Duncan run! He'll take your head here! Her mind called to Duncan, desperately.

She fought to move, to run to him, to intervene, to push him out of the way. But the llama by her side would not let her move toward them. Tessa struggled with herself to move, to push the animal away. But she could not. She watched helplessly as the figure advanced, sword raised.

Suddenly, the creature in the sky swooped down, positioning itself between them—halting the pair. Fire consumed the temple as she continued to watch. The scene finally crumbled to dust completely then slowly began fading into the flat watery background.

Alone with the llama, she stood on the surface of the water, blue from horizon to horizon.

As she stood, pondering what she had just witnessed, Tessa felt a dark presence behind her and slowly turned to see it.

Dark and ominous—it's coming for me, run! I can't move. Instinctively, she knew she was going to die and she was powerless to prevent it.

Something moved next to her, just at the edge of her peripheral vision—closer and closer it came until it was by her side. She turned her eyes away from what she knew was certain death, expecting to see the llama, and saw a large feathered snake.

Coiling, it reared up from the watery mirror still surface until it was eye level with her. His bright red and yellow feathers were flared out from its long graceful head and neck—its tongue licked the air in reptilian fashion.

Tessa recoiled momentarily from the strange reptile, then, against her will, she found herself reaching out with her open hand toward it, expectantly. The snake slithered across her open hand, and her hand closed on its neck. It stared up and into her eyes, knowingly.

"Strike!" it commanded forcefully.

Tessa shook her head. "I don't understand," and glanced back toward the menacingly dark figure advancing steadily toward her across the water.

"Strike!" it commanded, this time louder.

She looked back toward the feathered reptile in her hand. It was now straight, stiff and lifeless. *It's Duncan's katana!* she mentally gasped.

Duncan pressed his ear to the receiver. Had he lost the connection? There was a long pause at the other end of that phone where Grace was.

"Duncan, what were you thinking?" Grace's voice was sharp. "Kidnapped? Of course, Tessa was traumatized by that maniac and then when she finally thought she was free she was shot and nearly killed. Why didn't you tell me this in the first place? It all makes so much more sense now."

Duncan shrugged helplessly though he knew Grace couldn't see his actions through the phone. "Too much had just happened to us, Grace. Within a space of less than fifteen-minutes, I was in a bizarre *lights out* fight for my life—I killed the kidnapper, found Tessa and sent her to the car with Richie – they had just left the house, I had just found his computer and was trying to get some information— anything at all about him—when I heard two shots ring out. Grace, the situation went from the frying pan to the fire too fast for me to think of anything but keeping her from dying."

Grace gave a heavy sigh. "OK, I forgive you, Duncan. But as I see it there are two issues here now."

"Two? You've lost me. Tessa's mental state is the only one I am worried about. She has lost her temper in a way that is – well – just not Tessa. She was shouting at Amanda and Richie over next to nothing—she hit Amanda with her scarf—and this drawing—Grace, what it is suggesting, it is so emotionally dark, I am honestly a little afraid when I look at it."

"She's a sensitive, passionate artist—she communicates with her hands. The darkness of her emotions on that paper is a healthy release, Duncan. It's good she is getting it out so it can be seen in by her conscious mind. Talk to her, Duncan. Encourage her to speak about what she has drawn. It will help her to heal, mentally and emotionally."

Duncan shook his head. "This is not simply a mental pressure release or escape. There is nothing healthy on this page. There is something else happening here—I can't explain it to you, or myself, except to say Tessa has drawn the impossible, she has drawn me, exactly as I was in 1830 in Peru—clothes and all—down to the last detail and there is no way she could have known this. This wasn't just an educated guess, this is perfection."

"Is that all that's on that page," Grace pressed.

"No, she has also drawn a pyramid in the jungle, the Aztec stone calendar, and a faceless figure that appears to be preparing to behead me. Her blood is part of the picture too."

"What do you mean blood? What did she do? What is happening in the drawing?"

"It looks like she scraped her finger drawing my sword—well—it really isn't my sword in this drawing, if you want to call it that. She must have been stabbing at the page with her pencil. There are rips everywhere—so much violence poured out on this sheet."

"An artist can be very passionate, and that word doesn't always mean love. Art can be expressed in violence as well. Apparently you have never seen that side of Tessa. How does that make you feel?"

"Afraid. very afraid."

"For Tessa or yourself?"

There was a distinct pause before he answered. "What do you mean?"

"You heard me, Duncan. Are you afraid that the violent passions inside Tessa, the ones she used for that art, could overwhelm you someday?" There was a very long pause at the other end of the phone. Now it was Grace's turn to wonder if she had lost the connection. *Ah, you have just stepped outside of your comfort zone where women are concerned. To you, a woman has always been a delicate creature, filled with love or at least the need to be needed. You really rarely – if ever – have taken a woman's head. Now a mortal woman couldn't possibly approach your potential for raw violence in the heat of passion or battle could they?* She mentally made a note then continued as if she hadn't noticed the pause.

"Tessa is *fighting* someone or something. This came out during the Guided imagery session we had."

"Is that hypnosis?" Duncan asked

"No. Guided imagery is a subtle and gentle but powerful technique to relax one's mind, inhibitions, and get down into thoughts and experiences that need to come out or be reinforced. It can be a form of physiological therapy too. You can use sound, smell, objects, or all three as a trigger. These stimuli focus and direct the thoughts and imagination. They become the vehicle for the person to act on their desires. We call it *visualization* or *mental imagery.* It really uses all the senses, though. The end result is that it can activate the whole body, the emotions, and the inner psyche. It can make a lasting, powerful impact."

"What happened? What did you do?"

"I placed her into a relaxing—a quiet, darkened room. Then I gave her various objects to hold, based on what her body language, and a few verbal hints told me. I caught a few whispered words as she created and visited these scenes in her mind. Time is a repeating theme for Tessa. She is in a fight with time, or someone connected to it. It doesn't take a genius to figure out who that might be either. Her mortal life is measured by minutes on a clock and the man who shot her represents the *time thief,* stealing her precious time with you, away."

"She said that?" Duncan was given pause by Grace's words.

"She acted it out, she whispered the words, and tried to destroy the *clock* that was ticking away her time, with my sword in her hand."

"What? Grace, what were you doing in that room?"

"Calm down, Duncan. Tessa didn't hurt herself. She was startled and shocked when she realized what she was doing, but there was no harm to anyone. If anything, it brought her suppressed feelings closer to the surface. She responded rather angrily toward me afterward, but I don't worry about things like that when there is this kind of trauma. If you would please let Tessa know, as she heals, that I don't hold any anger she felt for me against her. We're still OK."

Duncan wiped his face with his free hand. *This conversation with Grace is also weird,* he thought. "You said there was something else—two issues?"

"Besides Tessa, I see a very real possibility that the man who shot her could be connected with her kidnapper. Duke and Sandy, the officers you met in the hospital—neither of them believes this was a junky. If that is true, they need to be made aware of the kidnapping. This might change everything in the investigation."

"There is one problem with that, Grace. I killed the kidnapper. Now how do I explain the circumstances surrounding that?"

Grace thought for a long moment. "I don't know, Duncan. I honestly don't know. Maybe talking to Duke alone—I just don't know. One thing I do know is if I'm right, and the shooter knows Tessa or Richie are still here, he isn't going to want to leave any witnesses alive. For Tessa's sake, let someone who can help track that guy down in on all of this."

"Duncan!"

The shout from the bedroom brought him to his feet in a microsecond. He never bothered to hang up the phone; he just dashed to the door and threw it open. He was by Tessa's side—pulling the comforter around her—taking her into his arms, unconditionally.

She grabbed for him, held him close, kneaded the worn shirt in her hands until her fingers felt his flesh below.

"Oh God, Duncan, you're alive and you're here now." She glanced away, through the open bedroom door, into infinity and beyond, then she took a deep breath.

"He's coming for you—near the end of time—whatever that means. He's going to try to violate the Rules of immortal combat and take your head on Holy Ground."

Chapter Seventeen

Hugh Fitzcairn poured Tessa's cup full to the brim with piping hot cocoa. She nodded, then wrapped her hands around the oversized cup and took a sip. Setting it on the stand near the couch she refocused her thoughts.

"It's like I've been trapped in someone else's nightmare. One moment I am working in my studio, the next, I was bound, blindfolded, and dumped in a tiny room with a madman who repeated the same words, over and over for days. I was frightened, but even more so, I was angry, angry that I was nothing but an object to be used against someone I loved so dearly, angry that I *personally* could be the ultimate cause of Duncan's death." She looked from Fitz to Duncan then reached for her cup once again.

"That's silly, sweetheart. You mustn't think like that," Duncan replied.

In his usual mollifying tone, she thought. *Will you listen to my exact words and take me seriously here.* She reached out and placed a firm hand on his arm. "Duncan, nothing about what I am saying is silly. I know you love me with your life—he was counting on that when he used me like bait to draw you into his flame. I was chained in there, helpless and knowing that my mortal love and life was likely going to cost you your immortal existence. I was angry with myself and at you for loving me with reckless abandonment."

Fitz placed a hand on her shoulder. "Guilt, Tessa—that's what he made you feel. You were his pawn and the reason Duncan would die." Fitz shook his head. "This one may have been a madman, but he was a devious, calculating one. He manipulated you, like so many trained paramilitary learn to do, so that you would feel and believe that you were Duncan's ultimate executioner. You have every right to be angry, but at him, and he's dead so this has to end." He rubbed her shoulder lightly and smiled. "Besides, you would have done the same if the situation had been reversed, you would have come for Duncan." Fitz gave a nod to punctuate his point on role reversals. "A beautiful young woman such as you has better things to do than stay angry at a dead man."

"Fitz, we're having a *moment* here—if you please," and he motioned with his head in the direction of the kitchen *Get out, would you. And keep your amorous hand off her shoulder.*

Fitz responded with a wave of his hand indicating he was, '*already gone*'. As he rounded the corner, Duncan pulled Tessa close to himself and looked her straight in the eye. "Sweetheart, I didn't die, and you have no reason to feel guilty or angry now. Fitz is right. You would have done the same if you had been in my shoes. The best way to say this is, when you're in love, as much as we are, you never have to say you're sorry for giving our all."

"When I was shot, the only thing that went through my mind was now my mortality would take me away from you. For me, time was ticking off its last seconds and was about to run out." She looked to the cocoa cup, which had grown cold, in her right hand. "I know that must be hard for someone whose immortal clock has no hands to truly comprehend the feeling that time's up." Tessa wrapped her arm around his neck and pulled him the rest of the way to her lips.

"No, not really that difficult," Fitz began, poking his head around the opening and into the living room once again and halting their impending kiss. "Not if we're truly honest with ourselves." Absently, he casually inched his way back into the living room under Duncan's thoroughly annoyed expression.

"Tessa, we Immortals die by a slightly different set of rules, as it were. But we can still die. We're not omnipotent, we're just, well— Immortals. Ten, twenty, one hundred, a thousand years or more, it doesn't matter how long you've lived. The stroke of a sword can quickly level the playing field between us all. Suddenly it can be over and in the end, we're all really the same. Dead is dead. If we're being honest with ourselves, we too acknowledge that there is no such thing as forever in this body." Fitz's expression was very telling and silence reigned supreme for several long moments.

The whistling teapot made the first sound sending Fitz racing to the stove to prevent a mini volcano from erupting, as Duncan and Tessa finally consummated their kiss.

Chapter Eighteen

Richie grabbed ahold of yet another shopping bag. *Does Amanda ever stop shopping?* he thought desperately and juggled the handles so the weight was even. *It would sure help if I had three or four hands. OK, so I'm not going to complain. I've got a place to crash for a couple days while Mac and Tess work the kinks out of their relationship. It will be interesting to try Amanda's cooking.* He shrugged as he followed her to the car. *So what if she can't cook. There is always pizza—I can live on that.*

Reaching her car, Amanda had Richie dump the bags in the trunk. Instead of getting in, she turned and motioned for him to follow again.

Why am I not surprised? He mentally heaved a sigh as she led him toward a specialty food shop.

A man was coming out of the dry cleaner store across the street. He looked casually around as he reached for his keys and headed for his car. Suddenly, something caught his eye and he stopped dead in his tracks and stared. A moment later he caught himself staring. He stepped quickly to his car, unlocked it and threw his clothes in the back seat, then slid into the passenger's side. Mark Roszca watched the pair intently as they walked to the next shop. Reaching into the glove compartment, he retrieved a pair of sports binoculars then made a few notes. A moment later, he reached for his cell phone then stopped. *If I activate this unit and someone is trying to locate me, I've just given my position away.* It was a disposable cell phone, but he left it turned off just the same. Glancing up and down the street he settled on a destination. He got quickly out of the car, walked to the restaurant and went inside.

"Where are your courtesy phones?" he asked the attendant. The man motioned him to the side of the lounge. Mark picked a phone at the end of the hall. He was using a pre-paid card—it was untraceable. Pallin Wolf had to be dead he reasoned. That was the only way that woman, Tessa, could have escaped. He had been called to finish the mortal woman off after Wolf finished beheading her Immortal boyfriend—just like the last time. He had figured taking out her other boyfriend was simply a bonus.

He flipped his notebook to the back cover. Wolf had given him another number in case something went wrong. In Mark's estimation, something was very wrong now. This phone would not tie him to a location for long. He pressed it close to his ear.

"Yeah, it's Roszca—I want to speak to him now," he said in an even voice into the receiver. He watched the customers being ushered to their seats as he waited. "Mark Roszca," he repeated to the man at the other end of the call. "Pallin Wolf is dead—he has to be. I shot the woman and her other boyfriend this week. Yeah, that's the problem, sir. The boyfriend didn't *stay* dead. I don't miss, ever. Put a slug through his chest, saw him drop like a stone—the woman too. No, he wasn't a big guy—no, he didn't have dark hair – that's not what he looked like. He can't be over five and one-half feet, sort of red curly or wavy hair—he didn't have a sword either. Yeah, he was with the woman." His voice was getting a bit loud and he forced himself to quiet down. "I don't leave witnesses and this guy is a *loose cannon*. Don't worry about that. I took care of the cop that followed me too. No, I am not sure how that came about. There was no one else in the area when I shot the pair. Doesn't matter what he is, I know how to deal with Immortals. The only thing I want to know from you is, are you picking up my contract from where Pallin Wolf left me—yes or no? Don't worry about that, I'll take care of that boyfriend too." He flipped back to the front of the book where he had written the license plate number. "I'll find out if that Tessa woman is dead—if not, she will be." A moment later he hung up the phone and left by the back door.

James Horton slowly and thoughtfully hung up the phone at his end in Paris, France. Pallin Wolf's methods—playing the Immortal's Game, with a *lights-out twist*, was too eccentric for his taste. He preferred the direct approach with a gun and meat cleaver. Never mind that Wolf had been on a winning streak with the last handful of Immortals, his luck had run out when he met Duncan MacLeod. *Who is this wild-card Immortal kid with the red hair?* For the moment he was willing to go with Wolf's assessment of Mark, '*When he shot someone, he didn't miss.*' *Then if that's the case, I have another problem to deal with.* He smiled and turned to his group of Watchers. "Pallin Wolf is dead. I believe it is time we expanded our membership." His grin widened. "A breath of fresh air is good for any organization, don't you think?" It was a rhetorical question – no one intended to reply.

"And I have just the candidate in mind. He has excellent credentials—just finished reviewing them today—didn't we?" He motioned to his men by the door. "Bring our candidate in – I think I'm ready to make a job offer—and if he accepts, I don't think we'll be beheading Xavier St. Cloud anytime soon."

Chapter Nineteen

Holding the large drawing out for a better perspective, Fitz pondered the images. "You say you didn't consciously draw this—but your *hand* did? Sorry, Tessa, I'm not a parapsychologist. I see the drawing looks pretty ominous, I agree. I can see Duncan as plain as life, but the rest is really up for grabs. What do you think it means?"

"I saw the same thing in my *vision.*" She looked to Duncan then back to Fitz. "I don't believe it was a dream, Fitz. I believe it was a premonition of some type. I had no reason to see what I saw. Nothing like what you see in that drawing was suggested to me, not ever. In my vision, I saw this figure descending that staircase and watched him behead the statue. I felt he was on Holy Ground and he angered something by doing this."

"In this picture Duncan is just standing by the statute," Fitz continued. "In your vision, you saw him walk toward this dark figure?"

"I have never been to Chichen Itza, if that's what this is," Duncan interjected. "I've been through parts of Texas, Old, and New Mexico. I have never actually seen the Temple of Kukulkan."

Tessa shrugged. "I am not sure this is Chichen Itza. I know what that monument looks like. I ended up on water. I was just standing on the surface. It looked like I was surrounded by the ocean. I don't believe this is any place in Mexico." Tessa paused. "I just know how the vision made me feel. He angered something by his actions. He will respect no boundaries and he intends to take your head on Holy Ground, I just feel it."

"Tessa, Immortals never fight on Holy Ground. No matter how evil they are, it doesn't happen."

"Oh, I wouldn't swear to that, old boy. There are rumors."

"Fitz, Immortals don't fight on Holy Ground." He paused and stared intently at him. "What have you heard?"

"Like I said, just rumors. I've been around a bit longer than you, a good 400 years longer. There is a rumor about two Immortals fighting in a Greek temple in Pompeii around seventy-nine AD, and we all know what a mess that volcano made of that entire civilization. There was also a bit of murmurings about an entire island nation in the western hemisphere being wiped off the face of the earth because an Immortal violated the Holy Ground rules." Fitz put a pensive finger to his chin.

"Then there was that volcanic eruption around 40,000 years ago, west of what is now Naples Italy. Some Immortals have speculated long and hard on the cause of that. That explosion may have wiped out a fair number of people on earth at that time, possibly even partly to blame for a whole race of humans becoming extinct."

"Come on, Fitz. Who lived in that part of the world then?"

"Neanderthals, Duncan. They are all gone now. No speculation needed. As I said, all just Immortal's rumors."

Duncan shook his head. "Neanderthal Immortals? You've got an imagination, Fitz I'll give you that."

"And why not Neanderthal Immortals? Do any of us know who the very first Immortal was or how long ago it was when they became an Immortal?"

"Is that possible?" asked Tessa.

"Ask Fitz. He seems to be an expert in immortal anthropology these days."

"Sweetheart, no matter what Fitz—or anyone else may have heard—beheadings on Holy Ground don't happen—certainly not in either of our lifetimes. What else did you see in that vision?"

Tessa collected her thoughts. "He was about to kill you and you did nothing to defend yourself."

Duncan shrugged. "That's unlikely."

"The stone Aztec calendar-clock, I think I understand. It's telling me time is running out in some fashion. I just don't know why I was shown this object, or when time is supposed to end according to it, but somewhere on that page is the symbol that tells when he will come for you."

"What about the statues themselves? What is the significance of beheading one, or something protecting Duncan—if in fact that is what was going on?"

"I think the offense was somehow related to the dragon or snake-like creature I saw in the sky." Tessa shook her head as a confused expression formed. "All this stuff about Immortals and Holy Ground. What constitutes Holy Ground? These cultures had pagan deities. I grew up in the modern world as a Christian. Yet, Duncan, you have always told me that Holy Ground is *any* place consecrated to any deity or any *Higher Power*. As a Christian we are taught that there are no other gods."

"A tough one," Fitz said, placing the unlit pipe between his teeth, preparing to launch into a philosophical discussion. "We Immortals can *feel* a power when we set foot on Holy Ground. Now that could be a modern church, or church yard, religious cemetery, but it could also be an Indian shaman's hallowed spot, or a Buddhist temple, or a temple to Athena, or Zeus, or Ra. It doesn't seem to matter if that deity has fallen out of favor, as it were. Once a place has been consecrated, through some acknowledged ritual of man, to that Higher Power, it becomes Holy Ground. We feel it, whether we choose to acknowledge that belief or not." Fitz sat back and pondered a moment. "No offense intended to the currently in favor deities, but since all of these places are felt by us Immortals as alike, if I were a theologian—which I'm not—I would say there is truly only one *Source* for that omnipotence."

Duncan sat back, truly astonished. "I never thought of it that way, Fitz. Sometimes you truly amaze me. Did you ever consider publishing your theological argument as a dissertation?"

Fitz chuckled. "I don't want to be burned as a heretic by *all* the major denominations today for telling everyone that they have been wasting their time arguing and fighting for hundreds of years over the same supreme power."

"Was that everything in your dream?" Duncan asked, changing the subject.

Tessa shook her head. "After the scene stopped, I was confronted by a dark figure as well."

"The same one?" Duncan asked, a bit concerned at the new twist in her vision.

"No, something different. I knew I was going to die and I couldn't run away. The dream wouldn't let me."

"The shooting," Duncan supplied hopefully.

Tessa shook her head again. "As this figure was approaching me, a large snake slithered up beside me. I put out my hand and grabbed hold of its feathered neck. It kept telling me to 'strike'. I didn't understand in my dream so I didn't act. That was the end." Tessa thought a moment. "I am certain that this is telling me someone is coming for me too, I can just feel it."

Duncan sat in silence considering what he had heard. *She grabbed hold of a feathered snake and it became a sort of sword. I remember thinking, for just an instant, I saw feathers on the neck of my katana today. I never believed in premonitions when Darius told me of his and he's dead now. I'm not going to ignore hers.*

This sounds like Kukulkan. But what does Kukulkan have to do with either of us? His mind drifted in the direction of the new pieces of art he just acquired.

Chapter Twenty

I don't care if the planet stops revolving today, she thought as she opened her eyes, just a crack and stretched herself out next to Duncan's warm body under the covers. *This past week has been totally enough for me. I'm taking the day off.*

The first rays of morning were just peeking through the window. It was usually a special time for them when neither was really asleep or awake, but both wanted to pretend they were when they hugged. Tessa closed her eyes tightly and pulled the cover over her head. Duncan was still asleep and Tessa began to think of all the things she was going to get him to do today. Between running the shop and running after her needs, this would be fun. Besides, she wanted to forget about her shooting, clocks, and evil drawings today she was going to focus on the *Tessa* that is going forward in life.

Initially she had viewed Fitz's arrival just after her return from the hospital as an ill-timed visit. But that had quickly changed. His varied conversations and points of view over the past two days had felt like a breath of fresh air in her life. It wasn't always what he said that was stirring her mind now. Sometimes it was what he *didn't* say that made her wonder, why not? In any case, she had awakened this morning with the feeling that she had just turned a corner in her life and though she was uncertain where this road might lead her, she had already been over the one she had just left more than enough.

Duncan roused and she wrapped her arms around his shoulders. "Good morning, sleepy-head. The sun has been knocking on our window for some time now. I vote we hang out a do-not-disturb sign."

Not fully awake, he gave his non-committal, "Uh-huh," and snuggled up to Tessa's warm body.

"I am putting you on notice today that you are the chief-cook-and-bottle-washer. I'm taking the day off."

"That's nice," he mumbled a little more coherently.

"And I think I would like something special for breakfast, made with your usual ruffles and flourishes."

"OK," he yawned.

Tessa propped up on an elbow. *You really haven't heard a word I've said,* she thought. A fiendish smile formed on her lips. Her imagination went into overdrive. "And afterward, for the housework, you can lick the floor clean, it's very dusty."

"Sure thing," he sighed; and rolling over, buried his face in his pillow.

"And I don't want your kisses to taste like floor-breath, so I think I would like a nice long shower—you can lick the body wash off of my shoulders. Oh, I like plenty of moisturizing body cream after I am towel dried, then when you are finished—"

Her sentence was cut short as Duncan launched himself off the pillow and on to his forearms, fully awake and alert. *An Immortal was near!* A moment later they heard the rapping on the bedroom window.

"I say there, is everyone up?" came Fitz's bright voice. "The morning is half over."

Duncan dropped his head back down in his pillow and shouted, "Go away, Fitz, I'm sleeping." It all came out muffled which made Tessa chuckle. A moment later the window, which was open a crack, was slowly pried all the way open. Fitz finally poked his head in their room.

"I say, the doors to the bleed'en shop are locked. How on earth do you expect me to get in? Oh, good morning Tessa. Lovely out here this morning," he added. Tessa smiled back warmly and pulled the cover around herself.

"Fitz, it's locked for a reason—we're in bed," he said coming up for air.

In true Fitz fashion, the most astonished expression formed on his face. "Well, I can see that, my boy. And I understand too – all that's been happening and such. You need a day off," he added with zeal and began climbing through the window.

"Fitz, what are you doing?" Duncan exclaimed, favoring him with a seriously shocked expression. "There's a lady in bed."

Fitz stopped, one leg in and one leg out, he motioned in the general direction of the door. "Your door is locked. How the bleed'en, well you know what I mean, am I supposed to get breakfast started for you two if I can't get into the kitchen. And Duncan, in case you haven't been paying attention for the better part of the last 400 years, I *know* what a lady in bed looks like. I've been in bed with one or two in my lifetime you know."

"Not this one, you aren't going to be."

Tessa giggled momentarily at the ferocity of Duncan's tone.

Fitz finally pulled his leg in and straightened his English suit. "Of course not. I have the utmost respect for the lovely Tessa. After all, I'm a gentleman first. Now you two don't mind me, I'm just passing through as it were. I'll have something whipped up and back in here before you know it."

Before Duncan could respond, Fitz scooted out of the bedroom and toward the kitchen.

"I guess we're up," Tessa said with a smile.

"Either we're up or he'll be in bed with us with breakfast."

Sandy picked up a wheelchair from the hospital lobby and started back to the elevators and Duke's room. Grace was coming past admission when she spotted him and picked up her pace. It was early yet and they were the only two who arrived at the elevator door.

"Good morning, Grace," he said, as the bell for the arriving elevator rang. "Came to help my convalescing partner home for his medical rest and mine too. I hear the fish are supposed to be biting today up the river a ways at Duke's secret spot," he said with an all knowing grin to the immortal doctor.

Grace looked about the car momentarily as it started up. An instant later she quickly reached out and hit the 'Stop' button. Sandy gave her a '*What?*' questioning stare. She took a quick breath then faced him. "You might want to reconsider that medical leave – both of you." Her eyes darted to the wall—to nothing—as she nibbled her lower lip.

"What's going on, Grace?" Sandy said gently, placing a friendly hand on her arm.

"I told him I wouldn't say anything, but Duncan is in way over his head, Sandy. It could get them all killed. This information can't go any further than you and Duke—it can't."

Sandy nodded. "OK. What have you got?"

"Tessa wasn't shot in a random shooting. She had been kidnapped by someone using the Tudor house, a couple houses up from where the shooting occurred. She had been held for several days by a man who was luring Immortals in with their companions as bait and then somehow overcoming and killing the Immortals. I am virtually certain that the kid, who shot Richie and Tessa, was a part of this kidnapping scheme. Someone hired to get rid of mortal hostages after the Immortal was dead. If I'm right, Sandy, Duncan, Tessa, and Duke are all in danger now."

Sandy unconsciously stepped back. *So that's how it went down,* he thought to himself. *Pallin Wolf was the one responsible for all those Immortals and their companions, as well as a few Watchers, who have gone missing recently. James Horton is dead. Joe said Duncan MacLeod got him in the factory several months ago, preventing him from killing him. He was a hell-of-a friend. Horton had some really sick people to carry on after him. Mark mustn't have known about Duke being an Immortal or he would have tried to finish him off.*

Sandy thought back to the incident that morning. *Or, maybe he did know and just didn't have time because I came in right behind Duke.* A cold feeling settled in Sandy's belly. *Joe didn't think the kid was a Watcher. What if he's wrong? What if he has access to the Watcher's database?* Suddenly Duke was front and center in his mind in a way he could not shake.

Grace saw the shift in Sandy's expression. "Sandy, what is it?"

He wet his lips. There was a far-away look in his eyes. "I was just thinking of Duke. He's a pretty impervious partner. Someone who's going to be sitting next to you in that squad car till the day you retire—or die. No one we ever go after thinks to do anything more than shoot and run. I never once considered there might be someone out there who knows how to end Duke's immortal life – more than two-millenniums of service suddenly finished. I simply can't even begin to picture myself attending his funeral service." The call bell rang and Grace flipped the 'On' switch restarting the elevator car.

"Find him, stop him Sandy. And please, watch yourself and Duke's back too. He needs your help now."

Sandy nodded. The door opened onto his floor a moment later. He exited as several other visitors got in with Grace. He walked on to Duke's room.

One of the young, female nurses was fussing over the instructions for Duke's wound care at home, pain medication, vitamin tablets, antibiotics and a few others that Duke had never heard of.

If she'd use the Latin names I might know what these potions were, he thought. Latin was his second language, right behind Greek. He sighed and nodded again. Duke had been through this routine before. He was putting on his best act. Holding the side of his chest lightly, he obediently listened to each and every instruction given. *And if I feed all that crap to the fish,* he thought, *will it make them easier to catch? Or would you want to eat them afterward? How do mortals survive the list of pharmaceuticals you push on every patient? What, more of this? I already have enough gauze and wrapping at home to make two mummies! And I am absolutely not putting any more of that gorilla-tape you call a bandage on myself anywhere—no, no.*

Sandy's arrival saved Duke from having her demonstrate the use of the at-home enema kit.

"Ready to go, Duke?"

He nodded and practically jumped into the wheelchair, anything to remain seated and away from that enema kit.

Sandy wheeled Duke past Station desks full of well-wishers. He waved and nodded, smiling. As they approached the elevator door

Duke began to relax. A quick ride down to the garage and he was home free.

The door snapped open and out stepped their high school work-study student with another bunch of flowers.

"Officer Maxim, you're leaving already?" she bubbled, with the biggest smile. Stepping from the elevator, she set the flowers in his lap and threw her arms around his neck. "You're looking really great. I know you're going to be OK soon."

Duke accepted the hug graciously and agreed he was on the mend and would be well soon.

She was absolutely overjoyed and rode down to the garage with them to help Duke into the squad car herself – all the while giving a thorough, non-stop, rapid-fire report of each and every duty-paper she had personally prepared, in what envelope, arranged in what order, on his now very neat desk which she reorganized, all waiting for him to sign when he returned. Closing the car door, she looked to Sandy.

"Could I get a ride back to the station? It would save me a bus transfer."

Sandy turned momentarily toward Duke. The expression on his face was priceless. He reached to the rear car door and, saying nothing, held it open. She quickly jumped in. A moment later her report continued uninterrupted *for the next twenty-six blocks!*

Duke could have cried! *By the Sons of Zeus,* he thought, closing his eyes. *I should have stayed for the enema demonstration!*

Duncan rolled over, stretched and yawned, then relaxed – moments turned into minutes. Before either of them realized that time never waits for anyone, the delicious aroma of a large breakfast was filtering through the door, which had been left ajar in Fitz's wake.

"Smells delicious," Tessa said and scooted up on her pillows. "Can't wait for it to get here—the aroma is making me crazy hungry."

"What?" Duncan exclaimed, suddenly realizing how long he had been laying there after Fitz's departure. Glancing over to Tessa, rather wide-eyed, he rolled quickly out of bed. "You can't get breakfast in here like that. You don't have a stitch of clothes on."

Tessa's impish smile broadened further. She favored him with an exaggerated, '*I'm looking at you too*' stare. "All I see is you in your birthday-suit," she replied with a chuckle.

Duncan returned the comical stare-expression and headed for the bathroom as Tessa fluffed the pillows up, propped herself up and smoothed the bed cover over and around herself very, very neatly. A few moments later, Duncan was back. He halted – his expression matched his tone. "What are you still doing in bed? That man will be in here with—"

"Breakfast is served," came the highly-caffeinated voice. A moment later Fitz elbowed into the room, a serving tray topped with two plates of food in his left palm, two large napkins looped over his left arm and a coffee-server in his right hand – all in true English butler style – right down to Tessa's long, flowered apron neatly tied around his English suit.

"Fitz! I'm not ready."

"Ladies first," he replied with a smile toward Tessa, cutting Duncan off, as he quickly moved to her side of the bed. Setting the coffee-server down on the nightstand, with his right hand he flipped the large napkin squarely over the bed cover atop her with all the flair of a bullfighter. Nestling the serving tray on top of it, he removed the second plate, unrolled the silverware from its napkin and repositioned everything in front of her before pouring her a cup of piping-hot coffee.

"Thank you, Fitz," she said as her mouth began to water. "I was becoming famished inhaling the aroma from the kitchen."

Duncan was still standing on the other side of the bed, his arms folded in annoyance with this self-made butler, when Fitz rounded the bed with the second plate.

"Fitz, does it look like I'm ready for breakfast?" his hands motioning to the obvious lack of any attire.

Not saying a word, Fitz waved his hand urgently—'*sit down*'—and reached for the second napkin which was still draped across his arm.

Taken aback, Duncan quickly sat – the wooden chair was a sudden *cold* reminder on his bare buns. Fitz flipped the napkin squarely over his bare lap then placed the large plate, with very hot food, directly atop. An instant later, Duncan's eyes opened wide and he grabbed the edges of the plate, lifting it off his lap.

"Ah—Fitz—this plate is—"

Without missing a beat, Fitz reached, grabbed the nearby pillow and placed it on top of the napkin, then pushed the plate, in Duncan's hands, back down on it.

"There you go, old boy." He looked to Tessa who was trying unsuccessfully to stifle a chuckle at Duncan's '*too hot to handle*' expression. "Oh, don't worry about any of that with him, he's an Immortal—he'll heal."

"Thank you for that news-flash," Duncan remarked between bites, as Fitz returned with the coffee pot to pour Duncan's cup. His eyebrows went up noticeably. "Fitz, this tastes great. I didn't know you were such a good chef."

Tessa, who was already well into her plate, stopped. The twinkle in her eye would have told Duncan there was a curve-ball coming if he would have been looking.

"I agree, Duncan, we should hire this man as our head chef and butler. Breakfast in bed like this every morning, can't you just see me, us? He would be fabulous."

Fitz's smile spread across his face as he made a short bow. "At your service, Madam."

Duncan nearly choked on what he was chewing! Looking quickly to Fitz then to Tessa. "Oh no you don't. I can see—too much, that is," he emphasized. "No way is Fitz going to—Tessa, put some clothes on."

"Now?" she said in a sickeningly innocent tone then reached for the side of her covers, threatening to throw them back.

"No, not now! Fitz, it's delicious—thank you, now get out of here."

Fitz gestured to the coffee pot. "Another round perhaps?"

"*Go*!" Duncan exclaimed.

Fitz scooted out the door. Duncan shoved the last delicious mouthful in his mouth, set the plate on his nightstand and went over and closed the bedroom door firmly. Grabbing his clothes, he quickly dressed, collected the dishes and headed out the door.

"I want to see you with your clothes on from now on. You've had entirely too much fun with this," he emphasized and shut the door behind himself.

Tessa stretched, a long comfortable contented stretch. Throwing back the covers, she got up. *Let's see what mischief I can get into today.*

Chapter Twenty-one

Stepping from the steamy shower, she removed her shower cap and fluffed her damp hair, then slipped into a lounging robe. Grabbing a towel, she wiped the mirror dry then paused. The image that stared back was positively glowing. *Is that me? Did I just step from the Fountain of Youth, or what is happening here?* She touched the mirror, her moist fingerprints leaving a telltale reminder of which side of the mirror she was still on. Fitz's delicious breakfast and her long, self-indulging, shower had rejuvenated her in ways she hadn't thought possible. *When was the last time I felt so hedonistic?*

The events of this past week had gone from screaming hectic to dead calm. Her life was finally quiet. Duncan and Fitz were together again—a man who was double Duncan's age. For all Duncan's fits of jealousy, she was very glad Fitz had come when he did and they were sharing some quality time together this afternoon. *Leave the store to them to tend and close today,* she thought. This used to be her function together with Duncan. The store as much her domain as it was Duncan's, with her carving out her art space beside his swords and various pieces of antiquity. But something was suddenly in the air and she felt a change from owning the task to embracing some serious me-time alone. Slowly she swept past the bed feeling as light as a feather. In fact, she was beginning to cherish these new moments by herself. The wheels of her imagination began to grind, slowly at first, then faster and faster as the dust from disuse fell away. Looking out of the brightly lit window, Tessa saw the morning in a new way, as if for the first time. The sunlight gently caressed every object that surrounded her—on the table, the bed, the chair, the wall—and they, in turn, showed their gratitude by reflecting each ray on her. It was like a silent, secret conversation. She found herself musing about the new scenarios her life could have. In that silence she was standing by the window, receiving all the warmth by herself when Duncan poked his head in the bedroom.

"Just wanted to check to make sure you were out of the shower. Thought I might have to come in and give you mouth-to-mouth resuscitation," he said jokingly, yet giving her a questioning stare.

"None needed," she replied, then turned her back toward him and resumed her gaze out of the window.

The expression on Duncan's face formed a question. "Tessa, are you alright?"

"Yes," she said turning once again toward him with a warm smile. "I feel great—better than alright."

Duncan took a hesitant step toward her then stopped short. *That smile isn't really for me. What phase is Tessa going through? Oh well, at least she seems at peace now. I better keep an eye on this phase too,* he thought. "Are you going to favor us with your presence?" And he motioned to the living room. Wordlessly, she swept past him through the open door and into the living room. *I know I'm going to keep an eye on this,* he reminded himself.

Fitz was attacking the living room floor with a vengeful broom.

"Fitz, you have done a great job removing the very last piece of dust off this floor. You can give that smoking broom of yours a rest now."

"I'll be done in just a 'spiff'," he replied. "I want this floor to look licked-clean."

"Oh, I assigned Duncan that job this morning," Tessa replied with a sheepish grin.

"You did what?"

"Never mind," she replied, and took up a comfortable repose on the couch, spreading her gown out across it. Her hand reached under the end pillow and found a book that had been tucked behind it. She brought it up to eye level only to discover she really had no interest in it. *It makes a good prop,* her mind told her.

Duncan favored her with another puzzled look. *What is with Tessa today? Fitz is here, I'm just standing here. Am I missing something? She is usually busying about me or in the kitchen, or in the store, or there is a new or old art project that she feels has to happen—always something. It isn't eleven a.m. and she is parking herself. This isn't the Tessa I know.* Duncan pushed out a place around her gown and sat down near the crook in her lap.

Fitz, finally satisfied he had banished the last speck of dust, propped his broom against the overstuffed sofa and sat down. His mildly tired expression was akin to that someone would have given if they had just fended off a hoard. Tessa lowered her book.

"Fitz, we really appreciate everything you have been doing today, but you are a guest in our home. You really didn't have to work."

Fitz smiled back gently. "I know, but I wanted to. It isn't every day that Duncan MacLeod of the Clan MacLeod gets married to the lovely Tessa. I know this is going to be a special union. I want to do my part to make it special. Friends of the bride or groom usually give some gift—something you don't have." He shrugged. "What do you give someone who's been around 400 years old and a bit? He has had everything any couple has ever wanted, or needed, to start out with in life, and then some. Simply giving you something that I walked down to a department store and bought. You've probably had it in your second and fourth lifetime. That special feeling would be lost. But laddie, when you give of yourself, that can never get old. Besides, I may not be here on that special day."

"Why not?" Duncan asked, a tinge of concern reflected in his voice.

"Well, I could be away in another country and can't make it back in time, that sort of thing. This way you will have my gift to you now."

"That's sweet," Tessa interjected. "Helping to make our wedding special."

"And speaking of special, you need something special about your wedding preparations, something truly unique that you'll remember the rest of your lives."

"With all that has come up, I haven't had time to pick up a marriage license, or set a date and place yet," Duncan replied, looking to Tessa. "But once we do, we'll hire a photographer to capture the moment."

Fitz shook his head and waved his hands in the air. *Stop, stop—this is not what I'm referring to, I mean truly memorable,* his gesture said.

"You two have been together now—what—about twelve years? What you're suggesting is about as memorable as going the Justice-of-the-Peace in the courthouse." *And he mimicked someone stamping postcards on an assembly line.* "*I now pronounce you man and wife—*you take my meaning here, Duncan? Look, if you had wanted to get that marriage certificate finalized and framed, you have had twelve years to do so – any Monday through Friday would have worked. No – this was a special decision on your part," and he leveled a stern finger at Duncan. "So this event has to be really memorable – in an immortal sense."

Tessa closed her book. "I couldn't agree more. Duncan, I want our wedding to have *uniquely us* written all over it – to be one for the books."

Duncan shrugged and nodded. "OK. Sure. What do you have in mind?"

"Well," Fitz continued as if Duncan had asked him. "There are as many ceremonies as there are denominations. I assume you are going to choose one of the currently fashionable faiths?" He looked to Tessa who was already nodding. "OK, then that part is already taken care of. So what we really need to spice it up, as it were, is come up with a prenuptial ritual–"

His voice faded out and he sat back and began rubbing his chin thoughtfully with a hand. "Something that hasn't been practiced for the last couple hundred years or so should do it, something to really get your pulses racing."

"Fitz, *we* are not getting married, Tessa and I are."

Fitz waved his fingers in Duncan's direction. *I'm thinking, don't disturb a genius at work here,* his action and silent expression seemed to say.

"You know, Duncan, it would be grand if we invoked one of the old Scottish or English prenuptial rituals," Tessa said.

Fitz's eyes lit up. "Tessa, there was a time when getting married was almost as challenging for the bride and groom as storming a castle." And Fitz leaned into his story like the best story teller. "You see, there was a time when—at the first hint of a wedding—the bride and groom-to-be were separated – torn apart from one another for many long days. They were subjected to grueling mental and physical endurance rituals. Both the man and woman, mind you," and he brought his arm down on the coffee table in a fashion reminiscent of a sword stroke. "Complete isolation from one another, both to be prepared for the exciting wedding night. During the week, after much bathing, feasting, or fasting, depending upon the family, of course, the bride and groom were separately stripped of their old clothes, made up in something entirely new, paraded through the streets in some fashion—him, his loins girded, weighted down with buckets of stones, soot covering his near naked body – her on a steed with all manners of cloth, beads and bows dangling from every place they could tie them, all amidst volleys of musket fire in the streets, all to announce to the world that they would meet one another at the ceremonial place."

"Sounds like an exciting idea. What comes next?" Tessa exclaimed.

"That sounds like a terrible idea, Fitz. Where do you dream this stuff up?"

"Oh, I'm not dreaming, laddie. Back when I was a wee lad, this went on in my village any time there was a waxing moon and several good kegs of ale."

"I'm a lot younger than you are—remember? Men were civilized by my time. Volleys of musket fire? I can just see our Seacouver police down here after the third musket went off and me being arrested on some indecency or insanity charge and by the way, we don't use muskets anymore. Have you checked lately to see what century we're in?"

"I think it is a romantic idea, Duncan," and she folded her arms crosswise on the edge of the sofa and lay her head on top in a dreamy fashion. "A knight in shining armor—facing the trials of destiny as the maiden rides off to meet him in Avalon."

"Absolutely not, Tessa," he favored her with a hard stare. Duncan's expression showed no indication of understanding what possible romantic or glamorous hallucination she was having at the moment. His offhand went to his hip as if reinforcing his position. There was a limit and this was it.

"Duncan," she began sweetly, ignoring his stare, "I am not asking for your permission; this is my decision too, and I am, after all, one-half of this union." Tessa's hand imitated Duncan's 'on hip' as if to say, *All right Highlander, here is a human being as stubborn as you.* After a moment she relaxed her hand and straightened her gown, then raised her book back to her eyes, totally disinterested in his silent fuming.

Duncan was not, by any stretch of the imagination, finished with his point. "I have agreed on everything in your life, so far. I have given my consent to all your ideas, but there is no way I am getting involved in some ancient ritual, or letting you do this."

Tessa glanced blithely toward him. "Sweetheart, I didn't hear myself asking you for your permission. I intend something unique and memorable," her tone of voice was clear evidence of her determination, her French accent becoming stronger by the microsecond and her cheeks were pink. "I suggest you reconsider." She absently turned a page and looked away.

"Fine, I am reconsidering—there, the answer is still a resounding no," one hand still pressed firmly on his hip, the other pointing accusingly at Tessa.

"Hey guys, let's go to neutral corners here. You're both still good on this wedding, aren't you?"

"Everything will be just fine, Fitz" Duncan replied without taking his eyes off Tessa. "Just as soon as Tessa comes back to earth—hey, Mission Control calling Tessa, time to land!"

"*Yes'um, Master,*" Tessa replied then giggled. "I think the Women's Suffrage Movement was finally completed in 1920. So when was it repealed? When did I stop having a voice or a vote? You know, Fitz, I think Duncan must have been lying about his age all these years. He is not a 400-year-old Highlander; he is actually a caveman from prehistoric times!" Tessa opened then slammed her book shut with both hands and her eyes lit up again.

"Now that would be a *real* pre-nuptial ritual for you. Fitz – just picture it, basic animal instincts. Duncan and I in loincloths and animal skins, barely covering our near naked forms—him on the prowl," and she pantomimed a crouched position with her forearms on the couch. "Searching—hunting for me. Of course I am in your protective custody."

"No! No! No!" Duncan affirmed each and every word. "You and Fitz are not going to be—"

"Absolutely not, dear boy," Fitz quickly sat up straight. "It has to be female-protectors, someone to fend you off good and proper while she is going through her purification ritual. Hum, now let me see – you are going to need a couple of skilled Immortals for that, I wager."

"Look, Tessa, *sweetheart,*" he exclaimed. "If I'm a caveman, at least I am one with more common sense than you are showing – a loin cloth? Give me a break. I'm not Tarzan! I am just a guy here who's trying to keep things under control and sane for our *normal* wedding."

"Of course—all under *your* control," and she reached back and gave his cheek a little tweak with her fingers. "Now, dear Fitz, let's talk about my purification ritual."

Chapter Twenty-two

Their apartment, with the attached store, had always felt like home to her, but today everything had seemed special. Maybe it was the light-hearted and playful Fitz with his over-the-top wedding suggestions. Maybe it was how funny Duncan seemed to look to her every time he thought Fitz was organizing his life or maybe it was her sudden acceptance that she wasn't in control of every moment of her life, and didn't have to be for it to go on. Whatever it was today had been full of precious and impromptu moments. Though they had left her alone in the early afternoon to tend the shop or talk outside, Tessa knew that Duncan wasn't far away.

This was the quiet time of the day when all the earth was slowing down. At this time, when the sun was setting, its dying rays played all kinds of tricks with the artifacts and antiques preciously guarded, making the place cozier, even when Mac was not around. They seemed to come alive and invite her to play games with them. Tessa often accepted their challenge and willingly participated—creating all kinds of stories about their origins and the circumstances that led them to their store. Not to mention the fact that some of these pieces had been picked up by Duncan himself along the centuries.

It was at this time of the evening she had gotten into the habit of taking a final walk past one small sculpture—Solo (lonely), the little  llama as she had taken to calling the tiny gold statue which stood in a special display case in the corner of the shop. She had become very fond of Solo and was glad no one had shown an interest in buying it. Lately, she hadn't had the opportunity. It had been almost two weeks since this ordeal began with her kidnapping. She poured her mug full of hot cocoa, made her way to the shop, and past Solo. Nearing the display case, she stopped and stared. Solo wasn't alone anymore—three others had joined it. Like Solo, the other statues looked like the same stylized llama. Solo was made of gold and the others were silver and metal-seashell mixes. *Whoever created these reproduced each llama faithfully. It was truly a work of art. So these are the new statues Duncan had gone to pick up the day I was with Grace. He must have been negotiating for the others. He mentioned Solo was part of a collection which represented a part of life that is now at least 500 years old. I wonder where the others were when he bought Solo?* she pondered.

"Have you named the others yet?" Duncan asked as he walked up beside her.

His voice momentarily startled Tessa. Lost in thought, she hadn't heard him approach. "I just found them together. I guess I will have to stop calling him Solo now that he has company."

Duncan was by her side, fingers tucked in his pants pockets. "He's used to that name by now – don't change it or he'll be confused," Duncan said playfully. "I just arranged the others around Solo to keep him company." He paused.

"Tessa, there's something I've got to ask you—seriously now. Do you really want to see me in a loincloth, swinging from the branches after you, before our wedding?"

Tessa nearly spilled her cocoa laughing. Composing herself, she slipped an arm around his waist. "No. And if we wed in the winter, it could be more than a little cold. I don't want a *cold blue* Highlander for a groom – it might clash with my animal skins. No, Duncan, it was just so funny the way you were taking dear Fitz so literally. I couldn't help myself. It was a delightful game. You aren't the only one who plays these games, you know."

She set her cup down and wrapped her other hand around him as well. "I do want my wedding to be unique – with something that is truly only us. Tarzan really isn't my style, and so I am still open for suggestions."

Duncan breathed a small sigh of relief. "So we can cross all of that purification ritual nonsense off the list?"

"Oh, I wouldn't go that far," and her eyes sparkled in the fading rays of the sun. "I think there might be a test or two we can endure to make our wedding extra memorable."

"Oh, that's just great," Duncan said not at all convincing.

Tessa released him, and retrieving her cup, she began studying the small figurines. "I really haven't studied the South American cultures. Did they exist during your lifetime?"

"No. When I think of it I feel rather small in some ways. An entire empire rose and fell. They developed art, engineering, and astronomy in complete isolation from Europe before I ever existed."

"What do you know about these new pieces—besides that they were unearthed on the border of Argentina, near a volcanic mountain?"

"All the llamas statues were found with mummified children who had been offered as sacrifices to their gods in a highly ritualized ceremony. This type of ritual sacrifice seems to be common among all of the cultured – Mayan, Aztec, and Inca."

Tessa looked aghast. "You mean they actually killed these kids for no reason?" distress clearly evident in her voice.

"They believed they had a reason. It was part of their culture. These children are just a few of the many that have been unearthed."

Tessa set her mug down again. It was cold now, perhaps as cold as she felt the poor mummified children of these misguided social orders.

Reaching into the cabinet, Duncan repositioned the other llamas, deciding which angle was best for the three additional pieces to call the customers' attention to them.

This was a pointless exercise, Tessa thought. *He knows how much I love Solo, he will always find an excuse not to sell the set. Just look how he handles them – they are like his children. Children,* she couldn't stop thinking about the kids and what they must have felt. *Did they know their fate? Were they afraid? What must their parents have felt?* "Mac, tell me more about the kids."

He closed the cabinet. "Well, the scientists and archeologists who have been finding these sites say they were participants in the act of *capacocha,* sacrificed to rejoin their deceased ancestors who watched over the villages from the high places nearby."

Tessa shivered. "That's horrible."

"Well, that's how things were back then. People used to believe in their gods and pleasing them was their main concern. Not much different from other cultures. Celts had their sacrifices, too. Many societies were quite determined to appease their gods."

"Do they know how these children died?" Tessa was near the shop's computer. An information Website displayed a picture of some of the mummies that had been found across South America. *They looked so real, so innocent, and so alive.* She was suddenly overwhelmed with sadness.

Duncan sensed the tension in her voice and sat by her side, warmly comforting her with a gentle kiss. *She could have been a great mother. She could still be if she wanted to. I don't have to be the father—there are other ways.* "I'm not sure." He lied—he had no intention of telling her all the gross details. "They were usually given coca leaves and some alcohol, so apparently they just fell asleep. For these people, they were not there to die but to meet their ancestors."

Tessa sniffed. "I bet they were good politicians," her anger clearly present. "I wonder how their parents must have felt."

"As far as I know, being selected for the ritual was supposed to be a great honor, and apparently it was a major offense for parents to show any sadness after giving up their children for the ceremony."

"I wouldn't care what anyone thought. I wouldn't give up my own flesh and blood for some brutal ritual and I would do more than cry –

I would wail." Tessa's body tensed abruptly, she sat up leaving Duncan's reassuring embrace. The picture of the children filled her with a mixture of horror and compassion. She could not, for even one second, and in her wildest imagination, begin to comprehend what these ignorant people were expecting would happen after death. They died – the end – there was nothing for them beyond death.

"Mac, are there immortal children?" she asked, almost pleading for a negative answer.

Duncan took a slow deep breath, giving him time to fully grasp all the connotations implied in that simple question. Suddenly he was sorry he brought the other pieces home. All his anticipation of her excitement of having additional llama statues had turned into this.

"There are a few, Tess. They do not survive long. They can't defend themselves."

"Have you ever met one of them?" *Have you ever beheaded a child, Duncan MacLeod?* she pondered the unspoken question.

"I remember one. It was during the Civil War period, in 1862, his name was Sean. He couldn't have been over nine-years-old at the most. He was a drummer boy."

"What happened to him?"

"He didn't make it. I left him with Catherine, at a 'safe house', one I had used for Negro slaves. An Immortal took his head while I was helping a couple of people to freedom."

"How could an Immortal do something like that to a child?"

"*¿No estás haciendo muchas preguntas?*" (Aren't you asking too many questions?). He brought her back to his arms and gently caressed her cheeks, pulling her curls behind her ear. He was grinning mischievously. *Something to distract her from this line of questioning.* He knew her curiosity would get the better of her. Hopefully, it would be strong enough to take her mind away from immortal children and sacrifices, and restore her to the playful Tessa he had seen earlier today.

"Duncan?"

It had worked; the sparks in her eyes showed she was ready to play the game. "What sweetheart?"

"What did you just say to me?"

"I said, you look really hot in that gown."

"No, you didn't. That was too many words. What did you really say?"

"*¿De verdad quieres saber?* (do you really want to know?). Try and guess."

"Maybe I will learn to read minds instead." Tessa closed her eyes and put her fingers to her temple, reminiscent of a classical fiction mind-reader pose. "You are all tired out from all the housework Fitz had you helping him with today and want to go to bed."

"Or, maybe I am just getting started," and he hugged her affectionately. "La cama es para el amor (bed is for love)."

Tessa gave him an, *I'll show you,* grin. "Well, be warned, l'amour inventé français (the French invented love)."

Chapter Twenty-three

Tessa removed her robe, folded it, and laid it neatly over her chair near her side of the bed. She reached for the covers then paused. In her mind, a bed had two purposes; Duncan, on the opposite side, was energetically positioning his pillow and warming up for its *secondary* use. *Not too much tonight, Duncan,* she thought. This entire day has had a different *feeling* to it. *Something is preparing me—for what, I don't know—but this day has been no other, for as long as I can remember.* To Tessa, it all somehow unconsciously felt like she was nearing a '*gateway*' to some incomprehensible destiny. Pushing back the covers she crawled in. She wasn't really that tired, but after a little hugging, kissing, and cuddling, she let Duncan know, wordlessly in her own female way, that tonight was not the night for a marathon of intimacy. Curling up together, they 'spooned'. Pulling his arm around her, and tucking her head in his hand, she drifted off to sleep.

Null:
Tessa was simply and suddenly *there.*
A warm, damp wind swept by her oriental-printed gown, pushing it against her otherwise bare legs. She was aware of her feet firmly on something hard and flat. Glancing down, and all around, the image formed and solidified.
I'm on a mountain, at the base of a stone staircase, she thought. Around the edges of that staircase were vines crawling, twining and reaching upward. Her gaze followed that sea of green as far as the eye could see until it touched a hard blue sky. *A pyramid built into the side of a mountain,* her thoughts spoke.
Where is the floor? a part of her rational mind asked.
"The Earth is your floor," something '*outside*' spoke.
More than just its appearance, the humid air she felt '*touched*' her as if it was a finger gently stroking her flesh. Her rational mind began calling up a previously experienced memory of her guided imagery session with Grace – Salvador Dali's painting, 'Persistence of Memory,' with its myriad of surrealistic clocks draped over everything. But here, as far as the eye could see, there were no clocks and no surrealistic Dali images of creatures and landscape. She was alone, at the bottom of a pyramid, built into the side of a mountain.
"A volcano," that *outside* voice corrected her thoughts.
A sensation touched her mind and she knew without knowing that someone was speaking to her. Looking around, she saw no one.
"Where are you?" she called out, into the wind. No human voice

replied.

Suddenly her whole being was shaken by a sound *lower* than any human ear could possibly hear.

"Look down," it called. *"Here I am—beneath you."* And the whole mountain began to tremble.

"Where?" Tessa gasped, hands instinctively reaching out into thin air, trying to steady herself against the shifting stone beneath her feet.

"Look up," it whispered softly. *"I am all around you."* She felt the gale pressing against her, almost pushing her off her unsteady feet.

"I don't understand," she cried fearfully. *"An Earthquake! I'll fall off this mountain and be killed."*

A part of her rational mind searched for a point of reference and found none.

"You are standing on my face. I am alive."

"Stop!" She screamed. *"Everything, just stop! I don't understand. Are you trying to speak to me, or kill me?"*

Suddenly, the earth beneath her feet was still.

"There's no one here," she spoke into the wind. *"What are you?"*

*"**The same thing you are!**"* came the booming reply from everywhere.

Her mind was a blank slate. She couldn't even begin to fathom the meaning of that reply.

In her pondering, she felt other presences near her. Something small and soft touched her arm—then another, and another—human fingers, a hand. Tessa felt small hands grasping her sleeve, tugging gently, seeking her attention. Slowly she turned, in a dream-like manner, to see first one small child—then another, and another. Children were clustering around her—their small hands reaching out to hold hers, encircling her arms, pressing against her body to be near her. The children—each with sparkling brown eyes and light olive, sun-kissed skin—wore hand-woven cloaks of bright earth-tone threads.

Do I know these children? She pondered. A part of her felt she did – but from where? Her thoughts began shuffling images as if she were viewing a scrap book. Without warning, the images froze then superimposed themselves over each of the bright, smiling faces.

Yes, I have seen them, each of them. These children are the mummies I've read about. An inner voice gasped as if giving a death-knell. Looking into those innocent eyes, Tessa was moved to tears.

How could anyone bring themselves to rob you of your precious, young lives – condemning you to nothingness? she thought. In an act of maternal compassion, she quickly knelt, reaching out to embrace as many as she could gather into her arms—holding them close, sharing her warmth—her maternal love. Tessa closed her eyes, as tears silently rolled down her cheeks, pouring out from a heart that was breaking.

One by one, small fingers reached up and touched her cheeks wiping away one tear, and then another. Tessa opened her eyes slowly to see the many fingers—each taking away a tear, drying her face. The eyes that stared back weren't sad or longing—the lips she saw were smiling.

You're all dead, her thoughts cried out. *All that you were, is gone – nothingness.*

Slowly they shook their heads. *You don't really understand,* their expressions seemed to say.

A tall girl spoke up in a language Tessa had never heard.

"Did you ask me a question?" Tessa replied. It sounded like a question. *"I don't understand you,"* she said once again, shaking her head. In the back of her mind it occurred to her, in passing, that this was her vision and she shouldn't need a translator.

The girl repeated the phrase once again. Realizing she was not being understood, she gestured the message.

Tessa watched, trying to understand what she wanted her to know.

Look all around, her hands gracefully motioned outward—to the other children, to the mountain, to the sky.

Look at me with your heart, her hands passed over her own woven tunic, one finally coming to rest over Tessa's heart. She smiled benevolently. *See me with your inner eye—not with your outer eyes.* A hand rested on her delicate brow concealing her sight. Then, standing on her tip-toes, she reached up with both hands into the wind as if trying to grasp something off of a shelf that was just out of her reach. Slowly, she turned this way and that, humming an unfamiliar tune. After a few moments, she stopped and returned to stand in front of the bewildered Tessa once again. Gently she grasped Tessa's arm, her hand following it down to hers. Carefully she turned her palm upward in her own small hand. First, she smoothed Tessa's palm flat with the pads of her fingertips then, one by one, she opened Tessa's fingers into a fan-like shape, inserting her slender fingers between each and every one. As Tessa watched, the girl raised Tessa's arm as high as she could reach into the sky. Hands—all around her the children were thrusting their hands upward – reaching, swaying.

"I still don't–" Tessa began, when suddenly she felt something touch her hand and draw it upward. She yielded to the gentle but persistent force. *The mountain winds?* her thoughts questioned – but,

no. Her senses were alert to this new sensation encircling her hand. It was strong, powerful, yet gentle and smooth; like silk cloth, it was wrapping and unwrapping itself around each and every finger. It felt, in one instant, like Duncan's hair, wavy, rugged, yet alive with dimension. But it was more than that, much more. *As if I can almost hear the sound of a voice,* she pondered.

Releasing Tessa's arm, the girl reached up and out with both hands—into the wind. Humming her ancient melody, she swayed with the others to the happy tune. And, as Tessa watched, their images all grew fainter and fainter against the crisp blue sky; until at last, one by one, they became dust in the wind.

Tessa stared after their wake, her eyes transfixed on the now empty spots where once children from the distant past had stood—all so loving and so alive.

In the midst of her gazing, her mind began calling forth the memory of a song by the group Kansas – *'Dust in the Wind'* – a song depicting the utter futility of all humankind's dreams and ambitions— man's life-work condemned to ultimately disintegrate in the face of time. Her train of thought was suddenly halted when she felt the familiar touch of a small hand in hers—carefully smoothing her palm. Looking up, she strained to see substance in that touch from an unseen hand.

Close your eyes and see me, Tessa heard in her mind.

Listen with your heart and hear me. We are both alive—I am with you, right here, right now.

"But you died hundreds of years ago," Tessa whispered. "*Your body is now—*"

"*It clothed us,*" she heard in unison, as if the children were still around her. "*It took us for walks through our island home – it let each of us reach out and hold others near. Our bodies were ours, but not us. Real life is not bound by death—real life is immortal.*"

In the midst of her astonishment, Tessa's heart heard the earth's song. It wasn't a rush of mountain wind that she had been feeling, it was the earth singing, alive. Life was all around her. Rippling around her gown, it swept playfully about her legs like a puppy—holding her hand skyward, it slipped between her fingers to steady her. It embraced her wind-flushed rosy cheeks, like a playful lover.

I understand, her mind gasped, reeling with the magnitude of that instant of understanding. "*I'm touched and touching a living spirit.*" She whispered into the everything. Life was all around her. "*You are here with me—all around me—we are alive now and forever. I understand.*"

"*Good*," came the voice from beneath her feet, and there was victory in that sound.

And as she swayed to and fro, keeping time with the sounds of the earth, heard by her loving heart, the mountain danced in unison – a perfect partner, beneath her feet.

Tessa felt the shifting earth and was not afraid, she was overjoyed! *My time in this life is worth something. My life—real life is forever—I too am immortal,* her heart sang.

The sound of shifting rock was heard as something rolled to a stop near Tessa's feet. She looked down, as a dark shadow fell across her right side, and the earth grew still.

A stone head, a snake's head, looked up at her with empty sockets.

"*Children*?" Tessa shivered as she called wistfully into the silence. There was no response.

Light was slowly being swallowed up around her as she turned her head to face the humanoid-shaped dark mass. Faceless and featureless, it was darkness itself.

Beside her—to her right—on the steps of the pyramid, stood a boy no older than ten or twelve years. Around his shoulders he wore a woven, brightly colored cape—about his head was a small band of feathers. His eyes passed from Tessa's to the dark shape before her. Reaching to his neck, he removed a leather strap with a small golden figurine attached and placed it in Tessa's hand. Carefully, he closed her hand, and then his hands around hers firmly and resolutely before vanishing.

Puzzled, she turned the small object over in her hand.

Slowly the dark humanoid mass reached an appendage toward her hand, expectantly, as the earth all around them began to shutter.

It wants this thing from me. It was entrusted to me. I dare not give it up. She shook her head, backing away as it followed. *There's something wicked – something deadly coming – I have to hide. But where?* Her mind raced as the images of the dream began crumbling around her. *What is this thing in my hand?*

She glanced down to her hand, to the necklace. It was gone. In its place, she was holding—

Reality:

"Solo." Tessa spoke the word audibly, awakening herself with a start. Duncan moved at the sound of her voice but didn't awaken.

After a moment, she looked around the dimly lit room, orienting herself. *I'm in bed—Duncan is asleep—all is quiet in the room.* She relaxed back against her pillow. Her vision was as crisp as if it had

occurred in that room. Carefully she pushed the covers back and
headed to the cabinet, to her small gold statue.

Chapter Twenty-four

"Are you sure about this, Richie," Amanda said as she closed her car door and turned the key in the ignition.

"Yeah, I'm sure," and Richie nodded as he closed his passenger's door. "It's been three days. Mac has smoothed things over with Tessa by now. Besides, they've probably spent the last three days in bed making up for lost time—oh, sorry," he added, catching a glance at Amanda's gloomy expression.

Amanda pulled out of the parking stall and on to the street. "You know, I didn't mind having you along as a shopping partner. You could stay, maybe just a couple days more." She gave Richie a wistful glance, one eye on the road.

"Come on, Amanda," Richie smiled and gave a half-hearted head shake '*No*'. "I was lousy in the fashion shoe store and you know it. If it's a shoe, and it fits, I'm good with it. Oh, not that it wasn't an interesting experience," he added to soften the blow. "And I didn't mind carrying all those bags and boxes—really I didn't. I guess shopping has never been my strong point. Now when I hit the store— bam—I'm in and out in ten minutes tops. I don't care if I'm buying a loaf of bread or a house. I've heard this shopping style is a *guy thing* you know." He stared at her sideways for a moment, pondering the half of her expression he could see. "Hey, Amanda. I really want to thank you for the last three days of quality time showing me sword maneuvers."

"In between shopping," she added dryly.

Richie's smile broadened. "Seriously, Amanda. I know Mac has other concerns right now, but I'm not getting any younger as an Immortal. If Axel is any example of what is waiting for me outside my door, I can't wait for Mac. You put me through my paces these three days. Granted I'm not trained but it is a lot more than I knew before."

"Sorry about the shirt," and she glanced over to him quickly. "I swung a little fast. Just not used to training Immortals anymore. The last Immortal I seriously spent an extended time training happened in about 1182. He was just a kid—Kenneth—about nine or ten years old and going on forever. That blouse seems to fit OK. One of my old lounging pullovers."

Richie pulled up the front and smiled. "The pastel flowers seem to go with my natural curls. At least you weren't swinging for my head. I'm sure I'll get lots of training cuts from Mac when he finally gets around to it." He paused and let his gaze rest on the passing buildings as he thought of a way to introduce the next topic. "Once you get to know Tessa the two of you will be able to shop in tandem."

"I don't think that's ever going to happen, Richie, no matter how much you are hoping."

"Look, you're going to have to sit down with her sooner or later. She's marrying an Immortal. Like it or not, Tessa is going to have all of Mac's friends on their shared doorstep eventually. She may want to pretend that he's just a typical guy, but that isn't going to happen. Someone is going to come for his head eventually and Tessa will just have to deal with the whole immortal thing. Immortal friends are important to Mac and me."

Amanda shifted nervously in her seat. "I'm on a twenty-five-year coffee-break, remember. Besides, the moment I walk in that door she'll probably hit me with another scarf."

"Big deal. As long as it isn't a sword, I'm sure you can deal with it. That wasn't Tessa—not really. She was just freaked out because of everything that was happening all at once. Give the poor, mortal woman a break, will you?"

"She's got enough 'fire' to use a sword, that's for sure."

"I'm sure if you just sat down with her on neutral ground, you could talk it out. Once she sees that you aren't going to make a play for Mac every time he's around, it will be OK."

"You mean I've got to keep my hands on the table as it were, and not all over Duncan for the next, however long they're married?"

"That's right, Amanda. You'll just have to learn to be a good girl around Mac."

"What if I don't really want to be? It's really hard with Duncan – I mean I take just one look at him and I want to—well, you know what comes next."

"Do you really want him that badly? I mean to marry him?"

Amanda thought for a moment then took a deep breath. "We've been together off and on over the last almost 400 years. I never really took any relationship seriously—not like that. Maybe it was me, maybe it was the other guy, but I've fallen in and out of love so much over the last 1,100 years I never thought it should be any other way with anyone until I saw Duncan fall for Tessa. He was suddenly different, right from the start—even before the whole 'marry me' thing came up. Kind of makes me want to play house with him just to see what it's really all about."

"Well then, you have a good reason to get to know Tessa – you know—girl talk and all. You can learn a lot about what marriage is and isn't as it happens to her. Someday it could be your turn with

Mac if it is what you really want. Right now, I don't think it's really what you want or are ready for."

Richie was so fixed on their discussion that he failed to notice the car that had been following them from the moment they left their parking stall.

Mark Roszca maintained a discreet distance behind Amanda's car. *Let's see where this boyfriend comes to roost.* His right hand slid down the side of his leg to the top of his tall boot, coming to rest on the handle of his Bowie knife, tucked in an inner boot scabbard, he smiled. A popular early nineteenth-century frontier weapon, its blade was easily a foot long and razor sharp. *Horton doesn't know how this Immortal fits in with the woman I killed. It doesn't matter, once the slate has been wiped clean.* His hand left the handle of the Bowie knife and slid expertly along the edge of the seat. His fingertips brushed the semi-automatic pistol he had hidden out of sight but within quick reach if needed. A fleeting thought crossed his mind and he gave a quick chuckle. *The Old-West expression was wrong. The Colt 45 didn't make all men equal, the Bowie knife and the sword did. The only way to kill these bastards is to cut off their heads—'Mr. Boyfriend'.*

Tessa hung up the phone and returned to the kitchen and breakfast.

"Who called?" Duncan asked, his hands fastening the hair clip as he entered the kitchen.

"No one I called the police station. I wanted to know if they had caught the man yet."

"And?"

She shook her head. "No, nothing. They don't even have any leads."

"I'm sure Seacouver's police are looking. They don't want a killer on the streets any more than we do." Pouring a cup he walked over to Tessa and put his free arm around her. "I know," he said absently. "Waiting for anything especially news takes time. I understand what you're feeling."

Tessa turned her head, looked him square in the eyes, and in a matter a fact tone said, "No you don't, not this time. You see, while we both know he's still out there, I know he's coming for me – soon. I saw it in that drawing I had no control over creating. We can't wait for the police." Tessa paused reflectively. "I had another vision— whatever you want to call it—last night."

Duncan set his cup down. A contemplative expression creased his brow. *This is what Darius said to me more than once. I just wasn't comfortable believing it then and I am certainly not now. But this is my Tessa, and I saw what happened to my friend.*

"Tell me what you saw."

Tessa had spent some time in deep personal thought during the night trying to decide what she was going to say to Duncan in the morning. This vision had left her with very mixed emotions. A part of it had had a deeply personal and exhilarating impact on her life – the revelation that all life was truly immortal – not her body, but *the real Tessa.* There were some aspects of this very personal vision that she would have to share later—not now, though.

"As before, it was a shadowy figure, and I had the overwhelming feeling of an impending evil approaching, only this time, it was somehow different. It didn't feel like the same menace as in my drawing. It wanted something from me. It felt like it wanted the statue, Solo. I was being swallowed up by the darkness as the dream was crumbling around me. I interpret that to mean he is almost here. Whatever it is, it wants Solo before time is up."

He grabbed her hand and tugged her in the direction of the bedroom.

"I want you to pack a few things in your travel bag, right now. I'm getting you away from Seacouver until this guy is caught." He shook his head. "There are too many loose ends, Sweetheart. I just haven't had time to follow up on each one and I want you out of harm's way."

Tessa pulled back halting their forward motion. "I have something else in mind. I don't believe what happened to me has ever been made public on our Seacouver news station. Well, I think it's time it was, and I know just the person to tell. Putting that information out on the street will send him scurrying off, probably get careless and get caught."

Duncan shook his head. "I don't think that's a good idea."

"And just why not?"

His gaze shifted nervously from nowhere to nowhere. "The situation is just too unpredictable – he's too unpredictable. There is no way of knowing how a professional killer is going to react to sudden exposure on the news."

"Well I know how I would react, I would get the hell out of town. Wherever this guy is, he's too comfortable. I think it's time to shake him up a little, make him play his hand."

"Sweetheart, that *hand* could be fatal. He stood his ground and shot a policeman—obviously he didn't know he's an Immortal—but that's telling me something about him right there. I'd rather take you away from here for now."

Tessa stood her ground. "Do you want to call Randi McFarland at the news station, or should I?"

"What are you going to say? If the kidnapping portion comes up they are going to start digging around in that house. He's dead over there—somewhere. I still can't figure out why that hasn't been uncovered yet."

"I'm only going to talk about the shooter and what happened to me alone. I'll describe him as best as I can." She walked to the phone. Flipping through the note cards, she dialed the news station.

Amanda turned down the quaint street to Duncan and Tessa's shop and stopped some distance from the building. Richie, in true guy fashion, reached out, grabbed the edge of the hood, and bailed out through the open window.

"The door works," Amanda quipped, and Richie grinned sheepishly.

"Why don't you come in—just for a while? I'll shield you from any scarf lobbed in your direction. Hey, I'm an Immortal now, I can take it," he finished with a theatrical bow.

Amanda shook her head once.

"Will you at least think about it—for later?"

"Maybe later," she agreed.

Richie walked over to his bike and planted a pretend kiss on the handlebars. "Hey gorgeous, with the silver spokes, did you miss me?"

Amanda leaned out of the passenger's side window.

"Ah—Richie, if you're up to talking to your bike like that, you seriously need to get out more often."

Richie chuckled.

Very slowly, a car turned the corner then stopped at the end of the street, behind where Amanda and Richie had just driven past.

Mark Roszca watched as the red-haired guy bailed out of the car window and walked to his motorbike. Not once taking his eyes off his target, Mark reached alongside his driver's seat. Drawing his semi-automatic pistol, he fastened a silencer to the barrel. *I may be able to get two Immortals for this single hit. Horton doesn't know who this guy is, but Amanda is an Immortal. I got to hand it to Mr. Redhead, he gets around. No love lost over his last girlfriend either.*

Slowly, he angled the barrel out of his side window and took aim at Richie, his finger tightened slowly on the trigger.

An instant later his car was nearly sideswiped by the Seacouver's Action News van as it plowed pell-mell around the corner, scraping his side mirror and nearly taking Mark's head and arm off in the process! Mark lurched back into the car and across the passenger's seat as he both felt and heard the contact with his car. The van continued past him without slowing. No sooner had he righted himself in his seat when a squad car rounding the corner just behind his position and gave a blast on the siren. Quickly he looked away, so the officer couldn't see his face as the squad car passed. Composing himself, he backed out slowly and smoothly so as not to attract attention then drove on. This was enough for him.

"**Geese! Slow down!**" Randi McFarland shouted at her cameraman-driver as they round the corner.

"You told me to put my foot in it, or get out and **push**!" Geese shouted back as he felt the van yaw sharply onto its two right wheels.

"Oh God!" Geese gasped and turned the wheel sharply as Mark's car came instantly into view around the corner.

Randi shrieked and leaned into Geese as the sound of metal scraping the passenger's door was heard. An instant later the van slammed back down on all four tires.

Geese glanced rapidly to the off-side mirror. "I think I hit that car."

"Was there anyone in it?" Randi asked.

The blast of a police siren sound and Geese slammed on the break. The van came to a stop just behind Amanda's car.

"Oh Damn. Now look what you made me do."

Randi clutched the dashboard as the van bounced to a halt.

"Don't hand me any crap," she snapped and gave him a thoroughly annoyed expression. "I'll get the ticket. Now don't forget the extra microphone—come on." Flustered, she shoved the door open and slid out.

"Someone's in a big hurry. I better get out of here," Amanda said.

"It's the Action News van," he replied staring at the very persistent Randi who was already smoothing her jacket and giving the impression she was preparing to pounce on someone. "Wonder what this is about?"

"I'm out of here. See you, Richie."

"Think about it," Richie called as she drove off.

The squad car lights were flashing as the police car pulled to a stop right behind the Action News van. Officer Kevin Kilgore got out of the car, put his cap on then retrieved his citation pad.

"Sir, Madam—unless the end of the world is coming in the next few minutes, the driver of this van is in for a colossal fine." He opened his book and noted their license plate. "And I'll need to see your commercial driver's license as well."

Randi spoke up. "OK, so we were going a little fast – **Hello** – we're news reporters on a breaking story here, OK?"

"No – not 'OK'," Kevin replied as he wrote. "And *a little fast* doesn't even begin to describe what I saw on my speed-gun when you were on that last street. This van was nearing triple digits just before you careened around that corner. I'm surprised you didn't roll back there," and he gestured absently back down the street.

Wordlessly, Randi silently fumed and held out her hand for the ticket.

But Kevin wasn't finished yet. "I don't believe you signaled before you turned." He flipped the page and continued writing.

"I always do," Geese replied.

Kevin looked up. "Oh – I didn't see it." He folded his pad. "In that case, I had better conduct a safety inspection of your vehicle. If the driver would just follow me."

"I need my cameraman," Randi exclaimed and stamped the ground.

Duncan stepped from the store, and greeting Richie, looked to the group. "What's happening here?"

Richie shook his head. "The news van came tearing down this street like a bat out of Hell. The Cop saw it and well," he gestured to the group engaged in a lively discussion.

Duncan took a deep breath. "Randi McFarland—nothing surprising about any of this with her," he finished with a grin.

The cameraman handed Kevin the keys then went to the rear of the van and began retrieving the equipment.

Kevin opened the driver's door and, after engaging the battery, began flicking turn signals, windshield wipers, and just about any other knob he could twist or push. Discreetly he brought the small Watcher's recorder up to his mouth and made a few observations.

Wow—Duncan MacLeod, Richie Ryan, and Amanda Darieux all in one place. I wonder what they are going to do with the news crew. I think I will stick around and find out. This safety inspection is going to take as long as it takes.

Duncan casually walked around the van to where Kevin was working. "Problems, Officer?"

Kevin put his head up from where he was pretending to inspect and Duncan recognized him.

"Officer Kilgore? We met at the station."

"Yes, Mr. MacLeod. The night Mr. Ryan gave a statement.

Nothing to be concerned about here. The van was speeding erratically. There may be some safety issues connected with the way it was moving."

"The only safety issues are likely related to the female reporter in the front seat," Duncan said dryly and started to leave.

"Sir, she said they were getting a breaking story here. I don't see an accident or a fire on this street. That's what they usually chase. What story are they covering here?"

"Tessa is going public with the shooter's details."

"That's a brave move, but a dangerous one too."

"That's what I said. Did anyone downtown at the station say they were getting close to an arrest?"

Kevin shook his head. "I haven't heard anything from the Detective Division. Of course, I am just starting out so I am shifted around a lot. I would be careful after this, though."

Duncan nodded and followed the news crew into the shop.

Kevin was making a few verbal notes about his conversation with Duncan when a female behind him spoke up.

"How long is this so-called inspection going to take?"

Kevin recognized the voice, it was Amanda's Watcher. Turning, he saw a woman about two to three inches taller than himself—high platform shoes accounting for much of the overage in height – a decorative scarf wrapped around her head, light reddish-brown short straight hair, and huge sunglasses covering a fair percentage of her face. Her stylish blouse—if you could call it that—could have been considered trendy, or camouflage tent material, depending upon your opinion. Her slacks were worn and nondescript.

"It will take as long as it takes," he replied quietly though there was no one within earshot. "What are you still doing here? Your Immortal left almost fifteen-minutes ago."

"In case you haven't noticed, this van has my car blocked."

"Oh," Kevin said, casually and walked to the front of the van. "Thanks for reminding me." He flipped his citation book open again. "This van is also double-parked, then." He dutifully wrote out a third citation for Randi.

Tessa and Duncan explained to the very eager Randi what they were trying to do and the limits to which this interview was to go. Duncan had used Randi's connection to the news media before and knew how much she craved a story and the lengths she was willing to go to get it. As Tessa was carefully working her way through the interview, both Richie and Duncan sensed the presence of another

Immortal approaching. Duncan whispered to Richie then quietly slid past him to the door. Cautiously, he opened it. A small cloud of very familiar smelling smoke assaulted his nose.

"I'm keeping it out here," Fitz spoke up and held the pipe out, away from the door." I'm awful curious, though." He motioned to the police car and the news van. "Is the lovely Tessa doing an interview about her art or being arrested?"

Duncan absently shook his head—a small grin on his face. "The news van was caught speeding." He motioned absently to Officer Kilgore who was diligently writing out something on the hood of the van. "Tessa insisted on going public with a description of the shooter. I'm not really comfortable with this." He glanced back into the shop. Randi was still talking a mile-a-minute. *Doesn't this woman ever take a breath?* he thought.

Fitz folded his arms, pipe in one hand. "I understand your concern here, Duncan. But try to see it her way. It has been—what—a week now? No word on this guy—no leads? Tessa is not one to sit still, old boy. I mean, who knows where this guy is by now. With any luck, he's off the continent. We'll just stay close."

Duncan looked back down the street once, briefly. "That's not what's bothering me now, Fitz. Tessa claimed she had another premonition last night. She believes the shooter—or something – is coming, and soon. I'm still not comfortable with this hocus-pocus premonition stuff, but my mind keeps going back to Darius. I just can't dismiss what might have been if I had taken him seriously. Would he still be alive now? Whether or not I am a believer, I would really appreciate it if one of us was always with Tessa until this investigation ages a little more."

Fitz smile broadened. "Whatever I can do, Duncan. I'm here. And I do think that is a good idea for now to stay close." Knocking his pipe out against the building, he stowed it in his pocket and entered.

Richie quietly mentioned that the shooter-victim interview had ended a few minutes ago and they had drifted over to some of Tessa's artwork.

Duncan nodded, relieved that they were off that sensitive subject and on to something Tessa was enjoying. He also noted that the cameraman was no longer shooting. Parking himself on one of the chairs, Geese waited for Randi to run out of steam talking to Tessa. It was obvious he wasn't interested in the artwork.

Kevin entered the store all but unnoticed, and removing his cap, casually began looking at a few of the art pieces near the door. Slowly he worked his way toward Fitz. "Interesting artwork," he said, trying to make small talk. "Is this all by the same artist," he finished motioning toward Tessa.

"All this pottery and these bits of mashed and mangled metal sculpture are, aren't they, Duncan?"

Duncan nodded then pointed to a section of the shop which Tessa had commandeered for her own work. "She has been working on that piece since graduating from the University of Paris, la Sorbonne. For the longest time, I called it a *work in progress*, though she has a different name for it." He smiled.

The bell sounded again and Richie excused himself to meet the new arrival. A moment later he was back with a woman who appeared mildly annoyed.

"Officer, that news van is still blocking my car. I would greatly appreciate it if you would have that driver move it."

Hearing their van mentioned, Geese got up and went to the police officer for his keys. He left with the new woman. Kevin waited until Randi was finished speaking to Tessa before he handed her a small stack of traffic citations.

Her mouth dropped open as her caffeinated expression reached an all new high.

"This is possibly every known violation in the book for this State. How did you find all of this on our Action News van?"

"On a brief inspection," he replied with an air of innocence. "It was obvious. You really need to get that vehicle off the road until it has been in the shop. I should call a tow truck for you."

Randi's eyes bugged out. "What is this?" And she held a pink citation slip ridiculously close to her eyes. "**Rust!**" she exclaimed. "I'm getting a ticket for rust? Are you joking? We're by the damn ocean. What in this State isn't rusting?"

"It's just a notice—and the rust in question is obscuring a letter on your license plate. I can cite the section that this infraction refers to."

"Never mind," she growled, collecting her slips she hurried out of the shop.

Duncan couldn't resist a big grin. He knew Randi would move an entire planet to get a story, even if it did mean getting a galaxy-worth of citations from whatever interplanetary forces policed it.

The evening crowd had begun to gather in the lounge at a large Seacouver all evening bar-and-grill. The chef had just thrown a quarter-side of beef in the open rotisserie and was just starting his cooking/acting routine when Mark walked past with a drink in his hand. The meat sizzled as it was turned in the open flame, which was flanked by artistic brick walls. A glass panel and hidden blower-vent combo behind the brick ceiling façade separated the patrons from the gas flame, smoke, and flying grease while giving them ample view of the meat and cooking activities.

Mark Roszca wasn't that hungry yet; besides, the drink in his hand would keep him busy while he relaxed by the TV. Dropping into an overstuffed chair, he stared at the lounge's new large TV screen. By and by, a waitress came around the lounge area with breadsticks, checking that everyone had their drinks order. Mark took the basket of bread sticks then ignored her. He only vaguely noticed that the Seacouver's news program was on. The scene slipped from a commercial break to Randi McFarland's Action News segment. Suddenly something brought Mark's eyes back to the screen.

"...Tessa Noel, shooting survivor, describes her attacker as a short, late-teens to early twenties white male, reddish curly hair, wearing an old denim jacket with a Mohawk Indian inked in..."

The breadstick slipped from Mark's fingers as Tessa came on the screen and spoke.

"Damn," he swore quietly. *You are still alive. Where the Hell are you, bitch?* he thought. His eyes riveted to every image the cameraman was capturing, trying to discern something from the surroundings. A brief clip of the store front sign, '*MacLeod and Noel's Antiques*', came into view and Mark nearly spilled his drink.

I was right there this afternoon, he mentally exclaimed. *So, you've got two Immortals you're playing house within your little harem. Well, Miss Tessa, you're as good as dead right now. Horton would love to know where your other boyfriend, MacLeod has been hiding. A pity he'll be paying me for the job because he won't get that information. Don't worry lovely lady, you won't die alone—MacLeod's head is mine!* Mark downed his drink then left.

Chapter Twenty-five

With a thoroughly floured fingertip, Tessa flipped a page then turned it back. *You've got to be joking – I'm supposed to add how much salt? Did they intend it to be sweet or salty?* Her mind cranked through the ½ teaspoon measurements. *No way—this is a cake, not a pickle or the Dead Sea.* She shut the cookbook certain she knew better anyway. Reading someone else's recipes—especially someone she never had the pleasure of dining with – told her nothing about their taste. Besides, she hated to cook by the book a pinch of this, and a pinch of that, was the way her grandmother had always done it. No matter what that woman made, it always tasted great.

It was mid-morning. The sunlight was pouring in the window and Tessa wanted to get back to her normal routine of waking up the kitchen with something special now that Richie was home and Fitz was usually seen hovering around these past few days. She had had a great night's sleep. No visions, no weird feelings of impending *'something'* approaching, and no clocks of any kind—ticking, staring at her, or shouting at her in her mind. Since that strange drawing had occurred, she had deliberately removed all of the clocks and put them in an out-of-the-way drawer. *I know Duncan thought it strange when he had seen me rounding up the clocks, but I know he understands. They will all come back out when I feel the time is right.*

Duncan was in and around the shop and Fitz would likely show up later. She had taken a quick shower and prepared breakfast for her two hungry Immortals. *Being an Immortal doesn't dull your appetite when you are a young man,* she mused. Richie still ate like a growing teenager. *I wonder, since he is stuck in that age forever if he will eat like this forever. If yes, he is in for one huge grocery bill in life.* Whatever they indulged themselves in her Immortals always came back to the kitchen starved. Today she decided fish would be nice for noon, even if she had to listen to Richie complaining throughout the whole meal. Fitz had mentioned something about fish the other day after Randi had left. She laughed to herself a bit. Here were two people with two entirely different tastes. To calm Richie down, she had prepared his favorite cream and spring onion sauce. Although she had prepared this sauce a hundred times, she had to remind herself of every step, the image of Duncan interfering with her cooking skills kept intruding. *Duncan is a good cook in his own right – actually there isn't much in the way of domestic chores that he can't do. His personal habits are fastidious as well.* Tessa admired him for so many things in life. She smiled inwardly. After the fish, there would be a homemade cake—made with her own special flair. She would make today a little bit extra special now that she was feeling like herself again, nestled in with her two special Immortals. *Immortals,* that word kept prodding one corner of her mind and she kept pushing it away. *No, I feel great today. I'm not going to give in to any gloomy thoughts of what I have no control over.* Satisfied, she shoved the cake into the oven, set the timer, left the kitchen and headed for the living room. To avoid looking into the oven every third minute to see how it was baking, she turned on the TV to see if she could take her mind off Duncan and the cake.

The image on the screen made her freeze. Burial of a Time Capsule. Unconsciously, that peculiar corner of her mind prodded again—*Duncan is an Immortal. Here is something I can do to stay with him a little longer.*

The close up of the unsealed canister showed kids of all ages placing objects inside the moisture and rot proof canister.

" ... *Kids are putting lots of different stuff in the time capsule ,as you can see. We wanted to show kids in the future what was important to us here in 1993...*" the commentator continued as the happy faces of children were seen crowding around the canister.

A time capsule! Her excitement about the possibilities overwhelmed her, causing her to lose track of time and forget there was a cake in the oven. The timer sounded bringing her mind back to reality. *Damn! I don't want to miss the rest of this segment. What are they going to do with the Time Capsule next?* With one eye on the TV for as long as was possible, Tessa finally made a mad dash into the kitchen, grabbed a towel and rescued the cake. *A little singed on top, but if he really loves me, I know he'll eat it with a smile,* she reminded herself. Shutting the oven off, she hurried back to the TV, cake in hand. Carefully, she began flaking off the brown top, as she watched. The expressions on the faces of all the children and adults seemed to jump out at her. They were all happy though none of them would be alive when this capsule was finally opened, it was as if they were placing not only objects into this capsule but their feelings and well wishes too. Somehow they were trying to send their celebration forward to people who they would never see.

What can I do to bring a smile to my immortal husband-to-be face – 100, 200 years, or longer into the future? How can I suddenly appear in his life, like a romantic thought from just yesterday? What can I give him of myself—for love's sake—to make him happy for the time we have shared together in love? I don't want him to mourn me, I want to be the surprise he needs from time to time—a reminder to

him that life can be precious when shared with someone you love.
The sound of human voices distracted her from staring blankly into
the TV. A commercial had replaced the news segment without her
even noticing.

Duncan and Fitz rounded the corner deep in debate.

"...and I'll say it again, dear boy, that very slender *Rapier* sword is
a sixteenth-century sword. And furthermore, it was not used by a
man, but a woman. I happen to know a particular woman who
showed me to the door, as it were, with one in her hand."

Duncan chuckled, "The bedroom door, no doubt."

Fitz coughed once then raised an eyebrow.

"Come on you two. Get the store dust off your hands and pick up a
plate," Tessa said with a smile and set a large pan of fish on the
kitchen serving counter. "Where's Richie?"

"Oh lovely," Fitz remarked as he grabbed a plate and headed for
the fish. "You must have had a vision and read my mind. This smells
delicious."

Richie jogged in, came to a screeching halt in front of the fish and
gave it an ominous stare.

Duncan gave him a look that would wilt a tree. *If you so much as
make one disparaging noise over this fish...* The message was
received and understood.

"Oh—this—looks, really delicious," he said with as much sincerity
as he could muster over something he really didn't like.

"Thank you, I know you will enjoy it," Tessa replied equally not
very convincingly. "And to make it up to you here is your favorite
sauce," motioning to the serving bowl near the potatoes. A more
realistic smile appeared on Richie's face.

Fitz and Duncan both dove in like a pair of hungry beasts. With the
exception of a number of culinary compliments, which Tessa
thoroughly relished, they worked their way steadily through the fish,
through the potatoes and through the other vegetables without their
usual mealtime discussion. Even Richie ate more fish than she
expected when it was drowning in onion-sauce. When they all finally
finished there were almost no leftovers. Duncan began collecting the
plates, as the earlier conversation slowly resumed and Tessa headed
for the cake in the kitchen.

"I have all the swords authenticated over at the metallurgy shop. If
I don't recognize some marking on them that's where they go."

Fitz shook his head and waved a hand. "They took scrapings from
the guard or some of the scrollwork no doubt. Look, any of that can
be repaired—and I say it was. You didn't just toss swords out in those

days, you fixed them. Here," Fitz got up and grabbed a piece of note paper and pencil from the pad and holder on the counter by the phone. He quickly wrote a name and address. "You take that sword down to him. He knows how to do non-destructive testing. He also knows how to really look at a sword. Let him take a look at it. If he says its seventeenth-century, I will shut my mouth. Oh, I would take this photo to him first and get an appointment," Fitz handed Duncan the Polaroid picture he had just taken of the weapon before lunch. "He is usually backed up with requests from collectors, so if you just take the photo to him and get an appointment, he will do the analysis while you wait. You won't have to leave it there. And, yes Duncan, I know you wouldn't want to let most of what's here out of the store."

Duncan shrugged and wrote his name and phone number on the back of the picture along with a few details of the sword. "I'll run this down to him tomorrow or the next day when I have time."

Richie was more energized and grabbed the photo. "I can do it now. It will end the debate you two have been having over this for the past hour or so. If I get a definite date and time – what about it?"

"Sure," Duncan replied. "If you want to. There really isn't any reason for you to have to rush out."

"No, no problem," he aid and quickly reached a piece of cake as Tessa passed by.

"Hey!" Tessa exclaimed, a bit startled as Richie suddenly lifted a piece of cake off her moving platter.

"Got to dash—want something to fortify me on the long trip." He glanced to the back of the photo. "This is on the other side of the city by that big bar and lounge, isn't it? You know what—don't worry I'll find it. How big is this city anyway?"

"Big," Duncan replied. "Just a moment." He got up and fetched a street map. After a few moments, he pointed to the location.

Richie nodded. "You had it placed correctly. See you."

Richie downed the cake and licked his fingers. He was about to reach for another piece when Tessa pounced protectively over it. "When you come back. You don't need that much fortification."

Richie grinned. He was out the door in the next instant. Strapping on his helmet he took off.

He had a street map with him but he hadn't intended to use it. About fifteen-minutes into his ride, he pulled over to the curb and took the map out of his pocket. *OK, so I should have turned here. I'll catch the next street up ahead.* He paused briefly then cut back into traffic. As he neared the next red light, a car pulled out of a convenience store rapidly just missing his bike, cutting him off in the process.

"Damn! Watch where you're going," he shouted.

The driver turned pointedly in his direction, preparing to return an insult, then he froze as both recognized the other.

"Hey! You're the guy who shot us!" Richie exclaimed as Mark Roszca hit the accelerator.

Plowing into the backend of a waiting car, he hooked his bumper and tore it loose as he forced his way through the group of cars at the red light. His foot was to the floor, his tires were smoking. He rammed anything in his path, hitting it hard enough to move it out of the way and give him an avenue for escape. Horns were blaring as Mark tore through the crowded intersection—swerving to miss an oncoming car—striking a pedestrian on the off side of the cross-walk, plowing down a bicyclist in the bike lane and finally recovering in his lane, he sped off at maximum speed!

Richie tore after him, his throttle wide open. The chase wend its way, at a high speed, around and through residential streets and main avenues. Richie, more maneuverable on his bike, was threatening to overtake Mark. *What do I do when I catch up with his car?* His mind pondered rapidly. *I can't force him off the road with my bike! If I can get him coming at the right angle I could ram him head on— OK, so I would die, but so would he if I hit him just right. To Hell with the Immortal's rules about dying in public, it's worth a shot for what he did to Tessa!* Richie was about to cut hard left and through an alley, reasoning he could come up around in front of the car, when Mark cut hard right, sending a front hubcap flying, almost rolling his car in the process.

Richie swerved to miss the rolling hubcap then, lying out across his bike, he went hard right with Mark at full throttle.

Mark could see Richie in his side mirror close enough to touch him. Ahead was a construction zone. At over one-hundred miles-per-hour, on a residential street, he was running out of options fast.

The park, his mind noted the bush-lined border—his eyes scanned for an opening. *Hell, I'll make one,* he thought as he plowed into the bushes.

Richie was caught off guard with that maneuver. Overshooting the opening, he hit the break—his bike skidded out from under him as the seat of his pants took the brunt of the concrete. Leaping to his feet, he ran to his bike, righted it and jumped on just as a police siren sounded. *Oh, not now!* His mind thought frantically as he hit the starter—then he felt the presence of an Immortal. The police car screeched to a halt in front of him, cutting him off before he could move.

"Switch it off son," Sandy commanded—one foot out of the car he stood up, leaning over the door. "Your ride is over today."

Richie waved his hand frantically in the direction of the car fleeing through the park and shouted. "Officer, that's the guy who shot Tessa. He's getting away! I have to get him!"

Duke leaned out of the opposite window. Leveling a hard finger at Richie, he shouted back. "You're going nowhere near him – do you understand me, Richie? This is our business now! You get your ass back to where you belong and be damn glad you aren't getting a ticket from me. You're not Apollo and that thing between your legs isn't His sun-chariot either," he finished as he hit the siren.

An instant later Sandy all but did a wheelie as he burned rubber getting around Richie's position. The squad car tore through the opening Mark had created as it roared into the park.

Thanks for the favor gentlemen—don't mention me and all, just cause I'm not up for a medal—gee Officers, just trying to make a citizen's arrest here, his mind ran through a half-dozen snarky remarks as the car disappeared through the trees. He took a couple of deep breaths to settle himself. *Mac will back me on a manhunt,* he thought as he took off in the direction for home.

The squad car raced through the park, following the path of destruction wrought by Mark's car.

Duke palmed his service revolver. Satisfied it was ready, he slipped it back into its holster. "I know just about what's going to happen when that mortal bastard sees my face again," Duke said with a grin and one hand on the dashboard to steady himself. "Watching him wet himself is going to be fun."

Sandy was silent. His eyes never shifted from the trail of torn up vegetation in front of them.

When he got no response from his usually talkative partner, Duke glanced briefly over his way. He was about to comment further when the car hit a dip in the ground and bounced hard. *Keeping his mind on steering through this jungle,* he reminded himself and he let his comment die.

Up ahead the pair could see the construction zone, as they neared it. Sandy cut the siren as Mark's car came into view. He slowed as they approached it. The car had visible damage everywhere and both tires on the driver's side were flat. Duke released his seatbelt—the other hand on the door.

"No, Duke. He's mine—I'll take him," Sandy spoke up suddenly, his voice a crisp command. He drew his revolver and started out of the door as the car rolled to a stop.

Duke grabbed his arm, halting him. "Not so fast, partner. I don't recall you getting immortal status since we got in the car this morning."

Sandy sat back down, his eyes never leaving the service revolver in his hand.

Duke stared pensively, waited for a response from his unusually silent partner. "We're alone this time—so maybe he shoots me again—then what is he going to do to me?"

"Then he'll take your head," Sandy said in a slow, matter-of-fact voice and stared at his partner with a look of fear in his eyes.

"What?" Duke's breath caught in his throat.

"Then he'd kill my partner forever. Name's Mark Roszca—he's one of the bastards who's been killing Immortals, Duke. He knows what you are and how to end you. I'm not going to let him get you. He's a dead man the moment I see him."

"Sandy—where did you get this information?" Duke asked slowly, deliberately, a stunned expression on his face for what he'd just heard—what his mind was suddenly forced to process—*Immortals, exposed!*

Sandy looked away, then leaned back in his seat and shook his head. "I gave my word—swore I'd never interfere in your life – observe and record only," he said quietly. Unbuttoning his sleeve he pushed back the cuff, exposing his Watcher's tattoo. "But you're my partner first before anything else." He held his wrist up so Duke could clearly see the tattoo. "Duke, there is something you need to know—right now."

Duncan was rummaging through the trunk of his Thunderbird when he felt an Immortal approach. Glancing over his shoulder he saw Richie on his bike and returned his attention to his rummaging task. A moment later he felt the pebbles hit his pants leg as Richie's tire screeched to a halt just inches from his leg.

"Whoa Richie!" he said, sidestepping instinctively.

Richie raised his visor, urgency in his voice.

"**Mac**, I saw the guy who shot us! He practically ran me down on the way to that shop."

Duncan was by his side in a second. He switched off the key as Richie pulled his helmet off.

"What happened? Where is he?"

"I saw him, he saw me then he just took off like a crazed rabbit!" Richie gestured wildly. "He took out cars—people—you name it. Absolutely everything in his path was mowed down trying to get away from me. Mac, the guy was doing something way off my speedometer up and down everyplace. He took out a line of bushes by the park. I spun out and by the time I got back on my bike a cop stopped me. Don't worry, it was Duke and Sandy—the two cops from the hospital," he added when he saw the worried look on Duncan's face.

"Then what happened?"

Richie was clearly spitting fire. "The immortal cop—Duke—told me to get my ass home, it was their job now, like I was just out for a joyride." He waved a frustrated hand into the air. "Mac, we have to go after him now."

Duncan grabbed the door handle then paused. "Get in the car," he said, as he dashed back to the shop.

Fitz was just walking out the door when Duncan grabbed him. "Fitz, I've got to take off now. Stay with Tessa—keep her safe."

Looking more than a little bewildered, Fitz nodded. "Of course," he said as he watched Duncan race back to his car and jump in. "Can I at least ask where you're going?" his words were lost in the dust from MacLeod's wheels. Fitz shrugged and headed back into the shop. *Must have gotten that appointment today, or a really hot deal on something,* he pondered and he walked back through the shop to a private corner where Tessa was working.

Richie filled Mac in on the details as he drove at a far more sensible pace than Richie wanted too. When they arrived at the park, Duncan refused to follow the obvious trail of destruction through it. People were gathering and a maintenance truck had arrived. Duncan thought a moment then continued around the park.

"Unless the Officers caught him, he had to have come out somewhere. We'll keep looking." Despite Richie's impatience, he drove on. They had driven around a fair percentage of the large wooded park when they came upon a construction zone. Far to the right of their position sat a car up against a construction pylon. Cautiously, Duncan and Richie drove in as far as they could before a barricade halted them. The damage to that car was obvious even at a distance. "He's not going to be anywhere near here," Duncan said to no one in particular then sat back against the seat deep in thought.

"So that's it then? He's out there and we still don't know anything about this guy?" Richie exclaimed a note of desperation in his voice.

"No," he said firmly, shifting swiftly. The Thunderbird went rapidly into reverse then spun around. "There might be someone who can help us," Duncan finished in a dead-serious tone. *Joe Dawson, a mortal Watcher—an organization of historian-agents, he claimed went back over 4,000 years. I trusted him once and he said he trusted me. Let's put that trust to the test.* He drove toward a newer section of Seacouver, to a newer building that was being renovated. A sign had recently appeared outside, *'Joe's'*.

Seated in her private retreat—an out of the way corner of the shop, Tessa was working with her sketch pad. She paused as Fitz casually ambled by to note his passage then returned to her work and private thoughts. The Time Capsule was on her mind. *There are many things to prepare and decisions to be made,* she thought. *How should I space this out?* The idea of the Time Capsule was developing into a full-scale mental project. *No, not a big one, but three small ones. The first, to be opened thirty-years after my death, the second one thirty-years later. Oh and a special one to be opened 'whenever you need it', the note on top would say. There are so many things I want to include.* Tessa mentally juggled a few room dimensions. *Three medium-size vintage trunks, now that might look good in any house if he wanted to use them as decoration. And, oh—two different sets of locks for each, so he will think twice before opening them too soon.* She chuckled to herself. *I think I will embroider a soft cream silk with the words 'Duncan, no cheating!' to cover the presents inside.* She paused and propped back on her sketch pad. *If he is going to keep them with him as he moves, they must remain a decent size or he will simply leave them in a safe storage depot somewhere as he does with all his ancient treasures. If he does that, he may simply forget them over time until one day when he is in a melancholy mood to look back he will remember the Time Capsules I created.* A slight frown creased her brow as reality began creeping into her logical mind. She placed the end of her artist pencil between her teeth and bit down. *I'm the most important thing in his life right now, but after I'm gone he'll simply 'move on' over time I would. That's what he has done with all the other mortal women he knew. So why should I be any different to him then? Am I so arrogant that I actually believe he would set his immortal watch for thirty and sixty years after my death to open a couple of old chests? Especially if another mortal or Immortal had long since found their way into his life? No, if I want this to really be meaningful to him, I am going to have to keep this project simple and have him open them soon. That way the wonderful memory of me will remain fresh on his mind for another couple of decades.* There was something sweet in that thought and she resolved to give the Time Capsule project a little further thought before finalizing anything major. One thing she was resolved to complete immediately was the drawing she was sketching a portrait of Duncan and Connor—both dressed in kilts with their swords drawn. The scant marks were forming Connor MacLeod, seated in an armchair. Duncan's features were already more distinct, as he stood by his cousin's side, his arm resting on the armchair. Their expressions would be benevolent—calm—a bond between these two gentle warrior clansmen. *This will be a loving tribute to two fine MacLeods. It will surely bring a smile to his face.*

Tessa had been working diligently on her drawing for over an hour when she heard the shop bell ring. "I'll get it Fitz," she said and laying her sketch pad on the chair. She peered around her work alcove to see—nothing? *Huh? Where is that person?* She absently thought as she rounded the column and hurried toward the front. Then she stopped and stared—*what is this?*

A white scarf dangled from a hand, protruding through the partially open door, near the top. Much further down, Tessa could see the top of a head and a pair of eyes peeking around the door frame.

"Come in Amanda," Fitz said from somewhere behind Tessa, as he entered the shop from the living quarters. "We can see your white flag of truce."

The scarf disappeared. In the next instant, Amanda stepped rather shyly from behind the door.

"You are always imaginative."

"Nothing imaginative here," she shot back, keeping an eye on Tessa. "Tessa, I came to talk with you, if it's OK?"

"Amanda," Fitz began, giving her a very all-knowing expressive stare. But Tessa cut him off.

"No, Fitz. Amanda and I need to talk. It's something that has been long overdue," she said turning to him. "Why don't you take a walk for a while?"

"Maybe down to the coffee shop," Amanda added smiling school-girlishly.

"But not for twenty-five years," Tessa finished sardonically.

"Are you sure about this?" Fitz asked quietly.

"Yeah, I'm sure, Fitz. I'm a big girl and no matter what Duncan told you to do here, Amanda and I need a little quality 'girl's time' together."

Fitz raised his eyebrows and shrugged, but said nothing as he walked past Amanda and out of the shop.

Amanda spoke calmly as she slowly worked her way toward Tessa, keeping a display case between them. Tessa did the same – at a right angle to Amanda's movement—their maneuver mirroring two warriors sizing each other up.

"How are you feeling now, Tessa? You look much better now."

"Thank you. I feel great, just great," Tessa said, placing her hands on the display case in front of her in a maneuver which suggested she was about to pounce. There was a lengthy silence. The next words were spoken simultaneously by both, breaking the silent tension that was building. Silence followed again. Amanda motioned for Tessa to go first. She composed her thoughts.

"Amanda, what happened the last time—I'm sorry. I'm not a child and I don't have to yell or throw things to make my point heard."

Amanda hung her head slightly and looked away. "I understand you were almost killed. That's a shock to anyone."

"To anyone *mortal* don't you mean? Yes, Amanda, I was almost killed by some guy I never even met before, some guy who came out of nowhere. Do you know what that feels like?" She walked purposefully to the end of the display cabinet. "Or, has that happened so many times to you now that you couldn't even possibly imagine how cheated I felt at the thought of dying."

Amanda mentally flipped a coin. *Is this woman expecting me to respond? Or, what kind of word game is she playing with me?* In the end she opted for honesty. "I've died dozens of times since the late 800s in Europe—most, but not all, as a result of my own misadventures, shall we say. We all feel it when it's happening, but we also know if it's by the hand of a mortal it's likely temporary. So you're right, maybe I don't have a real appreciation for what you just went through, but there is one thing I can relate to," and she moved closer, her steps careful and calculated. "That's having someone come out of nowhere—someone you've never seen before—someone who wants to take your head. Then your life is over. No matter how long or short it has been. We can't cheat death either. Yeah, I can relate to that."

"Well, my life—my already short life—was almost ended. And can you even begin to understand what was going through my mind at that moment. Not the fear of actually dying and not even a fear of what I *may* face afterwards, but a terrible feeling of having an existence, which is everything I had ever hoped for, stolen from me – through no fault of my own." She took a deliberate step toward her.

"And can you guess the next thing that went through my mind as I lay there with Richie, bloody and already dead in my lap? Let me tell you – it wasn't my life flashing before my eyes like you see portrayed in these sickeningly drippy romance movies—it was how soon you would find a way into my Duncan's arms and our bedroom."

Amanda raised both eyebrows but remained silent for a long moment. Then, casually glancing down the display case, she ran her finger around the rim of the glass.

"Duncan obviously loves you a lot. He would have been devastated by your death. Would you have begrudged him whatever comfort I could have offered if he had let me into his life?" Carefully she glanced back at Tessa. "You're mortal. Neither Duncan nor anyone else can change that, no matter how much he may want to. The real reason you dislike me is because I'm an Immortal. Is that what this is really about, envy?" Amanda met Tessa eye to eye.

Tessa caught her breath then nibbled her lip. *Amanda's not stupid— am I?* She considered her next words very carefully.

"I would be lying if I said I wasn't—envious of your immortality that is. I'm marrying a man who has no expiration date stamped on his forehead and these destructive feelings of envy are something I am determined to overcome. I know I must accept that his immortal friends will become a part of our lives because he needs them—we need them. He's already said it, we're in the time of the Gathering and he has no idea what lies ahead for him, or us. Neither do I. I know I must accept my inevitable death and you – or another like you – inevitably in his bed instead of me. Yes, I am learning to accept that I have to make our time together burn as fast and as hot as the sun because my mortal fire—my soul's passion for him—is as fleeting as a candle in the wind. It will burn out quickly."

Tessa's eyes shifted from Amanda to the sword holder by her elbow on the countertop. Carefully, her fingers traced the wood up to the handle of the slim, sixteenth-century Rapier perched in its grooves. "But you know what really bothers me about you, way more than any immortality issues I'm having to overcome right now, it's that you're a *poacher,* someone who just doesn't have the social, or ethical decency to keep their hands off of someone who is in a relationship or betrothed, simply because you truly don't respect what goes on between people in a mortal world." Her hand caressed the spirals of the sword's guard, her fingers touching then sliding down its smooth grip. "Grace has that decency. She has tried to be helpful to me, to us—but you?" Her hand slid smoothly into the grip, as if it had been made for her. "What happened in Duncan's life between you two before I came along is his business." Gripping the ancient weapon she raised it smoothly from the stand. "But I'll be dead and damned if I let another woman try to take what is rightfully mine, here and now." Eyes ablaze with inner fire, she smoothly lowered the blade to attack position and faced Amanda.

Chapter Twenty-six

Joe let his forehead rest against the thumb and forefinger of his left hand. Rubbing the bridge of his nose relieved the ache that had formed across his brow from what he'd just read. He shook his head once then looked to his two Watchers who, in his mind's eye, had seemingly morphed into kindergarteners.

To his left, two stacks of paper lay on his desk—the first, official police citations for every trivial and inane violation imaginable, several of which Joe never knew were still in existence in the State of Washington—the other, an unofficial stack of whining 'complaints', written on every conceivable scrap of paper, including a fresh stick of chewing gum. Joe picked up the gum once again and read, "Watcher Kilgore sucks, see back." He turned it over in his hand. The moisture was causing the fine ink print to disperse into the gum.

"I'll have to submit this report to our cryptology department to read. They're used to dealing with things that look as old as Methos' writing," he finished sarcastically, laying the stick of gum aside. "I swear I'm going to have this kept," he pointed in an exaggerated fashion to the gum. "It belongs in the Watcher's Chronicles. OK, let's have it—from the top—both of you."

Kevin and Joyce, seated in front of their very annoyed supervisor, looked sheepishly to one another. Like a pair of guilty children caught in the act, they stared silently and wide-eyed back at Joe.

"Well, I'm waiting?" Joe fingered the stacks of papers. "You both had plenty to say to each other in the field. I want to hear it all right now. Joyce, let's start with your issues."

"Sir, Kevin is so completely interfering with my duties as Amanda's Watcher."

"Uh-huh," Joe replied idly and picked up a few sheets of her complaints then nodded. "I see," he began facetiously. "And these are all your 'official and professional' reports. *'He's in my face all the time, I can't see Amanda'*—*'He started it! He's always distracting me and obstructing my view when I am trying to watch'* – *'He's never where he should be'*—*'Kevin is excessive'*—and I like this one too, *'Throwing his weight around.'* I don't think that is physically possible when you are standing, Joyce. And what is this? *'He planted his ass on my—'*

Joe closed his eyes and shook his head. "I don't even want to go there with this last one." He let the papers slide back onto the desk. "What is it with the two of you anyway? You, Joyce – wasn't the sidewalk big enough that you couldn't move over to see Amanda?

"It isn't that, Sir. It's—well—he's just there**,**" and she pantomimed her motions as if scooping up a pile of wet, disgusting muck and plopping it on the floor. "I mean right there! And he sticks to me like a pile of crap. He's so totally out of place in the field with a professional, such as me. It's laughable. When he's watching, he just gawks obtrusively. You can see him for miles around—he might as well have his tattoo emblazoned across his a—"

"Alright, Joyce, that's enough of that. Now, what do you think you really have on him? Has he interfered with or disrupted either of these Immortal's activities? Has he blatantly identified himself as a Watcher by handing out some *Watcher-leaflet* to everybody he met on the sidewalk, where you were trying to watch Amanda—well?"

Joyce sat back in her seat, sullen. Finally she spoke up slowly, her voice almost a growl. "He's like a fifth wheel on a unicycle—totally unnecessary and useless. I don't need or want him near me. He's interfering with my work."

"How, Joyce? Your entire complaint keeps leaving that part out," Joe scrutinized her closely. "For a Watcher, that makes you not very perceptive and articulate."

"In case you hadn't noticed, Joyce," Kevin began, his voice heated and rising in volume. "You started it all! My Immortal has been spending time with your Immortal. Where my Immortal goes, I go— that's the job description and tough if you don't like it! As far as I'm concerned you can take your bitching and shove it up–"

"**Enough!**" roared Joe, silencing the pair again. "In case you don't remember, Joyce, let me refresh you on Watcher's protocol. There is one Watcher to one Immortal when we have the manpower. So to illustrate," and he held up the fingers of both his hands in a ridiculous, childish fashion. "This means if there are ten Immortals *stuffed* into a phone booth, there are going to be ten Watchers, watching them. I don't care if they have to do it all bunched together on a space as large as a postage stamp—get it!" he finished sarcastically. "His Immortal, Richie Ryan, happens to have been spending time with Amanda. So, this means he is going to be there, right alongside you, doing what he is sworn to do in this organization—watch. And both Amanda and Richie are spending time with MacLeod, my Immortal. And don't you dare presume to tell me not to be out in the field watching him. I really don't care if you feel Kevin is unnecessary—or that you can handle it on your own, it's not your call – it's mine. I'm the area supervisor—get over it."

"And you—Kevin," he fingered through the stack of citations. "I'm not going to presume to tell a licensed police officer how to perform his official duty—when it actually exists. But don't you think some of these citations are simply asinine? Come on—I didn't even know a couple of these outdated laws were still on the books in the State."

"They are and I saw her doing every one of them," Kevin said in a defensive tone, reminiscent of a schoolboy trying unsuccessfully to bark-back at his teacher.

"No doubt you've spent a fair bit of time watching Joyce instead of Richie. So what the hell was this one for—Joyce was cited for, '*Loitering without a good reason*'? Isn't watching your Immortal a good enough reason to loiter? And this one, '*Exposing the public to a contagious disease*'?"

"It's a misdemeanor—still on our books—enacted in 1909."

"What? Did she deliberately sneeze on you? What did you figure Joyce had—the plague? It's curable now. And what's this one—'*Attempting destruction of a beer bottle?*' Who was drinking on duty out there?"

"She grabbed an *empty* lying in the street," Kevin quickly corrected Joe. "Law was enacted in 1897 – and its destruction was attempted on me, by the way!" Kevin piped up, an octave higher than normal, as he pantomimed Joyce's swing at him with an imaginary bottle. "Which prompted my–"

"Let me guess, that was followed immediately by this one – '*Assaulting a police officer*' and then, '*Resisting arrest*'."

"You can better believe it." he continued with gusto. "I tackled her—then as she said, I planted my ass squarely on her—"

"I got it the first time, Kevin. Just out of curiosity—while you were both wholly engaged in watching each other, did either of you happen to notice what your Immortals were doing? Or, perhaps the crowd of onlookers to your ridiculous public spectacle was so large that they blocked your view."

He looked back to the gum on his desk. "When did this happen, Joyce?"

"When I was in jail, Sir. He refused to give me any paper for an official complaint."

"You had your phone call – paper isn't mandatory," Kevin retorted with a haughty, official expression.

"Oh shut up—both of you," Joe barked. "I should pull both of you out of the field and give your jobs of chronicling to your Immortals. Maybe I'd get more cooperation that way." He rounded on Kevin again.

"I don't want to see any more of this crap on my desk ever again, Kevin—citations for fossilizing laws from 1897. If there is a real police issue out there, that's your business. But if you can't keep a lid on your citation pad every time Joyce makes a snarky comment, your department supervisor will be having a talk with you about your police protocol."

"And you Joyce—I'm seriously considering reassigning you all together."

"You can't—Amanda's mine," her voice rose in a cross between a panic and a challenge.

"I can reassign you anywhere I wish, Joyce. And just where did you get the idea that Amanda is your permanent assignment?" Joe roared back. "You knew you were only a temporary replacement after Amanda's last Watcher was found dead two weeks ago. I've been out ill and haven't been able to shift personnel around yet. There are plenty of good, emotionally mature, professional applicants for Amanda's post."

"Sir, this is a big part of my issue with Kevin. Amanda likely found out about her last Watcher and no doubt shot her. Kevin is so obvious in the field, he shouldn't even be anywhere near Amanda, as dangerous as she is. He's just a rookie and he's going to get us both killed."

Joe shook his head vehemently. "Amanda didn't kill her last Watcher, Joyce. With some rare exceptions during the early part of the first millennium and again around the time of the French Revolution, there is virtually no record of her killing mortals throughout her entire history. Haven't you studied her chronicle any better than that? And, except for a brief period in 1926 when she ran off with Cory Raines during their *Bonny and Clyde* escapades, she never carries a gun. The only people who *died* during that escapade were the two of them—repeatedly I might add. No, we don't know what happened to her Watcher," Joe paused. *Sandy and I have gone over several scenarios, none of which I'm willing to share with these two,* he thought silently.

"Joyce, Amanda isn't a danger to any Watcher and neither is Richie. Even if they both realized what you were and were doing, they wouldn't harm you. So if that's your concern and argument in all of this, you can drop it, understood?" Silence was all he got for a reply.

She glared back at Joe for a long moment. "Immortals are unpredictable and inhuman, Joe. Don't ever kid yourself, not even for one moment," she began quietly, her voice as harsh and cold as jagged ice. "Turn your back on any of them and you're dead. I don't plan to be one of their victims, even if you don't believe they're inherently evil," she finished in a whisper.

"Richie saved Tessa's life and MacLeod is devoted to her," Kevin chimed in. "He's going to marry her soon. They both watch out for her. That hardly sounds like a couple of savage, inhuman monsters to me."

Joyce looked to the wall for a long moment. "We mortals are just disposable play-toys for their immortal amusement. Duncan will be in Amanda's bed the second night after his wedding experience is over. So much for his normal human love and devotion. You just wait and see what that Immortal does when he tires of Tessa," she finished with a smirk.

"I don't think so," Kevin replied defensively. "Not the way he and Richie spoke about Tessa when I was in their shop."

"You want to make a bet on that naive faith of yours?" Joyce spat back, her eyes ablaze with challenge.

"Look—both of you—it's not our concern what MacLeod chooses to do. We observe and record. That's all, got it?" Joe followed his finger as it traced an idle pattern on his desk for a long moment then he looked back to his Watchers.

"For the record Joyce, I doubt seriously if MacLeod is going to treat Tessa like that. That wouldn't be MacLeod. When he takes an oath, makes a commitment, swears a promise, or whatever, down through the ages he has always carried it out or died at least once trying. That is just MacLeod and I know my Immortal."

A series of stray sounds in the immediate area alerted Joe that they were likely being observed by uninvited eyes. He stiffened momentarily, his arm instinctively brushing the concealed semi-automatic pistol he routinely carried, then he forced himself to relax. *Do not let on that you suspect,* he reminded himself. *If whoever doesn't suspect I know he's here, I have the element of surprise over him,* a well-trained professional mantra he fixed in his mind as he smoothly continued his speech.

"I'll assume our discussion is finished," he resumed in the same tone of voice. "Unless either of you become Immortals yourself – in which case you are to report to me at once," he added farcically. "Otherwise, I don't intend a repeat of today," he finished, dismissing the pair. They left without further comment.

Joe took a long breath, letting the tension and irritation of the last hour of non-stop reprimand ebb. He knew he wasn't alone. Whoever it was was still concealed in the side room and obviously he wasn't in a rush to make himself known. Despite the potentially dangerous situation Joe realized he was in, there was something else in the back of his mind vying for a sliver of his, as yet, uncommitted thoughts. Something Joyce had said in passing wasn't setting right—in fact it sounded very uncomfortably familiar. His present precarious situation kept him from examining it closely.

Chapter Twenty-seven

Joe was considering his options when he heard a light rap against his back door. The sound caused him to relax.

OK, so you don't intend to take me by surprise, he acknowledged. Turning, Joe saw Duncan and Richie entering. *Just the people I want to talk to. Now how do I begin a Watcher's conversation with a couple of Immortals?* He looked to the pair, an expectant expression mirrored in his face. He hoped he was coming off as casual though he knew he wasn't pulling it off very well. Fortunately, Duncan broke the awkward silence first.

"Joe, I need your help. There is something serious that loomed up from nowhere. Something that has made no sense from the beginning – and now Tessa's life may be at stake. I am not sure what this really is and where this is all going, but you're my Watcher and I hope you have seen something—anything—that can give me something to go on." Duncan watched Joe's expression carefully. Alarm, followed by recall flashed across Joe's face. This told Duncan he had come to the right place.

Joe glanced away trying to conceal what he knew his face was saying. "Could you be more specific?" he began his tone as casual as he could muster.

"Damn it, Joe, you're my Watcher. You must know who he was."

"Who was?"

Duncan shook his head. Irritated and impatient he took a very deliberate and forceful step toward him then halted, trying to recompose himself. "Come on Joe – please no Watcher-games with me now. You asked me to trust you once. I know you're out there watching every move I make and Tessa's too."

Joe gave Duncan a calculating glance. "We only watch mortal companions until we are certain they won't pose a danger to the Immortal they are with. Tessa isn't going to betray your secret. I realized that years ago, so I rarely keep tabs on her anymore. What does Tessa have to do with anything now?"

Duncan returned an odd stare. *What are you saying, Joe? I thought you were supposed to be the 'Big Brother' of our immortal world?* "Do you or do you not know what I've been doing for the past two weeks?"

Joe took a deep breath, glanced briefly to the floor—to nowhere—before meeting Duncan's eyes. He shook his head. "As a matter a fact, I don't. I have been out with the flu. It has hit this area very hard and out of season at that. For the past three weeks, we have been losing Watchers from the field daily. Except for the last five-days, I wouldn't know if you had been on the moon and back. There was almost nobody in the field ten days ago—including me." His expression softened. *Mac, do I dare ask you outright?* He took a leap of faith. "I would appreciate it if you would fill me in on what I don't know about your activities."

Duncan threw up his hands in an exaggerated, exasperated expression—his eyes everywhere but on Joe. "You're asking me to do your job now too?" he exclaimed louder than he had intended.

"Both of you—just stop playing games with each other. It's Tessa's life, Mac! Just tell him what happened," Richie cut in, halting Duncan's over-the-top response to Joe's statement. In the next instant, both their attentions were wholly on Richie.

"Look, it's usually me flying off the handle, but we don't have time for Mac to do that," and he motioned in the general direction of '*out there somewhere*'. "The guy who shot Tessa me and is still here—he almost ran me off the road—even those cops couldn't catch him."

Duncan passed his hands over his hair and took a deep breath. *OK, Duncan, old boy, get a grip. It's going to take a little diplomacy with this Watcher, you can do this, Tess is depending upon you.*

"Look, Joe, I'll tell you what happened over the past two weeks and if you know anything about this, I am asking you – for Tessa's sake – please fill in the blanks." He relaxed the tension in his jaw and readied himself. "About two weeks ago, Tessa was kidnapped."

"What? By whom?" Joe asked.

"That's what we don't know," Richie piped up. "He just walked into the shop, as casual as you please, stunned me without so much as a hello and grabbed Tessa."

"It was three to four days later before he began sending clues as to where I might find her. He wanted to make it a game of hide-and-seek with Tessa as the bait," Duncan said.

"Bait for what? Where was she being held?"

"You'll never believe how, but I finally found out through the most unconventional way that she was being held at a Tudor house. The man holding her was some kind of psycho. Tessa said he held her in a room, chained to a radiator while he constantly paraded around with a sword repeating something about, '*He'll come…Just wait and see…They always do*'."

"*They* always do? He wanted you specifically—an Immortal then?"

"Yeah, that's the part I don't understand. He was expecting an Immortal—me. He wanted me to find my way to him, by his game, with his rules. When I arrived, he was wearing infrared night-vision glasses. He switched the house lights out so I couldn't see him and tried to behead me. Needless to say I'm still here, but it was close, Joe. I never had a chance to find out anything about him. After I killed him, I found Tessa and sent her and Richie out to the car. I was going to check his computer when I heard the shots. I don't even recall shutting the door as I ran to find Tessa bleeding and Richie dead." Duncan fell silent and waited, his eyes probing Joe's face for any indication that a response would be forthcoming.

Joe nibbled his lip then closed his eyes momentarily. The expression on his face was such a mixture of conflicting emotions that Duncan could not sort them out. Joe nodded once then moved over to his desk and sat down. He flipped on the computer and pulled up the Watchers' database.

"The man you killed was Pallin Wolf. He was one of James Horton's Watchers," Joe swiveled the screen so Duncan could see Wolf's Watcher database photo. "We recovered his body, so it was never officially reported to the Seacouver police."

Duncan bolted from the door face he was leaning against. "Horton!" he exclaimed as his eyes riveted to the face of the now dead kidnapper. Duncan's blood boiled at the mention of Horton's name once again. How could a dead man seemingly reach from the grave and still influence followers – followers who spelled death for those with no normal expiration date to their lives? "I thought you Watchers took care of what remained of that madman's following."

"We never found them all. When the Watcher's Council learned James and his warped group had broken one of our cardinal rules—to never kill an Immortal—the Tribunal placed them all under a death sentence. They simply went underground and it has been hell trying to find the last of those renegades who were involved. We didn't piece together the Pallin connection until James disappeared then suddenly his Watcher couldn't be found either. The Watcher's Tribunal was sending security to bring Pallin in to be executed. You did the service for them."

"Do you know who shot Tessa?"

"Name is Mark Roszca."

"A Watcher too?"

"No. We don't know what his connection to Wolf really was." Joe typed in a web address and pulled up another image.

"That's the guy who shot us," Richie said as the image of Mark materialized on the screen. "What is he, then?"

"Someone with paramilitary training according to what we were able to find out. His connection in all of this appears to be to finish off the mortal companions for Pallin after the Immortal is dead. I know he killed at least one other woman—companion to the deceased Immortal James Fly. Amanda's Watcher was also killed, but we aren't sure yet if Mark was involved."

"Amanda didn't kill any Watcher," Richie affirmed. "Neither of us would do that, Joe."

"I know, Richie. Neither of you are ever likely to start using Watchers as target practice."

"Didn't sound as if one of your Watchers agrees with your faith in us," Duncan remarked his tone stern.

Joe gave a noncommittal shrug and looked away. Duncan's comment pricked his sub consciousness, but he did not want to open a Watcher dissension discussion with an Immortal.

"Mark is a professional, Duncan. Word on the street is he doesn't miss. If he knows she's alive, he'll likely hunt her down. The Seacouver police put out an APB for him the night she was shot. So far, Richie, Officers Sandy and Duke are the only people who have seen him and he's managed to elude everyone. Until he can be found, I would get Tessa out of town fast."

"You don't have to tell me twice," Duncan said turning for the door. He paused and turned back to Joe. "For the record, Joe, your woman Watcher is wrong. Once we're married, Tessa's bed is the only one I'll be in as long as she is alive. You can put that quote in my chronicle with absolute certainty."

A slight grin creased the corner of Joe's mouth and he gave a short nod, but otherwise remained silent.

Duncan and Richie were in the car moments later. Duncan turned the key and the engine roared to life.

"Where to, Mac?"

"Paris—this afternoon." He tossed Richie the cell phone. "The three major airlines are programmed in. See which one has four seats open today."

"Four seats?"

"Fitz could become a target too. Horton almost killed him the last time we all met. I am not taking a chance – we're traveling together." He glanced briefly to Richie. "You now know Officer Kilgore is your Watcher here in Seacouver. He's young and you're likely going to be seeing him every place. Just try and ignore him. A Watcher takes an oath of silence and secrecy. Letting an Immortal know they are a Watcher apparently has serious consequences in this organization."

"So what about Joe? What sets him apart?"

Duncan shook his head once. "I don't know. It was a bizarre situation we found ourselves in that day, in the alley – it just came out. I respect that man's ethics and oath. I haven't shared it with anyone I don't trust completely, down deep."

Richie gave Duncan a sideways glance. "Does that mean you also told Amanda?"

There was a long pause. "Yes," he finally said quietly.

Richie leaned back in his seat and thought about what he wanted to say, wondering if he was out of line to say it. "Mac, how is Amanda going to fit in with everything that's going to be happening with you and Tessa?"

"Amanda is an Immortal," Duncan began quietly. "Some things between the two of us are never going to change—in Tessa's life or any other," he finished resolutely, fervently hoping that Richie was at least wise enough to know when to shut his mouth.

Fitz worked his way through the living quarters of the house-store until he saw Tessa. He stopped and glanced around the shop. He needn't have, his immortal senses told him there was no other Immortal present. He peered around Tessa's work stall for good measure.

"I say, you seemed to have wrapped up your girl-talk session fast. Where's Amanda?"

Tessa—sword in a hand—was polishing the slender Rapier. She looked up to Fitz with a satisfied smile on her lips.

"Gone," she said with a note of finality in her voice.

Fitz considered both her statement and the tone it was delivered in as he watched her continue to polish that blade with a vengeance.

"Ah, Tessa—the way you're holding that, I would be careful, it is very—"

"Sharp," she said, finishing his comment. Setting the cloth aside, Tessa held the weapon up to eye level to admire. "This one is going to be mine, Fitz."

Chapter Twenty-eight

The Thunderbird skidded to a halt sending everything in the path of its tires flying.

"How are you coming with that flight?" Duncan demanded as he switched off the key and threw the car door open. Reaching around to the back seat, he grabbed his sheathed katana.

"Working on it yet," Richie replied. He shook his head and waving his hand to nowhere, returned his frustrated attention to the cell phone.

Unable to nail down a four seat flight to Paris on his first call only served to push Duncan's anxiety level up a notch and his foot down harder on the accelerator. Richie was trying with all the tact and finesse he could muster, to explain, without really explaining, why they absolutely had to be on the next flight to Paris this afternoon. *I'm serious here,* he thought. *There's plenty of room in the baggage compartment for three Immortals. So what if we die in the thin air, it's only temporary. We'll just come back to life when we land – honestly. Now how do I tell this to the ticket agent?* He cleared his throat and took a stab at a very lame explanation. A moment later he held the receiver away from his ear and grimaced. *OK, OK—even I wouldn't have bought that one,* he told himself as the ticket agent reminded him, rather brusquely, of the airline's rules against letting people travel as baggage. Finally, in the middle of the woman's sentence, he hit the call cancel button with a vengeance.

There should be an exception for us Immortals somewhere in the airline rules, he thought as he punched up the next airline.

"Fitz," Duncan called seeing his friend knocking his pipe out against the corner of the building. "Come on, you're with us just as soon as I get Tessa, we're all getting out of here right now."

Fitz raised both eyebrows at the alarmed tone the usually *un-ruffleable* Duncan MacLeod just handed him. "What's going on? What's happening? Why the sudden rush?"

He was at Fitz's side in an instant, his face a mixture of alarm and cold fear. "Paris—all of us just as soon as Richie can get a four-seat booking." He turned past Fitz and was about to bolt toward the door when Fitz grabbed him.

"Slow down, laddie," Fitz began, catching Duncan in mid-stride, halting him. "What's got you all in a panic?"

The kidnapper and Tessa's shooter—it's Horton's men all over again, Fitz. There were two of them working together this time. I killed Pallin Wolf—Horton's protégé—when he attacked me in that house. But there was a back-up who survived—Mark Roszca. He was there to kill anyone who got away from Wolf. He knows Tess survived and he's coming for her. He's trying to finish what he started—some code of honor about him never missing. I'm not going to play their game and endanger Tessa in any way. This is for Joe and his Watchers to deal with. We're clearing out right now."

"Good Lord, Duncan, I thought that was all over when you killed that maniac in the warehouse. Are the Watchers actually letting those crazy people go on killing Immortals?"

"No, Joe told me that's not what's happening. I think he's on the level. The Watchers are at a stalemate trying to find the last of Horton's people. These assassins are all under a death sentence by their Watcher's council—now they've gone underground. Joe and his people aren't able to find the last cells. The kid who shot Tessa is a paramilitary guerrilla working with the man who kidnapped her. You're coming with us Fitz. There is a real threat to you too with him out there. If he worked for Horton, I'm virtually certain he knows you're an Immortal."

"Mac," Richie called as he pushed his car door open. "I can't beg, borrow, or steal a flight to Paris today. Sorry, there's just nothing open. If we're going to Paris, we're going to have to flap our arms and fly like the rest of the birds," Richie said as he trotted up to Fitz. "So what do we do now? Just get back into the car and leave? To where?"

Duncan plowed his fist into his palm and looked about. *Options, options,* he thought frantically. *What can I do—what must I do to keep everyone safe? I don't have a clue which direction the attack will come from—he's not an Immortal—I can't sense him—I can't prepare.*

"Paris doesn't matter Richie," he finally said. "We'll go to my retreat house."

"Isn't that on Holy Ground," Richie asked hesitantly. "Immortals aren't permitted to kill there – be it against a mortal or an Immortal – those are the rules as I understand them?" He finished, turning first to Duncan, then to Fitz for confirmation.

Duncan nodded. "I don't have to kill him to put him out of commission, Richie. It's a defensible house. The only way in or out is across a lake."

Fitz gave him a quizzical look. "You mean you've built a castle with a moat around it?"

"Sort of. Actually nature built the moat. I just built the castle on Holy Ground – with the permission of the ancient Native Elders –

long ago."

"Well then, Duncan, as I haven't seen a home with a decent moat in centuries, I can't wait to see yours. I'll go pack."

Now it was Duncan's turn to halt Fitz. "Oh, no you don't. I don't want anyone leaving my sight. We're staying together. We're safer that way."

"Duncan," Fitz began again, as he carefully peeled his friend's hand from his sleeve. "You're going to have a full car with Tessa, Richie and all your bags. I am just parked in the lot around the corner, down there, that way," and he gestured a ways down the street. "I will just be off and get my vehicle – pack a few things from my flat – and be back fast."

Duncan was already shaking his head vehemently. "No, I don't want you to go home and get anything. I have no idea who might be waiting for you there. Stay here, I'll pack an extra change of clothes for you, a little big maybe, but—"

Fitz raised a finger, calling for silence. "OK, dear boy. If you feel it's too risky for me to go home I will get my car and pop-round the corner for some petrol. Wouldn't do any good to run out of fuel in a high-speed escape now would it? Besides, what can happen to anyone in the next twenty-minutes? I'll be fine, Duncan. We'll be off in no time." Ignoring any further protests from his friend, Fitz turned and started down the alley at a brisk pace.

Duncan shook his head as he and Richie started once again for the door.

Several paces up the road Fitz stopped and turned back. "Oh, Duncan, I meant to tell you," he called, gesturing for him to stop. "Something's a-foot with Tessa. Amanda came round to talk to her this afternoon and—well—when I returned, Tessa was polishing that Rapier and Amanda wasn't any—"

"What was who?" Duncan said as he grabbed the door, half his attention in Fitz's direction and the other on Tessa in the house. "Amanda, was polishing what? Fitz, Amanda can take care of herself. She's a survivor. It's Tessa I'm worried about. Come on Richie you've got less than fifteen-minutes to pack." His voice trailed off as they hurried inside.

Fitz took a deliberate step toward the retreating pair. He stopped and then shrugged. *I wouldn't give you odds on that survivorship, laddie,* he thought pensively. *I don't know what happened between Tessa and Amanda, but Tessa is still here.*

"Tessa, sweetheart, come on, we're leaving right now," Duncan called excitedly as he hurried through the door.

"Duncan, what's happening, what's wrong?" Tessa said. Hearing the urgency in his usually calm voice, she hurried to his side with the small metal sculpture she had been preparing to set up in the shop.

Duncan laid his katana on the ledge by Tessa's alcove. Catching her arm as she approached, he took the sculpture from her and set it on the ledge, then wrapped her hands in his, protectively.

"Sweetheart, I want you to pack a change of clothes and anything else that you can get quickly into your overnight bag. I've got to get you out of here now."

"Duncan slow down. Tell me why—none of this is making any sense. Why are you panicked?"

"The man who kidnapped you was Pallin Wolf – one of Horton's henchmen."

"Oh my God – Duncan. I thought all that was over when Horton died. You mean there are still Watchers loose out there who are killing Immortals? What about—"

"The kid who shot you? No, he wasn't a Watcher – some paramilitary mercenary Horton's man hired. Name's Mark Roszca and he was supposed to kill anyone leaving that house. I talked with Joe this afternoon. The man is on the level – they are trying to find the last of Horton's people to stop this killing. I have to get you out of here now."

"But I'm not an Immortal. What would any of Horton's people want with me?"

"Mark Roszca knows you are alive and he's coming for you, Tessa. He's trying to finish what he started."

Tessa froze as the future, from her precognitive memory, collided head-on with the present reality—her *mortal* reality. Her gaze shifted from Duncan's eyes to her inner thoughts, to the premonition which had etched itself in her mind's eye.

The dark ominous figure in my first premonition. My dreams were warning me—he's coming for me and I can't escape my fate. What will the real-life outcome be? Her eyes returned to Duncan as her gaze solidified.

"I know, Duncan," she began with a prophetic calm voice. "I have always known this would happen. I have seen it in my dream—my premonitions—whatever you want to call them. My hand drew the violence of it on that page. I now know that first faceless figure is really Mark Roszca." She released his hands and, reaching up, threaded her fingers through the hair which had fallen from his clip to his shoulders.

"I think I finally understand what you have felt all these centuries—what it feels like to have another human being trailing you for your head. Mark has been trailing me and I have been warned by some supernatural sense of his presence, just as if I was an Immortal too. He's coming for me, Duncan, and he's not an Immortal. There is no way you can sense his presence. It's my fate that's coming to a head and there's nothing you can do to stop it or interfere."

Duncan threw his arms around the woman he loved as if his force of will alone could halt the impending nightmare which was unfolding. His thoughts flashed back to that moment—the moment he heard the shots. Only this time, his mind's eye saw a different scenario.

His hurried steps slowed as the bodies of Tessa and Richie, lying sprawled on the ground, came into view. Only moments had passed since he had spoken to a vibrant woman that was so alive, only moments had passed since he held her warm hand, reassuring her all would be OK, only moments had passed since he had turned from her face to the computer, trying to find answers about the man he had just killed, and now those moments were gone. He was kneeling by a body, cradling the remains of the woman who would have been his wife. His heart ached to the point of self-destruction, even for an Immortal. His soul cried out in abject agony!

He shook his head slowly as a tear rolled silently down his cheek— "No" he whispered once—opening his eyes and refocusing on the living, breathing Tessa – so full of life – standing before him. "I will not close my eyes—I will not let this moment go—not this time. Richie," he half turned his head, "get packing **now**!" he shouted.

Richie hurried back into the living quarters and up to his room.

He released his embrace and held her shoulders at arm's length from himself. "I don't pretend to understand these premonitions you say you have been having, but Darius said he had them too and he's dead, just the way he said he would die. I'm not going to ignore yours. You don't know where this attack will happen, do you?"

Tessa shook her head. "It was all happening in surreal landscapes. God, Duncan, it could happen anywhere , at any time. I can't tell you any more than I have except that when that dark figure was about to kill me, something that looked like the Mayan deity was in my–"

The shop door sounded.

"Fitz, it will be just a few moments longer," Duncan interrupted. "We're almost packed," Duncan reached his katana from the ledge and turned quickly in the direction of their living quarters.

"Just another five minutes tops—the bags will be in the car." Something in the back of his subconscious mind shouted to his conscious self in mid-step. *Why aren't you sensing another Immortal?* Before he could glance back, he heard Tessa's cry of alarm.

"**Duncan it's him!**" she shouted.

Out of the corner of his eye, he saw a rapid movement by the shop door. *A gun!* His subconsciousness shook him. *Get Tessa out of the way!* There was no time for thought—he moved on conditioned reflex and instinct that was over 400 years in the making. Shoving Tessa through the alcove, he put her out of the direct path of that near-silent bullet—fired only a heart-beat after her breath had left her lips. The shot struck Duncan in the shoulder and he was jolted against the door frame—the second bullet hit him square in the back dropping him instantly. His katana was flipped from his fingers as his body recoiled from the force of that bullet-strike. The weapon slid across the floor to the wall.

Mark dashed toward him, gun in his outstretched hand.

Tessa was spun against the far alcove wall by the force of Duncan's shove. Recovering her balance in an instant, she grabbed the shoebox size, small metal sculpture from the ledge. As Mark's gun hand came rapidly into view besides the opening, she lunged forward and slammed the figure down on his hand. The force of that welded steel on his hand shattered a bone and knocked the gun from his grasp.

Pain caused Mark to lurch back, instinctively grabbing his wounded hand and throwing him suddenly off balance.

Duncan was hit, Tessa's conscious mind shouted. *Likely dead now—he can't come back in time to save anyone—it's my fate and his too that are on the line!*

Tessa was on the offensive and in Mark's face before he could recover his stance. Swinging her fist, she landed two successive blows, one to his chest, the other to the jaw, both connected hard. Tessa, ignoring the pain in her own hands from the impact of flesh-to-bone, grabbed his neck in an inexperienced choke-hold and leaped on him, trying to knock him to the floor. Unsuccessful, her female instincts sent her nails after his eyes.

But Mark was far more experienced in hand-to-hand combat than Tessa and grasping his opposite, uninjured forearm, he drove his elbow into her midsection, near the site his bullet had struck her a little more than a week ago. As Tessa folded from the impact and pain, Mark backhanded the side of her face, opening a fresh cut on her flushed-red cheeks and sending her violently against the opposite wall. She slid to the floor stunned by the force, as Mark, ignoring the blood oozing from the compound fracture in his right hand, reached to his boot and drew his long Bowie knife.

"His head's first—yours is next, bitch!" He snarled and turned his attention to the Highlander. Pouncing on the now lifeless Immortal's body, he grabbed the back of his head—his thick hair—pulling his head up and slid the knife under his throat to slit it.

From the very bottom of her darkest emotions, Tessa felt her most secret and violent inner passions explode to the surface – passions she had, until now, only allowed to trickle from her life-veins into the physical reality of this world through the white-hot molding of liquid metal – birthed as twisted steel images. A bolt of searing agony shot through her living being—casting a feeling of utter desperation and inconsolable dread of an impending eternal loss.

Mark's going to kill him forever – my immortal fiancé will die just like a mortal—just like me—time for him ends now, too! In the next instant, it all gave way inside her to white-hot fury. And then–

What's happening to me? The clock on the wall—movement is slowing—the world is slowing all around me – slowing before my eyes, a part of her mind noted.

"Listen to the ticking clock on the wall," a strange yet familiar voice hissed audibly in her subconscious mind, directing and riveting her attention to the hands in that instant.

"Feel the sound? It beats like a slow, disconnected drum. The hands struggle to move—to mark time, your time."

I'm living between the seconds? her mind asked, astonished. *Have I defeated time?*

"No, time has become your friend," the familiar, urgent voice hissed again.

That voice, where did it come from? Her eyes shifted rapidly to where her inner ear directed her attention—to her side—by her hand that was propping her against the wall.

Duncan's katana was beneath her fingertips. The ivory handle lay on its side, lifeless eyes turned upward.

But her mind's eye saw only the reptilian eyes and living face staring up into hers expectantly, her fingers felt only the smooth caress of the serpent's soft feathers beneath her hand as her fingers tightened around its neck – her inner-ear heard only the voice of the feathered snake commanding her.

"Strike!"

In one swift fluid motion, she was on her feet, both hands on the weapon. The moment she held it she felt power.

"Its power is a part of you now," came the disembodied voice of the feathered serpent once again in her mind.

"Strike!"

Tessa drew back the katana, her muscles as taught as an infinitely coiled spring.

The blade in Mark's hand found Duncan's neck, slicing into his carotid artery, inflicting a fatal wound that would, for any mortal, spell death. Duncan's blood began to run slowly across Mark's blade, pooling beneath his neck and shoulder, as Mark dug in. In the midst of the cut, out of the corner of his eye, he registered a motion and glanced back instinctively.

Tessa swung with all her might.

Steel which had been folded time and time again, producing a blade so strong and honed so sharp, in that instant contacted and severed flesh, muscle, sinew, bone, nerve, and finally splitting free air with the force of her swing. The blade burst forth from the opposite side of Mark's neck, sending his head to one side and a plume of blood spraying from the force of his now numbered heartbeats, up and out.

Tessa gasped once, not fully prepared for the warm, musty metallic scent the red spray carried to her senses as it hit her face, her hand, her shirt, spilling out like a fountain under so much pressure across the floor everywhere. Mark's beheaded body lurched, without intelligent direction, reflexively upward as the knife dropped from his spasming hand.

His disconnected head, which had been flipped to the side by the force of her swing, lay behind and to the side of Duncan's hip—face turned upward and angled over on its right cheek. Mark's living brain glimpsed his spasmodically flailing body, as his mouth contorted into a hideous agonizing scream from which no sound was produced. Looking up, his eyes met Tessa's.

Staring back, she did not flinch at the grotesque death-mask contortions, wrought by severed spinal nerves, permanently etching their final imprint into Mark's face. With a look infinitely colder than the bloodied steel in her hand, she slowly lowered the point of the blade until it was directly between his twitching eyelids.

"Time's up," her voice whispered, in the stillness between the seconds, to the dying brain. "It's on my side now."

The sound of Richie's hurried footsteps went unnoticed as he approached.

Slowly Tessa turned her head, angling her blood-sprayed front toward the approaching young Immortal.

"Mac, I grabbed a few things from everywhere and sort of stuffed them in the case—"

The sight of the body he knew to be his mentor—sprawled halfway across the entrance of the shop—his head nowhere in sight. Tessa bloodied with his katana in her unyielding grip, froze him in mid stride. The overnight case dropped from his grasp as his fingers sprang open—his hands moving slowly in a shocked expressive gesture.

"Oh my God!" he gasped, barely coherent, hands framing his face. "What the hell just happened here?"

The shop door sounded. "Tessa, Duncan, I'm out front. Whose car is that over on the curb?" His line of sight and immortal senses seized on Richie, his outstretched arm and pointing finger, an expression of absolute total disbelief written across his face. Fitz froze.

"Good Lord, Tessa," he gasped and stared down at the partially obscured body of the Highlander he had known for almost 400-years—at a head, which was tilted from his direct line of site—at the bloodied Tessa as she slowly turned toward him, swinging the blade smoothly with her motion.

I can't sense Duncan, his immortal 800-year-old senses screamed back and he swallowed hard.

The female eyes he met were still burning with unquenchable fire – a type of *mortal Quickening* of their own he had rarely ever seen. He quickly backed up a step. His sword was in his car and for the briefest of instances he pondered whether he would have even stood a chance in using it against this unknown Tessa, a Tessa with this much violence mirrored in her eyes.

Who is this woman? his subconscious mind prodded.

Duncan's gasp, as he came back to life, broke the silence which had been absolute—his immortal existence broadcasted in that instant to both Immortals standing there, suspended between the seconds. He coughed, clutched his chest and tried to roll over on to his back. Something heavy was across his legs.

Tessa reached with her free hand and grabbed Mark's belt, effortlessly dragging his lifeless legs off Duncan.

Duncan reached to the side of his neck. There had been a wound there; he felt the receding sting as the last of his skin healed without blemish. His fingers passed over his neck, his cheek—they were wet, dripping wet. Surprise, then shock colored his expression as he brought a completely bloodied hand, forearm and sleeve up to eye level. He was lying in a pool of his own blood. Quickly he brought his left hand around and down on the floor to prop up, his fingers found the Bowie knife. Startled—realization set in as to what must have happened. His eyes quickly passed, first between the knife and his opposing bloodied hand – blood that had drained from a severed artery in his neck—and then to Tessa—the bloodied katana in her grasp and the headless corpse that had lain across him.

"Welcome back," Tessa said, the first sound she had made in what, to her, seemed like an eternity. Relief was flooding her expression.

Carefully avoiding the katana's potential kill-zone, Fitz quickly slipped past her to Duncan and knelt by his side.

"Welcome back indeed," he said quietly glancing to Duncan, but with Tessa in the corner of his vision. "I thought for a moment there we had lost you," Fitz struggled to form a bright smile. *Laddie*, he thought. *I thought this helpless, vulnerable Tessa, you have been so worried about, had beheaded you! What the hell really happened to your survivor, Amanda?*

"It's alright now sweetheart, it's all over now," Duncan's smooth consoling voice began. Instinctively he braced himself up and leaned quickly forward, his hand outstretched to retrieve his katana.

Fitz quickly placed a wise hand on his chest, halting him in mid-motion. His eyes met and held Duncan's confused expression.

"No," he whispered softly. "Don't even think it."

Slowly, Tessa squatted down and placed her free hand gently on her immortal fiancé then smiled and spoke quietly.

"Yes, Duncan, it really is alright now. Mark is dead—we're both alive." She angled the katana's blade to her eye slightly, with a twist of her wrist. "And, I finally do understand. Time is on my side, too."

Chapter Twenty-nine

Richie emptied a tray of ice cubes into the blender and hit the pulse button. A second later, the cubes were reduced to the consistency of a rough snow cone. He quickly poured the slush into a bag, wrapped one of their table napkins around it and returned to Tessa, who was being questioned by the police. He paused at the entrance to the store, waiting respectfully for her to pause from her monolog.

Tessa was seated at a table in the viewing area of their modest antique store. Sergeant Maxim sat across from her conducting the interview – between them lay the bloody katana.

From across the room, Duncan stood near one of the shop counters with Fitz close beside him. Eyeing his weapon and the people surrounding it, Duncan's expression closely resembled someone watching a Popsicle melt whilst desperately in need of a drink. For some reason, which Duncan could not fathom, Fitz, by his actions and expression, had steadfastly insisted that he leave the weapon in Tessa's hands, wherever she wanted to go with it.

Glancing once to the bloody katana on the table between them, Duke flipped another page in his notepad and continued to write. Despite the ordeal, which he knew must have unfolded rapidly, this woman was giving him a remarkable amount of detail in a very calm and collected manner, he noted. *A very strong woman,* he thought, as a tickle of a grin formed on his face. He admired true strength of character—a rare quality in anyone.

Richie cast a nervous and questioning eye around the room—to the faces of the two police officers—to Sandy—as he casually examined Mark's body once again, then pulled the sheet back over his severed remains. He glanced at Duke, as he calmly, but officially took Tessa in hand and began questioning her. Richie glanced to the Watcher, Joe Dawson, standing silently against the wall observing. Mac had telephoned him within the hour of the beheading for assistance in this bloody matter of Horton's henchmen—to his mentor, who for the first time that he could ever remember was giving no indication of intending to comfort or hover protectively near his Tessa – and finally Richie glanced to Hugh Fitzcairn who, to him, seemed to have developed a genuine Immortal's fear of this very mortal woman.

Am I the only one who can see she's still bleeding and in pain, he thought? *What's the matter with everyone? Mac, Fitz—come on guys, this is our Tessa here. She hasn't suddenly morphed into Frankenstein. OK, so we all got a little freaked out for a while when Tess started swinging your sword around here like an evil Immortal* *on steroids, but hey everybody – **Hello** – Mac, it was either that or both you and Tess would have been lying side-by-side in a grave by tomorrow. You could show the poor mortal woman a little appreciation for saving your immortal head—literally!*

Frustrated, he shook his head then barged in, interrupting Duke's questioning. Handing the fresh ice bag to her, he took the original, hastily made makeshift ice-pack, which had become little more than a wet cloth on her badly bruised skin. He paused, not sure he was supposed to stay and not really giving a damn if he would have been told to go. Carefully he pushed back several locks of her blood-stained hair and ever so gently dabbed the blood from her still oozing wound. He tried for a smile as he cleaned her cheek, wiping the spattered blood from her forehead. She glanced briefly to him, a silent *thank you*, as she paused to let Richie minister to her before finishing her statement.

He knew his expression was coming off as pained as she must have been feeling at that moment. *Dammit Mac,* he swore silently. *Why aren't you over here supporting her and doing this?*

Seemingly inert, as he stood silently against the wall, the Watcher was mentally multi-tasking his senses. Tessa's story was very detailed, to say the least. And she wasn't leaving out any of the mortal or immortal details either. Obviously, she knew Duke was an Immortal and Sandy knew of his immortality. He sighed, briefly wondering if she would have given the same account at the station downtown to an unfamiliar officer.

Come on, Joe, he shook himself. *You know Tessa better than that. She refused to open up for the inspector at the hospital interview. I seriously doubt she would have said anything that would raise any suspicion regarding Immortals.* He glanced toward Sandy, who had moved next to his partner.

Joe had arrived as fast as he could legally drive after MacLeod telephoned. He had seen Tessa and the scene at the shop at its worst. He had called Sandy and explained what had transpired and what was needed. The squad car had arrived shortly thereafter without the usual sirens blaring.

From the moment Duke had entered the shop, Joe had felt the Immortal's eyes all over him. He strongly suspected Sandy had broken his Watcher's Oath of secrecy and told his partner about his affiliation with this ancient and secret organization. Joe heaved a short sigh. Calling Sandy on the carpet for this major breach of Watcher's protocol would be like the pot calling the kettle black. Besides, he totally understood, silently asserting he would have likely done the same in his shoes.

After Duke had finished his brief, silent scrutiny of the Watcher, he had simply gone about addressing the issues before him, pretending that Joe didn't exist. Sandy noted his partner's actions and followed suit.

Shifting his thoughts to his Immortal, Joe considered what he was seeing. *As far as I can recall, this is the first time the chivalrous Duncan MacLeod has not acted protectively where Tessa is concerned. Hugh Fitzcairn may be somewhat responsible for Duncan's behavior right now though it seems rather out of character as well for this historically happy-go-lucky ladies' man playboy. He's been eyeing Tessa ever since I arrived as if he, for some reason, had to worry about his head with her.*

Joe blinked and raised an eyebrow at what he was gleaning from the two Immortals' body language. *I can pretty much tell generations to come what Duncan had for breakfast a couple of days ago when Fitz slid through their bedroom window, but what happened in this shop in the past hour to cause this, I haven't a clue.* He seriously considered bugging the place as this was something that had blindsided him completely. He ran a few numbers in his head. *It has been years since I've made any entries on Tessa in her companion-chronicle. If she is going to start swinging a sword, perhaps it is time I reopened her file.* He paused from his mental monolog as a new angle suddenly formed in his mind. *Is Tessa a pre-Immortal? Is MacLeod starting to train her? Is this why she killed Mark with a sword? Maybe he could fill me in on this nagging suspicion – later.* Joe was getting used to the idea of discretely comparing notes with his assigned Immortal. *Sure makes my job more than a little easier,* he thought, though he knew the severe consequences for breaking his Watcher's Oath of secrecy.

Sandy was standing next to Mark's body when his uniform com-badge sounded. He spoke a few words into the microphone then muted it. Leaning over to Joe briefly, he spoke quietly. A moment later he crossed in front of Duncan and left the shop.

Almost unconsciously, Duncan's eyes followed Sandy's movements until the shop door closed. His focus on the pair at the table had been briefly broken. When his eyes returned to Tessa, he found himself rewinding an earlier conversation with Grace, one he never really took very seriously at the time.

"Tessa's a true artist, Duncan. She's a very sensitive woman, something never to be taken lightly. A true artist can be very passionate and that word doesn't always mean love. An artist's

passion can be pure love and unimaginably beautiful, or ragingly violent and grotesquely dark—in art there are no absolutes between ecstasy and abject agony. Apparently you have never seen the dark side of Tessa."

No, he hadn't. He hadn't considered that even possible in someone as slight in stature as Tessa was to him and as beautiful as a radiant dawn to his rugged Highland physique.

"How does that make you feel, Duncan—afraid? For Tessa—or yourself?"

What were his real feelings today? Having been within a heartbeat of losing his head to a mortal? Looking up into eyes he imagined were so innocent, a form so lovely, a nature so delicate he had devoted himself to guarding her – now holding his bloody katana in her unwavering hand—an expression so cold and, yes—sadistic—over the body of a man she had just beheaded.

"What do you mean?" he heard himself reply to Grace's cryptic comment. *"You heard me, Duncan. Are you afraid that the violent passions Tessa uses to create her twisted and tortured art forms, pulled white-hot from the flames, could overwhelm you someday?"*

Was he? He had dismissed Grace's comment as pure gibberish until he had seen what kind of death Tessa had wrought with his katana in her hand. He didn't really know what he was feeling at that moment, but it was not comfortable. As soon as the dust of today had settled he would begin to sort it all out, but not now, not at this moment.

The silence in the room alerted him. Tessa had finally stopped speaking. He shifted his stance and made as if to go to her side. Once again Fitz was in his way. Duncan's expression all but spoke *"What now?"*

Fitz motioned discreetly with his hand for Duncan to stay put. "She's doing fine," he whispered, barely audible. "Richie's taking care of all that needs to be done for now." *Duncan, I don't think you know this Tessa of yours at all—not really. I obviously didn't,* Fitz thought as he returned a confident expression to the Highlander. *She is not as helpless as you though and anybody that gets in her way is likely to find themselves at the business end of a sword, literally.* Fitz returned his attention to Tessa, then took out his pipe and placed it between his teeth in a manner reminiscent of Sherlock Holmes. Folding his arms, he leaned back against the adjacent counter. *That reminds me—I'm going to get to the bottom of what Tessa and Amanda really did together while I was out, before I say anything further to Duncan. Doubtful this proper, yet rather naive Highlander*

could take another shock like today without another fifty-years or so
between to smooth out the consternation he's bound to give it all.

Sandy re-entered the shop, walked to Joe, and had a few quiet words. Joe's expression took on a somber shade. Slowly he nodded.

Duke finally folded his pad, rose, and walked to Mark's body. Flipping back the sheet he grinned.

"A home invasion that really backfired," he huffed with a grin and cast an expert eye on the severed stub of Mark's neck. "I wish all such calls ended like this. There would be fewer people to chase down and I'd be off fishing more often."

"You're getting tired of chasing them old man?" Sandy shot back with a half grin, as he stood beside Joe.

"Nope. It's just nice to see the *perp* getting the death sentence and not the victim. Miss Noel,"

"Tessa," she said gently to Duke and smiled.

Duke nodded an acknowledgment. "You've got a strong arm and a good sure swing. I can't say in the last 2,000-years I've cut them off any cleaner myself." He glanced to one of the larger metal sculptures. "I can see why you do. You work the forge?"

"Not really very much. I fire all my metal and weld most of it. I only hammer when I have to."

Duke shrugged. "You obviously do enough of it. There is muscle hiding in those arms." He let the sheet fall over the body. "Tessa, it's my experience that people like this are very few and far between in this life. Nevertheless, you can't afford to let your guard down. This katana isn't really made for your arm length, height, and body size. It's best wheeled by a larger person." He picked up Duncan's weapon and took a few practice swings. "You need something that fits into your slender hand and fingers—something like a rapier." He cast an eye around to Duncan and Fitz briefly as he returned the weapon to the table.

Duncan's eyes opened noticeably wider with that comment and he glanced to Fitz as he mouthed the words silently, "*She is not going to put another sword in her hands—never, ever again.*"

"*Don't you bet your life on that on that, laddie.* S*he's already got one picked out,*" he mouthed the words silently back with a grin.

"*What?*" was Duncan's soundless reply. "Fitz, there is no way I'm going to let her—" he whispered audibly.

Fitz patted his arm briefly, waving his finger by his lips for silence.

Duncan opened his mouth, the expression on his face giving every indication he was warming up for a very audible retort when he heard Tessa questioning Duke.

"May I ask you, how did you become an Immortal? How long ago was it?"

Duke straightened his shirt, glanced once to Sandy standing next to Joe, then gave a slight shrug and leaned comfortably against the table. Almost simultaneously everyone present seemed to lean-in, making themselves comfortable against whatever they were propped.

Joe noted that everyone seemed to be quietly acknowledging that there were four Immortals and two Watchers present. Equally interesting was that no one seemed to be the least bit concerned who knew what about whom. *This is a new angle,* he mused. *I wonder where this is all going. Perhaps I could get more first-account stories down the road this way?*

"I started out in life as the son of a goat herder. The family who raised me had no sons, only daughters. They said they found me when their goats came upon me, at the foot of Mount Ida in Crete, the legendary birthplace of Zeus. They believed I had been left in the path of their goats in answer to their prayers for a son. They gave me the name, Diogenes, it means 'born of Zeus'. I became a Minoan Crete almost 2,100 years ago, celebrating the culture and customs—until the Roman invasion of 75 BC (BCE) when I was taken prisoner as a young man and sold into slavery in Rome. I ended up as a servant and entertainer during the turmoil period of Marcus Antonius, then ruler of the rapidly failing Roman Republic. Minoans were known for a peculiar sport that was enjoyed by some of the wealthy Romans too – an acrobatic art called 'bull dancing' or 'bull leaping'. I was taught how to approach and grab the horns of our young bulls. The bull then throws his head upwards. This natural instinct gives us performers the momentum necessary to do stunts in the air and on the bull's back before finally sliding off. As a Crete, we took care to work with our bulls, gentling them; unfortunately, Roman bulls were not given the same considerations. It was on a feast day—after a day of sacrifice to Hercules—the master of the house, with his esteem guest, began wagering on my skills in this sport."

Flashback – Rome 70 BC/BCE:

The music was getting old to Gaius Antius Antonia. Looking around to his guests propped on his dais cushions and lounges, it was obvious that everyone had filled their faces with as much of his food as they wanted. A yawn from his wife, as she idly reached over the armrest of their couch to finger another grape, brought a grunt of displeasure from his lips. Gaius could have cared less if she fell into an overindulged-induced coma. It was Marcus Antonius Maximinus, the appointed *ear* for their supreme ruler, Marcus Antonius, he wanted to keep happy.

Who knows where our next ruler is coming from? he thought ambitiously. *If it's my dear friend Maximinus, well, I want to become his official ear.* Ambition was Gaius middle name. Clapping his hands, he summoned his head servant and demanded that his Cretan slaves perform the bull dance for his guest. Bowing quickly, he left to find Diogenes and the others.

"Marcus, have you seen the bull-dance? It is quite a spectacle."

"A number of times, Gaius. I get around." He motioned for his goblet to be refilled – a slave obliged him. "Unlike yourself, I'm not stuck in the Senate chambers and forced to listen to those boring speeches by your esteemed colleagues," he replied somewhat patronizingly. "My affairs have taken me across our known world. In other words, if it exists, I've seen it."

"Really," Gaius chortled, waving his goblet in a rather unsteady fashion for a refill. "Well then, my worldly aficionado, how about a friendly wager? I wager you've never seen the bull dance performed the way my Cretan slaves can."

Marcus gave a nonchalant nod and reaching to his belt, produced a gold coin.

Gaius's eyes lit up when he recognized the luster. Almost as an afterthought, he elbowed his wife to join them on the balcony. A snore was her only reply. Glancing over to the plump woman, who was now draped over the armrest and passed out, he noted her lips were only inches from her goblet of wine that was responsible for her present state. Gaius waved her off as he rose. Three of his other guests were in the same state. They would, no doubt, keep each other company in his absence.

Diogenes was applying wrappings to his hands and arms for better grip when the bull was driven up from the field into an enclosure, which was in plain view of his master's balcony. His companion dancer, a Cretan woman, looked nervously from the obviously agitated and frothing bull to Diogenes.

"It's mating season, doesn't the fool up there know they're in a foul mood?"

Diogenes gave the bull a calculating stare. "We'll have to be quick. I'll distract him while you leap. When you land, get clear fast then distract him for me."

The animal handlers closed the gate then backed away as the bull mock-charged the door once again. Snorting, he stamped then paced quickly from end to end of his enclosure.

Gaius emerged onto the balcony ledge shouting for his slaves to present themselves and begin.

Marcus followed his host out a few moments later, only casually glancing down when suddenly he stopped dead in mid-step—his eyes searching down and around the grounds below.

Gaius noted his guest's sudden heightened interest and he beamed a smile. "Perhaps my world traveler, there are things about myself and my not so humble home that will surprise you."

I seriously doubt there are any surprises where you're concerned, Marcus thought behind his pained grin. *I, on the other hand, my ambitious fool, am an Immortal—full of surprises you can't even begin to imagine. Where is this feeling coming from? The person isn't an Immortal yet—but close.* Marcus' eyes followed the two slaves— the source of the *feeling* perceivable only to Immortals, as they emerged from under the balcony and bowed formally to their master. *The Cretan male is pre-Immortal,* Marcus acknowledged as he moved to stand front and center at the rail.

"Maybe you're right, Gaius," he replied, his words holding a silent double meaning. He watched as the pair climbed over the barrier and into the small pit of the private amphitheater.

Diogenes walked carefully around the edge of the wall, speaking quietly to the bull. Once his companion saw the animal was focused on him, she took a deep breath and carefully began her approach. At the last second, she sprinted to the head and grabbed his horns. The bull bellowed and threw his head up, pitching her high in the air. Somersaulting over his withers, she landed in a handstand on his back and was about to roll into a tumble when the bull bucked her off roughly to the ground then whirled, searching for what had landed on his back.

Diogenes waved his arms and shouted to the bull, distracting him, allowing his companion time to scramble away.

Turning from one distracting person to the next, the bull finally stopped, faced Diogenes and lowering his head, pawed the ground.

Checking the wrappings on his hands and arms, he uttered a brief silent prayer to the Cretan deity, Mistress of the Animals, then ran toward the bull. At the last instant, the bull charged him. Grabbing his horns, he hadn't time to shift his stance when the angry animal threw him to the side instead of up. Diogenes was slammed into his flank – an instant later he felt a horn ram through his back and out his chest. Gored, Diogenes was hooked on the horn of the maddened animal and flung about as if his body were a rag doll. Bucking, the bull threw his head up to free itself of his human victim. Thrown to the ground,

Diogenes back snapped like a dry twig under the weight of almost two-ton of furious bull.

Horrified, his companion screamed at the animal, running helter-skelter in front of him to distract him as the herders opened the door and waved whatever was in their hands. Seeing an opening, the bull broke off his attack and ran out of the amphitheater.

As carefully as they could, the herders lifted the broken, crushed and ripped human body—carrying Diogenes back to the slave quarters.

Marcus' eyes followed the group until they passed from view under the balcony. His host shrugged, his hands in a gesture of, '*you win some you lose some'*, was about to speak when Markus slapped the gold coin into Gaius fat hand.

"You're right—you won the bet. I've never seen it performed this way," he retorted, sarcastically. *I hope this piece of bright metal shuts your fat mouth, you mortal maggot,* he thought as he turned from the balcony rail and started purposefully through the archway, then paused. Seeing his host's expression was a query, he quickly added. "Once I've relieved my overfilled stomach outside of the vomitoria, I will be back for whatever delicacies your esteemed household will offer this *humble* world-traveler." Turning, he left the hall in disgust.

Gaius laughed. *So, I've finally won a bet against my dear all-knowing friend Marcus. Let's see what other surprises I can impress him with tonight.* Clapping his hands, he motioned for the server and sent him to the kitchen with the instructions to, "Kill something different this time and cook it well."

Marcus followed his immortal senses until he came upon the grisly scene. Pausing by an archway, he watched.

Carefully, they laid Diogenes' broken and bloody body on one of the servants' cots. With equal care, his female companion was trying to clean and soothe him with a hastily drawn bucket of water and washcloth. She spoke softly, encouragingly to him as she folded his skin back over to cover his visible insides – he was dying and nothing she or anyone could do would be of any help to this kindred slave. There was as much blood in the water as was spilling out of his insides onto the cot now. Another slave ran to her side and handed her wine he had stolen from the master's table. Perhaps this would ease his pain as he passed. Carefully she lifted his head and coaxed the cup to his lips, letting a little of the liquid spill. It mingled with his blood, brought up with every ragged breath and drooled away. She stopped trying and lay his head back down. Marcus entered startling all.

"You and you," he commanded. "Saddle my horse and bring him – you bring a large blanket and a rope. The rest of you leave – now."

The woman opened her mouth to protest, then thought better of it and bowed with the rest of the departing slaves. Marcus gazed shifted to Diogenes and he knelt briefly beside him as he drew his last few mortal breaths. "I'm Marcus Antonius Maximinus – I am an Immortal and by the gods, you will be too soon."

Present time:

"Marcus took me into his household, taught me how to fight with a Gladius—a Roman short sword—taught me the Rules all Immortals must follow, and gave me an education. He gave me the name Ducanus Maximinus and made me a Roman citizen, affiliated with his family household and lineage."

"What a horrible way to live and die, as someone else's property, someone who never cared for you as a human being—only as an object," Tessa said, her compassion reaching out to this ancient Roman who had been treated so cruelly.

Duke shrugged and glanced down, away from Tessa's eyes. "It was a long time ago," he replied quietly, his expression betraying his true feelings.

Tessa placed a solacing hand on Duke's arm and saw a flicker of a smile form on his face. His fingers slid up his sleeve until they touched the top of her hand, just briefly. Sandy's uniform com sounded and he looked to his partner.

"If we're finished, the coroner is ready for the body."

"I'm done," he replied and pocketed his pad. Rising, he left the shop, returning shortly with the coroner and his attendants.

Two men followed, then stopped in the doorway—waiting. To Tessa, they looked like plain-clothes police officers. She steeled herself for what she guessed would come next, handcuffed and on her way to prison.

"I'll write you," she whispered to Duncan, as the men approached her. Setting their oversized cases down by her table, they opened it and began assembling a portable floor scrubber. A bewildered look formed on Tessa's face as she watched. She looked to Duncan then to Joe as Mark's body was being packed out. "Now what?" she asked, totally confused.

"Now you get on with your lives," Joe replied with a half grin, looking to Duncan and Tessa. "And don't worry about the cleaning crew here, they're part of *my crew*." Joe followed the stretcher, pausing beside Duke who was standing by the door.

"I'm curious," he began. "Did your adoptive family really believe you were a son of a Greek god—Zeus?"

Duke shrugged, "Why not? The gods all had very healthy libidos."

"But we now know they're all mythical."

"Sure, right along with all the other stories about the Titans and of course, those Greek Immortals who fought for Olympus." Raising an eyebrow to Joe, he let his expression sink in and his comment hang for a long moment before he followed his partner out.

Yeah, I got it, thought Joe. *I'm going to get a hold of our research department and have them do a little fact checking on the origin of early Greek mythology. This is something Amy Zoll would love to sink her teeth into. Who knows, maybe Zeus was just another Immoral?* He shook his head. He wasn't sure he was ready to go there just yet.

Duncan and Richie followed Joe out of the shop. "So that's it with Tessa," Richie asked looking from Mac to Joe.

"Yup."

"She's not going to be arrested and hauled off to prison for the next one-hundred years?"

"Nope."

Richie stopped and stared at Joe. The question was written on his face.

"Richie, you are clearly aware of Watchers. Mark was a part of our mess—he, Wolf, and Horton should have never happened to anyone. That is not what Watchers are about—we are historians, not assassins. When we make a mess, we clean it up." He shifted gears. "Well, Mac, is the whole tribe here off to Paris now?"

Duncan gave Joe a brief *and just how did you manage to get that information—I won't ask because I know you're a Watcher and won't tell me,* expression.

"I couldn't get a flight out. Everything was booked at the airlines I called." Richie chuckled. "You should have heard the ticket agent when I suggested we travel as baggage. Joe, I'll tell you, there should be exceptions for Immortals—so it isn't first class, we'll '*come back*' when we land."

Joe shook his head, his grin widening. "Just as soon as you're willing to explain that you and Mac here are Immortals. I am sure they will reconsider when you tell them that you're old-hands at coming back from the dead."

"Yeah—right," Richie finished with a heavy sigh. "Hey, Joe, you helped us with Tessa, maybe you could help us with the flight," Richie began beaming his *don't-fail-me-now*, grammar school smile.

"Hey, I'm not a travel agent—but," and his expression took on a *wheeling-and-dealing* demeanor. "I think I can help this 'extended family' out. One just has to be particular about with which airline they book with."

Richie glanced casually down the alley a ways to the two squad cars near the end. "Kevin is going to love following me around Paris. I'll take him smoothly past all the exciting and cool places. I tell you, Joe, he won't even know he's getting the grand tour." Realizing what he had just said, he gave Duncan and Joe and apologetic expression. "Sorry, I know I'm not supposed to know about Kevin, but I do. I won't let on to him, though. I hope this doesn't ruin his job or anything, Joe."

Joe looked away for a long moment. "Kevin isn't your Watcher anymore, Richie. He was shot down today." He motioned toward the parked squad cars. "We're not certain yet, but we think he confronted Mark first, before he arrived at your door. If true, that's what bought you the time you needed to get home and warn Tessa, otherwise Mark would have gotten to Tessa before you returned."

"Oh man! Joe, I don't know what to say."

"There is nothing to say, Richie. Mark was the Watcher's fault, not yours or Tessa's."

"Is he still alive? Is there something we can do for him?" Duncan asked, concern in his voice.

Joe closed his eyes and shook his head. "Just barely alive. If he ever wakes up we'll ask him what really happened. We are anxious to put a period at the end of this Mark incident as well."

"He's just a kid, Joe—like me. He doesn't deserve to die."

Joe looked with sympathy to the young Immortal whose compassion for his Watcher was self-evident. "He's a year younger than you are. He just graduated—junior grade—a real ground-floor rookie."

Richie's expression was near tears. "So, because I didn't run that bastard down when we were playing tag in the street a few days ago, that kid—who just wanted to be the best cop he could be—will probably die. He gets the death sentence, Joe – and he may be partly responsible for saving Tessa today. Joe, I swear I—"

Joe reached out and grasped Richie's shoulder halting his self-recrimination. "It's not your fault. He knew the risks when he accepted that badge. There was an APB out on Mark from the day of Tessa's shooting. Kevin was simply acting in the line of duty. Hell, Richie, it's the same for every Watcher, too. We all know the risk before we take our final vows and have this tattoo inscribed on our flesh. We know we could be working with Immortals who are dangerous and who just might kill us if they knew. I'm just thankful that you, Mac, Fitzcairn and Duke aren't all out to kill me or anyone else – mortal that is." He pulled out his cell phone and placed a call. A few moments later he gave Richie the phone and let him finish booking the flight to Paris.

"Mac, you're one hell of an exciting person. I'm glad I know you."

Duncan smiled and nodded back.

The cleaning crew was hard at work when Joe and Duncan reentered the shop.

Seeing Duncan reappear, Fitz chose that moment to carefully pick the Rapier off its stand then amble over to Tessa. His smile was reminiscent of an English butler.

"If you don't mind, my friend here would like his favorite sword back. He's very fond of it and I'm sure he'll need it eventually. Besides," and he proffered the Rapier to her, "I believe you have already identified this one as yours."

Slipping her hand smoothly into the grip, she looked up and into Fitz's eyes as a curious smile formed on her lips. She briefly nodded her acknowledgment.

He made an ever-so-slight English bow, all the while thinking, *I hope I am interpreting you correctly Tessa—if not, every Immortal who pisses you off will have to watch their head—myself included. Brace yourself, Duncan, old boy. The Game may be about to pick up a mortal player – whether you know it or not.*

Chapter Thirty

Duncan sat in silent contemplation in Tessa's work alcove – chin resting on his folded hands, Tessa's mysterious drawing by his side. How long had he been gazing at the space where he had lain only hours ago? Over the years, he had lost track of the number of times he had passed by that space on the floor. Yet in this seemingly insignificant space, only hours earlier, a life and death drama had unfolded. *A space is never insignificant,* his conscious mind whispered. *It's only insignificant until something happens in it, then it is immortalized in time – as a beginning, or as an end to some event.* Unconsciously he gave the briefest of nods. It almost was an end – his end. That space on the floor had become the resting place for his line of sight – though he had long ago ceased to see what little it was showing him. *I have lived more than 400-years and survived countless dangers all over the world yet I almost perished in my own home.*

The Wheel of Fortune spun in your favor, his conscious thoughts offered up.

No, his subconsciousness corrected him. *Your luck had finally run out, Highlander. That space, in that moment, would have been immortalized as your last.*

Physical immortality – is there really any such thing, or are we all just kidding ourselves? The words of Connor MacLeod came to the forefront – as crisp as when they had been spoken by his cousin.

"You are an Immortal, Duncan—part with us—a race of Immortals. You cannot die in the way of mortal man, nay – only the stroke of a sword, which separates your head from you, will release the power of your Quickening, ending your existence here forever. It is the Game that threatens our existence now as we await the Gathering."

Slowly he shook his head. *Connor, you can't imagine how wrong you were,* he mentally told himself. "I always expected that if my end came, it would come in combat – at the hands of an Immortal whose presence I had sensed, one who possessed superior swordsmanship skills and Quickening power," he whispered then closed his eyes. *Not out of the clear blue by someone un-sensed and unseen, a mortal scum with a knife and no honor.* So lost in thought was he that the light sound of Tessa's bare feet on the floor was unheard.

"Penny for your thoughts," she asked gently, her hands wrapped around a warm mug of cocoa.

Unmoving, he replied quietly. "Gaze into your crystal ball."

Lowering her mug, she responded with a wry grin. "It's after hours – I've turned my crystal ball off for the day." Setting her mug on the ledge by her work-alcove, she moved to stand by his side, her gentle hand resting on his shoulders.

"You know, Joe's cleaners did an excellent job," she began, trying to lighten his obviously somber mood. "I can't tell that anything unusual happened in here today. I swear they even put my easel eraser crumbs back on the floor." She glanced down to the seemingly inert Duncan. The silence was absolute. When the seconds ticked by without a comeback, she quietly slid onto the bench seat beside him. "Let's talk about it," she said.

"I don't even know where to begin, or what to say right now."

Turning her head, she followed his gaze, keeping her eyes from meeting his, allowing him to shield his vulnerability which she knew had been laid bare today. "I understand what you're feeling even without my crystal ball. Your world came unglued today – just like mine did a little more than a week ago—I was staring down a gun barrel—" She left her sentence purposely hang on an ascending voice.

Almost inaudible at first, Duncan slowly began to speak. "How many times in our lives have we taken the moments we have for granted? I've lived more than 400-years which is enough for many mortal lifetimes, yet more often than not I've found it easier to philosophically convince myself that I'm just passing through life, generation to generation. That's what I told Richie, not too long ago. Then, without warning, it can suddenly all be over and no matter how long you've lived—it makes no difference."

Tessa's arm slid smoothly around his back, pulling him gently but insistently closer.

"Real life isn't a video game for us either. Cold steel—be it a knife or a sword—is an equalizer for both of us; you don't get any bonus points to trade in for extra lives just because you happen to be an Immortal." She angled her head, catching the corner of his eyes in hers, stealing a glimpse into his pained soul.

"Just listen to us, we really sound an awful lot alike. I seem to recall feeling and saying something very similar to it myself in the hospital. But that isn't the only issue you're battling with at this moment, is it?"

Duncan let his head incline further. "I've never felt so powerless, so out of control of my destiny as I did today."

Tessa steeled herself for what she instinctively knew he had left unsaid. A heartbeat and a half later, she took a deep breath and filled in the blanks. "In your eyes, a mortal never really quite merited the same attention as an Immortal—as a serious personal threat, or a defender. Mark—why of course he could kill me and steal my precious time with you away from me. After all, I'm only mortal. But not once did you ever seriously entertain the idea that he could also do the exact same thing to you."

Slowly Duncan lifted his head, his eyes never meeting Tessa's. "I never thought that you could ever bring yourself to—"

"Protect the one I love with all my strength and passion?" she replied softly, finishing what she thought should be the end of his sentence.

Slowly he shook his head. "No. I never thought that you could bring yourself to kill—like me," he corrected her. "So much explosive passion with this weapon as if it were a part of you, an extension of your soul—as if it belonged in your hands. I know what you must have done—how you must have felt – what it must have taken to—" he let his sentence hang with a hint of anguish in his voice, as his offhand slid down the handle of his katana. He sat up fully – his left hand moving slowly across her visibly lacerated cheek, his eyes pleading, trying to understand.

"Today, I looked into your eyes—and saw myself staring back."

She straightened noticeably. "A person doesn't have to be Duncan MacLeod of the Clan MacLeod to defend the one they love. All anyone needs to do is strip away their civilized veneer and draw on their darkest innermost self. I now know how strong mine really is. I guess deep down I always have. I never really felt I could let it out." Her last sentences came fleeting and halting and Tessa closed her eyes and looked away, knowing she was on the verge of a painful recall. When her eyes finally opened and met his once again, it was with a hint of reproach.

Duncan looked away too, his eyes misty too. "In the past twelve wonderful years we have been together, I have always felt that when the Game came to me, I had to shield you from the reality of my immortal conflict—from the ever present danger to you that exists as long as you are with me."

"If that's what you still believe after today, then you've asked a woman you really don't know to marry you. If twelve years isn't enough familiarity, just look around," and she motioned slowly in the general direction of everywhere. "There I am—and there—and over there. That's me—and me too. Duncan, what do you really see?"

In a rhetorical exercise, Duncan looked from one creative work to another. "I see your creative expression in that abstract metal work—I see the beauty your hands have molded in that clay—I see your smile shining from that figure. What else am I supposed to see," he finished, genuinely puzzled.

Tessa paused for a long moment and lowered her eyes, considering what she had just really heard.

"Have I really been that good at keeping the truth from you? Or have you always only seen in me what you wanted to?" she finally said, softly. Withdrawing her hand from around him, she rose. Turning to the large, twisted, tortured metal sculpture that formed the focal point of her portion of the shop's display area, she reached back into her memory—to a memory she hadn't consciously visited in fourteen years.

"Now it's my turn to say I don't really know where to begin or what to say right now." She turned sharply back to him. "But I'm going to find the words and I'm going to tell you because I really owe you that—right here and right now." Purposefully she reached down, took his shoulders in her rock-steady grasp and coaxed him to his feet. He was above eye-level to her smaller stature and she felt herself unconsciously straightening until she stood taller than she ever felt she had before.

"You have been zealously protecting what you believed to be a fragile China-doll, from the immortal world around us. I tell you now that porcelain is less than a breath thick. There is something you need to know about me—about my past. About the kind of person I ultimately became to someone I cared for and who died caring about me. It was a little less than two years before we first met—before you jumped into my life on that Seine tour boat."

Tessa took a deep breath and tried to compose the sequence of events into a coherent story. It was a painful story that she had kept hidden from her most intimate love—a story of her life and a relationship she had always felt guilty about.

"I met Ana when I was a first-year student at the Sorbonne, a little over fourteen-years ago. She was just a couple of years older than me and had a very distinct avant-garde art style that had already caught the instructor's eye. I had none when I first walked through that door, but she always encouraged the best from me. She helped me grow personally and I found my art style by knowing Ana. She would always say, '*Our works compliments each other in an avant-garde way.*' We became very dear friends at the Sorbonne, promising each other that we would take our unique duo avant-garde styles to the world. Then one day she just walked into class, folded up her sketch-pad and walked out. I found out she had been diagnosed with a terminal disease—Ana, who was so young, so full of life, was going to die."

"Duncan, you can't even begin to imagine in your immortal existence the emotional turmoil that we both went through – the thought of death at that age. Ana telling me over and over again that nothing was helping her, me always telling her everything was going to be fine, you're too young, it won't happen to you. Suddenly she was gone and I realized that what she was really saying was, '*Would you shut up and listen to me. I need to tell you what I am going through. Why can't you be with me through this part of my life too?*' I felt guilty afterwards because I knew she wanted to talk about her impending death and I never let her—I couldn't face hearing about it because I couldn't face my own eventual mortality. Duncan – that could have just as well been me. How cruel can anyone be to someone who was so close?"

"It was shortly after the funeral, that I left my apartment one morning and just started walking. It must have been hours—the downtown with all its shops and cafés became an unimportant blur as a sense of being lost in this world was building up inside of me. I was walking like a mad woman, my heart beating faster every second. I had no idea where I was heading, but I knew I had to get there. suddenly I saw the sign. *Perfect!* I remember thinking. *My feet have taken me to the city cemetery. Just the right place to come on a stroll and cheer up.* My feet took me through the gate without pausing. It was getting late and people were leaving. *This is not right, I should do the same,* I told myself repeatedly, yet my feet carried me on. '*OK*', I finally said, *if some urge has brought me here, I want to know why.* I knew I had better find it before night came. Suddenly my feet stopped—so suddenly that I almost tripped myself. I was in front of a grave—Ana's grave. There was nothing on that grave—no art, no flowers. I had nothing in my hands to make it less austere. I had come to my dearest friend's last resting place with nothing to give in memory. *No different than what you didn't give her in her last weeks of life,* I remember thinking sardonically of myself. My knees nearly gave way at that moment and I made it to a small bench that was nearby. In front of me was an empty grave. It looked as if the spot had just been dug—probably waiting for a newcomer. I closed my eyes—only for a moment and saw myself with Ana in a fleeting memory. When I opened my eyes again, I saw that a tombstone had appeared at the edge of the grave—a name was being inscribed on it by an unseen hand—my name, '*Tessa Noel 1958–1978*'. *No! No! I am not there! I am alive! I'm not a ghost! It's Ana who died! It can't happen to me! I haven't lived yet! I'm too young!* I felt absolutely furious at death, the ultimate cheat—the ultimate time thief."

Tessa took a deep breath, composed her feelings again, and continued. "After the Sorbonne, there was a brief period where I couldn't look at a piece of art. I wasn't going home, so to support myself, I took a job as tour guide on the Seine boat tour. Six months later, you literally jumped into my life when you leapt onto the boat. I thought you were insanely crazy, in an absolutely wonderful kind of way. I knew there was something very special about you. Three years later, when I learned you were an Immortal, something painful inside me just stopped hurting. My soul-mate, my lover was going to live forever—he wasn't going to die of some dreaded incurable disease, he was always going to be there—just for me. And from that moment, the furiously angry, agonizing woman that had been raging against mortality – Ana's and mine, went away. I locked that woman away. She only peeks out every now and then—there, and over there she is again." Tessa pointed to the grotesquely twisted polished metal on the stand.

"Then I remember the day Slan Quince came for your head, and you finally told me the truth about the Game and the Gathering." Her mind rewound to that moment—

"Damn you! Damn your Gathering! Damn your whole race!"

"You tore my dream world apart in that instant. Someone who could not normally die was deliberately committing *'immortal suicide'* right in front of me. I had lived, laughed, shared your dreams, your body, and yes, even glimpsed your soul, for twelve glorious years, and you were taking that all away from me by fighting in this insane Immortal's Game again and again. In that instant, I realized that the furiously angry, raging, pained woman I had locked away wasn't really gone. I had just opened Pandora's box and she had just slipped out. I was never going to be able to put her back inside there again. Your China-doll Tessa was really a lie."

She paused and wet her lips before looking back into his eyes – eyes that were now clearly confused, and yes—even a bit frightened. She nodded her acknowledgment. "I know exactly what you have been going through today, and I'm sorry—sorry for so many things that I could have done and should have done over the years to let you know that you didn't have to bear the burden of watching over me like I was a fragile egg. I didn't have to be shielded from every knee-scrape life throws at me." Her hands left his arms and reached to stroke the hair that was neatly captured in a Celtic clasp.

"Have you never let someone else be strong for you in your entire

400-years of life?"

Duncan slowly shook his head. "No—no I haven't. It's always been others looking to me for help—depending upon me for their safety – or looking out for myself, my head." He reached a strand of her hair and carefully twisted it around his palm.

"There are very few people I've looked up to in my life, but I've never thanked someone else for saving my head, when I couldn't help myself." Very slowly at first, his fingers gently brushed her lips and her cheeks as he held her creamy porcelain colored skin, skin that was so alive, in his hands.

"I'm so sorry," he whispered. "If I've ever taken you for granted – ever forgotten to tell you how much I loved you – I'm sorry. I have never, in all my 400-years, held a woman with so much passion, depth of insight, and strength of character as I'm holding right now. Whatever flaws or strengths you believe you have—however you perceive yourself to be, it's what makes you. You and I wouldn't have it any other way. Thank you for being you and for saving my immortal life."

A gentle smile spread across her face. "Come. There is something else I want you to see." Her hand slid down his arm and grasped his hand. She led him into their bedroom.

Tessa rummaged briefly in the closet, retrieving two small cardboard utility boxes. The top labels on the boxes were both marked in light pencil: 'Time Capsule project'. Setting the first box on the bed, she opened it, took out a sheet of paper and scanned it briefly then held it protectively to her breast.

"You have heard about Time Capsules, placing important bits of today into storage for a tomorrow's world that will, most certainly, have forgotten it; and, in its rediscovery, cherish it more than those who lived with it. I am making a Time Capsule for you – for after my inevitable, mortal death. I know I'm the most important thing in your life right now, but after I'm gone, I want this to really be meaningful to you, one year, five years, ten years, a hundred-years – however long you want to hold the memory of me in your heart. My Time Capsule isn't to prolong your mourning of my passing, but to be the surprise you need from time to time—that loving reminder that life can be precious when shared with someone you love. I first considered preparing one large chest of materials, but as I thought of all the places your life has taken you, and the women you are likely to meet along the way in the future, the project has shrunk considerably. It's still taking shape though." She glanced once again to the paper then slipped it back into the one-foot-square utility box, and set it on the floor. She placed the second box on the bed.

"Until today, I never considered the possibility that you could die before me—that I could conceivably outlive you, making this project of mine a futile exercise. I could never have imagined myself opening my own Time Capsule, ten, twenty, or thirty years into my future. Duncan, after what happened with Mark today, in my mind, there really is no such thing as unconditional physical immortality. You can die and be gone forever just as quickly and just as unpredictably as I can. The only difference is that your options for death are *limited,* while mine aren't." She held the box out to him.

"In the event that the inconceivable occurs in my lifetime, I want you to make a Time Capsule for me. Put something away, in here or whatever container you choose, for me to find when I open it in need of a Duncan lift of my spirits—something that I can touch and feel you with me—do it soon, please."

Duncan took the box from her hands and contemplated it. *She's right,* he considered somberly.

"I never really considered my immortal *mortality* in these terms. Immortality is simply a term for limited options for death—not impossible." Setting the box aside, he opened a drawer and reached deep inside. Taking a pouch he opened it and held a key with a tag attached, for Tessa to see.

"If I should be killed before you die, I want you to have this. This key opens the storage depot that you already know about." He dropped the key inside the box and handed it back to her. "Here is the sum total of my life to date. If I am dead, I want you to have my whole life with you, in remembrance of me."

Tessa set the box aside. Reaching Duncan she pulled him on to the red satin bedspread with her.

"Paris is our city—now and forever. Let our new life together begin there. Say you'll marry me—let it be in Paris."

"I will," was his only reply before they became lost in the giving and receiving of each other's love.

Chapter Thirty-one

"Are you sure you're packed?" he recalled Duncan asking, for the third time as the sound of his bike engine became background noise on the road.

"Yeah, Mac," he heard himself repeat. *"I must have packed enough for two lifetimes."* Their *'travel agent'*, Joe had managed to hook them up with a direct flight to Paris leaving out of Seattle International Airport, in forty-eight-hours. They were now on a twelve-hour countdown to departure, and to Richie, it looked as if Mac and Tessa were both packing everything out of the store. *Fed Ex is really going to cash-in on this delivery to France,* Richie mused. *At the rate they're going, I don't know why they don't just jack the building up and box it.* He smiled to himself. He didn't have so many things to pack. He hadn't lived as long as Duncan and Tessa, and he could hardly be called a pack rat.

"Our flight is going to be on time. We have to clear security early in international flights take longer to clear. I don't know why you have to take off now?"

He just had to go, it was a simple as that. There was something weighing on his mind and he couldn't shake it. *"Don't worry, Mac. I'll be back in plenty of time. It's something I have to do, OK?"*

His bike turned under the parking ramp entrance. He continued on until he came to one of the hospital service elevators. Switching off the key, he dismounted, removed his helmet, went inside and punched the button for the main lobby. His previous brief visit to Tessa's room had given him enough familiarity with the general areas of the visitor's sectors that he could find his way around without looking totally lost. A helpful young admission's woman was eager to please this red-haired energetic young man with a warm smile and he was on his way quickly.

Kevin Kilgore was in the intensive care section – reserved for the most critical conditions. The distinction between death and life in this ward was often blurred. People coming and going here were either in full clean room gowns, surgical garb, or religious garb.

Richie walked cautiously up to what looked like the main desk – *or the control console of a spaceship,* he thought. The monitors were an enigma to him, many registering numbers or displaying graphs – some simply flashing red or green—a loud 'beep' was intermittently heard. It seemed to Richie that all of this was simply bedlam in progress. Two or three people quickly came while others got up and quickly left this horse-shoe shaped station. Random nurses in the hall stopped briefly by the desk, noted what was flashing, pressed buttons, and went on.

"Excuse me," he began, looking to one of the women at the desk who had the largest official looking pin attached to her uniform. "I am trying to find Kevin Kilgore. Admissions told me to come here—said I could get right in."

"Are you family?" she asked officially.

"Yeah sure—well, sort of—actually no. You see, he watches me—I mean he watches out for me. We're together like brothers," he finished with a big smile, hoping he was coming off as a nervous wreck. He didn't have to hope, he was actually starting to sweat under her intense scrutiny. *Man, where do they recruit these nurses from – a prison ward! I could always get around Sergeant Powell down at the juvie section of the police station without too much effort – just smile big, and wear them down. I'm glad these ladies weren't working at the police station.*

"Immediate family only," was her reply. She turned back to the console.

She'll have to do a lot better than that to discourage me, he thought. "No, you don't understand nurse, Weston. I just got back from army reserves, and I always promised him I'd—"

"I'm sorry," she repeated, a little louder, her tired expression showing. "His condition is extremely critical. Unless you're immediate family, the rules say you don't get in." She deliberately turned her head and focused on the console in front of her.

"But if I could just get in to speak to him for five minutes – you see I came a long way, and it would mean so much to Kev, lighten his spirits to know I'm here."

"Look, he isn't conscious. It wouldn't matter whether you or anyone else, spoke to him." She shot back, far more impatiently than she should have.

"It might," came Grace's voice from somewhere behind one of the critical units. Grace peeled off her paper isolation cape and gloves, placing them in a biohazard bag before she joined Richie.

"He's in a coma," the charge nurse shot back, her voice elevated, defending her authority. "He's probably brain dead from–"

"I believe you're overstepping your bounds nurse," Grace spoke up, her voice an official reprimand. "You have no authority to make medical calls on the condition of a patient. It's time for you to take a break."

"I've only been on duty—"

"It's obviously already too long, from what I just heard."

Heads had already turned as the volume of the surrounding bedlam quieted down several notches. The nurse, realizing the implications of what Dr. Grace Chandel had just said, quickly stepped away from her seat and walked toward the lounge. A younger nurse took her empty station. The woman gave no indication that she was going to hassle this physician.

Grace turned to Richie and motioned for him to follow. They entered a glass enclosed room several paces down the hall. The three nurses, who were monitoring vitals, or recording readings, looked up when they entered. Grace went to the computer stand on their crash-cart and scanned the most recent physiology log. "Has there been any change in his status in the last hour?" she asked, flipping from screen to screen.

"No" they affirmed.

"Then I would like everyone to leave for a few minutes. This man needs a moment alone with him—don't worry, I will stay close," she finished and waved them to the door. Amidst stares, they left the room. Grace closed the door. "OK, Richie, what's this about?" she asked quietly.

Richie, trying to find someplace to rest his crash helmet shifted it nervously, not knowing what to do with his hands. "I had to come – we're all leaving for Paris tonight. I just had to see Kevin to say something to him—you know, before I left." He faltered, not knowing how to phrase his feelings at that moment. Richie looked aghast at the small figure lying on the bed. "What happened to him, Grace? How bad is it? How long is he going to be hooked-up like that?" and he gestured to the tubes and electrodes fastened to almost every conceivable place from his torso up.

Grace placed a gentle hand on his arm. "Kevin was clinically dead when the paramedics arrived. I don't know the details, but as I understood, a woman called the dispatcher with his uniform com. She stayed with him – trying to give him CPR until the paramedics loaded him up. They were finally able to get his heart started, but he isn't stable. The problem is, we don't know how long his brain was without oxygen, Richie. He may in fact be dead."

She paused and turned his head slightly to face her. "You still haven't told me what this is all about. How do you know him?"

Richie met her eyes and took a deep breath. *OK, Mac told me I can't tell other Immortals about Watchers. They might not yet know about them. Then when they find out, they might go out and kill some Watcher for being a snoop in their lives. Sure, like Grace is going to do that. But OK, I promised Mac I wouldn't, because it's a trust thing with Joe.*

"Tessa and Duncan were attacked in our home by Mark Roszca–Tessa's shooter, yesterday."

"Oh, Richie, not Tessa—not again. What happened to her?"

"She got a little beat-up by him, but she killed him before he killed Mac, *forever*—beheaded Mark with the katana."

Grace froze for an instant and processed what Richie had said. When she spoke there was a sense of closure in her tone. "She was finally able to defeat her *time thief* she had been battling. What happened to Duncan?"

"That's just it, Mark knew how to kill him—how to kill an Immortal. Tessa saved his life and hers. I didn't see it— it figures that I would be packing in a hurry when Tessa was taking her first head."

"Her **first** head," she said distinctly, emphasizing the words—cautiously hoping she was not hearing what she had just heard. "Tessa is a mortal, Richie. I understand she had to save herself and Duncan any way she could, but she is not part of the Game. I hope she understands that."

This was not why he came—time was short—everyone's. He moved it along.

"Anyway, the police that came to the shop, after Mac called them, said that they think Kevin went up against Mark, or something like that before he got to our house and attacked. If he hadn't – done whatever he did with Mark, we probably wouldn't have gotten back from—where we went in time to be there with Tessa. She would have been alone when he attacked. I think he would have killed her this time."

Grace bowed her head momentarily. "So that's what it was." Slowly she shook her head. "You know something Richie, I believe when this much happens to someone, and they still survive, they must have an important mission in their life that can't be stopped. How many people has this madman attacked in relation to Tessa?"

Richie shrugged. "Me, Mac, Duke, and Kevin that I know of, maybe more that I don't."

"And it was Tessa who finally stopped him." Her voice died on a descending note.

"Richie, Kevin was shot at close range, in the back. It just grazed his heart. I don't know what is going to happen. It may take as long as a week or as short as tonight to find out. He's unstable and in a coma now, but we don't know if someone can still *hear* on some basic level. We know talking to them can't hurt. It is hospital policy that someone is with the patient at all times when they're in this unstable condition, but—" and she angled Richie toward him, "whatever you feel you have to say, by all means say it. I'll step out for a few minutes. I don't think it will matter if medical people are in here or not for now—go Richie." Grace left closing the door behind her. Through the glass wall, Richie was only momentarily aware that the emergency room nurses were having an absolute fit that Grace had left the patient alone with him. Grace quickly quieted them. The eternal feeling of regret for someone was far worse than death. They really hadn't been doing anything to improve the patient at the moment Richie had entered—only monitoring him. They could do that from the auxiliary computer here for the next few minutes.

Slowly, Richie walked to Kevin's side and stared in silence for a moment. This man seemed like just a kid, dwarfed by everything that was around him and being done to his body. He closed his eyes—only for a moment and saw,

Kevin stopping him in the park:

"…There are no motorcycles allowed in the park…"

"Sorry officer, I was just—haven't we met somewhere before?"

"Yes, Mr. Ryan, at the station..."

Kevin by the Action News van near the shop:

"…unless the End of the World is coming…the driver of this van is in for a colossal fine…"

Kevin in the shop speaking with Fitz about Tessa's work:

"Interesting artwork. Is this all by the same artist?"

And suddenly the moment was gone. He was left staring at a human being whose life was hanging by the slimmest of threads—life or death—either way it was the only one he was ever going to get. Richie reached a hand toward Kevin, not knowing if he should or where he could safely touch him. He only knew he wanted to reach out to this mortal and pull him off the brink of death and back into life. As he did, the words of his mentor came to mind.

"No matter how much we want to, an Immortal can't give any portion of their immortality to a mortal. I would have done it a hundred times over by now if I could have. I've watched so many people that I have cared so deeply about, die and all I could do was hold their hand."

Richie slipped his hand very, very carefully, into Kevin's—into the one that bore the Watcher's symbol on his wrist. "I don't know what to say, man," he whispered. "Tessa's alive, she wouldn't be if it weren't for you, I'm told." He paused as his eyes grew misty. "I really just want to say thank you. God, straight out of school and all you wanted to be was the best Watcher-cop you could, and you had to get mixed up in this mess. The second week you're trailing me, you ran into Mark! Damn, is there any justice in this world for decent guys like you?" He paused. *This could just as well have been me – I could have been lying in one of these beds, my life on the line – had I not been destined to be an Immortal. We were both protecting Tessa – why do you have to die for it?* Unconsciously, he leaned closer as if speaking directly into his ear would somehow improve Kevin's understanding.

"I found out you were my Watcher—hey, don't worry, Joe is cool about it—said it wouldn't hurt your job. You're young, you still got a future—I'm planning to be around a long time so you'll have a job waiting for you after you get out of here. I swear I'll raise such a fuss about whomever they give me in the meantime, Joe will give me back to you just to shut me up. How about it—you can pull through. Come on, you're young—like me. Then you can stalk me all around the world—I'll show you things that – come on, Kevin, you can beat this. Everyone needs more guys like Joe and you. You're going to grow into one hell of a Watcher, watching me," he paused from his monolog. "Just please don't die."

The door sounded and Richie wiped his eyes before straightening and releasing Kevin's hand. "I'm going to be waiting for you out there, you better join me," he finished with all the bravado he could muster without his voice cracking.

Grace had averted her eyes. She knew the emotions that Richie had expressed—she had seen it literally thousands of times before in her ministering to people over the centuries. She placed a gentle hand on his shoulder as he passed through the door.

"Did you say what you came for?"

"Yes. Grace, do you know who the woman was that kept him going until the paramedics arrived? I would like to thank her too."

She shook her head. "There is nothing about her in the report we have up here." She paused then went to the desk and flipped the computer screen back to the opening notes. "If he isn't out on another run, here is the name of the senior paramedic who responded to the call." She wrote his name down on a memo pad and the area of the hospital he could likely be found. "He may have more information than we do."

Richie took the note, thanked Grace and headed off for the ambulance bay.

Working his way into the bowels of the hospital, after only having to ask directions a half-dozen times, he finally arrived at his destination.

The paramedic was busy loading up his trauma kit when Richie introduced himself and asked about the mysterious woman. The man paused only briefly to speak.

Yes, he remembered the woman—she was the most insistent Good Samaritan he had seen in some time. Even after they tried unsuccessfully to restart his heart, she wouldn't let them pronounce him dead – she kept insisting that we do more to revive him.

"Poor woman must have had a kid of her own go through something like this," he continued. "She just wouldn't stop CPR. He hadn't been breathing on his own, for who knows how long— whenever she came on him lying there—I suppose. Anyway, we shocked him, injected him—shocked him again and nothing. I was ready to tag him and bag him, but she jumped back on him – told me I could just '…*take a coffee break for the rest of your life if you're giving up this fast.*' She said he was just too young—he had a life and she was going to make sure he got it. She'd call someone else if we were giving up—she had the com in her hand while she worked with the other. We shocked him again and again and finally we got a heartbeat. It was touch and go keeping it going till we got him here. He almost didn't have any blood left from the wound. That woman was really something else again."

Probably his Watcher companion Joyce, Richie thought. "You don't know who she was? I would like to thank her for what she did for my friend."

He shook his head. "The call came from the police station. She left as soon as we told her his heart was beating again. She wasn't interested in giving autographs."

"What did she look like?"

"Not too tall—about your height or so. Slim, or at least not fat, I guess—dark hair and no glasses that I remember."

"You said dark hair? What color?"

"Either dark brown or black—why?"

"Nothing," he said trying to appear noncommittal. "Just made me think about someone, that's all." *Joyce has light reddish brown hair,* he thought. *So who was this? How could he find out?* "You took the call from the police station?"

"Yeah, from dispatch."

"Don't they keep a record of those things?"

"They're supposed to."

"Maybe she said who she was when she called in on his com."

The paramedic shrugged then excused himself and went back to work.

The police station wasn't Richie's favorite hang-out though he had been in and out of those doors more than he wanted to over the last few years of his mortal life. Curiosity was gnawing at him. He walked to his bike and was about to turn the key when his cell phone sounded. It was Duncan reminding him once again that they were now on an eight-hour countdown to Paris. He wasn't taking no for an answer this time. He wanted Richie home ASAP!

Richie reluctantly hung up and resolved to set his detective mission aside. He would place this project on the back burner. Sooner or later, though, he was determined to find out who that woman was.

Down at the police station, Sandy closed the door to the small office he was temporarily borrowing. Picking up the phone he paused and thought a moment before he dialed.

"Joe, it's Sandy. We've got another mystery on our hands. Ballistics just reported back on the bullet they took out of Kevin, it doesn't match—that's right, it wasn't Mark's gun."

There was a long pause as Joe spoke. Sandy considered what he had just heard before he weighed in.

"Joe, as I see it, that leaves two options and I would say the first one is pretty much out. Kevin wasn't shot anywhere near a potential drug hotspot in the city. I'd say given what's been going on with Tessa, Richie and MacLeod that this is somehow connected. I think we've still got one of Horton's loose cannons out there somewhere. I'm just not sure how Kevin fits into that picture."

Chapter Thirty-two

"Duncan MacLeod, Tessa Noel, Richie Ryan and Hugh Fitzcairn boarded the Washington-Tacoma to Paris flight at approximately 5:15 p.m. and settled in for the long twelve-and-a-half hour trip. There will be one stop-over at Amsterdam and it is possible that this immortal troop will take advantage of the de-plane time to stretch their legs for an hour. I am going to need a Watcher at the de-plane gate to keep up with this troupe in case they decide to split up."

Joe ended his call quickly as he shouldered his carry-on bag. The agent was already announcing,

"Final Boarding Call for Paris, flight..."

The Amsterdam coordinator had promised two Watchers would be at the gate tomorrow—Claire Bailey, and a recent young graduate from the Watcher's Academy. They would also board the last leg of this flight to Paris with everyone. Claire would take Richie on as his Watcher as long as he was in Paris. Joe wanted to have a long talk with the other individual first.

The flight departed on schedule into a beautifully clear, darkening sky—silver wings glinting in the fading rays of an early November sun. Once the plane reached the cruising altitude and the seatbelt light was switched off, Joe pulled his poker-cap on, his notepad out and began doing what he did best—discreetly watching. Trouble was, on a plane with Fitz, he soon discovered that there was no such thing as being *discreetly* incognito.

His pen moved smoothly across the pages of the Watcher's notebook. *As soon as the refreshments were distributed and drunk, Tessa and Richie settled in on their respective business seats and appeared to have both fallen asleep. Duncan selected* The Paris News *from the pre-board rack of newspapers and chose to read instead of sleep. I haven't located Hugh Fitzcairn's seat yet—*

"Begging your pardon, Joe? It's Joe, right?" He began as he, ever so delicately, peeled back the visor portion of Joe's cap. "My, you do look a world of difference in that getup—a real card shark I'll wager. Funny choice of words on my part—all things considered," Fitz's effervescent voice bubbled as he leaned over and down the side of Joe's headrest with the biggest of English grins.

Joe—momentarily startled by the voice until he realized who was speaking—peered up at the Immortal who had literally uncovered his cover.

"Hello, Fitzcairn. Fancy meeting you here at 40,000-feet." It was an incredibly lousy line, but he had nothing better at the spur of the moment.

Fitz patted Joe's vest once. "Oh, I shouldn't think so, dear boy. You've been following Duncan for years—where he goes you go. That's the way it works with you Watchers, ay?"

"Shh! Would you keep your voice down, Fitz," Joe retorted as quietly as he could and still getting his point across.

Fitz waved a hand in front of his mouth in an '*I'm being shh,*' motion, then slid around the aisle seat and zipped into it, next to Joe and leaned in.

"It isn't the 40,000-feet that should be a surprise, dear boy – you see, my seat is directly behind yours. And as far as my indiscretion in letting the word Watcher slip, Joe—everyone I've seen passing by my seat has their wrist conveniently covered—and I must add, not absolutely covered, with something, either." He motioned to a young stewardess serving beverages in the front. "I would have had to be blind to miss the tattoo poking out from under her delightfully shapely blouse—sleeve that is."

Joe exhaled and rolled his eyes. *Does this guy ever think without his libido?* He favored Fitz with a *come on now* look.

Fitz stiffened and returned the expression. "I'll never stop looking at beautiful women—not until I've been dead and gone at least three days. You've read enough of my chronicle, I'll wager, to know better than that by now. At any rate, my point was that from what I've already seen, this entire flight must be made up of Watchers. I doubt if there is anyone who doesn't know." He casually glanced up and down the aisle once again. "So tell me, which one of these lovely young ladies is my Watcher?"

"That's confidential, Fitz. We Watchers don't make public announcements to Immortals," he retorted a bit sarcastically.

"Well then," and he slipped out of his seat, "since I don't know which one it is, I'd better bring them all up to speed with my exploits." He started down the aisle then turned back briefly. "Joe, you did say this was a twelve hour flight? I hope so, because there are a lot of women back there. My entire years of exploits—I'd better trim a few centuries off if I want to make the rounds, as it were – or maybe, to save time, I should just make an *immortal announcement,*" and he made as if to grab the intercom.

Joe buried his face in his hands.

Smiling sheepishly, Fitz relented. "Don't worry, Joe – just putting you on and all. I'll be discreet of course." He moved energetically to follow the young stewardess who had just passed their position.

Joe groaned and sank further into his seat. *Does he ever give it a rest?* Trouble was he knew Fitz was right. Joe had gotten this immortal gang booked onto a charter flight, one where a number of people on board were either a Watcher or a Watcher's Council member, retired or present, in some capacity. True, almost everyone, with few exceptions, was ultimately heading back to the Watcher's Academy in Switzerland. Quickly he made a few notes about Fitz – conveniently leaving out the part about being recognized as a Watcher – then, switching off his reading light, he laid his head back to rest. Other than to visit the bathroom, he doubted if Duncan and his party were going anywhere off this plane at 40,000-feet. A snarky thought crossed his mind briefly as his brow furrowed. *He is after all an Immortal. If he chose to take a walk outside, that 40,000-foot first step wouldn't really be a lasting issue for him.* Silently he reprimanded himself for that nonsense. He had been awake too long.

Duncan flipped the page back and rubbed his eyes. What had he just read? Was he really that tired, or had his thoughts been wandering? He glanced over to Tessa, peacefully lying beside him and carefully pulled the blanket completely around her back. She had had no trouble falling asleep in these newly renovated airplane seats. He was glad. Considering all that had happened over the past three weeks, he was having trouble falling asleep himself.

No, his mind had not been sleeping; it had been turning over the events of the past weeks. One of the many thoughts still plaguing him was this business of the renegade Hunter-Watchers. He had tried to convince himself that with Horton's death this had ended. But with the incident involving Wolf and Mark, it was obvious that there was more than one cockroach left in that vile nest Horton had created. He silently hoped he wouldn't have to deal with it further, but something wasn't letting the thought go. *What if,* his mind began all over again, *seriously, what if Horton wasn't really dead? What if he was like a cat, with nine lives? A zombie? What if—*
He shook himself to break the train of thought. Horton was mortal. He had killed him that night in the warehouse. True – I also died and when I came back everyone and everything was gone, but I had mortally wounded him before I went down. He exhaled and switched off his reading lamp. Change the subject, Duncan, he told himself.

Married—this was a big step for him in his 400 plus years of life and he turned his mind to those married mortals he had known and what they had felt was important at various stages of their lives together.

Stability—*first make a secure home, one that is surrounded with love and financial security. These first two weren't going to be issues. We will would start out with the barge—maybe build a house, maybe buy a condo, maybe rent. There was time enough to decide—later, though.*

Pursuing a career—now that we are on the verge of the twenty-first century, Tessa might want both of us to explore one or more different professions. He pondered several options. *There is any number of things that I could be. I could adapt one of my older trades to a today's industry, or I could try my hand at something completely new. I have never been afraid of trying new things in each lifetime. Tessa, on the other hand, has always been involved in the art industry— either as an artist or as a gallery curator. I can't see her giving that up entirely. Will she want to make a change and if so to do what?* This thought sent a little ripple of excitement through him. The thought of embarking on a new adventure by Tessa's side was a whole new concept in his life. He had always embarked on his own adventures alone. Here was a woman who had long ago indicated clear objectives—recently those personality traits had intensified. He doubted seriously that Tessa would be content to simply sit by a potter's wheel and give random art shows anymore. No, something else was brewing in her life and he too was beginning to catch fire with her new found excitement.

Children—almost all my mortal families and friends wanted children in their lives. His thoughts ground to a halt. Both of them had discussed the subject. An Immortal was sterile. The only way children could enter into their lives was with medical help or by adoption. However Tessa had given him no indication that she was willing to give up her personal freedom by adopting. Could he? A child would become an adult, ultimately Duncan would bury him or her. *Does that make them a burden? No, not if it is ultimately what we both want. The child will simply be taught about Immortals and the Game.* This repeating thought surfaced once again. *Would I be fair to that other human being by bringing them into a dangerous situation, in proximity to myself?* The words of Ceirdwyn – a woman who had married a young man, lived fifteen happy years, finally losing her husband in a random act of violence, came to mind.

"They're not children, Duncan. They can make up their own minds. If there is love in your heart, don't push the one you love away, don't make that choice for them."

OK, I promise I won't make that choice for another. Look at Tessa and me. If she truly wants children I won't stand in her way. You know, I think it would actually be fun to have someone grow up—and yes, grow old in my company—someone who was calling me Dad.

And what else, he pondered, *is a mortal family concerned with as they go through life?*

The end of life, his subconscious mind reminded him. He closed his eyes and leaned back against the seat. *Yes, I know what Tessa would want me to do— what I have to do.*

"You're not asleep, are you, laddie?" Fitz's insistent hand on his shoulder nearly caused him to jump.

"I was just resting my eyes. Where are you sitting?"

"Over there, back a ways—right behind Joe. Duncan," and he leaned in close. "Did you know this plane is infested with Watchers?"

Well that explained all the stares he and his party were getting when they first boarded. "Why am I not surprised?" He commented retrieving the paper from his lap. "Fitz, Joe got us this flight, literally out of nowhere. Richie had tried for more than an hour, with all the major airlines, to book us for that night, or the next day for that matter. Joe got us on a flight, at a bargain price, in just forty-eight-hours after placing one call." Casually Duncan looked around. The immediate cabin area was quiet, few people were standing and even fewer were moving about. No one appeared to be paying either of them any attention.

"Well, I just want to let you know that there are more tattoos on more wrists, with something pulled almost over them than you could ever imagine. I've made the rounds with all these women."

"All the women on this flight?" Duncan's eyes opened noticeably and he took another deep breath. "Why am I also not surprised to hear that?" he emphasized.

"Dear boy, I'm not one to let moss grow under my feet where there are beautiful women."

"Everyone, Fitz?"

"Well, there are a few who are—and Fitz gestured *so-so* with a wave of his hand. "But I don't fault them. Not everyone can look flawless. Besides, they all have charming personalities and look," Fitz pulled out his pocket notebook. "I have so many phone numbers now. I should be busy for weeks."

Why am I really not surprised, Duncan thought, returning his attention to his paper and trying real hard to ignore Fitz.

Joe was dozing lightly when he *felt* a presence near him. Raising his head slightly he opened an eye. His Watcher's notebook, which he had inadvertently left in his lap, was now in Fitz's hands.

"Hey!" he exclaimed, a bit louder than he had planned. "That's official business in there. What are you doing?"

Fitz flipped another page. "Checking it for accuracy." He closed the book on his finger. "And let me say that you have a lot of holes in this story."

Joe pulled the book smartly off his finger. "And just how would you know?"

"Because I've been watching up close—you have been watching," and he waved his hand *out and away*, "from who knows where. There is a big difference in perspective and interpretation."

"For instance?" Joe asked, a bit intrigued by the opportunity to gain another Immortal's personal perspective.

Fitz slipped the book out of Joe's hands before he could protest. "For instance, let's step back a number of days to right here." Flipping the pages back to a spot, he placed the book firmly in Joe's lap and pointed. "It's what happened between us at the café. You have the basics, but that's not what it was about. You weren't sitting there listening, I was. If all your chronicles are this full of holes, I can easily see why I could be interpreted as anything between Don Juan to Attila the Hun. Let me tell you what really happened that day between Duncan and me." Fitz settled in and began an uninterrupted, blow by blow, account of the cafe discussion regarding Tessa's ordeal—told from a Fitz perspective—for the next four hours of the flight.

In self-defense, Joe finally fell asleep. He awoke when the flight attendant announced they would soon be landing at the Schiphol-Amsterdam Airport. Fitz was still beside him, now writing with gusto. "Now what are you doing with my book?" Joe asked as he recognized what he was writing in.

Fitz closed the Watcher's notebook. "I'm finishing the story the way it's supposed to be—the way it really was. Here," and he handed it back. "You'll just have to patch in with more of your distant observations—I ran out of room in this book—unless you've got another on you?"

Oh God! Joe thought. *The book was almost empty. He must have recorded every breath he took.* He paused then brightened. *When have Watchers had a first-hand account written for them?* He couldn't wait to start reading this novel when it suddenly dawned on him – *I have no paper left for when we de-plane, damn!*

Schiphol was alive with activity when their flight pulled in. As soon as he located the connecting flight to Paris from the board, Joe made straight for the nearest stationary shop and restocked his supply of note paper. *Let's see Fitz fill these pages on the next leg of this flight,* Joe mused as he pocketed the notepads. Casually he began looking around. It wasn't long before he spotted his troupe of Immortals.

A woman stepped away from one of the flight monitors and passing Joe's position gave a nod. When he didn't respond in kind, she pulled out a brochure from her jacket pocket and walked up to him. "Joe?" Claire said, breaking his train of thought. Holding up the brochure, she made as if she were asking directions. "I got your message and the Immortal's photos. Where is he?"

Joe casually motioned to Richie, who was perusing the magazine stand in a vendor's storefront. "Richie Ryan—a very new Immortal—about two weeks ago."

"And he isn't dangerous?"

Joe shook his head. "The most 'dangerous' thing he's done so far—as a mortal that is—is steal hubcaps off of cars. He's been in juvie several times. Nothing else, no violence. After he broke into Duncan and Tessa's antique store, a couple of years ago, he has been on the straight. Duncan and Tessa have seen to that. He's been growing up, so to speak, in a home with values. They both treat him as family. Tessa seems to see him as a younger brother, or at least that's the impression I have gotten from my observations. I don't know what will happen after the wedding, probably nothing for the immediate foreseeable future. He hasn't learned to defend himself yet so he will likely stay close to MacLeod, who intends to train him."

Claire nodded. "I've read your report on his history. I'll take him from here." She moved off casually, eventually wandering back and ending up at the same paper stand as Richie. Seeing Richie was engrossed in a Motorcycle Magazine, she thumbed through the magazines on the rack next to him, casually exchanging a few words with Richie as she pretended to look for several titles.

Joe turned his attention from Richie to where he last saw Duncan and Fitz. Sandra Ficke, Fitz's regular Watcher, had been held up in the States and she had missed the flight. *No matter,* thought Joe, *I can keep an eye on him too for a day or two until she arrives in Paris. Besides, with Duncan and Tessa making wedding plans, I suspect Fitz intends to be fully involved—at least in the beginning. He won't stray far.* He walked past Fitz's position discreetly and followed after Duncan.

"Hey Joe," Tessa called as she came quickly up from behind, startling him. "That was a good flight. I slept almost as good as in my own bed." She casually slipped a hand around his free arm momentarily. "The next time we need to travel, I will be sure to consult Duncan's *'travel agent'* again," she said a bit facetiously.

Joe smiled and shook his head once. *So much for me being discreet,* he thought. "I got lucky. I'm usually no better than Richie when it comes to booking a trip," he replied, trying to make it all sound casual and genuine. *Would you please leave me before Duncan starts looking for you,* he wished silently.

"Then I'll just say, thank you," she finished with a smile, releasing him. Something in a shop next to her position caught her eye and she wandered over to look.

Duncan had slowly been wandering up the corridor past the myriad of shops and cafes on the way toward their connecting flight when he abruptly halted. Some distance behind him, Joe stopped as well and turned toward a store's display.

Out of a lounge-bar stepped a man with medium olive-colored skin and collar-length dark, almost straight hair. Joe noted he was wearing a very formal business suit and carrying a thin briefcase. Slowly Joe moved up the side of the hallway, near a confectionary stand, to watch the exchange. There were no shops any closer to their position and he was still too far away to hear what was being said clearly with the ambient noise level of the shops and foot-traffic. He also noted that Tessa had been casually ambling after him as well. She was almost standing next to him again. Silently he wished Tessa would go somewhere else. It was impossible for him to move closer. He also knew he wouldn't remain unnoticed for very long with Tessa nearby. Sooner or later MacLeod would look for her.

I don't recognize the businessman and I can't say I ever remember MacLeod meeting with someone who even resembled him during the time I've been his Watcher, he thought as he searched his memory. He considered Tessa once again. *Maybe this situation can work to my advantage.* As casually as he could, he turned back to her and, without giving the question any great significance, asked, "Duncan seems to know that businessman—do you?"

She focused on the pair then shook her head once. "I've never seen him before, Joe." Tessa watched their exchange briefly then took a couple of steps to join them. As she did, a strange feeling began creeping into her. There was something that felt familiar about this stranger whom she had certainly never met—and whatever it was, it was becoming *uncomfortable.* She stopped dead in mid-step.

Joe noted the subtle events as they happened but couldn't glean any more information from anything. When their encounter appeared as if it were about to break up, Joe quietly moved away from the immediate area. As he did, Duncan turned away from the man and seeing Tessa, rejoined her. A moment later they grabbed Richie and continued along to the departure gate without stopping. Joe checked his watch—there was more than enough time before departure. *Who did Duncan meet and what was it about?*

As Claire was passing him, he stopped her. "Have you ever seen that man? MacLeod seemed to know him, but I've never seen him before."

"That's Kawill—Kawill Rockford these days—he's an Immortal from South America. He reinvented himself again about fifty-years or so ago."

Joe mentally flipped back through Duncan's chronicle but couldn't place him. "Was this a chance meeting, or is there a connection here? What's his line of work?"

Claire turned a few thoughts over before she spoke. "I think this was a chance meeting, Joe. I've never been Kawill's Watcher, though. His work is brokering antiquity art—specifically Aztec, Inca, and Maya antiquity. He doesn't get out much on this side of the planet, travels mostly in Mexico and South America – when he isn't in New York that is. Did you hear anything of their conversation?"

He shook his head. "Too much noise around theses bars and shops. Whatever it was about, they weren't loud." *I know Mac has a habit of acquiring art from far-flung places. I wonder if he is one of the dealers he has used in the past. If so, they've been working exclusively by phone all these years,* he considered. He shrugged and mentally made a note to consult the Watcher's database regarding Kawill and when he may have come into contact with Duncan.

Paula Roca, the Watcher academy's latest graduate was waiting for Joe in the departure lounge. After MacLeod and his troupe boarded, Joe briefly took her aside and told her where to meet him after they deplaned in Paris. He couldn't risk briefing her on the airplane. Once they had arrived he would orient her for a field assignment.

"What?" she exclaimed. "I've been training for a desk job. I've never even considered working with an Immortal," she finished at a whisper. "My instructor has given me references for the research division. No one said anything about field assignment after graduation," she finished, her eyes widening, a distinct hint of fear in her voice. "I understood I would get to do what I loved – research in paleoanthropology, or something similar along those lines in this organization."

Joe nodded, halting her discussion as the desk attendant called for all rows to board. "I have a suspicion about something and I'm playing a hunch, Paula. Let's call this a potential practice exercise only—I'll explain later."

"Who was that businessman? You seemed to know him," Tessa asked as they were boarding.

"He is an antique broker and yes, I do know him." He was silent for a long moment before he spoke again. "I consider him a cultural thief. He mines art from one culture—various periods in a civilization's history and sells it to the highest bidder, away from the people to whom it belongs."

"Is he doing something illegal," Tessa asked, concern coloring her voice.

"No, not according to the law. Ethically reprehensible, I believe. A people, a civilization, should be the keepers of their own antiquity. It's their national treasure he is selling. He has no respect for them."

Tessa fell silent briefly. Her voice took on a very serious tone the next time she spoke. "Was he an Immortal?" she whispered as they neared the airplane doorway.

Duncan nodded '*Yes*', then considered her question further. "Why do you ask?"

She thought about her reply for an even longer moment before speaking. "Duncan, I got a very bad feeling about him."

"Nothing could possibly happen between us in the airport, sweetheart," he replied at the level of a stage whisper now that they were in the airplane.

She closed her eyes and shook her head once. "That's not what I was suggesting. I *felt* that there was something very familiar and very bad about him somehow. What kind of cultural art does he mine?"

"Mexican and South American art treasures from the past."

Tessa shrugged. "Why these cultures?"

"His ancestry – he is a descendent of the Olmec civilization. They were forerunners of the Mesoamerica cultures – Maya, Aztec, Inca and—" Duncan's speech halted as a red flag went up in the back of his memory. He turned sharply in his seat toward her, the question framed in his expression.

Tessa wore the answer on her face. *My drawing—the figure on the temple steps—it's him!*

Chapter Thirty-three

Standing on the sidewalk above the Seine, Joe raised the Dictaphone to his mouth, shielding the microphone from the Paris breeze.

"Duncan, Tessa, and Richie have settled in to the barge. MacLeod now has a neighbor, Maurice Lalonde. He moved his barge next to Duncan's while Duncan was State-side. From what I can gather, they've spoken on the phone and he has been seeing to some minor upkeep on Duncan's barge while he has been away." He paused as a string of motorcycles passed his position.

"Wedding plans are underway. Duncan has been making some of the regular wedding-related inquiries around the city – photographic shops, cafés, and caterers. Tessa appears to be the main planner for this event, though. Several people have been coming and going for the past week. My assistant has done a little checking and they all appear to have been attending the Sorbonne at the same time as Tessa did."

He paused as Duncan and Richie came on deck. Joe inched closer to one of the sidewalk trees, his gray-brown overcoat blending in with the drab bark and bushes coloring. It was doubtful that Duncan and Richie would have any reason to look up to street level and almost a block away from their position, to see him. He was mortal and there was nothing special about him to sense. But Joe was a professional Watcher and he wasn't going to be an obvious person of interest for them either. Besides, his oath demanded that he *Observe and Record* in secrecy. *Well,* he thought. *I'll do that most of the time—when it is convenient.*

There were any number of casual passersby on the sidewalk around him this beautiful Paris mid-morning and he knew he didn't have to try and keep up with the spunky duo—not with Claire now taking on Richie as his Watcher. Joe considered what he saw. *Likely going off again to train in the same place. Claire's last report said Richie was quickly making progress with his practice sword. He even managed to disarm MacLeod once.* Watching them walk to Duncan's car, Joe considered Claire's latest report.

Claire sat quietly with her Dictaphone by a stand of tall trees on the upper bank. She raised her binoculars to her eyes once again. She was almost a block away from the clearing, by an expanse of water, where MacLeod and Richie were training.

I'm far enough away that they won't hear my whispering into this mike, she assured herself. *"MacLeod is guiding Richie through the basic moves. He is a very patient teacher. Richie appears to be focusing as MacLeod shows Richie various sword-fighting stances in slow motion: en garde, attack, defense. Richie is mirroring his moves."*

She paused. The wind was in the right direction—toward her. It was carrying bits of their conversation to her ears. She strained to hear between the rustling branches. When the breeze abated, Claire sat back against the trees. Her muscles were sore and it dawned on her that she must have been squatting—no, balancing on the very edge of her toes to hear them. She considered what she had been watching for the past few days. Richie had barely been able to hold his sword correctly—shaking and out of breath by the end of their first lesson. It wasn't a full week and he had come a long way from falling on his ass during a simple swing to disarming MacLeod.

Claire switched on her Dictaphone and added a few brief comments. "From what I've observed with other Immortals, it takes a tremendous physical commitment to use a sword well. If Richie continues to learn at this speed, he might actually have a chance at long-term survival."

The midday smells of French cuisine being prepared by the many street vendors up the way began vying for Joe's attention. The area around the barge was quiet. Tessa was obviously hard at work on some aspect of wedding planning inside. His attention was fighting a losing battle between his Watcher's job and the smell of the food. He shrugged. Lunch was calling his mortal stomach. He turned from his post by the tree just as his cell phone rang. It was Watcher Sylvia Krause.

"Immortal Sean Burns will be on his way to Paris within the week. He received a call from MacLeod sometime yesterday and he has been speaking of the wedding and nothing else to the entire staff at the University."

Joe acknowledged the call from his European Watcher colleague then headed for one of the vender's stands. He was in the middle of his lunch when the phone sounded again. *Can't a man get a decent bite to eat without a report from somewhere about someone,* Joe grumbled and washed what he was chewing down fast. It was Watcher, Jeanette Fallon from State-side.

"Joe, I just want to give you a heads-up. Grace Chandel is leaving for Paris by the end of the week. She spoke to the director yesterday about transferring her duty shift to one of the other physicians on the

floor for about two weeks or so. She told him she was helping a friend out who was getting married. This is MacLeod—right?"

Joe acknowledged her information and told her they would compare notes when she arrived, following Grace. He hung up and dug back into his lunch. He was filling his glass when his phone sounded again. He closed his eyes momentarily. *I didn't hear that,* he thought as he re-corked the bottle—the next ring confirmed his suspicion. *Oh, yes I did.*

Ceirdwyn's Watcher, Debra Adkins, was calling with more of the same news. She had not heard about the MacLeod wedding and was surprised when her Immortal broke the news to the office. *"And she is planning to use all her vacation time. Joe, what is happening over there? A wedding is only a day-thing—not a two or three-week ordeal."*

Joe couldn't offer an explanation for the protracted stays he had been hearing about today. He ventured a guess that they were going to have an immortal celebration—perhaps? He hung up and was about to pocket the phone when he thought better of that and laid it on the stand next to his wine glass. In the middle of a sip, his phone sounded again. *How many Immortals are going to attend this wedding?* He wondered as he answered the call. This time, it was Cassandra's Watcher, Melanie Hind—same story. Closing his cell phone, Joe seriously considered asking the Watcher's council in Paris to reserve an entire hotel. There were going to be Watchers from everywhere, all converging on this wedding.

His fork was buried in a large slice of soft and aromatic cheesecake when his phone sounded yet again. Watcher, Rebecca Running Bear just learned of the MacLeod wedding from her Immortal, Coltec's conversation.

"Let me guess—he will be arriving within a week," Joe said almost as if he were reading a script. "No, I didn't read your mind. You're the fifth caller in the last hour. This is shaping up to be an immortal conclave."

"Or a Gathering. Joe, what's really going on? Immortals don't come together in any numbers," she reminded him with a touch of foreboding in her voice. *"Is this it?"*

"Come on, it's just a wedding," Joe replied, but even he was starting to wonder. *No, he hadn't heard of Immortals associating in significant numbers. Could it be that this wedding was really just a front for the beginning of their fateful and final Gathering?* Joe blinked—he couldn't believe he just thought of that. *MacLeod, consciously or unconsciously, initiating their Gathering with this event? If there was any truth to this suspicion, Joe wanted a front row seat—him and all the other Watchers as well,* he thought. Suddenly, that train of thought came to a screaming halt.

The final Gathering was rumored, amongst Watchers, to be an event of sheer bloody mass mayhem, with every Immortal after each other's head—certainly not a joyous celebration of love, as a wedding is supposed to be. The amount of power released and absorbed from every Immortal, in every direction, would make that site literally *Ground Zero.* Was he really so sure he wanted a front row seat to an atom-bomb explosion?

Stop it, Joe, this is silly, he told himself again. *It's a wedding—Duncan and Tessa have invited a couple of friend—nothing else. Stop imagining things.* His thoughts turned to Tessa. *What excuse can I use to see where she is with invitations? More importantly, how can I get one?*

Chapter Thirty-four

Tessa took out her pocket notepad and scratched a line through another number on her wedding list. *Another one down,* she thought, smiling to herself. *Only an infinite number of tasks left to complete. I never realized that getting ready to say 'I do' entailed crossing off so many 'I dids'.* She was at the flower shop. The beautiful buds and blooms were eye candy, filling the air with the most delightful aroma. She had come with an idea of simplicity for her wedding bouquet but was having second thoughts. *What would Duncan like to see?* As far as she could ever remember, he was rather terrible at picking out flowers or making arrangements. He preferred to leave that detail to a floral shop. He would just buy them.

She shrugged. She wasn't the floral genius either. She only knew that for her wedding, she wanted something simple and lovely to show up and accent her light pink dress. She was filling out the floral caterer forms when a modest size, rather unusual arrangement caught her eye. Walking to the thin, flat rectangular vase, she pondered the arrangement of partially submerged calla lilies shaped in a near perfect semi-circle and wondered what the artist was trying to say. *A wave? A spray from an ocean swell? A spiral? A circle or a cycle of something? If so, to what end?* There was something almost literally drawing this arrangement into her hands. Of all the others in the shop, this was almost completely out of place.

"Excuse me," she asked as an attendant passed her position. "Who made this? What is it supposed to mean?"

The assistant shrugged. "It was brought in by our delivery service. We usually make our own arrangements here, but we do have another designer helping from another location, on occasions. Do you like it?" she asked.

"I just know I want it. There is a place waiting for it," she replied enigmatically, her eyes never leaving the arrangement.

The attendant quickly paper wrapped the arrangement in floral tissue for her.

Suddenly, Tessa blinked as the shops across the street registered in her field of view. She was suddenly standing on the sidewalk outside the shop with this strange arrangement wrapped in floral paper in her hands. To Tessa, it was as if no time had elapsed between when she picked up the vase in the shop and this moment. *How can that be? I recall speaking with the assistant and paying for the purchase, having it wrapped, then—,* she pondered. Her thoughts ground to a halt.

"*Why are you pondering what is truly unimportant, just go,*" the insistent mental reply came.

Go where? She asked the inner voice. As if in reply she just started walking.

The shops, the cafés all became an unimportant blur as she walked on. She didn't feel lost—somehow she instinctively felt as if she knew where she was heading. She knew she wanted to arrive somewhere, but where? Around the corner and down the block—block after block—there was urgency building in her steps.

"*Don't you know where you're going? Haven't you always known where you have needed to be for so long?*" that inner voice reminded her. The sign came into view—the Paris city cemetery. She stopped by the gate. *Yes, I really did know,* she thought resolutely to herself. *And there is someone, someplace, waiting for this and yes, it is long overdue.*

Her feet took her through the gate without further hesitation – straight to Ana's grave. The feeling welling up inside her was not one of sorrow or recrimination, but one of finally achieving closure. *I've come to my dearest friend's last resting place—for her mortal remains—with something she would have found very special.* Tessa knelt beside the headstone and positioned the vase so that it complimented the weathering stone.

I know you would have found this arrangement as avant-garde, as I did in the shop today and taken it home. She knew the flowers were ephemeral, as was she, but somehow that didn't matter. She would enjoy what they had to offer the eye and heart, right here and now. She had lived between the seconds once before, tipping the balance of life and death, and changing an outcome of a place, a time, and an event, for all eternity. Somehow, there was an amazing amount of power in that ability and she held on to it fiercely. She would exist with the living memory of Ana here and now, between the seconds, which had the power to stretch out for almost an eternity. *If you can feel, experience, live—every infinitesimal instant between two seconds with your whole being, time for you will become infinite.*

"*Don't you really mean your existence will be immortal?*" that small inner voice prodded.

Tessa's smile radiated inward toward her small, inner voice, offering it a quiet reassurance. The time thief was truly no more—she didn't need to answer.

Chapter Thirty-five

Joe watched as Duncan left the cemetery administrative building with a card in his hand. He followed at a very discreet distance as Duncan walked slowly up a long row, past the many varied headstones and slabs that decorated what seemed to him like innumerable graves in this city cemetery.

Joe pondered what this must all mean to an Immortal—to someone who cannot die. *How many times throughout history has this man visited the graves of people with whom he ate, laughed and shared camaraderie? How many of these people were his yesterday friends? When he's standing before their final resting places, how does he find a place within himself to set these sorrows aside so he can remember only the joys he shared and not their ends?* Lowering his eyes, he shook his head. *It was Vietnam in the mid 60's—a fair chunk of my lifetime away from today's 90's. I lost a couple of good friends – for nothing and over nothing. I don't need to stand by their graves to remember how we made each other laugh, to remember their faces – hell, I can't stop seeing their faces now. What's it like for someone who's seen that and done that for more than eight life times? I almost put a gun to my head after my last active day in Nam – the day my legs exploded along with that mine. How does he keep his sanity seeing what he's seen and knowing that putting a bullet through his brains will only give him a headache?*

Duncan slowed as he entered a newer section and appeared to be searching for a marker, a name, something.

Joe halted and stepped to the side of a large grave marker. As a Watcher, he had sworn to observe and record in secrecy, but his actions now had little to do with his oath and everything to do with ethics. To him, Duncan MacLeod wasn't simply an assignment—an object to be hauled out of a case and studied. This was a man, a human being. Time and time again, throughout his history, he had shown an amazing amount of compassion for mortal man—he deserved to be treated the same.

After some careful searching Duncan finally stopped, straightened and stood in silence. A light breeze was blowing this cloudy Paris morning and it seemed to be a perfect backdrop to his somber frame of mind. By and by, the breeze caught the few un-captured strands of his highlander's hair and played them out in the wind.

Who is he considering? What is he remembering? Joe pondered. He had already noted the date and time Duncan had entered the cemetery. There was simply nothing else he could add standing a ways off, as he was. A Watcher didn't speak to their immortal assignment the way he had spoken to MacLeod and Joe hoped that today he could do the same.

How does a man simply walk up to another who is looking down at a grave and ask him, "What's in your soul?" Joe took his courage in hand and walked slowly to Duncan. He stopped an arms-length beside him. When Duncan did not look up, Joe looked down. For a brief moment, he deeply regretted disturbing this man's privacy. *Damn my Watcher's curiosity,* he swore silently to himself. *Would I have done this to him if he wasn't an Immortal?* He already knew the answer before his thoughts were finished.

As Joe focused on only undisturbed earth in that marked out zone, it occurred to him that there was no one buried there.

"Expecting someone soon?" he asked. It was really a misspoken thought at best and insensitive at worst. He gritted his teeth for what he knew MacLeod had every right to throw at him for it.

But Duncan stood unmoved. "No, not today—hopefully not for a very, very long time to come. This one is for Tessa," he motioned to a small space on the left of the marked plot. "And that one, Joe, is mine." He looked up and into the eyes of his Watcher.

Joe braced as if he were careening out of control into a brick wall. It was the last thing he ever expected to hear from a man who had lived 400 plus years and could not die a natural death. He stood there aghast, unable to give a reply.

"Are you ready to call it quits on life?" he finally asked, very quietly.

"No," Duncan said. "I'm not planning to put you out of a job," he added, in a lighter tone. He turned back to the marked ground. "You know we're all living a lie, don't you? Immortals that is—that's what we call ourselves. Truth is Joe, you and all the other Watchers over the millenniums have been wasting their time watching these people called Immortals. Do you know Tessa told me the truth – what I really am? I'm just a mortal with, *limited options for death.* And you know something, she's right. There really is no such thing as physical immortality. I have an Achilles' Heel. All that has to happen is for me to lose my head. I'm going to die someday, I know it – and it will be no different for me than for Tessa, or you. Dead is still dead no matter how you finally achieve it. We are more alike than you realize, Joe, then I ever did." He paused and looked away briefly.

"I am about to become a married man. I have known many good people, who have given me many fine examples in my life, of what it takes to make a good union between a man and a woman. Three of the most important things are: consideration, stability and responsibility. If I die before Tessa, she would want to know where I – my mortal remains are. I don't plan to leave that decision to her at a time when she surely won't need it." He shook his head once, knowingly.

"I never realized what a strong woman she really is. Even so, it's no reason for me to avoid obvious responsibilities to her in life."

Joe thought a moment in silence, before placing a hand on Duncan's arm in solidarity.

"Immortals' existence gave me a reason to live when I was ready to put a bullet in my head." He motioned absently with the end of his cane to his two prosthetic legs. "I don't really care how you want to define an Immortal. The fact remains that seeing a person with *limited options for death* was a good enough excuse for Ammaletu the Akkadian to found the Watchers more than 4,000 plus years ago. It's my life's work now and my time to waste, Duncan – if you want to call it that. Come on, you've done your duty well for today." He tugged at Duncan's arm. "Let's go pick up Tessa, Richie and Fitz and head over to a pub that I think is truly noteworthy. I haven't had the opportunity to properly congratulate you yet on your upcoming wedding."

"Richie, I think I just saw the courier car pull up. Would you go check to see if there is a box for me?"

Richie bounced up the steps of the barge and out across the deck. He was back in no time with two shoe box size boxes. "Is this about what you expected, Tess?"

"Perfect!" She exclaimed and relieved him of one of the boxes. Setting hers down she tore into the packing. "Oh Richie, will you look at this. They're absolutely beautiful." She held up a beautifully printed wedding announcement with its accompanying RSVP and specially embossed linen envelope.

A taxi pulled slowly up to where the delivery car had been parked. A single occupant got out then retrieved a long object from the trunk. A moment later, the car drove off.

"Yeah, Wow," Richie exclaimed and held the announcement up to view. The finely detailed script stood out, crisp and bold. "What do I say here? They really do look great. This is almost – well – artwork in itself." He pondered a moment at the second box under his arm. "Tess, you're planning to invite this many people?" he said, motioning to both boxes. "Some of them probably have husbands and wives. Where are you planning to put all the people? They won't all fit on the deck of this barge? We'll have to rent a tugboat or two," he finished, grinning.

Tessa gave him a wide-eyed stare and nodded. "Of course there will be a number of husbands and wives that will attend too. Don't worry. We have options in mind for places to hold a reception. We don't have a restriction on the number of family members who can attend."

"What if some of them can't make it for the big day?"

She set the open box aside and reached for the next one under Richie's arm. "We have already arranged alternate days for our friends who can't make it to the wedding. This RSVP was specially printed with options."

"Smart," Richie replied. His Immortal's senses suddenly detected the presence of another Immortal approaching.

"Mac!" he shouted through the partially open porthole. "You've just got to come and see these wedding announcements." He bolted up to the top of the steps and pushed the door opened. "Mac, they just came in and –"

It wasn't MacLeod.

Joe let Duncan guess for a while as to where they might find the amorous Fitz before he quietly called Fitz's Watcher to get his position. Duncan was wrong in all three guesses. Joe and Duncan both drove to the area and parked. Joe asked Duncan to get him alone. He couldn't risk being seen together with him knowing Fitz's Watcher was here—somewhere. When pressed for details, Joe refused to go into the Watcher's Oath. He simply said there would be grave consequences for him if he was seen flagrantly violating that oath of secrecy.

Duncan shrugged. That cloak and dagger secrecy stuff made no sense to him.

Joe shrugged also then reminded him that all Immortals were not safe to work around and mortals have only one life.

"Besides, if we all interfered or became involved with you Immortals, as I am doing now with you, it could change the entire immortal history."

Duncan didn't respond. He simply walked to where Joe told him Fitz was. He had also said Fitz wouldn't be alone – naturally, he was with a couple of young women he had happened to meet by the Seine.

As soon as Duncan left, Joe called Fitz's Watcher and sent her off on an errand. Joe promised to keep tabs on Fitz while she was away.

Fitz, mandolin in hand, was doing his very best to entertain a couple of young female Italian tourists. He had apparently mastered a few chords and was improvising on an Italian love song, much to the delight of the two girls he was serenading.

Duncan waited until Fitz sounded like whatever he was half singing half speaking was about to come to an end before he walked up beside him. "Bravo Maestro," he said in a dubiously serious tone.

Fitz made an English bow then clearing his throat, he attempted yet another phrase in broken Italian. "Thank you signore belle. Il tuo apprezzamento del mio modesto talento è più gentile" (*Thank you, lovely ladies. Your appreciation of my humble talent is most gracious*). Amidst giggles and applause from his young admirers, Fitz readied himself to strike another chord. "Lasciare il mio modesto talento per trovare il vostro favore, ancora una volta" (*Allow my humble talent to find your favor once again*).

Duncan seriously doubted there was anything humble where Fitz was concerned. "Un momento" (one moment), Duncan quickly interrupted. "Fitz, Joe is taking us all out for a pre-wedding celebration. He thought you might like to join us."

"Oh, I would be delighted. Just let me excuse myself from my admirers." He turned to the two girls. "Perdonami, ma devo andare. Questa povera anima è il mio manager, e lui insiste condivido il mio talento con il resto del mondo," (Forgive me, but I must be off. This poor soul is my manager and he insists I share my talent with the rest of the world), he finished with the utmost sound of regret in his voice and handed the musical instrument back.

The reaction was immediate.

The girls gave a hearty laugh then exclaimed, "Oh, non ci lasciare adesso! Vogliamo sentire di più." (Oh, don't leave us now! We want to hear more), and leaping from their perches on the boulder, flung their arms around Fitz. Fitz attempted to gesture '*what's a person to do*'.

"As you can see my lovely fans just won't let me share my talent with the world just yet," he said with a big Cheshire cat grin on his face.

"Oh sure," replied Duncan with an exaggerated nod. "Do you want to come or don't you? I don't want to wait here until your entertainment style has run its course."

"I would like to leave, but these lovely young things won't understand if I go."

"Fitz, you're full of it." Then turning his comments to the women, said,

"I need to borrow Fitz for a small celebration this evening."

Fitz favored him with the oddest expression. "They don't understand a word of the King's English, dear boy."

"I seriously doubt that Fitz. This isn't the sixteenth-century is it ladies? You do understand me?"

Fitz was about to interject a comment when one of his lovely ladies spoke up.

"Of course we do."

"Well, why didn't you say something earlier then instead of letting me babble on?" Fits said, wide-eyed.

"Because you were so sweet and this was just too much fun," the other replied. Before Fitz could move, the girls quickly hugged him close, kissing him on both sides at the same time, leaving perfect red lipstick impressions on his cheeks. Releasing him, they giggled and walked briskly away.

Fitz threw up his hands. "Women, I'll never understand them and I'll never leave them alone."

"It figures, come on." And they headed back to where Joe and Duncan were parked.

Joe had also called Richie's Watcher and sent her off as well.

It was actually a short ride back, but Joe wanted to take Duncan by the pub first to make certain that this choice would be OK.

As Duncan and Fitz pulled into park by the barge, their immortal senses told them that there was another—no—two other Immortals present. Duncan switched off the car, all the while giving Fitz a puzzled look. Before either could get out of the car they saw Joe's attention rapidly shift toward the bow of the barge. Glancing back, once to his immortal companions with an urgent expression, he began walking with purpose toward the bow.

The moment Duncan opened his door, the all too familiar sound of metal on metal—sword to sword clashing—resonated in his ears. Reaching in the back seat, he retrieved his katana and hurried after Joe. Reaching his position, his ears took only microseconds to locate the source of that sound.

From their position they looked up at a steep angle – high above, on the bow of the barge, they could see Grace Chandel dodging, parrying, and swinging her sword with all the speed and force she could deliver on her aggressive attacker.

"Grace," Duncan gasped as he watched a woman, who had spent far more time saving mortal lives than she had practicing her own survival skills, in a fight to save her own immortal life. In a reflex action he bolted toward the gangplank then halted.

"You can't interfere, laddie," he heard Fitz remind him. "The battle is joined," Fitz finished as he approached, jockeying to get a better view of the action above.

Duncan silently cursed. The *immortal Rules of Combat,* no interference was allowed. Duncan bit his lip hard. No one ever violated this rule, no matter the consequences.

"If she loses her head Fitz, I swear, before her Quickening is absorbed I'll have whoever's head myself," he said with vengeance in his voice and he began pacing beneath the bow, trying to see her attacker.

Grace dodged yet another advance then advanced herself, slipping from their view momentarily only to reappear an instant later, seemingly on the verge of being forced off the boat and into the water.

Her attacker is aggressive and relentless, thought Duncan, fearful of the outcome against this gentle woman. *Who dared to issue a challenge to a guest right on the deck of my barge?* Duncan pondered in anger. Popping only partially into view now and again, Duncan saw a white jacket sleeve and a sword swinging on Grace. Fervently, he began wishing and whispering for her to fall into the Seine. This would officially end the battle and Duncan would take over her challenge and take his head fast. Desperately he watched her, subconsciously wishing for the telekinetic ability to throw her into the Seine himself.

Out of the corner of his eye he saw something on top of the barge's wheelhouse. It was Richie's head popping into view. Duncan blinked—was he seeing what he thought he was seeing? He focused, it was Richie, and from the little he could see of him, he appeared to be just sitting on top of the wheelhouse, watching. With Grace fighting, he had completely forgotten about him. *So why is Richie just sitting there as if he is watching a football game?* Duncan glanced back to Joe, with a most confused expression on his face. "How many Immortals do you sense up there," he asked without thinking.

Joe threw up his hands. "How would I know? Why are you asking me?"

Quickly he shook his head as if to clear some unseen cobweb from his immortal radar then quickly glanced to Fitz.

"Only two," Fitz replied with the same puzzled look on his face.

Duncan took only an instant to process a mental calculation. *OK, Richie isn't fighting, and Grace I can see—so why can't I sense the third Immortal?* Katana in hand, he crouched low and slipped up the gangplank as soon as Grace disappeared from view again.

They're on the other side of the wheelhouse, he thought. Raising his katana, he calculated their position then sprang around the corner.

As Grace and her attacker's blades collided and crossed once again, Duncan swiftly brought his blade crashing down on both of theirs together, binding and halting them.

"What is this—who are you?" he exclaimed, his voice a mixture of aggression and bewilderment. It was an instant later Duncan realized the attacker was masked—a fencing safety mask.

Lowering the blade, the attacker removed *her* mask—it was Tessa.

Duncan was speechless. He straightened abruptly and a moment later he lowered his blade.

"I don't believe a third person is allowed in standard saber-fencing," Tessa said brightly as she flipped her hair back, her rosy cheeks glistening with sweat.

"What?" he exclaimed staring first at Tessa then at Grace. "You later," he pointed to Tessa. "Grace—you now."

"Well, hello—nice to see you too, Duncan," she said reminding him, in an off-handed way, what he had forgotten to say.

During all of this, Fitz and Joe had been slowly, and cautiously, making their way up the gangplank. Now, with the rest of the story in front of their eyes, they both stood at the rail watching the exchange.

Oh don't look so shocked, Duncan, Fitz thought as he removed his pipe from his vest pocket and placed it between his teeth. *If you couldn't see the way the wind was blowing with your so-called helpless Tessa, back in your store that day, you truly are a dumb Scott. Oh – don't blame Grace. Better her than no one. You certainly wouldn't teach her, I'll wager and yes, she is going to learn to use a sword – and use it well. Truth be told, laddie, Tessa is going to be more involved in our immortal world than you would have ever imagined in your wildest dreams. That sixteenth-century Rapier is eventually going to be hauled out of retirement, if it hasn't been already,* Fitz pondered. *That reminds me, there is a question I've been meaning to ask the lovely Tessa.*

Joe watched Duncan take Grace aside. Though he spoke quietly, Duncan was obviously upset.

MacLeod is upset with Grace for the training exercise with Tessa. Obviously he wanted to be her only teacher, Joe reasoned, trying to justify Duncan's behavior. *I wonder if there is an Immortal's rule concerning the training of pre-Immortals. Come to think about it, I have never read any chronicle where a new Immortal has ever had more than one instructor. Hum? Tessa isn't an Immortal yet. Duncan would have sensed her and not asked me what he did. I wonder why he asked me at all?* Joe shook his head once. That bit of mystery would have to wait for another day. *Grace probably violated some rule of protocol by stepping on Duncan's toes. Duncan and Grace have been good friends for centuries. I don't think Duncan will fight her for her head because of her breach of protocol,* he calculated. *Interesting? First Richie turns up an Immortal and Tessa—who is obviously still mortal—has already killed once with a sword and is now obviously being trained. There is a lot of action around MacLeod that has blindsided me lately,* and he nodded to himself. *But, no longer. I've got a solution for that,* he mentally concluded. Once their social at the pub broke up, he had several phone calls to make.

"Grace, exactly what do you think you were doing with Tessa?"

"What did it look like, Duncan? These are fencing sabers," and she held up her blade. "I am teaching Tessa to saber-fence."

Duncan blinked several times. *Did I actually hear you say that?* his expression screamed. "Why? She is mortal."

Grace returned Duncan's awkward expression. "So? What does that have to do with anything? We Immortals aren't the only ones who learn to use a sword. It happens to be a worldwide sport."

Duncan favored her with a hard stare. "Grace, don't play word games with me now. I think you know what I am really saying here. Tessa beheaded a man with my sword a little over three weeks ago. We are Immortals, we kill with swords in any century. She is going to marry an Immortal; there will always be Immortals and swords all around her and throughout her world for her entire life. She is the odd woman here, Grace, she is mortal. Don't give her imagination the fuel to think, for even one moment, that she can compete on our level in our immortal Game."

Grace took a step backward and returned the hard stare. "I don't believe you just said that, Duncan MacLeod of the Clan MacLeod. If you truly believe that of Tessa—that this is all leading to some fantasy of hers, call off this wedding now, mister. You don't really know who you're marrying." She let her comment sink in. "Tessa is going to learn to use a sword—there is something inside driving her to do it. Whether it is because of the shooting incident, her visions, the confrontation with Mark, or something else I just can't put my finger on. She is determined to learn how to use a sword, however. I learned to saber-fence according to the original rules of the sport about eighty-years ago." She cocked her head, her expression softening somewhat. "Well, you aren't going to teach her. And I'm going to be here in Paris for three weeks. I've already arranged to be away. Don't worry, Duncan. She has a strong arm and a good sure swing. She needs practice to gain the skill and the stamina needed. I'll see her on the right path to learning before I leave. She can find a good fencing school here in the city, if she wishes to continue."

Duncan adjusted his stance and placed a gentle hand on Grace's arm. "I know what you are saying Grace, but there is a voice in the back of my head that is frightening me when I see this. I don't want to lose Tessa in a situation that is preventable." He paused and forced himself to say what was really on his mind. "I don't want her to go up against an Immortal for me. She would be killed. No matter what determination she has to learn, or inner fire that's fueling this urge, she is never going to be that good. Grace, you know that the Immortals who survive have had decades if not centuries of practice. Tessa will never have that."

"Are you really so certain that you know what Tessa can and can't do? Or is this whole sword thing becoming an issue—something that's just one step outside of your comfort zone with Tessa? Please, take my professional advice and take this new Tessa one phase at a time. Life will go on no matter what." She walked back to where she had laid her towel on the corner of the wheelhouse roof.

Duncan put a hand to his mouth and thought for a long moment. Glancing first to Richie, then to Grace and finally Tessa, he walked back to her and pausing, opened his mouth to speak. A hundred-and-one thoughts vied for his voice—a hundred-and-one concerns fought for space on his tongue; and yet, as he stared into the eyes of the person he was about to wed, a person who was dressed in full fencing attire, he remained speechless.

"I don't think I'm quite ready to take you on just yet," she said quietly, with a twinkle in her radiant eyes.

"You're not part of the Game," he whispered very softly. "Not now, not ever. Do you understand me?"

"Yes," she replied, still smiling. She turned back to join Grace.

Chapter Thirty-six

In an otherwise quiet Paris pub, glasses were raised in celebration of the upcoming wedding of Duncan and Tessa, with many additional toasts for a long and happy marriage.

"And an exciting one too, filled with lots of adventure," Tessa added as the last glass clink sounded.

"So, what are your future adventurous plans?" Grace asked as the waitress brought the appetizers.

Tessa set her glass down and gave a pensive stare at the bubbles as they rose.

"At this very moment in time, I don't know. I only know that I feel more alive now than I have ever felt. I'm ready for a change— something challenging and adventurous."

"Well, does that mean you are going to open your own public art gallery in Paris?" Fitz asked.

Tessa shook her head. "I have been an artist all my life. I was involved with an art gallery after the Sorbonne. I have sat at a potter's wheel long enough. I have fired, welded, sculpted and well – everything that's art. I have created so many beautiful things, but I need a break from myself in all of this. No, I don't want my existence to be defined by a workspace, by my workshop. I want to be more limitless. I just don't know how I want to achieve that yet."

"Do you plan to stay in Paris?" Joe asked, carefully trying to gain insight into where his Immortal might end up.

"For now," she replied. "I really want to explore this new me – find out who this new Mrs. Tessa MacLeod of the Clan MacLeod is going to be." She tossed her hair, her smiling eyes coming to rest on Duncan.

"It suddenly feels as if we just met, as if Duncan has just jumped into my life all over again. It's as if there was a final period at the end of our years together and now everything is new once again."

"That's normal. It's the expectations forward-thinking people have – when two people are really in love and are eagerly looking forward to a new chapter in their married lives, that is. The two of you have been together now—what, twelve years?" Grace paused and considered her next words. "For many people they may not think that there is any newness left in life. But you have had a very traumatic series of recent events. The feelings you are describing can be summed up as, *'I've died and come back to life – now I'm starting over'.*"

There was a distinct pause in the conversation after Grace's unspoken analogy to becoming an Immortal was given.

"Whatever you would like to try next in life, I just want you to know I am with you, you have my support," Duncan affirmed, breaking the silence.

"So, Mac, what are your plans?" Joe asked.

"Ask Tessa – my plans are her plans."

"I hope is one of them is seriously training me," Richie spoke up. "Unless you're sending me back to Amanda to be trained."

"Absolutely not, Richie," she exclaimed. "You are a part of our lives and always will be. You need to keep your head and it won't happen without Duncan's help."

"Hey, Tess thanks, but realistically, the two of you are getting married soon. Mac doesn't have a moment to think of me with all these plans you have. Then there's the honeymoon afterward. I doubt Mac here will want to be swinging a sword from your honeymoon bed."

"Don't worry about it, Richie. We'll start again—in earnest this time—tomorrow. I have just a few more things to arrange for the wedding and Tessa already has the rest finished. Besides, the wedding is still a week away."

"And that's closer than you think," Grace reminded Duncan. *Men—typical. They think they have all the time in the world to accomplish something. Then the day arrives and 'boom', it has to have been done yesterday and they are standing there with their hands full.* Grace gave her head a little shake and grinned. Something about men – mortal or immortal – never changes.

Joe glanced from Fitz to Richie, to Grace. His expression remained pleasant and with the spirit of the conversation, but his thoughts were troubled.

Grace was the wild card I didn't count on today. I sent both Richie's and Fitz's Watchers away so I wouldn't be seen socializing with Immortals. Grace's Watcher must have observed me at the barge. She could be trouble if I am reported to the head office. The penalty for breaking my oath of secrecy and consorting with Immortals is severe and could even earn me an execution. I am going to have to try to convince her and Jack Shapiro that I am here because I have known Tessa from whenever. I'll have to come up with something fast. In a few days there will be many more Watchers descending on this wedding. I'm really going to need a good alibi if I want to stay close. Dammit, Mac, why couldn't the two of you just elope!

During the lull in the conversation, Duncan reached into his pants pocket and pulled out a small wrapped box.

"Here you go, sweetheart. A little something I think would look lovely on you for our wedding."

Tessa carefully peeled away the paper so slowly, that even Duncan appeared to be on the verge of jumping in to help get it done. "I'm getting there," she said with an impish smile. "I just want to prolong the suspense."

"For us too," Fitz said as he leaned in giving the impression he was trying to see through the box's wrapping with x-ray vision.

Tessa finally peeled off the last shred of paper and opened the box. "Oh, it's lovely," she said softly and held up the necklace.

"It's a Celtic bridal love knot," Duncan said, filling in the details.

The beautiful silver and diamond studded pendant was roughly two inches across. It was suspended from opposing ends of the diamond knot by a delicate eighteen-inch silver and diamond studded chain.

Duncan took the ends of the chain and helped her slip it on. The table and ceiling lights were reflected from everywhere to everywhere in the small individual diamonds that caught and played, in prismatic fashion, with each and every beam.

She's more beautiful than I could have imagined with it on, Duncan thought as he gazed at the woman who—in his heart, could radiate light from the darkest cave with only her presence.

"That's very lovely, Tessa. And on that note," Joe interjected. "I see our lunch is approaching."

"I can't wait," Tessa replied as she caressed the pendant. "All these marriage plans and toasts have made me famished."

As the evening wore on, Joe noticed the trend in conversation was becoming one-on-one. With Grace giving Duncan advice on how to cut the ceremonial wedding cake so the photographer can get the best shot and Fitz pantomiming for Richie how to make the best sword swings when in-fighting, Tessa was turning her attention more and more to some of the posters on the walls of the pub. The pictures depicted random shots of various adventures—rugged hikes, mountain climbs, skiing, rafting and she seemed more and more engrossed as the evening wore on. Grace, noticing Tessa drifting towards one of them on the far wall, excused herself from Duncan and rose to follow.

Duncan reached for another breadstick and slid his chair closer to Richie to correct some of Fitz's swordsman advice.

Joe's eyes and, to some extent, his ears followed Grace.

"Something here on the wall catching your eye?" she asked.

Tessa hugged herself. "I don't know, Grace. This is all starting to look romantic and appealing. You've no doubt done some of this over the centuries. Is it really as exciting as they picture it?"

Grace stared at the three posters before them. "Yes and no. It all depends on you and where you are in life. What are you searching for in these experiences? Excitement? Danger? Adventure?"

"A little of everything and a little of none of these – if that makes any sense to you. As I said earlier, I am ready for a change. I don't know where this change will take me, but it won't be sitting at a potter's wheel anymore, that's for certain." She paused and tried to glean what was so fascinating about each of the posters. *They are all different. So, what is the basic appeal that I am a responding to in each?*

"Why don't you ask yourself in a vision?"

Tessa considered Grace's comment, not really knowing what to make of it. "My vision? I don't understand."

"You are a very sensitive person. You are expressing yourself in inner visions. I believe that, at least in part, it involves how you are comfortable discussing things with yourself." She paused and gauged the feeling she was getting from Tessa before continuing. "Let whatever you see in your thoughts and dreams be your guide to exploring the next step. Don't be afraid to try new things, even if a few of these are failures, at least you've tried."

She watched as Tessa's finger began following the curve of the sword in the lower corner of one of the posters.

"You know, you can become a very skilled saber fencer. You do have the speed and stamina. You just need to mentally incorporate the maneuvers. It will take work if you are truly interested." She peered around her to catch her gaze.

"I'm interested, and yes it's something I want to do. Thank you for taking time from your obviously busy medical schedule over the next couple weeks. Between the wedding and all the arrangements, I feel that I am keeping you at my beckoning call, when I have an hour here and there, to instruct and practice with me. Duncan obviously doesn't approve and won't help me."

Grace placed a hand on her shoulder and turned her gently back to face her. "Duncan is afraid he might lose you, that you might go up against an Immortal someday to save him – and be killed."

Joe was only catching snatches of their conversation over the quiet, but persistent, pub din as he tried to listen inconspicuously.

Tessa obviously wants Grace to train her—probably because of her fighting style, he reasoned from the bits of conversation he was half-hearing. *Duncan, on the other hand, is objecting, probably because he feels he is the better master of the sword.* He nodded to himself. *Makes sense. Mac has been in more sword fights and wars before the 1800s than Grace ever was. He has had more casual instructors and advisors on swordsmanship than Grace. What did I just hear Grace say? I think she said something about preparing Tessa to fight other Immortals? Training a pre-Immortal? If true, this will be a first for the Watcher's chronicles.*

It was then and there Joe reached a final decision and when the gathering broke up he would make several calls.

Duncan had verbally pushed Fitz out of the swordsmanship conversation and was now demonstrating swings and parries (somewhat discretely) to Richie with one of the table knives. Fitz wandered off to get another basket of breadsticks for the table as Grace returned to her dessert.

Seeing her alone now, he maneuvered the basket with its hot and savory garlic bread, to where Tessa was standing.

"The conversation has taken a serious turn into the swordsman realm. Care to rejoin us? This is certainly right up your alley, I would think."

Turning, she gave him a puzzled look. "Why would you think that?"

He shuffled in his space a bit as his eyes focused on his well-polished shoes. "Oh, your fondness for that sixteenth-century Rapier and Grace as an instructor for starters."

Tessa favored him with a wry smile. "You've become very observant where I'm concerned," she remarked, then leaned in close. "One would think you were practicing to become a Watcher, Fitz," she whispered.

A grin spread across his face as he shook his head once. "No, with my social schedule I really don't have the time or the patience to write about another Immortal, even if I wanted to." Fitz took a deep breath and pressed forward.

"I have been making some unofficial observations where you are concerned; and, there is a question I've been meaning to ask you. What happened to dear Amanda the day you sent me off for that *coffee break*, shall we say. Oh and don't just say '*gone*'?" he quickly added. "There are many types of *gone* I am sure you understand."

Tessa's expression shifted from the girlishly-playful, '*What makes you think I am involved in anything*?' to a small, cold satisfied smile.

Fitz noted the sudden, smooth shift in her expression and inwardly nodded to himself. *I've seen the same expression on many a faces of those opposite me and they always had a sword in their hands. Duncan, old boy, this Tessa is a book with many chapters. She's making plans.*

"Why, are you really worried, or just curious?"

Fitz didn't verbally respond, but his expression did.

Tessa faced him, eye-to-eye. "You're a smart old boy, Fitz. I told her that if I ever caught her pawing and trying to seduce my husband, that I would take her head myself and I wouldn't give a damn where her Quickening went. She turned and left—so, *gone.* Curiosity satisfied—OK?"

Fitz raised an eyebrow and glanced off to another area of the pub. His expression giving every indication he was warming up for one involved retort. Wisely, however, he let the pauses between their conversations stretch out as he fingered a breadstick. Setting the basket on a nearby unoccupied table, he began to nibble on the bread.

"You don't really know Amanda, Tessa – no matter what you may wish to believe. Oh, you know the part where she's after Duncan – you probably even know the part about her being a cat burglar. But there is a lot more about Amanda that you don't know."

"Should I care to know?'

Fitz bobbed his head slightly in a quaint English fashion. "Probably should, it is always nice to know who you can count on in certain situations. In the Immortal's world, you'd be amazed at how many times these strange situations come up and they bring people together—makes for the strangest bedfellows, if you take my meaning."

"No, I'm not sure I do. Why don't you speak English or French? I'll do a lot better at either language rather than trying to decipher your quaint, enigmatic expressions."

OK, he thought. *Maybe I should just put my cards on the table. Tessa just did.*

"The name Amanda means, *'worthy of being loved'.* She was given that name by the Sisters of the Abbey of St. Anne in Normandy. The good Sisters gave her that name for a reason and many a time, throughout her life, she has lived up to it. Oh, not as a thief, but as someone who has saved children and women throughout the generations, people who were at the mercy of men who didn't know the meaning of the word."

"Thank you for that interesting tidbit, Fitz. Do you have any other gems or pearls of wisdom about Amanda that I should care about?" she finished, sarcasm coloring her voice.

"Just this, no matter what you may believe about Amanda, you will never be able to take her head."

"Because she has had more than a millennium of swordsmanship up on me and I wouldn't stand a chance? It's my funeral if I do. Is that it?"

"No, because she wouldn't let you even try a stunt like that. You see, it's like this—Amanda knows that the outcome—any outcome from that confrontation, would hurt Duncan in a way she would never want to see him hurt. She cares too deeply for him and is truly too compassionate a human being for that."

"And just what are you saying? That I'm really—"

If the shoe fits, Tessa dear, wear it. Fitz expression seemed to say. "I would consider caring very much to know about Amanda, certainly a lot more than you do, if I were you." *You've got a lot to learn about Immortals if you are willing to learn it. And if not – it could be Duncan's undoing one day if you decide to try and put yourself in our immortal place.*

An instant later his expression switched to one of polite dismissal. *I'm finished here,* his expression seemed to be saying. Retrieving the basket, he glanced back once to her before returning to the table with the cold breadsticks.

Chapter Thirty-seven

The light Paris rain had ended almost a half-hour ago, just as Joe had left the pub. Turning off the road, he parked in the last parking slot–tires making a *'whooshing'* sound as they splashed through the receding puddle. He got out then looked toward the footbridge ahead—toward where he knew the Watchers would be waiting for him. Pausing, he gave a brief thought to the upcoming conversation that might transpire, to the potential possibilities and potential dangers of it.

The sidewalk was still wet, reflecting the streetlights as a distorted blur. Joe walked toward the pedestrian footbridge at the far end of the street, his cane producing a light tap, a *third foot* sound to his deliberate steps.

On the nearest end of the bridge, Grace's Watcher–Jeanette Fallon–was waiting for him. Another figure, which was barely perceivable, stood nearby.

Jeanette's cold stare, as Joe approached, was lost in the darkness. "Quite an evening," she quipped as he approached.

"Quite," he returned, trying to ready himself for whichever way this conversation was about to go. "It isn't often Watchers get to observe an Immortal's wedding, including all the festivities that surround it."

She shrugged. "From the chronicles I've read, Immortals usually don't bother with mortal weddings. Grace did, a couple of times–as have a few others. It's rare. This Tessa must be someone very special to him."

"She is and that's why I want to stay close to this troupe," Joe finished leaving the door open, inviting the obvious next comment.

Jeanette glanced away for a moment. "You were rather *close* to the Immortals all day. You're not really getting *involved*, are you Joe?"

OK, here comes the accusation. Now, how do I defuse the bomb before it explodes around me? He returned an expression and body posture, reflected in a nearby bridge light, which said *'And what is that supposed to mean?'*

"Are you sure you were really *watching* today, or just looking over your shoulder, Jeanette?" his voice deep, direct and smooth.

"And just what's *that* supposed to mean, Joe?"

"I know how to do my job," he emphasized. "Sometimes doing that job means getting close to someone in order to get the facts. You work around Grace in the hospital daily. Grace knows you as a coworker. She thinks nothing of you working near her." He shifted gears a bit.

"Tessa has known me as the neighborhood gentleman for some time now. It allows me to stay closer than usual to someone like MacLeod, who has been a shopkeeper for twelve years in the city." That wasn't exactly the truth and Joe had to focus to pull it off with a casual expression. He was thankful for the darkness which he hoped was obscuring his telltale body language giveaway that this was a lie.

She raised an eyebrow. "A neighbor who–coincidently–just happens to show up in Paris the same time they do to congratulate them on their wedding plans? You must be a neighbor with ESP."

Joe let the silence hang momentarily. "So? Duncan sees me around Tessa now and then. It is a non-issue. He naturally thinks nothing of my coming and going," he finished, unconsciously holding his breath –tense, the last word hanging.

Jeanette let the silence hang, her thoughts inscrutable.

"Tell me," Joe continued, on the offensive now. "What did you gather from what you saw today, starting with the barge? You must have been on the bridge near where it is moored?"

"No," she began shifting slightly so she was out of the direct line of Joe's unrelentingly hard stare. "I followed Grace in another cab. I had the driver stop a block away so I could pick up a paper as a prop. I was on the pedestrian walk—the same level as you, MacLeod and Fitzcairn, a little further up the street, though, when you all pulled in. Grace went right into the barge the moment she arrived. I was there for about an hour before I saw Richie leaping up on the wheelhouse. A few moments later Grace came into view, swinging her sword against someone on deck."

"And did you happen to recognize who that someone was?"

"No. The angle was wrong for me. I didn't want to leave my spot to get up on the bridge in case Grace was beheaded, or she beheaded whoever it was. All of you arrived just then and I never got to the bridge and the right angle."

OK, Joe thought. *Let's see how this next line hits home.* "Grace's attacker was Tessa." Joe grinned at the obviously shocked expression on her face. "You see, from where I was standing I couldn't have gotten any more information than you did. Because I have been close to Tessa, I could walk up onto the barge deck with everyone else and saw Tessa was wearing a fencing jacket with her safety mask in hand. She had been sparring with Grace."

"Why?"

Joe didn't respond to that question but instead fired back another. "Tell me, did you happen to hear Grace and Tessa's discussion in the pub?"

"How could I, Joe? I was at the farthest standing-table, behind the plant. I can't be seen here. You know that. Did you?" she retorted a bit defensively.

Joe nodded. "At least a part of it I did—enough to lead me to believe that we are getting a rare glimpse into the training of a pre-Immortal. Did you know Tessa has already killed once with MacLeod's sword?"

"What? Another Immortal? Who?"

"No. A mortal assassin who tried to kill her back in Seacouver."

"Do you really think that's what that business with Grace was all about? Tessa is actually in some pre-Immortal in training?"

Joe's grin beamed back like a spotlight. "Tessa was wearing a safety mask and jacket so she wouldn't be hurt if Grace hit her. Grace was obviously being careful, but as a pre-Immortal, she could have been badly wounded and wouldn't heal rapidly. I was up on the deck when MacLeod was arguing—rather unconvincingly—with Grace on training techniques for Tessa."

"You heard that conversation?"

"Some of it. Not every word, of course. After all, Immortals are very private when they are around mortals regarding their immortal existence – and he was standing off to the side with Grace. I heard enough though to believe that Duncan was simply worked-up and reaffirming he is the better trainer for Tessa–no doubt because of their relationship. It is obvious that Tessa wants Grace, though. That was clear to me from their conversation in the pub, when they went off to the side for a few minutes. Grace mentioned something to her about Duncan being concerned that she might go up against an Immortal. It was obvious to me that Duncan was simply concerned she wouldn't be properly prepared. That's the direction the conversation was going anyway." *Now top that one, you smart-alecky Watcher,* Joe mused.

Jeanette looked away for a long moment, her face a mixture of astonishment and surprise at Joe's unique discovery. She tried to compose an intelligent reply that would bail her out of the awkward situation she had dug herself into.

"If that's actually what's happening, it would be quite a discovery you've just made and a first for the Watcher's chronicles."

"And just why would you think it isn't what's happening? Immortals can sense a pre-Immortal when they are further along in their development. We have several records of that already throughout history."

She was silent. "We have no record of any pre-Immortal being trained by an Immortal before they became an Immortal themselves. Unless it was during a period when sword use was common and every boy learned from their youth anyway. Have you heard any plans–I mean for when Tessa is to become an Immortal?"

Joe shook his head. "I'm guessing Duncan, or Grace, or both will train her first. I have no idea what the plan is after that. But I do have a plan to find out."

He looked to the side, to the nondescript figure standing next to the other side of the bridge and beckoned with his arm.

"I told my supervisor in the hospital I had an emergency and had to be away for some time. I'm assuming this wedding is going to be over quickly. If I end up staying with Grace for as long as I think she intends to stay, to train Tessa that is. I will likely lose my position at the hospital. You're going to have to find another Watcher to take my place there."

Joe shook his head. "You don't have to stay. Go back to the hospital and preserve your cover for now. I'll ask Jack to assign someone else to her while she is training Tessa." *But I'm not going to be in a rush to call Jack. I want a little breathing room with these Immortals. And not having to dodge another Watcher, when I am with Duncan, is just fine with me. Grace is likely going to stay close to Tessa—so will I.*

"Then I will leave the details of Grace to you," she finished as Paula approached. Jeanette walked back to her car. A moment later it pulled away from the curb.

Joe mentally patted himself on the back for a job well done in defusing the potential bomb regarding his oath. This had been a dangerous game of words. The last thing he wanted were questions from a Watcher's Tribunal in Zurich.

He turned his attention to the new Peruvian graduate—Paula Roca. "I've got an assignment ready for you." Reaching into his overcoat, he handed her an envelope with a diskette and a couple of data sheets on Tessa.

Paula took the envelope, removed the sheets and scanned the contents under the bridge light. A moment later, her face gave her impending emotional eruption away.

"What! You want me to watch some mortal, modern artist?" Her voice was louder than Joe wanted to hear and he hushed her. "Mr. Dawson," she began again, only slightly more composed this time.

"Joe," he corrected her.

"Look, Joe," she continued without missing a beat, "I am the wrong person for this job–really! She's a modern artist–I think that art sucks! This Tessa is probably an egotistical, temperamental, prima-donna. I would be condemned to following her through endless, monotonous galleries filled with canvas that look like they had crap flung at them. Besides, I don't think there is such a thing as a modern artist who has a grasp of reality," she finished in rapid-fire without so much as taking a breath.

"It's obvious you aren't one of the more tolerant art critics in this world," he remarked sardonically.

"Look, I'm not asking you to develop an appreciation for modern art. I'm giving you an assignment. And since when did you stop looking at art in your field," he finished in a snarky tone of voice.

Her caffeinated expression hit a new high. "I wouldn't, in the same breath, compare anything this Tessa may have done in her mundane existence, with the prehistoric cultural markings I study," she finished more than a bit miffed.

Joe bore down on her with a hard expression until Paula realized what she had just done. Waving her hands in a gesture of, *'Alright, I'm a subordinate and I know I really just screwed up big time.'*

Rule number one, Paula—don't shout back at your superior. She bit her lip and taking a deep breath, remained silent for a long moment.

"I'm sorry, Joe. I have a little trouble keeping my mouth shut sometimes."

"Oh really, I couldn't tell," Joe commented sarcastically.

"I know I'm the new graduate," she continued. "I know you are my supervisor now and I have nothing to say about what bones you decide to throw my way."

"OK, Paula, I got what you think about this assignment in the airport. You didn't have to mouth-off just now. I know you'd rather be sitting next to a box of prehistoric bones, or a rock with something etched on it that looks like someone crapped on it, to study."

"Crap! Those are historically significant, primitive expressions of artistic—"

"Just shut up, will you? You've got an attitude problem. And, if you want to remain in this organization and someday get a chance to study those rocks with their primitive expressions, in the context of a well-disciplined Watcher—which is what you're supposed to be— you are going to have to learn how to work with supervisors and take assignments. You have absolutely no experience young lady–none outside of the classroom. You know zip. In this organization you never know when you are going to be dealing with an Immortal or something they influenced. It is time you learned–up close and personal. How do any of us know whether or not some of those primitive artistic expressions weren't influenced or done by an Immortal? That's why we recruit a broad range of professions in this organization. I'm giving you more of a chance to learn something practical, as a Watcher, than you realize. I suggest you apply yourself."

Paula's fiery Peruvian temper boiled under the lid she was trying to keep on it. Keeping her mouth closed when she wanted, or didn't want something was a lesson she had never really learned. With real effort, she softened her voice.

"Joe, would you just tell me why you picked me for this job?" she said slowly and deliberately, her accent thick in her voice. "The only thing I really know and love is paleoanthropology."

"I'm playing a hunch here, Paula, in several areas." Joe leaned back on his cane. *How much do I tell this young graduate? It is only a gut feeling about MacLeod and Tessa, but my gut is rarely wrong.*

"You may just be the best person for this job–if I am reading Tessa right. You see, Tessa has a special llama statue she calls, Solo—"

Joe placed a hand on her arm, directing her toward his van. As they walked slowly back, Joe briefed her on two pieces of information not in the packet–Tessa's strange visions inspired drawing of an Aztec stone calendar and menacing shadow-figure at a temple–and her favorite little llama statue–all the statues Duncan recently acquired–and their important connection to various new archeological finds in South America, including a recent find near Mount Llullaillaco in Salta, Argentina.

A car turning off the main highway passed by unnoticed on the road up ahead of the pair as they walked. Inside, one of the occupants did a quick double take before settling back, rather uneasily, in his seat.

"What's Joe doing in Paris? He should be at home in front of the TV." James Horton commented to no one in particular.

"So maybe he got tired of watching the Late Night Show," the Immortal Xavier St. Cloud replied in the most sarcastic tone, then looked to Horton. "We have more important business than your extended family's travel plans."

If Joe Dawson is here then so is his Immortal, Duncan MacLeod, he thought quickly, his eyes darting cautiously to his Immortal puppet in the seat beside him. He smiled and settled back as he considered Xavier's comment.

My dear Joe's travel plans are going to be of the utmost priority to us all soon, but you don't need to know that just yet. Once you've taken care of MacLeod, I'll have no further need of you—you immortal cancer.

Chapter Thirty-eight

"Purification ritual—are you joking?" Cassandra shot back, a distinct grimace on her face and in her voice. "Those rituals were positively brutal. Cleansing the body, purging any evil spirits before a union was permitted, was an ordeal that a few girls died from. Believe me Tessa, I've seen hundreds of those tribal rituals and I don't want to see any more."

Picking up a large flat box, Tessa scooted past Cassandra and into the bathroom. "I can pass on the purging of evil spirits part," she replied. "That's not what I had in mind." She paused before pushing the door partly closed. "I want to make this an extraordinarily special event—for me especially."

"I would think marrying Duncan MacLeod would be extraordinary in and of itself."

"That's not what I meant," Tessa began over the sound of crinkling tissue paper and other wrapping that she was removing. "Or, maybe I did." The sound halted and she poked her head around the door. "I love Duncan very much, Cassandra. But we have already been together for twelve years. It's not like he jumped on to my Seine tour-boat yesterday. After what I went through these past two months I have felt truly alive in a different way. My former world was pastille—my eyes are hungry for vibrant colors. So you might say I want to make a little magic happen around this wedding."

"Tessa, remind us why you are dressing in the bathroom?" Ceirdwyn called back as she fetched a hot pot of water for their tea.

"Because Richie has been floating between the upper deck and this kitchen more times than is necessary over the last two hours. He is just gathering bits of information to take back to those bulls up there. I don't want him, or Duncan, to see my wedding dress before the wedding—a ritual I intend to enforce." Her eyes sparkled. "Besides, I think a little mystery is fun."

Tessa and Duncan had greeted his immortal friends as they had arrived in the morning. Soon after the immediate events of their lives had been told and glasses had been raised in a toast, the men – Duncan, Sean, Coltec, Fitz, and Richie—headed up to the deck with a couple of bottles of wine and a large pot of tea. The women had stayed below for some serious and private girl talk.

Richie, Tessa noticed, had apparently become a self-appointed observer—popping down for hot water refills more times than she had kept count. She seriously doubted that they were drinking it all, as no one had been by for the bathroom in hours. The concept of an immortal bladder sent Tessa's imagination into overdrive until Ceirdwyn corrected her biological misconception—being unable to die had nothing to do with bladder control.

"Alright—if Richie doesn't know they won't either. I intend to keep them guessing, for now."

As if right on cue, Richie's footsteps were heard on the landing above once again.

"I am just heading for the stove. The pot needs to be reheated." He looked about, noting Tessa was absent and the two other women were hovering near the bathroom door. *OK,* Richie thought as he went through the motions of heating the pot, *either there's a rush for the john, or Tessa is up to something – this should be interesting.* "Don't mind me, ladies," he began in a smooth tone. "Whatever you're doing just pretend I'm not here."

"I'm modeling my wedding dress for the girls," came the muffled voice from behind the bathroom door, "and neither you, nor Mac, are going to see it until the big event."

"Ladies, my lips are sealed," he replied with a grand sweep of his free arm and a smile absolutely no one would ever believe.

"Yeah, right," Tessa replied, her eyes peering around the door. "You've been floating around here for hours. You just float back to those 'bulls' up there and stay there."

"I'm crushed," he replied. "I would never peek and tell," he finished, his spread fingers over his eyes, and a naughty smile on his face. He headed back up the steps.

Once the door was closed, Tessa walked out of the bathroom.

"Oh, that's lovely, Tessa," Ceirdwyn said as she turned slowly, her form accented by the barge's wall trappings and backdrop.

The shear, baby-breath pink, above the knee dress, both caressed and flowed with her body as she turned. The sleeves were a gossamer lace-work, form-fitting and below the elbow design, which ended in a delicate fringe. The otherwise pink, opaque bodice of the dress was covered with a delicate white, floral-lace-work pattern, which extended to the hem. The design featured a plunging neckline that was fully open, allowing Duncan's gift – a sparkling diamond studded Celtic love knot necklace to be perfectly framed against her smooth, fair-skin.

"I loved this dress from the moment I saw it," Tessa said, as Grace examined the sleeve trim. "I was on my way to order the announcements. I saw it through the open door and I just walked in, put everything I was caring down on the floor I was caring and said to the person adjusting the dress on the stand, *'I'm trying this on—right now. And, if it doesn't fit, you can just take a needle and thread and re-sew it while it's on my body'*. Fortunately for me it was the manager."

"What happened? Did it fit right away?" Grace asked, curious.

"No—actually, he had to adjust it." She moved over to one of the small mirrors. "There were people coming and going by the door the whole time he was working and no one stopped or acted as if there was anything unusual happening—like it's normal to be sewing clothing on a woman in a shop. He said it was because I made a very good mannequin," she finished with a grin.

Out of the corner of her eye, Tessa caught a motion by one of the open portholes. "Oh no you don't," she said and grabbed a pillow, about to throw it, when Grace stepped in front of the opening.

"There—you see what I mean?" she exclaimed, pointing toward the open porthole where Grace was now peering out of. "They can't go twenty minutes before curiosity gets the best of them. Duncan – Fitz," she called out. "I know it's just killing you because Richie didn't come back with any information."

"There's no one out here," Grace said as she leaned out of the port hole. "And no one could have gotten back on deck that fast. Are you sure you saw something?"

"Positive—it was only for a second though." She shook her head. *OK, so maybe I saw a bird sail by.* She shrugged it off. Turning, she tossed the pillow aside.

"My wedding is in four days—think girls—I'm ready for an adventure. Come on now—you've been around longer than I have. You have to have seen something new under the sun—something that will make my wedding one I'll never forget."

Cassandra rolled her eyes. "I thought we were off the subject of Purification. How about it if us girls take you out for a pre-wedding shower—you know—lunch, then we make it an all-day shopping trip?"

Tessa pantomimed a total letdown droop and then straightened. "Oh, I'm sorry. I know, I know—but that's just not doing it for me Cassandra." Placing a finger against her chin she tapped it pensively. Suddenly she whorled on Cassandra—the strangest look mirrored in her eye. "Yes, I'm up for shopping, right after I wrestle a lion under the *Arc de Triomphe*, bungee-jump from the Eiffel Tower and break into the Louvre at midnight, just for the fun of it. Then of course we can go shopping."

Has this mortal lost her mind? Cassandra stared back, speechless.

"Would that make your wedding special?" Grace spoke up, breaking Cassandra's incredulous stare.

"Yes, it would." She glanced in the direction of the porthole. "I want to do more than just walk down an aisle in the church Darius served. Fitz said it—and he was right. Duncan and I could have done that on any weekday for the past twelve years. For some reason it wasn't important to us then and the closer I get to our big day now, the more dull it is feeling already. I could almost say to the photographer, just meet us there, snap a photo for the record and forget the photo session afterwards. Duncan and I have boxes of photos together already." Her smile dropped into a very real downer this time.

Wordlessly Grace walked over and put her arms gently around Tessa.

"Rituals are important, Tessa. They define who and what we are and how we frame the rest of our lives. Up till now you've been sailing along, with Duncan as captain at the helm. Now that you have the wheel, you're searching for a new game to play that will define who and what you are and how you are going to frame the rest of your life. That's OK." She looked to the two other Immortals. "You're right, we have seen and experienced the more unusual. I think we can help you design a special wedding ritual."

"I still say purification rituals were brutal," Cassandra reiterated and shook her head again.

"Oh, not always. Many of the families I became acquainted with in the 1400s—here in France—focused on ritual washing and dressing the daughters in new clothing before presenting them to be married."

"It was a lot more fun if you were a young woman in a wealthy Roman household," Ceirdwyn interrupted with a one-upmanship challenge to Grace in her voice. "In the household I was taken to serve in—just before the first century—there was a week of feasting, bathing and gifts of expensive perfume and clothing before the wedding ceremony. It almost bankrupted the father. He had three daughters and I remember him complaining that he would have to sell every servant in his household just to pay for his last daughter's wedding! Fortunately it didn't come to that—I rather liked that household."

Cassandra had been sitting, curled up in catlike fashion against the armrest of the sofa, listening as Grace and Ceirdwyn traded ritual one up-manships. Eyeing the two in a calculating manner, she waited until the younger Immortals ran out of verbal steam before she spoke.

"Tessa, do you want to just have fun—or would you like to have a pre-wedding experience you'll never forget?" she entreated, using the *'voice'* she had used many times from antiquity—when she had been known as Cassandra the witch.

Tessa's eyes lit up with inner fire at the challenge those words promised.

"Yes!" she exclaimed and smoothly leaned over and onto the back of the couch above where Cassandra sat. Her facial expression beckoning for more.

Cassandra leaned in closing the gap. "And I know how Duncan can't resist a mystery. Do you want him to play in your ritual too?"

"Yes! Yes! Yes!" she exclaimed, feeling the suspense mounting around her.

She leaned back, her hand reached smoothly for the phonebook under the stand and she began thumbing rapidly through the pages.

"In Egypt, a young woman was being purified in preparation to marry someone." Her finger came to rest on an entry in the phone book and she turned her eyes back to Tessa, smiling. "Before that purification ritual ended, Osiris himself was invoked."

"Who's Osiris?" Grace asked, a tinge of concern coloring her voice at the unknown with which Cassandra was presenting Tessa with.

"Egypt's God of the Dead," she replied smoothly, with a purr in her voice.

Grace and Ceirdwyn looked to one another—their breath momentarily caught in their throats. But before Grace could utter a sound, Tessa was already in motion. Her hand reached up to a small shelf.

"And I know just the way to make Duncan want to play," she replied as her hands retrieved Solo.

A second car horn sounded, as Watcher Dudley Dillon wend his way precariously through the pre-noonday traffic, while balancing the two enormous pizzas he had just purchased. Huffing and puffing a bit from his rapid trip across the street, he quickly slid the rapidly cooling pizzas onto one of the micro-tables lining the Parisian walkway above the Seine. The pizzas almost swallowing the table.

A mild look of disgust formed on Melanie's face as Dudley unloaded the pockets of his large overcoat onto what was left of the table's surface—a bottle of cheap wine and a pack of cigarettes—tossed squarely on his latest 'Health and Fitness' magazine.

Working as Cassandra's Watcher in an up-scale modeling and fashion agency, Melanie was used to seeing people at their best. Dudley, in her estimation, appeared to be nothing less than a hippo trying to squat on a small mushroom seat while stuffing his face with more unneeded calories. The cigarettes and the health magazine were a fatalistic, ironic duo. *If he lights-up I'm moving upwind! I'm not immortal and neither is he—no matter what he thinks,* she mulled over in her mind. *The way he's been eating, drinking and smoking today, I wonder if this guy is going to live through this assignment. If Joe doesn't pick Watchers better than this—*

Her thoughts were abruptly halted as Rebecca's rental van pulled up near their position.

"The immortal men are all leaving. Joe took off a few moments ago. He thinks they are taking Richie to a place he already knows about for a sword training session. He said he plans to circle back here shortly if that's what they are up to. There will be three of us out there anyway—Claire, Sylvia and me."

Melanie nodded and turned to see if Dudley had gotten the message as Rebecca was pulling away.

Oblivious to the world around him, Dudley finished licking his greasy fingers then reached smoothly for the second pizza.

Melanie groaned audibly at the sight and re-focused her attention on the barge.

Coltec raised his Confederate Cavalry saber in one swift graceful movement, preparing to attack. Richie followed his lead as the others stood watching. This Native American's maneuvers, Duncan thought, were strikingly similar to those he had seen during spear hunting exercises he had participated in when he was with the Sioux tribe and *my woman—Little Deer—*his subconscious mind reminded him. Sword usage amongst early Native Americans was almost foreign, yet James Coltec had been forced to master the art, or lose his head in the Game. He reminded himself to ask his friend who his mentor and teacher was in 1190.

Born to the Cahokia Tribe of present-day Mississippi, Kol T'ek—now James Coltec in the twentieth-century—was a person with the ability to take the hate of others into himself and render it impotent. He had taken relatively few heads during his existence, preferring instead to remove the evil he saw as the reason for their lust for violence. When this failed, Coltec was as skilled with a sword as he had originally been with a spear.

Duncan considered the differences in fighting style from his own. He had been instructed under numerous mentors—beginning with his cousin, Connor MacLeod. His last important mentor—a Japanese Samurai master—had further refined and honed his skills into more smooth, rhythmic motions with a sword that had truly been created for a master.

Sean suddenly waved his hands, '*halt*'. The combatants froze as Sean approached Richie with further advice on how to deflect a side blow. Duncan grinned just a bit. Richie was already sweating from Fitz's exercise (which, in Duncan's opinion, was a bit lame). He held his comments though. He was thankful that everyone wanted to show Richie something new. Richie's training had been neglected for almost three weeks after he became an Immortal, because of the affairs surrounding Tessa. Tessa notwithstanding, Duncan knew the consequences of that tardiness. He reminded himself that he and his friends, had helped make up for his initial deficit. He was resolved to work Richie to near exhaustion regularly for the next two months. *And my wedding—Tessa—my honeymoon,* he thought. *I can accommodate both. After all, I'm an Immortal. I won't die from an arduous night of lovemaking no matter how exhausted I become training Richie during the day.*

The wind, sweeping out of the hill above the small ravine they were training in, was variable; and Duncan, who was standing further back from the group, began hearing sounds that were not from nature.

Voices? Where are they coming from? His ears raced to locate the origin of that sound. *If we're being observed by mortals,* his mind thought nervously. Slowly, he slipped back into the forest then circled around in the direction his hearing told him the sound was coming from.

Sylvia and Rebecca were deep in discussion about what Coltec had been doing. As Duncan silently approached their position, he could see one of the women pantomiming Coltec's sword maneuvers to the two others and in some cases improvising and rearranging his actions in *what if* types of scenarios. Occasionally one of the other women would break in with a few maneuvers reminiscent of things he had seen Fitz do. Though he was still some distance away, to Duncan's eye, one of the women appeared to be of Native American descent. His initial concern about being seen sword practicing faded fast when one of the women raised a pair of bird watching field glasses briefly, then resumed her note taking.

Duncan nodded to himself. *Watchers. Well, Joe probably can't make it up and over the hills to where we are on his prosthetic legs. Who's watching the Watchers now?* he thought as he shrugged. Smiling to himself, he quietly backed away before returning to the group.

As quietly as he possibly could go, Joe walked up to the inert form of his newest Watcher, scrutinizing what he saw.

Dudley, slouched back in his seat with his Donegal cap pulled over his face, was snoring loudly. The table in front of him showed the carnage wrought over some of Paris' finest cuisine.

Melanie walked briskly up to Joe, pausing only momentarily to favor the unconscious Watcher with a look of thorough disgust.

"The women are leaving now."

"Tessa too?"

"All of them."

Joe nodded, in the same motion acknowledging the information and indicating that she should go.

Melanie patted Dudley's shoulder roughly. "Come on, they're leaving," she said with one eye riveted on the barge.

Dudley awoke with a start, so much so he nearly slid off his seat. "I'm on it now," he said between a snort and a cough. "Which way did they go?" His hands caught the table edge and he oriented himself. Finally fully awake, he realized Joe was standing beside him. He struggled to his feet.

"Just conserving energy, Mr. Dawson. I'm in it for the long haul as it were. On top of Grace every instant."

Joe kept a straight face and said nothing as Melanie grabbed his lapel roughly, propelling him in her direction. "They're all leaving together. Hurry up—get in your car and follow me."

"I came by bus," he said halting and with a wide eyed stare.

Oh God, where did Joe find this guy, she thought, favoring him with an exasperated expression. "You're with me then. Come on, move it! Debra has already left with them."

Dudley waddled after her huffing and puffing as he scurried along until he reached a street vendor's stand.

Melanie was nearing the car when she realized Dudley wasn't with her anymore. Pacing angrily back, she grabbed his jacket. "Oh no you don't—not in my car," she exclaimed, nearly hauling him off balance, just as he was reaching for an item. "Move it, mister! We have a job to do."

Joe's grin widened from ear to ear. *Good man Dudley. Just the guy I want on Grace—a real no-hassle Watcher for me to get around. Exactly what I need now. Hum, I do hope he survives the assignment.*

Chapter Thirty-nine

"This place gives me the creeps," Ceirdwyn said quietly as her eyes scanned the large room and dark interior décor of the Egyptian Oasis spa, which had been modeled after the interior chamber of a pyramid. Complete with a life-sized statue of Seth, the Egyptian god of war, storms, and darkness in their lobby, the imposing expanse beckoned only those who dared.

Cassandra looked about casually then glanced to Tessa. *Well, what will it be mortal?* her expression clearly said.

"I'm ready—bring it on," Tessa said with anticipation and challenge in her voice as she eyed the room's expanse. It appeared to be filled from floor to ceiling with Egyptian mysticism and lore. She took a deep breath. "What do I have to do first?"

Cassandra nodded formally, "Enter. But all who do must pass the *test."*

"Test?"

"Osiris judgment—the weighing of a human heart against *Ma'at,* the '*Feather of Truth*'."

Aghast, Grace looked to Cassandra. *Are you out of your immortal mind,* she thought. *This is a mortal woman.*

Cassandra's only reply was silence as Tessa stepped up to the desk to register.

"None of you guys are going to have to fight very hard to get my head. I'm sure I'm already dead," Richie said as he sprawled across the back seat of Sean's van. "You guys worked me pretty hard today and I'm starving."

Duncan looked at his watch. It was later than anticipated and he was beginning to feel a little hungry himself. There were so many things that really needed to get done before the wedding and their second honeymoon that the hours of each day seemed to pass faster as the event grew nearer. *I know there are still twenty-four hours in a day—that hasn't changed—but somehow those hours are going faster,* he told himself. He even felt a twinge of guilt about training Richie today. *That's nonsense,* he told himself once again. He had left Richie's training to Amanda and Fitz far too long. The bits of swordsmanship Richie had mastered before they arrived in Paris wouldn't save his head. *The consequences of doing nothing,* Duncan reminded himself sternly.

"You'll survive until we get back to the barge," Duncan said with a half grin. "You know Tessa always has something special for us when we finish these training sessions."

"I doubt it today Mac. Tessa has better things to do three days before the wedding then make a lunch for us," he replied as his stomach growled audibly. "Couldn't we just stop for pizza or something? I'm still a growing boy you know?" he added with a big, *whose leg can I pull now,* grin.

"Yeah sure you are. If you fill up on pizza and those girls have taken the time to make something good, you're never going to hear the end of it," Duncan replied, a smart reprimand in his voice.

"I promise—no matter what Tessa has set out—even if it's a bowl of lettuce, I'll eat it. I could swallow an entire cow right now and still be hungry."

"Come on, Duncan, the boy is starving. A little repast won't spoil Tessa's fine cuisine," Fitz said sympathetically.

Duncan had been tempted himself to suggest they stop at one of several cafes after they had turned onto the main road, but the image of Tessa had come immediately into his mind; and along with her, the reminder of the long list of groom-duties he had to complete before the big event. That wedding list—the one she carefully placed in his pocket—was now more than a week ago. *I'm working on them,* he told himself, assuaging the tinge of guilt that was tugging at the corner of his memory. *Oh well, no need to panic, there's plenty of time yet to get it done.* *"Sure,"* his second subconscious voice reminded him, *"since when did three days become a long time to an Immortal?"*

The van was making good time on the main road. *Richie's right,* he thought. *Tessa doesn't have time to prepare anything, not with our guests around all day.* He mentally patted himself on the back. He had already planned for their guests' visit. There were just a few miles between them and the delicious selection of cold meats and cheeses he had bought the other day—all waiting for them in the refrigerator. The thought of this gave him the energy he needed to refocus on something else.

"You can relax. I went to the delicatessen and bought ample supplies in advance of everyone's visit. They're waiting for us in the refrigerator—that is, if Tessa doesn't have something already prepared. Oh whatever," he finally said after several moments of silence. "You're driving, Sean, you choose—the barge refrigerator or a café."

Sean nodded in Richie's direction as the van turned off toward a quaint, old family restaurant in the country.

"Now remember, Richie, not a word, and you better be hungry no matter what she has prepared," Duncan reminded him as Sean pulled the van into park near the barge.

"The cars are all gone," Coltec said as they got out of the van.

Sean looked about but didn't comment until they reached the gangplank. At the deck, he paused and placed a hand on Duncan's shoulder as he passed. "I don't sense another Immortal here. Everyone must have gone out for the day."

Duncan was already several steps ahead of him when he realized Sean was right. *There are no immortals here—that's odd.* There was urgency in his next steps until he reached the door.

"Tessa," he called. "Tessa, are you here?" Silence was the only answer. "You're right, they must have all gone out," Duncan said as he began looking behind the door for a note. There was none. *She wouldn't have left without leaving a note somewhere,* he thought, trying to minimize what he felt in front of his friends. There was something about all of this that made him visibly uncomfortable.

"She probably left something special for us in the fridge before they left," Richie said as he sprang toward the refrigerator and grabbed the handle. Moments later Richie called. "Hey guys," his voice expressing an unusual urgency, "you've got to see this."

Duncan's mouth dropped open as he rounded the corner. They bunched together in front of the open door and bent down, staring incredulously into the completely vandalized refrigerator. The only nutritional treasures left on the otherwise bare top shelf were a dozen eggs in an open carton and two avocados—all of which were sitting one shelf above a sketch pad and – Solo!

Tessa! He mentally screamed. *What are you up to now?*

"I'd say, Duncan, if this is what you call ample supplies, you must have meant for us to all be on an egg and avocado diet," Fitz quipped dryly, staring at the exposed eggs.

Duncan waved his hand in front of the virtually empty refrigerator. "This is all your fault, Fitz."

"Me!" Fitz exclaimed with an incredulous stare. "I've been with you the entire time. What could I have done to empty this refrigerator?"

"You know exactly what you did and what I'm talking about. You and your purification ritual nonsense that you put into Tessa's head. That's why this refrigerator is empty now."

"Purification ritual?" Sean asked. "What are we talking about here?"

Duncan and Sean straightened abruptly. "Tessa was planning some pre-wedding activities back in Seacouver. Naturally, Fitz had to go and suggest something outlandish like a purification ritual to spice up her life—as if she needed it with me."

"Huh? And you think that's what this is all about?" He gestured to the opening.

"Positive," Duncan said his hands going to his hips. "There is no other way she could have possibly come up with such an idea. Why else would she dream up this absolutely ridiculous, whatever?" he waved his hand by the opening of the refrigerator. "If it weren't for Fitz and his antiquated, pre-marriage practice advice, she would have never gotten the idea in the first place. He put it in her head."

"Oh, now wait a minute, Duncan. Don't blame me for your Tessa being somehow brainwashed. I don't think you really know her as well as you think you do," Fitz replied. "Tessa has plenty of her own ideas. I can assure you of that. She wanted to spice up her pre-wedding activities. I just helped by supplying a few suggestions."

"All the wrong ones," Duncan shot back, a bit heated.

Sean maneuvered between the two refrigerator combatants. "Just calm down boys. Now, Duncan, Fitz may have given her the idea but he certainly didn't make her carry it out. If Tessa is responsible for what we aren't seeing here now, there's a good reason for it."

"What possible reason could anyone have for clearing our refrigerator with the exception of a box of eggs and two fruits," he motioned accusingly once again toward the void.

"Duncan, you must understand, rituals are important to us all, in every age. They define who and what we are and what we intend to become in life. If Tessa did this, there's a reason and I think she wants us to discover it and get involved."

"No chance," Duncan remarked as he very carefully reached into the refrigerator and grabbed the top shelf. Pulling it slowly and carefully out—as if the eggs were likely to explode, he placed it on the table. His hand then grabbed Solo—an instant later he realized the feet were taped to the sketch pad. He reached to peel up the tape.

"No, Duncan—don't disturb anything. Take it out carefully," Sean encouraged.

Duncan raised an eyebrow to Sean's insistence, then very carefully lifted the sketch pad, with the statue still attached and placed it on the table next to the refrigerator shelf.

"OK detectives," Duncan began a bit testy. "What can you make of all of this?"

The five men took up positions around the table in a manner suggesting that they were scrutinizing an archeological puzzle.

"Well," Sean began after examining the contents of the first shelf. "Let's take it from the top—literally. We must assume she arranged things in an order for a reason. Let's consider what food she left in the refrigerator. Eggs, for instance, could represent a couple of things."

"Such as what? It's just breakfast food to me," Duncan said, following Sean down as he scrutinized the eggs.

"Such as new life, fertility, renewal, rebirth. The symbolism has been borrowed from various cultures—the Teutonic goddess **Eostra** for one."

"You're joking," Duncan replied.

"Not a bit," Sean continued. "The egg is a very feminine symbol." He switched, gesturing to the fruits. "The word '*avocados*' on the other hand, comes from an Aztec Indian word meaning 'testicles'—a very male symbol. They probably named the fruit in reference to the shape of the avocado, grown in that part of the world."

Duncan's very poignant and surprised stare was all Sean got for a response.

"Don't look at me like that, I didn't invent the concept."

"Do you realize that I'm not going to eat another avocado without thinking about what you just said? Correction—I'm not eating another avocado—period."

"All I'm saying here, Duncan is that we have two powerful opposing symbols—one female and one male sitting right above this," he gestured to the sketch pad.

Behind them, the refrigerator cycled on once again and it suddenly dawned on Duncan that he'd forgotten to close the door. He reached back and shut it quickly.

"Now this is interesting," Sean said as he shifted his attention from the produce to the sketch pad.

The drawing, a hasty sketch of the great sphinx at Giza near Cairo, was normal with one difference—the face was Tessa's. Across the paws ran a banner with the words, 'purification location'. Beneath the paws stood, Solo.

Sean squared his chin between his thumb and forefinger in a contemplative gesture. "Oh, I see that Tessa has some seriously grand events planned for herself in all of this," his finger following the image of the sphinx from end to end. "There are a number of interpretations as to what a sphinx actually represents. For example, one of the Egyptologists I know relates the symbolism of the human head, attached to a powerful animal's body, as a transformation or metamorphosis, in which there is a link between mankind and the gods—mortal and immortality if you will—as if the person is constantly on the threshold of these two worlds." Sean raised both eyebrows at that. "Tessa may be presenting us with imagery of how she is viewing her connection with Immortals—with you, perhaps. Or it could be intended to represent a subconscious message of her own intended transformation—from mortal to immortal—" Sean's voice halted abruptly as his expression shifted to one with a hint of trepidation.

"I don't like the sound of that," Coltec said quietly. "Their supposed immortal connection was through mummification."

Duncan shook his head. "That's enough Sigmund Freud for today. This is all getting just too weird for me." His eyes shifted to Solo.

Solo rested on a large square beneath the sphinx's feet. The square loosely appeared to be an open scroll. The first section contained neatly drawn hieroglyphics followed by rows of words in a language that Duncan did not understand. He studied the strange symbols.

"I haven't a clue what it says. Can either of you read any of this?"

Coltec shrugged and shook his head. "Whatever the message is it appears to be repeated," he offered, pointing, "here and here – over and over again, like a Rosetta Stone."

"That's exactly what it is," Sean said. "I can't read hieroglyphics, that must have been Cassandra's writing, but the second line is from the Viking language, which I've seen before. Ceirdwyn must have written this. It says, "To find me—follow Solo.""

"Follow Solo?" Duncan repeated, looking at the statue. "To where?"

"To Egypt?" Coltec asked.

"But the wedding is in three days?" Richie exclaimed. "Guys, are you telling me that Tessa is off to Egypt to somehow get purified in some Egyptian mummification ritual? That's totally gross."

"How do we follow a statue? This doesn't make sense." Coltec replied. "There must be something else here—other clues or something—somewhere."

Duncan pulled the statue loose from the paper. As he did, the paper flipped up—there was something on the next page. It was a picture of Solo lying on a pillow in their bedroom.

"What? I don't get this," Duncan said throwing up his hands, frustrated. Quickly he flipped through several blank pages in the sketch pad. These were the only two she had used.

"Follow Solo?" Richie repeated. "OK, does that mean we are now supposed to go to Egypt, or to the bedroom?"

"No, that means now I call the police," Duncan said in a stern tone of voice that indicated he was in no mood for this nonsense anymore. He left the table.

"Wait a minute, Duncan," Sean said, halting him in mid stride. "Tessa has obviously made a game of her purification ritual and she's inviting us to play." He gestured to the sketch pad. "This could be fun for the two of you."

"It's silly and I don't feel like playing childish games."

"Mac, what are you going to tell the Paris police? That a group of ladies are preparing for a pre-wedding fling—they left the barge a couple of hours ago and when we got back, they weren't here to serve us lunch. Where is the emergency in that?"

Duncan slammed the receiver back on the phone. Richie was right. For all his fuming and complaining, the police were going to say nothing more to him then '*Someone has to be missing for three days before you file a report with us.*'

Duncan ground his teeth—he was trapped into playing this ridiculous and somewhat embarrassing game of Tessa's. In the midst of his frustration, something in the back of his mind began tugging at his protective senses, making him feel a bit uneasy. After all that had happened to them over the past couple months, he wished he simply knew where she was and that she was safe. How could he find out?

"Hey guys—number one priority here and now is just this—tell me how to find her. She couldn't possibly have gone to Egypt and I have nothing to call the police on yet, so short of using a crystal ball, come up with a suggestion for finding my missing Tessa, please."

"How many museums and art galleries are there in Paris whose focus is on Egypt?" Coltec asked as he retrieved Paris' version of the Yellow Pages. "I'll check in here."

"I can check the Internet for references to Egypt in Paris," Richie said as he started for the computer. "I'm sure there will only be a couple of hundred."

"Why don't we just find her by playing her game," Fitz said pointing to the sketch pad. "If Sean is correct, all we have to do is go to the bedroom for the next clue—like a treasure hunt."

Duncan rubbed his forehead and was about to comment once again that he had no intention of playing when, out of the open porthole, he saw the small outline of a familiar person on the walkway above the Seine.

"I've got a better idea, everybody," he said with a satisfied smile on his lips. "I'll consult an all-wise oracle." And as quick as that, he bounded up the steps and out over the deck of the barge.

"What oracle?" Sean exclaimed – but the highlander was already gone.

Duncan set a lively pace down the Seine walkway. Glancing occasionally up to the sidewalk above, he calculated his distance from the barge. *It isn't likely that Joe is going to stop and talk to me until we are both far enough away so that the other Watchers don't see him*, he thought.

Joe was dropping further and further behind Duncan on the walkway above. *Slow down and take a deep breath*, Duncan told himself. *This man is walking on two prosthetic limbs—he's not able to keep up.* He slowed and noted that Joe was continuing to follow him, more casually now.

After he had walked about three blocks away from the barge, Duncan took a speedy turn up the bank and intercepted Joe in an area of the walkway where the trees were a bit thicker.

Joe gave every indication of walking past Duncan without acknowledging him. Duncan's keen reflexes reached to grab Joe's arm, but he halted his hand before touching him. *The man isn't being rude, he's just protecting himself, so go with the flow.*

"Fancy meeting you here," Joe said casually, looking straight ahead as he continued slowly.

"Sure," Duncan remarked dryly.

"So what brings you out this fine Parisian day?"

Duncan ignored the small talk and cut to the chase. "I am looking for my Tessa—I seem to have lost her," he added with a whimsical twist. "You wouldn't happen to know where I can find her would you?"

"Nope." He paused and faced Duncan. "Like I told you, I don't watch Tessa." Joe looked away and made as if to continue on.

The statement caught Duncan momentarily off guard and he faltered. Catching Joe's obvious evasive answer a heartbeat later, he recovered swiftly and placed a hand on Joe's forearm carefully, halting him.

"OK, so you don't watch Tessa—but she is with three other Immortals and you have Watchers on them," he emphasized.

Joe winced. His lame excuse had failed to get around Duncan.

"So how about it—where's my Tessa?"

Joe stared at him with a standoffish expression. "In case you don't already know it, we Watchers take an oath of silence."

Duncan bobbed his head and gave Joe a really annoyed stare. "OK, now that that's been said—where's Tessa?"

"That oath of silence is to the death—in case you didn't know that either," Joe finished in a deadpan voice.

Duncan's hands went to his hips. "Don't stalemate me, Joe. This is serious. I know that you know you can find her. I'm just asking you where she is."

"And when you find out, then what?" Joe replied in a serious tone of voice. "If I were to share that information with you and you were to go charging off to her, someone's going to put two and two together reasonably soon and figure out how you found out. I can't have that—for my sake."

Duncan put a hand to the bridge of his nose and rubbed the ache that was forming there.

"Look, Joe, I promise I am not going to go charging off anywhere and do anything. I just really need to know that Tessa is safe. She took off earlier this morning with three of our friends—she's playing some sort of pre-wedding game. She left a strange message in our refrigerator."

"In the refrigerator? What—did she make a casserole and write something on it?" Joe finished in a jocular tone.

Duncan wasn't in the mood for this from Joe. His hard annoyed expression wiped the silly grin off of Joe's face fast. "She cleaned out the refrigerator except for two items and left her sketch pad in there with her favorite statue, Solo, on top of it. There is some enigmatic message in the picture she left us—something about a purification ritual."

Joe's expression did change which made Duncan wonder if this Watcher had acquired x-ray vision this morning.

Joe reached into his pocket and pulled out his cell phone. Flipping open the cover, he kept his eye on Duncan as he stepped several paces to the side before dialing. Joe was on the phone for several long minutes before he closed it.

"Tessa is safe. She's at one of those trendy health spas—you know the kind—sort of a New Age thing you see in Paris all the time."

"Where, Joe—details."

"She's safe—that's what you wanted to know." Joe could feel the Highlander staring a hole straight through him. But he didn't flinch. *You'll have to do better than that, Duncan old boy*, he thought, *before I give you any more information.* Duncan continued to block Joe's path and stared harder. Joe finally let his head fall in a gesture of submission. "An Egyptian theme health spa—alright? Are you satisfied?"

Duncan breathed a sigh of relief. *So that's what the picture was about,* he thought. "Thanks, Joe. You just saved me a lot of hassle and worry. Don't worry, I'm not going anywhere near it. Your cover is safe. I'm going back to the barge and put my feet up for a relaxing rest of the day. Let Tessa and the girls play their games."

There was a decisive spring in his step as Duncan wended his way down to the lower level of the bank near the Seine and strolled back toward the barge.

Joe followed him with his eyes. *I hope he does just that and nothing else today,* he thought. *If he doesn't, I'm in big trouble.*

"OK, everybody, you can stop whatever you're doing—the mystery has been solved," Duncan said with a real zeal in his voice as he sauntered down the steps into the barge. "The drawing of the sphinx has been unraveled. Tessa and the others are at a health spa in Paris with some strange Egyptian theme. That's what this whole purification thing is about. We can all relax now," and Duncan did a sideways leap, reminiscent of what Richie usually did, landing full length on the sofa.

"Everyone will be home as soon as the business closes tonight," he said with a lighthearted voice. "So, now that that is out of the way, what would we all like to do? We've got the day free."

Silence was the only answer he got as his friends looked to one another.

"What?" Duncan held up his hands in a gesture of, '*I don't get it*'.

"Who said she was at an Egyptian spa?" Coltec asked.

"A friend from the State's—he's vacationing here." Duncan quickly supplied hoping that would end it.

"If he's just vacationing here, how would he know where she was? I didn't see anyone else stop by this morning since I arrived," Sean added.

Duncan saw a knowing grin forming on Fitz's face and he shot him a, *don't you dare say a word about Watchers,* expression. "Well, he's one of those guys who are always in the know and he does get around a lot."

"And you believed him?" Coltec looked back to Fitz with a rather surprised expression. "He must be using a crystal ball if he's just vacationing and he already knows what's going on in every corner of Paris."

"That's about right. If he says it is, it's a fact."

Smiling, Sean shrugged. "I wish I had him for my stock broker. It's just that you're getting married in three days and well—we're here to become involved in your life. Tessa has obviously set the tone of what is going to be happening with these ritual games. We're here to get involved too," he nodded.

Duncan sat up straight. "You're joking—no, you aren't—you're dead serious. You can't be. Come on, Sean, this is ridiculous."

"Ladies going to a health spa is ridiculous?" Fitz remarked, puzzled.

"No, her making a game of it and expecting me to participate."

"I don't get it?" Richie said holding up his hands in the same questioning gesture. "This detective work and the treasure hunt thing, sounded kind of fun to me."

Fitz nodded, his expression telling. "Duncan, you're just embarrassed to be caught having fun, that's all it is. It all seems so silly to you. That drawing—that statue in the refrigerator—you having to become detective Duncan Macleod of the Clan Macleod," he finished with a jovial wag of his head.

"Right, it's silly! That's what I have been saying all along," Duncan replied as he got up from the couch. "I'm an adult—I don't play childish games."

"In case you haven't noticed, dear boy, we don't care if it looks silly." Fitz looked about gesturing to no one in particular. "It's just a bit of pre-wedding fun—like a stag party."

"So *you* go to the spa and have *your* nails done," Duncan shot back to Fitz.

"Adults go to Disney World all the time," Sean said. "They ride the rides originally made for kids, they meet actors dressed as characters—Mickey Mouse and Donald Duck. They're having fun, Duncan and they don't care who sees them doing it. What's the harm in that?"

"So how many times have you been to Disney World, Sean?" he asked with a wave of his hand.

"Twice actually, since Disney World recently opened in France. I had a great time."

Duncan placed his hands on the chair back, lowered his head and leaned in. "OK, OK—I get the message. You guys want to play and you're taking me along as an excuse to do it."

"We just want to play along with *you*. It's not every day that you're getting married Mac," Richie interjected. "This is all very special to us too."

"So what do you guys want me to do—and don't anybody say go to that Egyptian spa to get a pedicure." Duncan retorted, defensively.

"Well, since the puzzle has been solved, why don't we focus on preparing you for the wedding?"

"**What?** You want to make a purification ritual for me—no

way. You're joking—please say you are."

Sean chuckled. "Well, not quite like that. The origin of purification rituals had to do with the purging of, or removing, specific *'unclean'* spirits prior to a particular activity. I doubt seriously that Tessa had any intention of becoming involved in a ritual that had anything to do with spirits. It's more likely that she's engaged in this to undergo some personal experience—perhaps, even subconsciously, she intends this experience to somehow prepare her for her new role in life with you."

"More Sigmund Freud, Sean?"

"Well, you know that's what I'm good at," Sean said with a wink. "It doesn't take Freud to see that Tessa felt she needed to experience something special in her life as a part of her personal pre-wedding preparation." Sean shrugged. "Throughout history, women weren't the only ones who went through rituals before being married, or on other occasions. I'm sure we've all seen or experienced something that would be appropriate for you now."

"I'm an adult. I officially became a man in my clan a long time ago, so we can skip that ritual."

"But have you ever sought the wisdom to become a husband?" Coltec asked.

"As a matter a fact I did—from many people I've known throughout my very long life. I must say that the pearls of wisdom they left me will serve me quite well, thank you."

Coltec smiled. "A long life? Compared to the three of us, Richie excluded of course, you're still wet behind the ears." That brought a chuckle from everyone.

"It has always been customary for a young man to seek wisdom in a ritual," Sean finished.

"And that ritual is always taken quite seriously," Coltec added.

"Oh really? And what exactly are we talking about and who does this yet?"

"Many Native American tribes practiced the *Vision Quest*. For centuries, perhaps for millenniums—maybe for as long as there have been Native Americans in existence. Seeking a vision quest experience could occur for many reasons—for becoming an adult man or, at a turning point in life where they were seeking direction for their future."

Duncan had heard of this, but like so many bits of information he had felt were not of use in his life, he had simply shelved it in his memory. "What did this ritual consist of?"

"It is still practiced today to some extent. A person would usually go off into the forest spend one to several days and nights alone, fasting and sleep deprived to better *hear* the *voice* of nature or an animal spirit guide."

"My wedding is in less than three days. I don't have time to go off to the forest to commune with nature for a week. Isn't there some way we can hurry this up? I'm already hungry—that should at least get me started—right?"

Coltec grinned. "We'll use what we've got. The whole point of going off into the forest was to eliminate distractions and provide time for deep communion with the spiritual energies of creation around them. But you don't really have to go anywhere. It's your frame of mind that is important. We can do it right here, right now."

He got up and grabbed a small pouch from his duffel bag. Inside was a Native American flute. Coltec showed the instrument to the very curious Sean.

"It's a river cane flute. The Museum at the University of Arkansas has one almost like it in their collection." His grin widened. "It may have actually been one of the ones I made when I first became an Immortal and spent time as a healer in my tribe. They call theirs, 'The Breckenridge Flute' and it is dated towards the end of the twelfth century. That's about right for me." He shifted his attention back to Duncan.

"I recommend a vision quest for you to seek guidance in creating a new life together, with today's Tessa, Duncan." He said in an official manner and gestured with his hands, '*How about it*?'

"What do I have to do in this ritual?"

"Eliminate distractions, make yourself comfortable—focus on your upcoming marriage and what it means to you to be joined to Tessa. Once you have this focus in your mind, open yourself to receiving guidance from a spirit—an animal councilor."

I'm not going to offend Coltec's beliefs, Duncan thought, *but for me to seek an animal guide is more than a bit strange. Something spiritual is supposed to come and tell me something I haven't already learned in 400 years of living? This I've got to see, or at least experience, once.* After a moment Duncan nodded. "Alright, what am I supposed to experience by communing with this animal guide?"

"Anything and everything. It is considered a time of intense spiritual communication. The seeker can receive a profound vision—some insight into themselves and their place in their world. It relates directly to the purpose of the question being asked."

Oh really, thought Duncan, as he began fluffing the sofa pillows. "So, what animal is my spirit guide supposed to be?"

"I don't know—you subconsciously already know your animal guide. This creature will come to you and identify itself and well, you'll both take it from there."

I've done enough Far Eastern traditional meditation exercises. All right, I know how to get started—I'll get into a relaxed, trance-like state. I suspect that this is all very similar. OK, here goes—think 'animal guide', he repeated silently to himself as he rested his back squarely against the pillows of the sofa. Sitting in an upright and relaxed position, he closed his eyes and pictured his lovely Tessa, someone he rarely stopped thinking about anyway.

Somewhere in the background of the quiet room sounds, he heard the soft sounds of a reed-flute playing.

Sean and Fitz made themselves scarce by slipping up to the deck. They had just settled back into the deck chairs when Richie joined them.

"You picked up Tessa's second clue from the bedroom," Sean said when he recognized what was in Richie's hand.

Richie settled into an adjacent chair as a rather sheepish look spread across his face.

"Guys, I wish Mac would have just played along. Look I don't really care if it's all kid's stuff. It's just for fun after all. Some guys have Stag Parties before a wedding and do really dumb things. So, Tessa knew we would all be seeing this. That means she wanted us all to play, not just Duncan—right?"

"Curiosity is just killing you because MacLeod didn't take her bait," Fitz said with a big smile. "Of course she did. Nothing saying we can't still find her clues." He leaned forward eagerly, with Sean, to examine the second drawing. "Besides, you probably can't read this language either."

"No, can you?"

"Yes, I've seen this one. This language is an almost prehistoric Saxon and Jute mixture. This is Ceirdwyn's writing again for sure." Fitz nodded. "I see what the ladies have been doing. Each clue has a different language on it. Duncan might be able to read this one, but he certainly couldn't read the Viking script or the hieroglyphics." He looked up to Richie with a *'by Jove—well done,'* expression. "By adding these various languages to the clues, Tessa obviously did intend for all of us to play along."

"So, who else but Cassandra can read hieroglyphics?"

Sean and Fitz exchanged bewildered glances.

"Neither of us," Sean said. "Cassandra, I believe, is almost 3,000 years old. She has a small bit of history which includes a period in Egypt, I understand."

"Maybe I can get help from the Internet—later," Richie suggested. "There aren't too many symbols. It's worth a try."

Tessa's second drawing was a sketch of an opening into a pyramid. Fitz translated the phrase above the door as 'Gateway to rebirth.' A few hieroglyphic symbols flanked the sides of the opening. A series of llama tracks scrolled around the edge of the drawing, ducking in and disappearing into the intricate design of the pyramid wall then, reemerging—teasing the reader's eye to follow.

Richie turned the drawing whilst being urged by Fitz to hurry up.

"I'm going, I'm going. She drew strange shapes in this wall – they might mean something. I don't want to miss anything," he said as Fitz began tugging at the corner of the paper, impatiently. "Fitz, will you just wait a minute," he finally exclaimed.

Following the irregular marks, Sean found a small drawing of Solo almost hidden within one of the designs of a wall. Solo was being drenched by a waterfall – the English inscription read: 'Go to the falling waters'.

Sean looked around and out onto the smooth Seine. "I don't see any water falling from anything anywhere." He sat back in his chair. "The last two clues were on this barge," he pondered.

Fitz took out his pipe and placed it unlit between his teeth. A moment later his eyes lit up. "The shower!" he exclaimed.

Richie's leapt to his feet. Sean grabbed his arm before he could bolt off.

"Coltec is helping Duncan with his Guided Imagery session right now, Richie. We shouldn't disturb him for an hour or so. Whatever Tessa left in the shower will be there when they are finished." Sean could see it was going to take more than a few persuasive words to keep Richie in his seat for more than a few seconds now that he knew where the third clue was hiding. He looked to Fitz and saw he was going to get no help from him. Fitz was already eyeing a length of rope.

Oh, what the heck, thought Sean, as he put a glass on top of the drawing to weigh it down against the wind. *We can have Richie over the side and through the bathroom porthole in a matter of minutes.* Treasure hunt fever was getting to him too.

Slowly, carefully, rhythmically Duncan inhaled and exhaled, absorbing the calm around himself and gathering it inward. His mind narrowed its focus to Tessa—to their love and life together that was to come—beautiful, peaceful, tranquil imagery filled his senses. His stomach rumbled. *Where did that feeling come from?* His consciousness asked himself. Another rumble. *I'm so hungry I could eat my animal guide. Where's my Tessa? What is she doing? Purification?* Another rumble. *Richie is always hungry.* An image began forming in his subconsciousness.

"Richie!" he heard himself call. *"Where's my meat and cheese? The refrigerator is empty. I swear if you've raided my fridge again."* He was suddenly aware that he was standing in the middle of an empty space, shouting into nothing. The only object in front of him his eyes could discern was the empty refrigerator.

"Richie, where are you? There's not a crumb inside—you've eaten everything." Duncan stopped. Strangely, the sound of his last frustrated words were still echoing around the space he was frozen in.

I have existed for more than 400 years. I remember everything that's happened to me in that time, but right now, nothing is making any sense. I know I'm here to meet someone—I'm waiting for someone—or is it something? An animal?

A giggle from somewhere behind him, broke his train of thought, distracting him from the image of the empty refrigerator. *"Concentrate,"* he told himself. *No distractions until—who arrives?*

Another giggle erupted from outside of his peripheral vision breaking his concentration once again. Trying to turn, to see the source of that sound caused his knees to suddenly weaken.

"What's happening to me?" he voiced. *"My immortal senses just lit up, or did they? There are no other Immortals approaching—are there? Why can't I reach my katana?"*

Duncan focused on the quiet sounds of human voices slowly growing louder. As he did, he found he could turn toward it.

"Tessa, you're here—who is that man with you?" he exclaimed.

Tessa was lying forward on a chaise lounge in the living room of their barge, one leg bent upward at the knee, her bare foot waving lazily to and fro in the air. Wearing a short, vibrantly printed, silk robe, she was smiling broadly back to a tall, muscular, handsome man who was wearing an Egyptian *shendyt* – a kilt-like, wrap-around skirt and a short sleeve tunic.

Duncan stared incredulously as he watched the man's hands play slowly through her hair, unwrapping the strands as they followed his fingers, almost as if they were being gently caressed. He was smiling back proudly to Tessa.

"You must relax now—there is tension in these strands. I must

purify you for what will come next in life."

"*Excuse me. She's obviously relaxed enough,*" Duncan said in an agitated tone. "*I'll take it from here if you don't mind—and even if you do, you're finished.*"

"*But, I see there is still a little bit of tension right here—right at the base of your neck—it's in these strands.*" His fingers played down the wisps of hair to the base of her neck, his fingers inching ever closer to the back of her robe and the clip that held it closed.

"*That's far enough with my fiancée, mister—just leave.*" Duncan's voice was noticeably louder and more aggressive.

"*Here they are—those naughty strands were hiding from me,*" he continued, his fingers disappearing under her loose collar and between her shoulder blades. "*I'm just going to have to teach them a lesson—would you like that Tessa?*"

Tessa purred with pleasure. "*Oh yes,*" she moaned. "*punish them—punish them all.*" She sighed. "*Thank you, Rob. I so desperately needed to be purified today. All this pre-wedding stress. Your hands are magic on my body.*"

"*I'll bet and a few other things too. Rob, get out of here, right now!*" Duncan roared, confused why he was being ignored.

"*Oh please—let's do it again the next time I need to be purified. Oh, say you will.*"

"*OK, that's enough of this purification crap,*" he growled. Struggling to move he found he could not. *Incredible! What's going on? They don't even notice I am here.*

"*I have really enjoyed every minute, Tessa,*" Rob reassured her as his hands caressed hers, sliding down along her arm. "*Purification is such an intense ritual.*"

Duncan struggled to reach his katana – to get rid of Rob one way or the other, when—hands—many hands and arms—from somewhere behind him, wrapped around his waist, his chest, entangling his arms like an octopus, preventing him from reaching out to where he knew his weapon lay.

"*Oh, don't do that,*" the lyrical and all too familiar voice cooed. "*They're busy de-stressing. I'm here now to de-stress you.*"

That voice, he thought. "*Amanda, where did you come from?*"

"*Did you miss me? I've been away on my coffee break, remember?*" Amanda's head popped up on top of his shoulder, as her fingers popped the buttons on his shirt then crept underneath to explore his muscular chest.

"*Amanda—would you stop it. My fiancée is standing—ah—lying right there, next to Rob.*"

"They're very busy, they won't even notice, besides we're busy too. My, my—I see I have my work cut out for me," she purred as the probing fingers of her right hand played down his rock-hard abs while her left hand finished unbuttoning his shirt.

"Just look at all these muscle knots I am going to have to knead out," she finished with a satisfied smile as his shirt finally fell away.

"Amanda—don't do that. Now Rob is looking our way."

"Hi Rob," she panted as she nibbled Duncan's neck, tugging on several of the hairs at the nape. She wiggled a few fingers '*hello*' in Rob's direction, as her free hand slid smoothly beneath Duncan's belt.

Duncan gasped and flinched. *"Amanda—please, will you stop that. I'm waiting for my—"*

"Animal guide?" she whispered into his ear as she kissed the edge. *"Well, here I am, and I'm all yours."*

"What! *You're a lady."*

"This lady is a tiger," she exhaled, nuzzling his earlobe between her wanton lips. *"Pure, intense and totally animal,"* she whispered into his flesh. *"It's all you really want in a woman anyway, isn't it?"* A coquettish expression beamed from her big brown eyes as she angled her head around to see his face. *"You have so much built up tension in here."*

"Would you get your hand out of my pants!"

"Oh my—you've got a lot of stressed out hairs. I'll just have to work all that purification stress that you've been worrying about, out of you, one strand at a time—starting from the bottom up."

"But Tessa is right there."

"I don't think she will see anything new. Now just relax and let your tiger do the rest." An instant later, she took him down on the floor.

The impact was a hard jolt back to reality and he gasped as if his breath had just been knocked out of him – or he had just *come back* from being dead. He was suddenly aware he was flat on his back. A moment later he realized something still had a hold of his arm.

Coltec grabbed Duncan's arm then paused, waiting for him to fully recover from his trance-like state. Studying his friend's face with a practiced eye, he nodded knowingly.

"That must have been a powerful vision to put you on the floor," he said as Duncan focused on his friend. "Many times the first experience is very intense and unsettling."

"The *first* experience?" Duncan emphasized, as he leaned into

Coltec's grasp and got to his feet. "You mean there'll be more? Is this going to happen to me again?"

"Only if you invite your animal guide into your spiritual life regularly."

Not likely ever again! Duncan thought vehemently. He was about to speak when Coltec raised his hand.

"The vision quest is a deeply personal experience. It is meant to reveal a person's most inner desires of the soul to themselves. It is not shared with anyone or it would offend your animal guide."

Oh really, that's not the impression I got from mine. I doubt if anything could have offended her, Duncan thought as both eyebrows went up.

Coltec hesitated, the question begging to escape from his lips. "I am forbidden to ask for any details, but would you at least tell me— have you seen this creature before in this physical reality and life, I mean?"

Duncan gave an exaggerated nod, *'Yes'*, as he headed for the bridge. *Whatever Tessa is doing, she's done doing it—just as soon as I find Joe.*

Chapter Forty

"I've got it," Richie said waving a large piece of paper as he struggled out of the porthole. Fitz and Sean pulled hard on the rope to help him out and Richie lost his grasp on the side of the ship. Flipping upside down, he looked like a poor imitation of a trapeze artist.

"Don't drop the paper, Richie," Fitz called.

"After all this work—are you kidding? Don't worry, even if I drown, I've got it."

"Monsieur, what happened? Did you lock yourself in the bathroom?"

Hearing the thick French accent, Richie twisted around to see a very stout man sporting an earth-tone chapeau. "Hey, Maurice—no, not exactly. Mac is kind of busy in there right now and he doesn't want any disturbances.

"What? He doesn't even let you use the bathroom? Inhumane!" Maurice shook his head.

"No, Maurice it's not like that. He's just well, meditating. It's bad karma or something like that to be disturbed." He waved the paper in his hand. "It's kind of hard to explain when you're hanging upside down. You see the ladies have concocted this pre-wedding game."

"Oh, of course. You're playing their game. Very clever and very sly." He wagged his finger. "Detective work, Richie. Have you found your food yet?" He shook his head. "Of course not—Maurice is too impatient."

"Our food? Do you know about that? Hey guys, would you pull me up? I feel like a spider here. It's awkward. Maurice, come on board and let's talk."

"Sean," Richie said when Maurice had joined them, "this is our neighbor, Maurice Lalonde. He has the boat next door."

Maurice touched the rim of his cap and bobbed his head. "Bonne journée, everyone. Oh, I must confess those ladies have recruited me as their accomplice in this game. They are very clever—their secret maps and this strange treasure hunt."

"So you know about all of this my good man?" Fitz asked.

"Oui—but of course. I was there when they drew this." And he motioned to the paper. "Tell me what deep secrets this reveals to you."

The four men each grabbed a chair and began scrutinizing the strange drawing.

There were clearly two different things going on in this picture.

The first was Tessa being escorted into a room by a cat and a dog. The words **Anubis** and **Bastet** were written into the carpet below their feet.

"Do you know who they are?" Maurice chided, eager to share what Cassandra had told him. "That dog, Anubis, is the royal Egyptian hound and that feline is the goddess of the sun," he finished with a knowing nod. "Miss Tessa is being prepared like royalty."

Solo, on the other hand, was saddled with baskets and laden with food. The tracks led away from Tessa and to the second of two boats—this one, a small rowboat.

Maurice sat back and smiled. "Well," he said looking at the puzzled faces in front of him. "Messieurs, haven't you figured it out yet?" He let his comment hang only a few moments before impatience overtook him. "Oh, come on now. There are three of you here to think. Can just a few beautiful women outsmart all of you very clever detectives? Look—see where the little llama has gone?" And Maurice walked his fingers in the tracks—across the water and onto the boat. "What is that telling you?"

"That Solo is on a boat with our food? That doesn't make sense. It's a tiny statue."

Maurice motioned something grand with his hands. "Sean, you must think of the big picture. Don't think of it as a little statue."

"OK, so the llama has our food on a boat." Sean looked around. "I don't see anything here that looks like a llama pack."

"Now you're thinking too practical. You must use your imagination just a bit," Maurice said.

"Can we just cut to the chase here?" Richie interrupted. "Do you know where this is?"

Maurice nodded. "Of course I do, but what would be the fun in the grandiose adventure if I told you the answer to everything. That is the point of the puzzle—to search, Richie."

"We're kind of hungry, Maurice. I could eat that llama. It would be a good time to help here."

Waving his hand in the air. "Ah, youth—always hungry and too impatient! OK, Maurice will help—but just this once. Look, there are two boats in the drawing and conveniently there are two boats here," he gestured to the barge and his boat behind it.

"So the ladies shifted our entire refrigerator over to your boat for safe keeping," Richie finished and patted Maurice's shoulder. "Guys, lunch will be returning in just a few moments. Come on, Maurice, your de garde is at an end."

"It was an énorme challenge for me to rise to," he began poetically.

"And I regret to say, Richie, not all of those under my watchful eye survived," he finished a bit apologetically, whilst patting his bulging stomach.

Duncan and Coltec emerged from below just at that moment. "Hey Mac, we found our food," Richie called as he started down the gangplank. "We might need a little help bringing it all back." Coltec and Fitz joined him.

"How did the vision quest go? That was quite fast. The spirits must have obliged your tight schedule," Sean asked lightheartedly. His expression shifted when Duncan didn't smile. "Is something wrong?"

Duncan smoothed his hair back with both hands then looked away briefly. "Wasn't what I was expecting it would be, Sean."

"What did you expect would happen?"

"I don't know what I was really expecting to happen, but what happened wasn't anything I would have ever expected," he replied, clearly uncomfortable.

"What did you experience?"

"Let's say it was a bit disturbing." He paused and glanced back to the receding trio. "I don't want to offend Coltec's beliefs, Sean. What is this vision quest experience really about? Why do you see—well—whatever you see?"

"There can be many reasons," Sean began, gentle professionalism in his voice. "Guided imagery – soul searching, or whatever you wish to call it, reveals directly what is in your subconscious mind. And what it has in mind, so to speak. It comes out. I take it from what you're not saying it was something not too pleasant. Have you been worried about Tessa recently?"

"I guess so. I'm wondering if I shouldn't be a bit worried about myself as well."

Sean returned a pensive stare.

"Let's just say I don't want to believe my relationship with Tessa over the past twelve years has been—let's say, that *shallow*," he finished awkwardly.

"You experienced something which is causing you to doubt the seriousness of your future relationship with her? Duncan, we are on the last countdown, so to speak. It's no time to be getting cold feet about the wedding."

Duncan shook his head. "It's not that at all, Sean. It's just—" he struggled with his sentence. Trying to choose his words and avoid what he did not want to say out loud was leaving him with little to say. He lowered his voice—embarrassed. "I never considered that sex could possibly be the only reason for our continued relationship."

Sean's eyebrows went up rapidly, but he held his comment for a long moment.

"Sex is naturally a part of both your lives, Duncan. What you really have is a very normal case of the pre-wedding jitters. But if you really want to psychoanalyze yourself, ask yourself very seriously, what is *this* Tessa to you today? How do you view her in your immortal world and in your personal life, going forward?"

Duncan gave an exaggerated, *come on now,* expression. "How many hours do we have before the wedding, Sean? I could go on and on describing her."

"Do it then," Sean folded his arms and rocked back on his heels.

"OK—she's smart, funny, creative, exciting, and beautiful. Sean, how many adjectives would you like me to use?"

"Well, at least your conscious mind didn't say sexy," he finished with a small grin.

"Look, Duncan, a lot has happened to the two of you since you first proposed. And there is no doubt a lot of hidden fear yet that you haven't really expressed verbally even to yourself. You may also feel a little guilty about some of the earlier passion you've shared with Tessa after she came so close to death. There may have been things you had wanted to say. When the shooting happened you feared that there was no time left to say them. Whatever you saw or experienced is likely the result of fear—personal perhaps, but for Tessa's life— certainly."

"You know, Tessa has chosen to undergo this thing she's called purification, or a personal renovation experience. I know they have made a game of it, but at the core, Tessa does somehow feel that she is sweeping out the old Tessa and her former life and remaking herself for what is to come next. I think it would be of value to you if you took a serious look inside yourself, privately this evening, when everything is quiet around you. Ask yourself, how you want your relationship to grow together? This might clarify what's bothering you and get it out in the open. Nothing is ever as dark as it originally seems when you shed some light on it."

Duncan grimaced. "Promise me I won't see my animal guide in this one."

"Only if you really want to see it," he returned.

Chapter Forty-one

An enormous glass and marble desk, flanked on either side by royal cheetahs, stretched out before the women. The desk, in and of itself, lent to the grandeur of the ambiance that was this room—the gateway to a great pyramid and all its eternal mysteries.

Statues lined the perimeter. Great and small, all of Egypt's finest man-animal gods were here. Their lifeless eyes looking out to those who had entered their abode.

The décor was heavy and dark—sconces with their torches wafted their synthetic flames up the hewn sandstone appearing walls. Golden cobras arched with hoods flared as if ready to strike. Some trailed from the wall sconces giving a sense of awe and foreboding to the customers who were waiting their turn at the desk. A sarcophagus, propped by a veiled corridor, suggested to the imagination what kind of immortality this establishment might just be offering behind their printed services.

Cassandra smiled as she watched Tessa's eyes light up like a schoolgirl on her first field trip. When Tessa was drawn to a large statue of Horus, Grace stepped in and took Cassandra aside.

"What really goes on in here, Cassandra?" Grace pointed to one of the masked attendants in a dark robe. "It is absolutely the creepiest, most macabre place I have ever seen in Paris. This is not a place you take someone who is preparing for a celebration of love in marriage in a little over two days. Tessa should not be here. Are you out of your mind?"

Cassandra drew back and stared at Grace as if she were a stupid child.

"Get a hold of yourself. I think some of your fourteenth-century superstitions are getting the best of you in here. This is just a business—nothing more. And I don't know what you're talking about—what in here is creepy? Nonsense—it's Egypt and it's not even their darker side—trust me—not even close. Besides, Tessa is a big girl, in case you haven't noticed. And she's hungry for something different—something truly out of the ordinary. She wants a big adventure so I'm giving it to her." *And you're not her mother, so stop acting like you are. There's far more in that little mortal's head of hers than you realize. She may have fooled you into thinking she is vulnerable, but I am millenniums older and wiser. She's not fooling me. She wants to move up from her mortal existence and join our kind—I can use that,* Cassandra mulled over in her mind.

"Well I don't agree with this," and she made a sweeping gesture.

"Call me parochial, call me old-fashion—if you dare—but this is not a happy place for someone who has gone through multiple traumatic experiences in so few months."

Her eyes scanned the large bust of King Tut and its multi-headed cobra candle stand as well as the masked attendants who were occasionally escorting people through the curtains.

"If there is any possible danger to Tessa in here, she will be leaving your party immediately. I say this is all macabre."

The silence was pregnant between them and Grace searched Cassandra's eyes for any sign of a hidden agenda. *I don't care how much older you are, if any harm comes to Tessa in here through your folly, you will answer to Duncan and me,* she silently promised herself.

The desk attendant was dressed in a white silk wrap around robe with a golden sash and delicate headband. Tessa stepped up to the counter and was about to speak when Cassandra walked up beside her. Using her hypnotic voice on the check-in attendant, Cassandra spoke.

"This maiden is destined to marry someone who has tasted the '*waters of eternal life*'," she began cryptically and with a grand gesture. "She must be purified before her wedding can take place. Give her the royal preparation—before Osiris and through your Waters of Eternal Life treatment—the works—everything."

The desk attendant stared blankly back at Cassandra as her hand moved, almost mechanically, past the registry which resembled an open scroll, to a lighted panel. She pressed a button.

Cassandra smiled to herself secretly as two attendants emerged from behind a cloaked entryway, one wearing the mask of the Egyptian king's loyal hound Anubis and the other, Bastet, goddess of the sun.

The mask-costumes were in the style of '*Cirque du Soleil*' where half of the human face was partially covered by the brightly contrasted gold and black mask and the rest was painted on.

"The sun goddess and imperial hound will guide you to your destiny," Cassandra added, still using the *voice*, as the attendants bowed formally to Tessa, then gently took her hands.

"All who enter within are forever purified and renewed," Bastet said as she parted the large drapes revealing a hallway that seemed to stretch on forever.

"I'll see you at the Waters of Life room," Cassandra called after

Tessa as she disappeared behind the curtain.

It was with a certain pleasure she also noted the desk attendant's trance-like state had made her forget to register Tessa in her log-book as a paying customer. *As far as anyone is concerned, Tessa doesn't exist in—convenient,* Cassandra thought.

Bathed in warm, soothing droplets, Tessa rolled slowly over. A deep sigh escaped her lips. *This is virtual ecstasy,* she thought as the warm Vichy shower's water pattered down her body, gently touching, stimulating and soothing every nerve and muscle fiber in her being.

Her attendant, who was wearing a simple Egyptian robe, was getting as wet as she was as she worked the length and breadth of Tessa's body with an exfoliating natural sponge. Every so often she worked the long metal bar suspended above the waterproof massage table, adjusting the heads and intensity, offerings variations in this hydrotherapy sensation as she continued to work.

Tessa laid her head back down. This was a pleasure she had not known before. *I could get used to this,* she thought to herself. *It's as if one thousand aqua-fingers were probing every pleasure cell on my body.*

This—the 'Washing Room'—was the first room she had been taken to in what she was told would be a long series of preparation rooms, leading up to the 'Waters of Life' treatment. A statue of Thoth, the Ibis-headed god, stood before her.

"What is he known for?" Tessa asked.

"That is the god of learning, writing, and measuring the passage of time."

Time – it had been a long time since Tessa had thought of time in any form. She propped her chin up on her arms and considered the statue. *I don't feel threatened by what you represent,* she said to herself. *I understand time now. I have lived between the seconds.*

The attendant turned off the water and began drying Tessa, one side at a time. The towel felt a little brisk on her newly exfoliated skin and she asked, "Don't I get a little moisturizer now?"

The attendant shook her head. "Your skin must be receptive to the anointing elixir so that you can properly be wrapped."

"Wrapped?" Tessa asked as she was helped from the table.

"Wrapped," the attendant repeated. "All of Egypt's greatest Pharaoh's kings passed through anointing and wrapping before they were sent on to eternal life."

Tessa's expression shifted noticeably to one of trepidation.

Grace and Ceirdwyn stood in the lobby watching customers milling about, uncertain what they wanted to do.

"OK, I don't see anyone being eaten by crocodiles," Ceirdwyn said dryly, "and except for the weird get-up everyone is wearing, this is probably nothing more than a high-end spa."

Cassandra had disappeared through another veiled doorway more than ten minutes ago, and it dawned on Grace that they were on their own now to decide how far they wanted their experience to go.

The desk attendant was looking toward the two women waiting expectantly for them to make a decision.

Ceirdwyn shrugged and stepped up to the counter. "I would like to get a manicure and a pedicure with a foot massage," she said. The attendant logged her in.

A few moments later a gentleman wearing a headband and wrap-around tunic came and led her into a side room.

Grace decided to take her time and look at the services on the spa menu. As she was browsing the menu, she became only vaguely aware that a gentleman had joined her at the counter. Though she was not trying to listen, parts of his conversation were filtering into her conscious mind.

"This is my first time… I'm not really sure what to request. Maybe just a little off the sides?"

Grace suddenly felt a gentle tapping on her arm.

"Excuse me, Madam," Dudley said quietly as he removed his Donegal cap. "This is my first time in here. Could you recommend something?"

Grace leaned over to the obviously obese man with rosy cheeks and spoke quietly.

"I recommend as little as possible in here," she replied with a smile and twinkle in her eye.

"I couldn't agree more," he replied as his eyes quickly scanned the immediate surroundings. "I never knew anything like this existed outside of a haunted house."

Grace winked. "I'm sure there's nothing different in here than in any other spa-salon in Paris. All these dark and heavy symbols just give me the creeps, that's all."

"If I may be so bold as to ask—what are you having done today?"

Grace closed the spa's brochure. "I will have hand reflexology and a manicure treatment. I think that much is relatively harmless."

"Me too," Dudley exclaimed with a large boyish grin as he began to visibly perspire. Taking out his handkerchief, he wiped his face.

As soon as they were signed up, the attendant took them back into a room across from Ceirdwyn.

Dudley sat down on the small chair, nearly overbalancing himself.

The attendant grabbed him before he fell—apologizing for everything and nothing, then went to fetch a larger chair—one that could hold the weight of a marble statue.

Further unnerved, Dudley wiped his face again. *Calm down. Grace doesn't suspect anything. You've never been this nervous around an Immortal before—come to think of it, you've never been this close to one either. Dudley, old boy, you can handle yourself, after all you're a professional Watcher. Mr. Dawson is a US area supervisor. He wouldn't have given me Grace if he wasn't confident in me. So why aren't you feeling so great just now?*

Tessa sat comfortably in her ergonomic chair. The room lights were dimmed. Before her hung a balance—reminiscent of Lady Liberty—except on one side of the scale rested a feather.

Her new attendant wore a dark hooded robe and carried an Ankh—the key of life.

"Before you can continue, you must pass Osiris' test—weighing the purity of your inner heart against the Feather of Truth."

Tessa gazed around the perimeter of the room. The Eye of Horus looked silently back. Firepots with their blue, yellow and red flames, licked upwards, casting eerie shadows around the otherwise darkened room. Flanking the scale was a pair of crocodiles.

"Who are they?" Tessa asked as she stared at the gaping dark jaws.

"That is Ammut—the Eater of Hearts—the devour," he said in the most solemn of tones. "Those who fail the test of Osiris are thrown to him."

In front of Tessa was a table with stones—broken and fragmented—they were in the shape of a heart. The attendant took Tessa slowly through meditation exercises of breathing, calming and stretching. After what seemed like a half an hour, her priestly attendant told her she was ready to face the test.

How can a heart equal the weight of a feather? Tessa considered this strange violation in the laws of physics.

Egyptian music was playing softly in the background, as her guide asked her to consider the puzzle. "These stones represent a human heart. What of all these stones will not burden you in life?"

Tessa looked closely at the stones and saw they each had gold printing on them. The meditation session was coming to an end and she pondered her decision.

"Take only what you need with you as you pass through this life and are purified for your next," her attendant said.

She pushed the stone sculpture apart trying to decide. Only one small heart-shaped stone remained in the middle; the inscription read '*love*'. She smiled, rose, walked to the scale, and placed it in the center of the pan.

The balance equalized.

Her attendant bowed formally. "You are now ready to be anointed with the elixir of the Pharaohs," he said. Making a grand sweep with his arm, he motioned her to another curtained hallway.

Ceirdwyn was relaxing in her chair as her feet were gently exfoliated, massaged from the tip of her toes to the base of her heel. As the first series of moisturizers were being applied, she sank into the plush chair. She was so deeply enjoying this entire pampering experience.

OK, she thought, *if you can get past the freaky costumes when you first walk in the door, this place is actually a high-end luxury that is just heaven to the senses.* She leaned forward briefly and saw Grace through the open archway sitting at a table with her manicurist and another gentleman.

Dudley was clearly uncomfortable with the manicure and hand massage. The attendant repeatedly assured him that she had worked on many gentlemen who came in for just the same thing. Not to worry—they all left with as many fingers as they had arrived with.

Grace exhaled and settled comfortably into her chair as her hands were gently exfoliated and massaged with moisturizer. Reflexology to the palms sent a warm and comfortable feeling through her whole being. When was the last time she had allowed herself to be pampered? She was always so caught up in helping and healing others that she often forgot about herself.

Maybe Cassandra is right—maybe I did overreact when I saw the décor. She reminded herself to loosen up. She had seen many things in her entire life which spanned the early 1300s until today. Maybe this is exactly what Tessa needed—something a little out of this world, and yet safely *freaky*—to get her into the excitement of the wedding with Duncan. *After all, she is marrying an Immortal.*

Lying on the table in a room lined with sarcophagus and statues alike, Tessa's skin was anointed with fragrant oils until she was completely slippery. The scent was intoxicating. Slowly and carefully, her attendants began wrapping banana leaves around her feet, legs, torso, arms and neck, stopping just under her chin. This was followed by carefully placed, and loosely wrapped, pure linen that was intended to hold the leaves in place.

Tessa thought, *I'm being wrapped up like a mummy.* Somehow, as strange as it was, this all seemed normal to her. Her imagination indulged itself. *I am on my way to join the immortal realm of the Pharaohs—fitting, as I am marrying an Immortal.*

The room was warmed with gentle air jets that kept the temperature high enough to be comfortable when wet. At the conclusion of their wrapping, her hair was anointed with a volumizing moisturizer and wrapped with a terry cloth.

"Now we will leave you to the gods." Carefully her two attendants picked up what appeared to be the top half of a sarcophagus. This open-weave, wicker-framed lid allowed the client to see out into the room with minimal visual obstruction. But when Tessa first saw it her breath caught in her throat.

"How long will I be in here?" she asked a little timidly.

"Until their anointing oils of life take effect," they answered cryptically. They bowed formally before lowering the lid, securing the hinge and finally giving her instructions on how to open it if she felt claustrophobic. Then they left her in peace.

Tessa was not afraid of tight spaces, but despite her initial exuberant burst of imagination, this whole idea of being placed in a sarcophagus was now a bit unnerving. Tessa speculated—in the time when this was practiced as a way of life and death—*did the immortal souls of the Pharaohs watch over the preparation of their body in a room similar to this?*

Time passed. In an absolutely still room, Tessa's ears caught a faint sound of something moving. Slowly she pushed the lid open and looked out.

To her right and left were the lifelike edifices of Anubis, each in

alert reposes – heads angled toward her as if waiting for her—their lord and master—to arise from her cocoon to eternal life.

Very slowly, so as not to disturb the wrappings, she sat up. With her arms outstretched before her, she gave a deep groan reminiscent of a classic 'C grade' mummy horror film.

"I am Tessa MacLeod of the Clan MacLeod, bound for immortal life," she said in the lowest pitch voice she could speak. A moment later, she giggled uncontrollably. *I can't believe I just did that,* she chided herself mentally. *It was fun. I would be a natural as a mummy! That sound must have been in the hallway,* she told herself. Slowly, she laid back down closing the lid carefully over herself. She was starting to enjoy the cocoon.

Behind the far curtain, Paula focused on slowing her breathing and calming herself. Dressed in an Egyptian's servants robe, she clung tightly to the curtain, keeping it between herself and Tessa.

Was this supposed to be 'it'? Is she an Immortal now? Doesn't she have to die first? I wish I would have spent more time listening to the Watcher's field advisor course instead of doodling on my notepad in his class. This is the first time I have ever been this close to an Immortal—I mean a pre-Immortal. I don't belong in this assignment—I can't be found in here! What will Tessa do to me if she finds me? Some Immortals are killers. Everyone's heard how gruesomely some kill. Taking a small pad and pencil out of her pocket to make a few notes, she dropped the pencil. It clattered on the floor and rolled out toward the sarcophagus.

Paula froze, trembling ever so slightly. Quickly she made the Sign of the Cross before herself. *She's going to find me now—I know it! I'm a Watcher and I'm going to die!* The longer she stood silently the more obvious it became that nothing was going to happen. As the moments ticked away, Paula got up the courage to crawl to the pencil, which had stopped near the first statue.

Nice dog, she unconsciously mentally commented as she retrieved the pencil then turned to retreat.

"Is someone there?" Tessa said from inside her cocoon.

Paula quickly flattened out on the floor. "Just a servant here to pay homage—I saw you arise," she responded quietly, nervously.

Tessa pushed the lid open just far enough to see and saw the back of a woman lying prostrate on the floor near her table. Her face was completely hidden from view.

"It's OK," she began gently. "The hounds can keep me company— I don't know how long I will be in here. You don't have to lay on the floor for me," she finished, a bit in awe of the service she was receiving in this unusual place, and in the same token, a bit embarrassed to have someone hired to grovel at her feet.

Climbing to her feet, Paula kept her face averted as she quickly left the room.

Chapter Forty-two

"Guys, I always thought hieroglyphics were so cryptic and so complicated," Richie said. Leaning over, he grabbed a couple more pieces of cold meat for his sandwich. "I really think I could get the hang of this. Look, these characters—a lion, a snake and so on—are all just the sounds of letters. It's like our alphabet only more graphic."

"OK, so you'll have a great future as an Egyptologist," Duncan said with a grin. "Have you figured out what it says yet?"

Richie scowled. "As near as I can tell from this Website, all of this—on each page—is just a couple of words. It has something to do with 'death' and 'rebirth'."

Richie turned the computer screen around so Sean could see. "I still don't get what Cassandra is trying to say?"

Sean set his glass down and leaned over to take a look.

"Hum? From what I have read, the Egyptian priests were consumed with studying the 'Book of the Dead'. It seems that everyone, almost from the moment they were born, started preparing for their afterlife."

"So how does this apply to what the ladies are doing now?"

Coltec washed down his last bite of sandwich and pulled the screen around to his eye.

"Purification could mean rebirth. Whatever Cassandra has written is probably intended to mean a form of transformation. You'll have to ask her."

"Death on every page—sounds delightful," Fitz said and made an, '*I'm grossed out*' face. "Death is the last thing I think of when I see beautiful women. Those Egyptians are positively morbid. I hope Cassandra isn't indulging Tessa in the darker side of Egypt's passion. That's the last thing she needs before her wedding to her illustrious prince over here. All this morbid stuff is not in my *book of love.* A wedding is a time for a wild romantic celebration."

"Yes Fitz," Duncan remarked, giving Fitz a knowing glance. "We know where your libido resides."

"Amour—oui!" Maurice exclaimed and gestured his punctuation. "A glorious night of '*romantisme sauvage*," (wild love) he finished, winking and elbowing Duncan.

"Maybe Cassandra just put these phrases in because it is what she remembered after almost 3,000—ah—hours of study," he quickly added for Maurice's benefit, a man who knew nothing about Immortals. Richie looked to Duncan for a yes vote but received none.

Duncan's brow was tinged with concern. *Cassandra has a dark side,* he thought. He scanned the walkways for any telltale sign of his

Watcher. "It's time I see how Tessa is doing. Richie, would you pull up the spa list in Paris. Check anything that has the word 'Egypt' or similar references in their name and get me an address."

"Aw, Messieurs—you don't want the last clue then?" Maurice said a bit disappointed. "And Miss Tessa worked so hard on this game." He pulled a folded drawing out of his jacket. "This is the most important one," he finished as they crowded around. "As I said—I, Maurice was recruited in this adventure too."

This picture showed Solo near their barge. In the final image, Solo was drawing a chariot which was waiting at their door. The inscription, under a cartouche, was in French. 'Venir à moi mon amour' (Come to me, my love). Richie was already deciphering the cartouche, having learned it was only a name.

"Tessa!" he exclaimed, gesturing a *ta-da* with his hands for his translation success. "And look at this—it's next to a royal symbol." Richie chuckled. "Tessa, 'Queen of the Seine'."

"She's always been a princess to me," Duncan added.

"You'd better go to her, Monsieur Duncan—before the other one beats you to it. You have competition."

"What are you talking about, Maurice?" Duncan asked.

"The other man—the one who stopped by while you and the ladies were away—he asked about the two of you."

"Who?"

"Aw—Maurice is bad with names but good with accents."

"So where was he from?"

"Everywhere!" and Maurice spread his arms. "He had so many accents he was obviously from everywhere."

Duncan shook his head. "Is there anything you can tell me about him?"

"He was very clever. I told him that you were playing a game to find Miss Tessa for the wedding. He looked at this drawing and said he would play too. I think he figured the whole thing out with just this one clue. You better hurry if you want to get to her first. I think he secretly plans to rescue her like a knight—you see, he had a sword and—"

"What?" Duncan exclaimed as adrenalin flashed from his head to toe. A moment later he forced himself to put a lid on his emotions. He glanced at the picture once again. *Who was after Tessa now? Had they really left their troubles in the States? Was there someone who wanted to play cat-and-mouse with them here?* He glanced to his companions—they understood.

Coltec, Fitz, and Sean exchanged knowing glances, agreeing with their eyes to protect Richie if necessary. Smoothly, Fitz distracted Maurice as Duncan slipped away and retrieved his katana.

Ceirdwyn was relaxing in the guest lounge as a group of people, wearing elaborate robes and headgear, entered and began milling around statues. She watched as the manager quickly walked up to them.

"I thought I'd told you people not to come back in here," he said quietly trying not to attract the attention of his clients.

"We aren't bothering your customers. We're only looking at your statues," one of their numbers replied. "I told you before, we're Neo-pagans. We worship these gods."

"This isn't a House of Worship," the manager whispered and glanced around. "The statues are for ambiance and for the customers, not for your devotion. I am going to have to ask you to leave now."

The group leader stepped between the manager and his boisterous subordinate devotee.

"This is a public place. We'll just stay for a few minutes. There won't be any trouble."

The manager looked about, fervently hoping that they would just go away.

Ceirdwyn shrugged. She wasn't a pagan—not in this millennium at least. How many times had she seen various faiths discriminated against? She couldn't count anymore. Shaking her head, she returning her attention to her beverage and the feel of her heavenly soft feet.

Stepping from her Imperial dais, that brought her from her sarcophagus room, Tessa nodded to her litter bearers. They bowed formally then left.

This time, she had paid attention when she was being carried through this strange infinity corridor. These rooms were actually laid out one across from the other, but a very clever artist had created a group of murals which gave the impression of infinite distance. She smiled to herself having figured it out. *One artist to another she thought—you're a mighty good artist to have fit all this together.*

Removing her large, plush Turkish bathrobe, Tessa draped it over a bar and descended the steps into the bubbling Waters of Life pool.

Someone has taken great pains to make this look like a grotto, she thought.

The three-meter long oval pool—complete with hewn rocks flanking the sides, and vapor-pots carefully concealed in the crevices—were changing color as their eerie mist rose, all completing the magical scene. The warm jets were pulsing slowly, caressing her with bubbles.

The feeling they were imparting brought another idea to the forefront of her mind. *I need a song for our wedding service—it's going to be* 'Eres tú' (It's you). *That is a beautiful Spanish song of love by Juan Carlos Calderón.* The lyrics, as sung by the Mocedades, began pouring through her head as she sank into an ocean of bliss.

Paula was quietly making notes in the corridor when one of the costumed spa team members walked through. Reaching into one of the rooms as he passed, he grabbed two large wicker baskets and continued toward her.

Quickly, she popped the notepad into her skirt. An instant later he shoved a basket into her hands and continued past.

Paula stared at the basket filled with flower petals. *What am I supposed to do with this?* she thought. A heartbeat later he halted, having not seen her move.

"Well?" he asked a bit irritated. "Get going. This should have already been done."

To where and then what? her hands motioned.

He stepped back to her. "The Waters of Life, of course—room number three. This is the rose petal part of the package—how long have you been working here, Ms.—"

The last thing she wanted was any questions. "Paula," she blurted out. "I'm new—just started today—I'm temporary." *What am I supposed to do with all of this when I get there,* she thought frantically.

The team member scowled then repeated. "Take these into room three, and pour them slowly into the water while the guest is relaxing—the rose petal rejuvenation segment—got it? Now get going. Our guests expect their full time." He propelled her forcefully in the general direction of the room.

Paula hurried off, stopping at each door along the hall to check numbers. Pushing the large laundry-size basket against the door, she entered. Rounding the curtain she froze—then quickly backed behind it.

Tessa was semi-floating on a cushion of bubbles when something tickled her chin—she ignored it. Another and soon another tickle— *what is tickling me?* Her senses told her to open her eyes. Tessa blinked. All around her they were floating, bobbing, drifting—rose-petals. She was absolutely surrounded. Quickly looking around, she saw the source.

A woman was kneeling and leaning over the edge of the stone railing. She was almost concealed by the rock outcropping at the far edge of the pool. With her face almost covered with a veil, this woman was scooping petals into the water.

She smiled at the absolute luxury she was being treated to. "Thank you, they're delightful."

The woman bobbed her head several times but remained silent.

Curious? Tessa thought. "Can you hear me? Parlez-vous français?" she asked again and drifted toward the woman cutting a path through the petals.

"Yes—I heard," Paula finally responded in a very small voice as she backed up a step from the edge of the water.

"It's OK—I don't bite," she said sensing trepidation in her visitor. "I always wondered what it would be like to do something like this. I'm, Tessa Noel—soon to be a MacLeod," and she reached her hand out of the water toward the woman. "This is sort of a pre-wedding present. How long have you been working here?"

Paula barely let Tessa touch her hand before she resumed scooping rose petals with real zeal. *How can I get out of here without being obvious?* she thought frantically. *I am not supposed to be talking to an Immortal, or pre-Immortal either. Observe and record only.* "I just started—it's my first day."

"Did you go to beautician school to prepare?"

Paula shook her head. "I'm a paleoanthropologist," she blurted out without thinking and regretted the sharing an instant later.

Tessa gave a startled shake of her head. "That's a mouth full. It's something to do with studying ancient cultures, isn't it? Why are you working in this place with that kind of educational background? Is it the Egyptian theme here?"

"No—I just got out of college—I need a job. I've got to earn some money. College was expensive," she said in rapid-fire succession, hoping to end the questions.

"I understand how that feels. When I graduated I didn't have much to live on either. I took a job as a tour guide on the Seine. It was about as far away as I could ever imagine from what I was training to be and wanting to ultimately do—but as it turned out—it was lucky fate. I met my future husband that way." Her smile warmed hoping to dispel what she now saw as the first job jitters in this young woman.

"You know, as strange as this all may seem to you now, today might be a very important part of your future."

You've got that right, thought Paula.

"Tell me, Paula, why did you study to become a—what was it—paleoanthropologist? What is so important to you about a culture that may have existed 400 or 500 years ago?"

"That isn't really old to me. Four-hundred years is almost yesterday. I look at the origins and predecessors of groups, tribes, loose associations of people who became a part of our present human species. That could be over a million and even two-million years old. I use their fossils and their art to understand them. They are extinct members of what would become us." Paula's voice gathered steam as her Peruvian passion began to peek-out from behind the self-imposed shell.

"Do you think art was invented by modern man? No chance. Anything that you may have ever done, or thought to do in your life, has already been done in some form at least one-million years ago or more. They were the real artists—they invented it—today we just copy and call it original."

Paula bit her lip as she unconsciously backed up another step. *When am I going to learn to shut my mouth! I might as well have just told this pre-Immortal, modern-artist that everything she's ever done is just a cheap knock-off of some monkey-faced Homo hominid's work. Oh God, Joe. What were you thinking when you threw me into this assignment!*

Tessa moved in closer and leaned against the rocks, studying this very curious woman. *A frustrated scientist—no, an art detective – in a place with nothing real to appreciate. Everything is only a show for the customers who want to enjoy an afternoon's fantasy. I feel for you,* she empathized. *Maybe I can reach out to her and learn something in the process.*

"I am fortunate enough to have a fiancé who appreciates art. We have acquired several lovely llama statues from South America—near Argentina I understand. Perhaps you could tell us a little more about their significance from a paleoanthropologist standpoint—why they were created the way they were and for what purpose."

Paula gave her head a nervous shake. "Don't know—maybe—doubt it. Anything you could ever get from a culture there would be just yesterday to me. They were all highly advanced already, almost two millenniums ago."

"Oh," Tessa said quietly, and a bit disappointed. "I suppose you are right. It seems they were working with astronomy, calendars, and time back then."

"They were obsessed with calculating the end—that's what the Aztec calendar is about—the end of time—or so they believed. On that date, it is really the beginning of a new world to those ancient cultures. As we near the end of time, the 'Prophecy of the Sun' must be fulfilled for the shift to occur. They believed a god who governs war and creation will return to make something right that is now wrong or at least out of order."

"How is that supposed to happen," Tessa asked, intrigued.

"Through a type of ritualized sacrifice which will end this cycle— at least that is what another Mayan archeologist interpreted the script on that damaged stone in southern Mexico to say."

That statement got Tessa's attention. *The end of time? So time is almost up now.* She rocked back on her heels in the water. Suddenly the violent picture she drew flooded back into her conscious mind in detail. Her mind churned.

"There is some talk that as we near that date, there are plans to hold ancient ceremonies at various sites in central and South America," Paula continued casually.

Duncan—my Duncan—what role is destiny calling you to play? Is he the sacrifice needed to end the cycle? Is that why he refused to raise his sword in my vision? Suddenly it was yesterday. Tessa's mind went into overdrive, as every detail and every scratch and scrape of her pencil—lead and blood—came vividly to mind.

Paula saw the dramatic shift in Tessa's expression—she felt the tension rise in this woman to whom she had been assigned and her own instinct for self-preservation kicked in. *What have I said? What secrets of hers have I stumbled on? I'm out of here!* Paula turned rapidly—at the same instant the sound of a door opening was heard. Startled, her foot hit a wet spot on the stone floor and she fell head first into the rail, flinging the entire remains of the basket at Tessa. Her hand caught the edge of the rail an instant before she would have joined Tessa in the pool.

Tessa stood up in the waist-deep pool covered with red rose-petals and looking every bit the *abominable rose-petal* monster.

Paula looked up as she worked her way back over the ledge. Stammering apologies in two languages she was visibly shaken as she eyed Tessa with abject fear.

As Tessa looked at the upper half of her body she heard Cassandra's laughter. Tessa broke down completely. *This was what I needed just now. That will teach me to stop thinking of morbid calendar-clocks before my wedding.* Tessa ducked under the water and let the rose-petals drift away.

"It's alright – no harm done, Paula," she said as she emerged from under the water. "You showered me with rose-petals, not rocks. Are you OK?"

Paula was speechless. *An Immortal too!* She bobbed her head 'OK' several times as her foot sought to find a hold on the damp floor. Climbing to her feet she left quickly with her basket.

"That was weird," Cassandra said as she removed her robe. Placing it and a long rolled towel by the cloak rack, she walked down the steps and into the pool.

"Poor kid. It's her first job. She wants to do everything right."

"She doesn't get my vote. You looked like someone tarred and feathered you just now. Wonder from where they scraped her up from?" She set her long bag down on the teak-wood shelf, laying her wrap and towel over it.

"Oh, it wasn't so bad," Tessa replied, a bit surprised at Cassandra's forceful criticism over something Tessa actually found funny. She shook off the comment.

"Anointed with rose-petals," she laughed and bobbed in the water once again. "Thank you, Cassandra—this has been all at once fun, exciting, a little mysterious, and I have to confess, a bit scary when I was being wrapped up like a mummy. There was one point where I was just lying there saying to myself, '*No way! Any higher and I'm out of here!*' It was an experience I won't forget." She moved closer to speak softer in the event the attendant came back.

"Cassandra, how long have you lived?"

"Since the bronze age," she said pensively. "I'm that old – give or take a century or two."

"I'm curious," Tessa continued as she eyed the large statue of Osiris. "Why did you choose an Egyptian theme for today?"

Cassandra flipped around and drifted with the bubbles. "It was my first really positive memory after I became an Immortal. I hadn't been an Immortal long when I made my way to Egypt. There I met a man. He was a simple Egyptian craftsman. He was a good and kind man and I fell in love with him. I hadn't yet become accustomed to recognizing pre-Immortals, as I am now. I just knew that I was falling in love with him. He was the first man that I really trusted after my village was destroyed by the marauding Immortals—the 'Four Horsemen', they came to be known as."

"What happened to him—the man you loved?"

"He became an Immortal after an accident. At the time, I didn't know what I should do as he was dying, so I begged one of the novitiates, in the temple of Osiris, to beseech the god to send his soul back. My poor man wasn't of noble blood, but the minor priest let his body be brought into the temple. The priest was in the middle of his prayers when he came back to life—an Immortal."

"I'll bet that was a shock."

"No kidding. The priest probably thought, *I can really talk to the boss – down there.* It wasn't long though before we both had to flee. It seems that being an Immortal, even in a culture where preparation for immortality is considered the norm, doesn't earn you acceptance."

"What happened to the two of you?"

"We drifted apart soon thereafter."

"And what about you *now* Cassandra," Tessa asked. "Do you want to marry in the twentieth-century?"

Cassandra considered her answer very carefully. "I thought about it several times, but I was never brave enough."

"How about an Immortal?"

"I have thought about that—the ones that didn't try to take my head that is. It never happened." *I'm not going to speak to you of how I felt about Duncan—how we felt about one another at various time in the past—and how close we may have come to being together for a long time.*

Paula was standing in the utility closet across from the Waters of Life room, finishing her notes. She folded her book and looked across the hall to the door. *If I want to gather any more information on what's happening in there, I'm going to have to be in there. An Immortal and a pre-Immortal—what secrets are they sharing?*

Edging out of her hiding place, she was about to venture back to the door when she saw a man at the far end of the hall. Paula quietly backed into her closet and closed the door to a slit to watch.

He was dressed in street clothes—not the costumes of the spa attendants. The man appeared to be looking for something when suddenly he paused, giving her the impression he had heard a sound. From his mid-length outer jacket, Paula watched him draw a sword.

An Immortal! He's going for Cassandra or maybe Tessa. Paula held her breath. Had he heard her? A moment later she saw him turn, and with a sword at the ready, slowly opened the door to the room. Paula bit her lip. *I've got to get in there. There is a large role of curtain near the doorway. I can hide behind that,* she told herself then quickly followed after him.

Cassandra stopped her monolog abruptly as her immortal senses told her another was approaching.

"Ceirdwyn, did you finally get brave enough to take the plunge and join us in the Waters of Life?" Cassandra asked as she drifted over to the edge of the pool by the door, expectantly.

"Not quite," came the unfamiliar male voice as a young blonde-haired man pushed the curtains aside. In his hand, he held a sword.

"Roland Martin," he said as he approached the steps of the pool. "Nice of you to get all cleaned up for me. I hate dirtying my sword."

Cassandra was caught off guard but recovered in a heartbeat. She pushed Tessa quickly up against the pool's rock wall and out of sight.

"I know who you are, Roland, and my answer is still the same. I'm not interested in you—not now, not tomorrow, and not in this, or any other, lifetime. Why don't you just gather yourself and toddle back to your mentor Harry Long. Where is he? I am surprised he let you out unsupervised."

Roland chuckled in a nasty sort of tone. "Bravo, I see you are still full of yourself, Cassandra. That's just fine if you're not interested in me because—surprise—I'm interested in you. You're not worth me. I've come for your head, not your love. So why don't you just float over to the steps so I don't have to get my feet wet coming in after you, and we'll take care of those immortal formalities of the Game."

Roland mounted the steps as Cassandra drifted back out of his killing sweep.

"Oh, Cassandra," he groaned. "I see you are going to make me get my nice cardigan wet. It will probably take me all day to get it dry. I thought you would be a better Immortal than that with me." He started down the first step.

"Very well, Roland. Let me get my sword and we'll step outside."

"Oh, I'm not interested in fighting you, Cassandra. I just intend to take your head—right here and now. Come on—be a good girl and swim over here." He raised his sword as his foot found the next step.

"You're crazy—we can't have a Quickening in here. It's too close. This building will go up in flames. There are people all through this building. They'll be killed."

"I don't give a damn how many of these mortals die because of your Quickening. Their lives are meaningless to me anyway."

"Didn't you bother to listen to your mentor on why we must remain a closely guarded secret?"

"It's just you and me in this room. I'm only interested in your head. Let's dance."

Cassandra's eyes flashed briefly, nervously, between Tessa and Roland.

Tessa hugged the boulder tightly as Roland's leg came into view. Her motion disturbed the water near the step, catching Roland's attention.

Shifting rapidly, Roland angled his sword to strike the unseen observer.

"Roland, No!" Cassandra shouted and lunged toward him.

Seeing her move, Roland recovered in mid-stroke and thrust the point of his sword outward—to the edge of his reach—and into Cassandra's chest. His foot slipped onto the third step with a splash.

Cassandra gasped as the blade pierced her skin. She quickly pulled herself off of his blade before he could drive it fully through her body and disappeared under the surface.

The moment Roland's foot touched the third step, Tessa lunged out from her hiding place. Grabbing his leg she pulled it out from under him.

Caught off guard, his feet flew out from under him and he toppled backwards, slamming down on the hard concrete steps. His head hit with a resounding *crack*. Blood began seeping slowly into the pool from somewhere near him.

"Cassandra!" Tessa called loudly then ducked under the bubbling surface. Searching with her hands, she quickly found and brought her to the surface. Cassandra wasn't breathing. Instinctively, Tessa positioned her head and prepared to give her mouth-to-mouth resuscitation when her subconscious thoughts reminded her, *she's an Immortal—she'll come back by herself. Just keep her head above the water.* Fighting against the action of the pool's jets, she pulled Cassandra around in the direction of the steps—then stopped.

Roland lay sprawled across the entrance to the pool.

Draping Cassandra's arms over the rock-ledge, Tessa worked her way as quickly as possible to Roland. Grabbing his arms, she hauled him up the steps and onto the landing as Cassandra came back to life.

Coughing and sputtering, she reoriented herself. "What happened?"

"We're getting out of here before he comes back to life," she replied, dropping his arms.

"That's not the way we play the Game, Tessa. Immortals don't run—we fight it out."

"What are you talking about? Come on—let's get out of here before he—"

"Too late for that," Roland suddenly said, grabbing her ankle and twisting it hard. "I didn't die—but you will," he finished with a ruthlessly cold smile.

The pain dropped Tessa to her knee on the hard floor, as she struggled to pull herself free from his vice-like grip.

"Let go of me! How dare you come in here like this," Tessa exclaimed, fearful and furious all at once. "You don't even have the good decency to adhere to your own rules, and take your sword business outside. You just couldn't wait, and too bad for any mortals who might be there."

Roland coughed, wiped his face and rolled over. His eyes scanned her naked form covered scantily in rose petals. Her blushing red cheeks, her milky white and tense bare breasts, her delicate skin beneath his fingertips were all ripe for his desire. It wasn't the look of lust his eyes returned to hers, but a look of disgust—he was viewing something that was inferior—mortal garbage!

"You're just another mortal. What do I care about you?"

"I would care an awful lot about this mortal if I were you," Tessa retorted angrily as she kicked and struggled on the wet floor trying to free herself. "Let me go, and **get out of here!**" she shouted.

A very nasty smile formed on Roland's face as he rose to his all fours on the slippery-wet stone floor.

"You're not worth my desire. I've raped better-looking bitches with their clothes on. There's nothing you can possibly do to me anyway. But there is something I'm going to do to you."

"Oh yeah—think again!" Tessa snapped as she quickly swung around. Her fingertips touched then grasped Roland's sword from the far edge of the landing.

"You're not worth the powder to blow you to hell!" With all her might, Tessa quickly swung the heavy weapon up, over and across in an arc severing Roland's head with a vengeance.

Ceirdwyn walked to the counter. "Excuse me," she said to one of the attendants. "Can you tell me how soon Tessa will be finished with her spa package?"

The attendant scanned the scroll registry.

"I don't see a Tessa listed," she said. "When did she come in?"

Huh? What are you talking about? She was the first one in line when we came in. "She was with us when we all registered—that was several hours ago. You signed us all in."

The attendant scanned the registry once again then shook her head. "Then I must have been asleep. I'm sorry there's no Tessa listed in here."

Ceirdwyn stared incredulously at the woman. Her consternation was broken a moment later as her senses detected the presence of another Immortal. Ceirdwyn looked expectantly towards the curtained doorway for Cassandra. But as the moments passed, the feeling faded. Puzzled, Ceirdwyn left the desk and walked to the doorway and peeked behind the curtain. There was no one there.

Dudley finished his spa treatment. Grace watched from the lounge as the man rose and walked rather unsteadily toward the doorway. *There's something seriously wrong,* Grace thought as she set her latte on the table.

"Mr. Dillon, wait a moment," she said, placing a hand on his arm. "You're not looking so well—how are you feeling? Please sit here a moment."

Dudley smiled and waved her off. "It's nothing," he said. "Comes and goes. This place is affecting my mood—a bit silly I know. I'll just step outside for a quick smoke." He patted his jacket pocket.

Grace shook her head as she studied his face. "I don't think that's wise. Sit here—please, for just for a moment let me look at you. It's alright, I'm a doctor." Grace passed her expert eye over his lips, his face and his fingers. A worried look formed on her face.

"I want you to take deep regular breaths and sit quietly. You need help. I'm just going to the counter. I'll be back in a moment."

Trembling, Paula stood aghast behind the curtain—a hand clamped over her mouth at what she had just witnessed.

Sword gripped in both hands, Tessa tried to use it to push herself up on her sore foot – to steady herself on her twisted and aching knee. Her leg suddenly buckled as her foot slipped out from under herself on the wet floor. She went sprawling across Roland's bloody and decapitated corpse.

"*Run!*" Cassandra shouted—but it was too late—a mist-like fog quickly welded up from that body and engulfed Tessa.

That energized wave—a preemptive buildup to the overload discharge and the ultimate release of an immortal Quickening—began to spark and swirl around the closest living being—the being who had released it.

In a purely instinctively human response, Tessa froze like a deer in the headlights. A heartbeat passed, then another—she hesitated—uncertain whether she could move. In those milliseconds, Tessa was in the eye of a living hurricane as the conscious, raging energy engulfed her, swirled and entangled itself around her legs, her arms and the sword in her right hand.

Confused by the mortal presence at its center, thin tendrils of pure Quickening reached out and touched Tessa's sword and arm repeatedly, probing with uncertainty. The feeling was that of static electricity jumping to her skin.

It's trying to enter me—it wants to enter me, Tessa thought. *To impart its power—no—to unite with another Immortal—with mortal me! Something isn't right—it knows I freed it—it can feel me. I'm not an Immortal. Oh God, Duncan—it's is pure soul stripped of any physical humanity—unimaginable violent and raw immortal power. To see the past of another, as if you've lived it, taste the intensity of his passions—the passions of another—the knowledge—the limitless feeling of 'forever', all given and taken in an act of violent possession—over and over again and again!*

This physical Quickening wave—now a palpable presence—finally washed over Tessa's naked body sending every hair straight up.

To know that feeling and be mortal! Can I possibly become an Immortal?

She reached out with her hand—sword in her open palm—into the thick mass that now felt like a thousand small pins pricking her skin. Her hand suddenly hit an elastic wall and was thrown back.

It's rejecting me!

A heartbeat later, a ball of pure energy hit her sword hand, crawled up her arm, then exploded around her, sending her off of Roland's body and onto the floor.

Tessa cradled her hand and arm, screaming in pain.

Finding no further attraction to the mortal form, it made straight for the nearest immortal presence—not as a fog, but as an enormous bolt of pure white energy.

That first bolt hit Cassandra straight on like a cannonball, knocking her off her feet and under the water. In rapid succession, energy bolts shot from Roland's lifeless form striking the water, the walls, and lighting. A blast struck the towering statue of Osiris which overlooked the pool, blowing the large overhanging cobra sconces into splinters.

The pool's water boiled and heaved upward like an erupting volcano, mood-lighting and skylights exploded sending glass in every direction. Incense pots in the statues hands fired up like flame throwers—the glass eyes of Osiris beamed like beacons into the water. The grotto itself radiated the energy as the living electrical discharge systematically overloaded every control in the room. The Quickening was everywhere and on everything simultaneously.

Awestruck beyond words, Tessa could only lay at *ground zero* in pain, watching the immortal energy welling up around her in a room that was literally disintegrating in front of her eyes. *The power of an immortal atom bomb,* Tessa thought. Another thought—fleeting—crossed her mind. *Is this what the final Gathering will look like? Explosion upon explosion everywhere? What will the final battle*

resemble if all of this power is pouring out from one relatively young
Immortal?

You arrogant mortal woman, her subconscious mind shouted at
her. *You cannot join with an Immortal's Quickening, or stand in an
Immortal's world—there is no place for you in this. Get away—fast!*

Painfully, Tessa found the presence of mind to scoot herself
carefully across the wet, glass-strewn floor. With the sword in her
hand, she clear away the debris in the path of her bare skin, as she
tried to put some distance—any distance between Roland's corpse
and the power that was pouring out from it.

Cassandra shot to the surface, her arms raised as bolts of
Quickening power appeared to grab her—hauling her into the air until
only her toes touched the water. A split second later she was dashed
back into the pool—a pool now resembling a boiling cauldron
awaiting its prey. An ethereal image of a pair of balances formed in
the air high above the pool—held by Osiris—the test of a true heart.
The Quickening swirled again and it was gone.

Clutching the curtains, Paula gasped—a dozen emotions—ones
she had not experienced in her entire lifetime—welled up and
collided. Her survival instinct screamed '*Run'*, but her feet wouldn't
move. She was frozen as she watched the raw, violent power of an
unstoppable Immortal's Quickening send the room up in a fiery glow.
The Quickening was near her everywhere.

The curtain supports above Paula burst into flames as the door,
struck by an energy bolt, exploded. Thrown against the wall, Paula
screamed as she was knocked unconscious by the force. She never
saw the final acts of the Quickening power.

Cassandra heard the screams, but she was still caught in the
Quickening – powerless to move on her own volition—as the
thoughts, the feelings, the conscious knowledge and experience of
Roland flooded into her along with the power he possessed.

Grace quickly walked to the counter and caught one of the
attendants.

"Call the paramedics immediately, I believe this man is having a
heart attack," she exclaimed. She never received a reply. An instant
later the curtains and King Tut wall trappings were blown off the
doorways as a double bolt of energy—the Quickening power—lashed
out striking and exploding anything in its path.

Good lord, thought Dudley, wiping his face with a trembling hand.
A Quickening—and it's massive.

Like volcanic lightning, it exploded in pairs—blasting the outer door, the lobby statues, the register, and all mood-lighting out of existence.

The eyes of the statue of Horus lit up, as did the Ankh in Anubis' hand. Two of the awestruck worshipers stared up at the almost eight-foot statues as their golden eyes came to life, beaming down at them. Living energy raised the statue's arm toward them as if it were offering the sacred symbol—the 'Key of Life'—to its devotees, beckoning them to join him in Egypt's eternal realm of the Pharaohs.

"Oh mighty Horus and Anubis, we accept your invitation," they gasped. Raising their arms as if in a state of rapture, they fell to the floor in supplication. An instant later the massive stone statues collapsed on top of them insuring their *spiritual* passage out of this life.

Another bolt of white-hot immortal power looped through the lobby. The statue of the goddess Bastet appeared to rise from its crouched position. The cheetahs flanking the check-in counter called out in a loud growl. The sarcophagus propped by a doorway rattled as if its occupant was desperate to flee the melee.

Hiding under the dubiously safe sarcophagus, a worshiper felt the sarcophagus shake violently. Before he could lunge away, it collapsed on top of him, concealing all but his priestly scepter.

Another bolt of energy ripped through the lobby blowing out the last of the windows. An instant later the fire alarm sounded.

With curtains and wall hangings ablaze, pandemonium broke out in the lobby.

One of the surviving Neo-pagans got up the courage to crawl through the smoky room to the opening and look down the hallway. The falcon-headed god, Ra, with his sun-disk ablaze above his head, was shining like a star—eyes beaming back as bright as flood lights.

"Ra has spoken," their leader gasped falling on his face in supplication as fragments of the crumbling building continued to burn around him.

"**Everybody out!**" the manager shouted and waved the customers toward the door as smoke began filling the rooms. Explosions could be heard in the hallway as Ceirdwyn looked quickly to Grace.

"Where's Tessa?" Grace shouted over the sounds of the Quickening explosions.

Ceirdwyn raised her hands in a gesture of '*who knows.*'

"The desk attendant doesn't even know she exists in here," she shouted back.

"What are you saying?" Grace replied, but she didn't have time to sort that comment out.

"Cassandra must have lost her head. Who could have taken it? I didn't sense another Immortal come in here."

"I did," Ceirdwyn replied over the screams.

"Who?"

"Don't know—never saw the person. The feeling came and went fast."

Out of the corner of Grace's peripheral vision, she saw Dudley collapse flat out on the floor. She was by his side in an instant. "Find Tessa and get her out of here," Grace called.

"What about Cassandra?" Ceirdwyn said as she paused.

"Cassandra is likely dead – and if she isn't, she can take care of herself. Find Tessa and get her back to Duncan fast!"

Placing an expert hand on his carotid artery, Grace turned to the manager and shouted. "Call the paramedics, and help me get him out of this burning building. This man is in cardiac arrest!" She pounced on his chest and began trying to resuscitate him. *What have you been doing to yourself for so long,* she thought as she tried to compress his chest and administer CPR. Fighting her way through his bulging, fat lined chest, she threw all her weight on top of him, trying to compress it as the building burned around them. *Come on – beat! You're too young to be gone forever,* she thought fervently. "Stay with me," she whispered. "You're too young—you've got so much to live for. Please stay with me now. I won't leave you—don't you dare leave me."

Ceirdwyn grabbed the remnant of the flaming curtains over the doorway and tore them off their hooks.

"**This way,**" she shouted, motioning that the door was clear. Then coughing, she quickly turned and darted down the hallway until she felt an Immortal's presence.

I'm alive, Tessa thought to herself, as her hand reached out for something to support herself. *What has just happened to me? Was I hit by the Quickening power?*

Fewer and fewer waves of power were being released—the Quickening was fading fast as Tessa rose to her knees, clinging to the sword still in her hand for support. All at once she felt a large, soft Turkish robe being thrown over her naked form—she felt herself being grabbed, hauled to her feet and steadied. She forced her eyes to focus through the haze. Looking around, a startled expression formed on her face.

"Connor!" she exclaimed.

At that moment, Ceirdwyn shoved the remains of the door aside and pushed her way into the flaming room. Connor's presence made her pause momentarily.

"Help me get her out of here," Connor said, motioning to the Quickening-stunned Cassandra who was trying to crawl up the steps.

Ceirdwyn grabbed Cassandra and pulled her from the pool. Connor tossed her robe to her and then grabbed her sword.

Connor made as if to pick Tessa up, but she protested.

"I can walk—my head is still spinning—just help me."

"Come on, Tessa we got to get you out of here."

Cassandra and Ceirdwyn had already left as they started for the doorway. Tessa spotted Paula, partially covered by the burning curtains on the floor.

"Connor," she exclaimed, "it's Paula. I've got to help her."

Connor hesitated, stopping Tessa as she tried to hook the curtain rod off Paula with the tip of Roland's sword.

He shook his head with impatience then, releasing Tessa, kicked over the flaming curtains and holders. Reaching through the fire, he threw the burning remnants aside. His hand was singed in the process—he knew he would heal. Helping Tessa to lift the woman out from under what would have surely been a fiery grave, they half dragged, half carried the woman out of the building.

"She's hurt," Tessa said, ignoring her own painful arm. "The entire room was exploding around us. She needs help."

"Sounds like a normal Quickening to me," he remarked in his usual raspy voice and dry sense of humor. He turned Tessa's arm over and examined the strange mark. His eyebrows rose noticeably.

"Did you beheaded him?"

She nodded.

He nodded his head back towards the building. "That's why you don't take heads in a wooden building. The Quickening is so forceful it can send a building up in flames and bring it down around you. Only an Immortal can escape that. Come on, I have to get you out of here and back to Duncan."

The screaming sounds of the ambulance and fire truck sirens approaching were heard. Paula was aware of several people with her—holding her.

"It's alright Paula, we're out of the building now. We'll get you some help. You'll be OK," Tessa fell silent.

Paula blinked several times and focused on Tessa. She was staring at her wrist Watcher's tattoo. Her heart leaped into her throat.

Tessa quickly glanced to Connor. His attention was occupied elsewhere as Ceirdwyn and Cassandra rounded the building.

"Shh," she said quietly. "I know about Watchers," she whispered and pulled Paula's dislodged Egyptian armband back over the tattoo. "It'll be alright."

"What about Roland's body?" Cassandra asked, pushing her hair back.

"Leave it. Roland's sword is out of there," he motioned briefly to it in Tessa's hand. "They will think he died in the explosion. Come on everybody."

"I have to get my clothes," Tessa said and turned back to the door.

Connor stopped her.

"No, you can't go back in there. You'll be overcome by the smoke. Let the fire department do their work. Besides, you both look great in those Turkish robes."

Everyone heard the emergency vehicles pulling up in front. With Tessa and Connor's help, Paula walked slowly around the building to the street. The paramedics and Grace were working fervently on Dudley.

"This ambulance is going to be full," one of the paramedics said as several men hoisted Dudley into the back.

"She can ride with me," Grace said. "I'm on my way to the hospital. Tessa, are you alright?"

Tessa nodded then brought her blistered and Quickening-burned arm up briefly. "It's a long story—I'm going back with Connor now—I'll tell you later."

Grace paused briefly, took hold of her arm and scanned it with a professional eye. "What happened here?"

"The Quickening," Connor whispered. "Seems Tessa has been taking heads in there."

"What?" Grace gasped. Her eyes flashed between the red streak and Tessa's eyes. "This isn't supposed to happen—not with a mortal. It touched you?"

Connor nodded then glanced quickly around. "Let's go, Tessa. Unless you want to go with Grace to the hospital to get this looked at."

Tessa shook her head. "I want to get back to Duncan."

"But the burn—that wound should be—"

Another fire truck jumped the curb and headed for the off-side of the building interrupting Grace's next sentence.

Connor grinned. "Tessa is full of surprises. You'd better get going." He steered Tessa away and back toward the rear of the building. Connor motioned for her to grab Roland's sword from the side of the building where she had left it.

"My arm doesn't hurt as much as it did before. It still looks bad, though. Connor, I have an idea."

"So do I—and it involves getting you into my car. It is parked behind that building." He motioned to the building adjacent to the Spa. "Lucky I left it there and not here." Suddenly, he stopped dead, and stared at Tessa in the most peculiar manner, then chuckled. "You're ready for another adventure, aren't you? Even a Quickening can't stop Tessa," he said with a quiet laugh. "I always told Duncan he seems to get all the good women," he finished with a twinkle in his eye as they headed back around the building.

By the time they arrived, Cassandra had ducked back inside to rescue their clothing.

"Cassandra went back in," Tessa said.

"Cassandra is an Immortal—she'll survive no matter what. I still say you don't need them."

A moment later Cassandra emerged, coughing and with something unrecognizable in her hands. She flung the entire wad into the dumpster.

"Wasn't worth it," she said between coughs. "Entire dressing room went up or is smoked out." She looked around. "Where's Grace?"

"I think someone had a medical emergency in the lobby," Tessa said. "She's on her way to the hospital with someone else we rescued."

"Today is finished as far as I'm concerned," Cassandra said with a rather sour expression.

Ceirdwyn glanced back toward the street. "My car is near that ambulance."

"I'll take care of that." Connor winked then disappeared around the corner again.

"What were you thinking?" Cassandra asked once Connor had left. "You can't take an Immortal's head."

"What?" Tessa stammered. That comment came at her out of the blue. "Excuse me?"

"What are you saying, Cassandra? Tessa took Roland's head in there?"

"That's exactly what happened—and with his own sword. What were you thinking? You're not part of the Game."

Tessa stepped back and eyed Cassandra. *I just received a cold slap in the face for managing to stay alive in there—never mind that I also saved your head,* her unspoken expression said. "And you're welcome," she retorted sarcastically. "That's a mighty strange way to say 'Thank you' to someone for saving your immortal life."

"Didn't you hear what I just said? You're not a part of the Game. You can't go around interfering as you please. Whatever happens to me—to Duncan—you can't violate our rules when it suits you. You won't be thanked for interfering."

"Cassandra!" Ceirdwyn exclaimed. "What's the matter with you? He had no business challenging anybody in a public place, especially with a mortal present. He broke our immortal Rules of Combat. Did you expect Tessa to simply stand there when he finished with you and wait for him to kill her too? Leave no witnesses—few Immortals are that dishonorable."

"He didn't see her until she moved, Ceirdwyn. So stop mouthing off like you were there. I pushed Tessa behind a rock. It was her choice to attack him."

"That isn't the way I saw it from where I was supposedly 'out of sight' and hiding. Oh—did you have a plan, Cassandra? I didn't see one." Tessa spoke up, her cheeks taking on a rosy blush. "The only plan I saw was you losing your head in the same pool I was standing—in and frankly—I don't like swimming in blood. I don't care whether you think some immortal honor was disrespected. That bastard waltzed in and was in the process of taking a stroll into the pool for your head—and anyone else's for that matter. Maybe his 'humanitarian'—*'Oh how I respect mortals'* speech floated over your head along with the rest of the bubbles? There is no way in hell I was going to let him kill me—mortal or immortal."

"And, after you killed him—you knew what was going to happen. You could have run. But no—what did you do? You just lay there—sprawled all over his body—like some vulture waiting for a piece of his Quickening." A very cold expression formed on her face. "You dare to think you could ever be one of us? Marrying Duncan won't make you an Immortal. Did you like the experience you had today?"

"That's enough, Cassandra," Ceirdwyn said and stepped up to her. "What are you talking about? The Quickening won't touch a mortal—not directly."

Tessa held out her hand and arm. Her palm was lightly burned with the impression of the sword's handle, and a branched streak was emblazoned on her forearm all the way to her elbow.

"Don't worry, Cassandra, you got the lion's share of what didn't burn me."

Ceirdwyn gasped as she carefully turned Tessa's arm back and forth.

"This isn't possible—the Quickening never touches a mortal."

"She had a sword in her hand—it's metal—the floor was wet—OK?" Cassandra interrupted, trying to downplay the event as much as she could. "The energy was attracted to it and nothing more."

"Then why wasn't I simply electrocuted if that's all this Quickening is supposed to be? Why did I feel as if Roland's conscious presence—his living essence—was probing me before it finally went into you? Something did reach out from his body and touched me."

Cassandra looked away annoyed by how much Tessa was trying to make of her experience.

"You felt Roland in the Quickening? Cassandra, this shouldn't have even happened."

Cassandra turned back sharply. "Alright, Ceirdwyn—is Tessa one of us—is she an Immortal? Can you sense her? Well? I can't. And we both know what another Immortal feels like—a pre-Immortal too. Are you getting anything off of her at all? I'm not," she finished, miffed.

Looking at Tessa, Ceirdwyn focused all her immortal attention on the woman. After a long moment, she shook her head slowly '*No*', then added a cautious, "Maybe—I might be feeling something."

"You're dreaming," she snorted.

Cassandra was about to open her mouth again when Ceirdwyn spoke up. "I think we have both heard enough of this subject, Cassandra. Just drop it. This was planned as Tessa's day."

"You go and play games if you want to, I'm done." Cassandra turned to leave.

Ceirdwyn threw up her hands. "You're going to walk through the streets of Paris barefoot and with only a Turkish bathrobe on—in December?"

Cassandra held up her car keys as she walked away. It was the only thing she saved of her burned and smoked belongings.

"I've been ogled for millenniums. There isn't a single look these Parisians could ever give me that I haven't already seen. Have a nice playtime—both of you."

The occasional person was still exiting the spa when Connor rounded the corner of the building. Fire personnel were unrolling their hoses in as flames were now seen leaping from the roof of the building.

"Alright, everyone," Connor spoke up, flashing something palm-sized and shiny at anyone who looked his way. "You—are you the Spa's manager? Help me move these people over there," he motioned to a spot far away from Ceirdwyn's car.

"Inspector?" the Spa manager began as he glanced at this nondescript man in a wrinkled, tan overcoat who was flashing what he thought was a badge.

"That's right," Connor interrupted, failing to supply a name. "Way over there—back behind that tree." Catching the manager's arm, he switched tactics to keep him off guard.

"I don't want to say this too loudly—frighten everyone and start a panic—do you understand? I have reason to believe your establishment was targeted by terrorists. You know the type—fanatics. One moment they're sipping lattes and babbling nonsense in your vestibule—the next thing you know, they're planting bombs."

An image of the Neo-Pagans came immediately to mind and he raised his finger to comment. But Connor cut him off.

"Good—I see you understand. There might be more bombs in the area. Now, if you could help me quickly get everyone away from that car," and he pointed to Ceirdwyn's rental. "I need to get that vehicle away from here now."

The man bobbed his head and hurried as many people as he could grab away from the car as if it were ticking and about to explode.

Connor jumped in and shoved Ceirdwyn's key in the ignition. Quickly he drove away as the real police inspector's car was pulling up.

Quietly, one of the Neo-pagan devotees walked around the off side of a nearby building. Looking about, the young man pulled the Velcro free on his robe. Wadding it up, he put it in the dumpster then reached for his cell phone exposing his Watcher's tattoo. His call was acknowledged and before speaking he glanced about to be sure he was alone.

"Roland Martin lost his head in the spa just now—no—I don't know which Immortal took it—there were several immortals inside. It wasn't Ceirdwyn or Grace—they were in the lobby the entire time. Cassandra and Connor MacLeod came out the back door with the Watcher, Paula Roca, and another woman."

The man listened for a long moment before responding.

"Yes that woman had a sword in her hand but I was too far away to hear anything that was being said. If there was another Watcher inside, maybe they know what happened."

He closed the cover. He would wait for an update before finishing his Terminal Report on Roland.

Before turning to leave, he removed his Egyptian headband, tossing it into the dumpster as well. He wouldn't need his cover anymore. His Immortal was dead, as were some of the others in that bizarre group he had been placed. He would be reassigned next week.

Connor pulled up near Ceirdwyn and stepped out of the car.

Ceirdwyn looked to Tessa for acknowledgment that she was riding with Connor. "See you on the barge tonight," she called as she drove away.

"How did you find me?" Tessa asked.

Connor looked her straight in the eye then winked. "By playing your game," he said and grinned.

"What about Duncan and the rest of the men?"

"I don't know. No one but your neighbor was there when I stopped in. He was eager to share his part in this elaborate treasure hunt you designed. Are you ready for the ride back?"

Tessa nodded and picked up Roland's sword once again.

"Throw it in the trunk," Connor said, reaching in his pocket for his keys—that sudden strong sense of immortal presence halted him in mid-step. A motorcycle screeched to a halt in front of the pair, and the rider removed his helmet.

"Harry Long," he exclaimed over the engine noise and dismounted. "I sensed a *ripple* in my apprentice's Quickening when he passed it on. I came for whoever took Roland's head today." Reaching to the sword scabbard tied under his seat above his bike's exhaust, he drew it and faced Connor.

"I didn't take anyone's head," Connor said as he smoothly maneuvered Tessa behind himself.

Harry slowly leveled his sword at Connor. "I was told you were in there."

"So? Do you feel the power of a new Quickening about me?"

"No," he said cautiously. "But I do sense something strange—somewhere here," he finished very slowly, trying to make sense of the new sensation.

"I beheaded that bastard when he came after me in there," Tessa spoke up defiantly.

"Impossible, you're a mortal. He wouldn't have challenged you."

"No—he had something better in mind. He was going to rape then kill me. So much for your immortal *Rules of Conduct*."

Harry saw Roland's bloody sword in her hand.

"You don't have to be an Immortal to use it," Tessa finished coldly.

The look of absolute shock on Harry's face was inescapable as Connor nodded.

"She did indeed. That place will burn to the ground because your apprentice didn't adhere to our immortal Rules of Combat either."

Harry swung the point of his sword toward Tessa.

"You mortal bitch," he growled. "Let's see you take me now."

Chapter Forty-three

Joe's cell phone rang. Retrieving it he flipped the receiver open. The message was anything but settling.

"Yes, I have a couple of Watchers on the inside—" He paused to listen. "What? Come again? What happened?"

The reply was alarming. Grace was on her way to the hospital with Paula Roca. The building was burning to the ground from a Quickening. Several people were confirmed dead inside. Dudley Dillon was rolled out on a stretcher and may be dead.

Joe wiped his face nervously. "Who else got out?" Joe asked as he began to sweat. Tessa had been there all day. *Did she make it out or not,* he thought frantically.

Connor MacLeod, Ceirdwyn, Cassandra, and Grace were the Immortals reported to be leaving the area. He hadn't recognized anyone else.

Joe swallowed hard and thought. *Grace is on her way to the hospital where she used to work—what went on? Is Tessa with her too or not? There was no positive ID on the Immoral who lost a head. This man thinks it was Roland Martin, but who took it? Was it Connor or Cassandra?* Joe's expression darkened. He hung up and considered his next action very, very carefully before he dialed.

Duncan, Fitz, Sean, Richie, and Coltec were all waiting on the bridge of the barge for Tessa to return.

"I'll bet the ladies have hired a limo," Richie said, leaning back against the rail. "That's probably what this part of the drawing means."

"How do you get a limousine out of a llama pulling a chariot?" Fitz asked.

"Fitz, that statue is solid gold—expensive, OK—so naturally you think limousine. Simple logic," he finished with a tug on his T-shirt as if he were wearing a tie.

Duncan's cell phone rang. Flipping open the receiver he heard Joe's worried voice.

"Duncan, it's against my oath and better judgment to be telling you this, but you'd better get down to the Egyptian Oasis spa. A Quickening inside the building just sent it up in flames. Tessa was there all afternoon—go—hurry."

Duncan flipped the receiver closed and quickly relayed the message to his companions. "I'm going after her. Everyone—just stay put." Retrieving his katana, he was in his car and away.

Firetrucks—their sirens blaring—were making their way through the crowded Paris streets ahead. Duncan swerved to avoid a motorist who had drifted into his lane. Smoke could be seen in the distance down the street. Duncan hit the break as a motorist came to an abrupt halt in front of him. His hands slammed the steering wheel in frustration. The Paris police were cordoning off the road up ahead He could go no further in this direction. Shifting rapidly, he threw the car in reverse and wheeled around hard. Speeding across an empty pedestrian zone, he snaked around a traffic restrictor and speed up a side service road toward the spa.

Connor reached a hand to his sword but didn't draw it. He could see people in the distance. If he could see them, they could see him. A moment later both Immortals felt another approaching.

Duncan's car speeded up the service road, jumped the curb, and skidded to a halt near the trio's position. He bolted from the car—katana in hand.

"Glad you could make it, cousin," Connor said, keeping Tessa behind himself. "Harry here is determined to kill Tessa for beheading his student."

"**What!**" Duncan exclaimed then readied his attack. "I'm Duncan MacLeod of the Clan MacLeod."

"Harry Long—and I'm not here for you—but for her!" he snapped.

Tessa raised the sword in her hand around Connor, but Connor reached back and clamped a hand on it, forcing her back behind himself.

"One Quickening is enough for you today," he said with a sideways grin. "Give Duncan a chance at Harry's Quickening, will you?" he finished facetiously.

"Come again?" Duncan said taking his eyes off of Harry for a long moment. "What did you say?"

"That woman killed my student, Roland Martin."

"Tessa is full of surprises, Duncan. There's a long story connected to her day."

"I'll just bet there is."

"I'm not leaving her alive."

"You can't challenge Tessa. She isn't one of us."

"I don't know what the hell she is, MacLeod. She took Roland's Quickening—somehow."

"That's impossible—she's mortal," he finished, his eyes flashing between Tessa and Harry.

Tessa held out her injured hand and arm so Duncan and Harry could see it. The branched red streak was now thoroughly red and swollen.

Duncan stared momentarily but remained silent.

"We had all better get out of here," Connor said anxiously, as flames began licking out of the open building exit. "You don't want to do that here, Harry—Duncan. The fire department is going to be back here any minute now hosing us all down."

"If you want her dead, you'll have to take my head first," Duncan said defiantly. He motioned with his head. "Down that alley—now."

"I'll be back for you—bitch," he finished. Tucking his sword under his arm, he jumped on his bike and took off in the direction of the alley.

"Take Tessa home, Connor, and keep her safe. I'll be along in a while."

"Be careful, Duncan," Tessa added wistfully as Duncan started off after Harry.

Connor shut the door firmly as the roar of a motorcycle engine was heard in the distance.

Duncan rolled the smooth dragon's head and neck of his katana in the palm of his experienced hand. Up ahead, Harry made a tight circle and stopped, facing Duncan.

Duncan swept the blade into several lazy strokes, waiting for Harry to dismount and advance.

But instead of dismounting, Harry swung his sword around and over the handlebars then gunned the bike forward in jousting style.

Momentarily startled, Duncan leaped to the side and countered with a sword stroke.

Harry spun in a tight circle around Duncan, his sword whipping around, his cuts in an ever tightening circle of death.

Duncan was forced into an almost continuous parry as Harry spiraled, using the bike's momentum as leverage against the force of Duncan's defensive blows. A cut to the shoulder—a cut to the neck—a thrust to the side—all barely deflected.

Harry swung and thrust for the rapidly shifting Duncan. His swings were powerful, but he was at the mercy of the laws of physical which kept his bike upright. Harry, a master of the joust in the fifteenth-century, could not make his bike maneuver with the flexibility of a horse.

Duncan switched tactics. Blocking a downward cut, he dropkicked the side of the saddle as Harry passed, toppling him.

Harry pulled out from under his bike as Duncan bore down on him, the katana's blade striking the seat where he had been.

Rolling, Harry was on his feet in an instant, driving his two-handed weapon with the force of an ax—again and again—each swing seeking to cut his opponent in half.

Duncan parried then thrust out and upward—his blade absorbing and deflecting the force of Harry's crude but deadly chops. A split second of timing brought his blade across Harry's arm, slashing deeply into his muscle.

Harry hollered once and maneuvering away, trying to buy time while he healed.

But Duncan kept the pressure on, forcing Harry's back against a wall—forcing him to stand and *in-fight*—something for which his sword was ill-suited. Duncan's blade drew a deep slash across Harry's midsection and he folded, but not before his blade struck home on Duncan's upper thigh, cutting nearly to the bone. Duncan went down as much with the pain as the surprise that Harry had actually found an opening that low.

Holding his gaping belly, Harry launched himself at Duncan—sword poised like a giant chisel—ready to impale him to the ground, to sever his spine and rendering him helpless for the final blow.

Duncan rolled over. As Harry dove for him, he raised the point of his Katana like a pike.

Connor had just pulled up to the stop sign at the edge of the busy Paris street when the sky behind them exploded—lit up with the power of the Quickening.

"Connor," Tessa exclaimed and turned to face the light. "I should be there with Duncan, no matter what has happened. Turn around!"

Connor shook his head and flicked the turn signal on. "There are some things you simply cannot be a part of, Tessa. This is one of those things and times."

"I've seen Duncan fight and take the Quickening before, Connor. There are no Immortal's secrets that I can't share," she protested.

Connor shook his head briefly then returned his attention to the traffic.

Tessa sat back sullen. *If that man has taken Duncan's head—I'll get his, I swear it,* she thought silently.

Chapter Forty-four

Joe knocked quietly on Paula's hospital room door then entered. Paula was sitting up in bed writing in her Watcher's data book.

"How are you feeling now, Paula," Joe asked gently.

She glanced up at him but didn't immediately speak.

"The Egyptian Oasis spa is a total loss. That must have been quite some Quickening," he finished, with a grin.

Paula closed her book slowly. "I'm just making some final notes. Whatever details I can recall yet, then this is yours," she said and nibbled her lower lip. "¡Lo dejo!" She exclaimed all at once. Her tendency to gesture her punctuations was being hindered by an IV in her arm. She took a deep breath and composed herself. "I had no idea what to expect with Immortals—pre-Immortals—whatever. ¡No me importa!" She shook her head, frustration building. "I don't care – it's not something I ever want to see again. Don't you understand? That's not why I became a Watcher."

Joe balanced his weight on his cane and gave her an inquiring look. "Shh. Keep your voice down. You're a Watcher Paula. In this business, the unexpected is expected. We're dealing with Immortals—pre-Immortals too. We just happen to have been lucky enough to identify one. This is what is meant by getting experience outside the classroom."

"No one ever knows what they are going to run into when they go out in the field."

"Joe, you knew I had never trained for a field assignment with Immortals. I was nearly killed yesterday—I would've died if it weren't for Tessa and Connor Macleod. I understand the building was burning down around me. I wasn't conscious when they pulled me from the flames." She shook her head.

"After what I saw, you're going to have to find somebody else to follow Tessa. I'm finished—do you understand? ¡He terminado aquí!"

"You take a Watcher's oath for life in this organization," Joe reminded her firmly. "You just don't jump ship when you feel a 'speed bump'."

"¿Estás loco? What speed bump are you talking about? I watched Tessa slice a man's head off. If this is a speed bump to you, I'd hate to see what you're calling a train-wreck. That woman is an insane killer. There is no telling who she'll kill next. I have only one life, Joe, and I want it. I don't care what I have to do at Headquarters—I'll peel potatoes in the kitchen. I just don't belong in the field near that killer."

Joe lowered his head and sighed. "OK, I'm not accepting anyone's resignation today. I'm just here to listen." He let several moments pass in silence.

"Would you tell me what happened out there with Tessa?"

Paula took a deep breath and concentrated.

"I was in the stock room—across from the Waters of Life room that Tessa was in. Roland just walked into the room with his sword in hand and went after Cassandra. I followed him in, slipping through the partially open door, I hid behind the curtain. I saw him stab Cassandra in the pool and then attack Tessa. She beheaded him with his sword. I've never seen anything so gruesome in all my life."

Tessa? Joe thought. A very puzzled look formed on his face. *Was that what Grace was talking about in the restaurant? Preparing her to take her first Immortal's head? Is Tessa an Immortal now or what?*

"Where did his Quickening go? What did it look like?"

"It looked like a raging tornado had engulfed Tessa—one moment it was sparking everywhere around her—and then it just exploded like a bomb and she was thrown off of his body."

"So, the Quickening went into Tessa?" he asked puzzled.

"I don't know—I don't think so—I'm not sure. It was all around her—it looked like a massive beehive. One moment she was lying across his body, the next she was on the floor screaming in pain. After that, it went for Cassandra—not like the beehive that was around Tessa, but like a bolt of lightning. Joe, it was all over the room and on everything. Every place was on fire. I saw things appear in the Quickening fog I've never seen in my worst nightmare."

"Did you actually see the Quickening go *into* Tessa or not," Joe pressed. "Did it behave the same way it did with Cassandra?"

"A bolt struck near the door where I was standing—it just blew everything apart and I must have passed out. I never saw the whole Quickening event. When I came to, I was outside of the building— Tessa and Connor were there with me. Oh God, Joe, Tessa saw the Watcher's symbol on my wrist. She knows I'm a Watcher. I can't go near her anymore."

"You don't have to worry about Tessa knowing—she's not going to hurt you. She knows about Watchers—so does MacLeod."

Paula shook her head vehemently.

"This isn't right, Joe. None of it is. I'm lucky to be here. I was in there—the whole building was burning. I saw the flames all over— everything seemed to come alive with Quickening fire. The next moment I can remember, I was in Tessa's hands. I never felt so scared in all my life. That woman butchered someone right in front of me and I was lying in her arms. I didn't know if I was going to be next."

"Paula, she isn't violent, and neither is Connor with mortals— usually," Joe added none too convincingly.

Did Tessa take the Quickening or not? Joe pondered Paula's description. *Something happened he had never read about before— but what did it mean?*

He considered Paula's last statement about Tessa—the woman who was less than forty-eight hours away from marrying Duncan MacLeod. He was silent for a long moment.

"No matter what you feel at this moment, you wouldn't be alive now if it weren't for Tessa and Connor. Immortals behead each other to survive," Joe said in a matter-of-fact voice. "The good ones don't hunt others, but they have to defend themselves from those who do. Duncan MacLeod is one of the peaceful ones. His chronicle has recorded him only going after those who have harmed others— usually they are Immortals—but not always. He has to be pushed pretty far before he draws a sword. Tessa, on the other hand, doesn't have a criminal record. In the twelve years I have observed her—on and off—she has never exhibited any violent tendencies."

"Well she did yesterday," Paula interjected.

Joe nodded. "Since the kidnapping and shooting with, Pallin Wolf and his henchman, Mark Roszca, Tessa's personality has changed radically. It's almost as if she were exhibiting some form of Post-Traumatic Stress Syndrome. She beheaded Mark back in the States when he entered their shop to finish her and Duncan off. Mark was a mortal."

"She has graduated to taking Immortal's heads now."

Joe shook his head. *There is something else going on here—I just feel it. I wish you had seen more and could give me more information. I really need to know if Tessa took any of his Quickening.* His expression was almost pleading to Paula.

She studied Joe's expression with an unsympathetic eye.

"My instructors worked very hard with me so I could get an appointment in paleoanthropology. I am not going to watch people be butchered for a living."

At least a dozen thoughts fought for a voice, but Joe held his comments. Paula was getting worked up and he needed more information from her. Her description was the carrot at the end of the stick and Joe had already taken a big bite. Something in the back of his mind wasn't settling right about this and he just couldn't put his finger on it without a better description.

Is Tessa an Immortal now or not? If not, why did she take his head? Just to save herself? To save Cassandra? Why didn't she run? Why didn't she escape while Roland was coming back to life? Cassandra has been alive for about 3,000 years and is well adept at using a sword. Why did she let Tessa take his head?

Lowering his head, he looked up from under his bushy eyebrows at his Peruvian Watcher. *You had a ringside seat to something I would have desperately liked to have seen. I've got to get more out of you than what you've given me before I will even think of letting you go anywhere.*

"I'll let you rest—we'll talk later." He turned to go.

"You're absolutely right about one thing Paula, you wouldn't be here if it wasn't for Tessa and Connor MacLeod. She can't be pure evil incarnate if she took the time to save you—a complete stranger—think about it."

A hospital assistant was leaving Dudley Dillon's room when Grace reached his floor. She waited until the lunch cart left before knocking and entering his room.

Dudley sat up straighter in bed—several monitors were flashing by his side. Grace noted he was staring at his lunch tray which was untouched.

"Mr. Dillon," Grace began with a smile, "how are you feeling this morning?"

He managed a half smile. "Pretty good I would say for a man who was brought back from the dead. The assistant told me what happened this morning. He said the ambulance paramedics would have given up on me except that you wouldn't let them. You almost couldn't get through all of this to give me CPR," and he prodded the fat on his chest. He looked down and licked his lips.

"Thank you, dear lady, for saving my life. I have no words to express how grateful I really feel."

Grace pulled up a chair and sat beside him. Carefully she placed a hand on his shoulder.

"I don't know what your situation has been in life, Mr. Dillon."

"Dudley, madam—please."

Grace's smile broadened. "OK, Dudley. You're such a young man, with so much life left to live. I want to try and understand why you have been killing yourself for so long."

Dudley looked back at her, his mouth quivering. A moment later he lowered his tear-filled eyes.

"You're morbidly obese, Dudley. And you apparently have a history of smoking as well. Do you know how grave your condition is? You just had four stents put in those veins that feed your heart. Normally we would have done a quadruple bypass but this was faster and the surgeon didn't want to try and grab something from your body that was in equally bad shape."

Her hand slid down to his wrist and turned it over, revealing the Watcher's symbol. "I've seen this before. I don't know what it means—would you like to talk about it?"

"No, doctor," he said very quietly. "I would prefer not to." He kept his eyes averted.

"It's OK, Dudley. I'm not going to force you if you aren't ready. I just want you to know that no matter what kind of history you have had—what gang or cult you may have been involved with in the past—today is a new day for you. Today you've got another chance for a new life. Everything that happened before today is over. You can start again right now. If nothing in your life changes after yesterday, the next time you collapse, I'm afraid you're going to end up in a box."

He slowly bobbed his head but never met her eyes.

"Dudley, before you leave this hospital in a couple of days, I'm going to write a medical order that our counselor is to speak with you daily."

"About my weight," he said.

"No," Grace replied gently and slipped her hand into his. "About your life. Your weight is an outward symptom of a life that is a mess."

"Mr. Dillon," she began again in a more official tone, "you're going to be in the hospital for a couple of days. I will stop in and talk to you as often as I can. When I see someone crying for help as loudly as you are, they most definitely deserve to be heard and I'm a good listener. I don't care what you were involved with, I just don't want to see a young man like you, die."

"Because for me there is no return," he said quietly, cryptically, not expecting a reply.

No there isn't, Grace thought puzzled by his comment. *You'll only go around once and you've barely had a glimpse at life now.* She patted his hand and rose. "I promise I'll be back. If you want to talk further about anything, I'll be here for you."

She started for the door as a second knock was heard. Opening it she met Joe in the doorway.

"Are you a friend, Joe?" she asked, holding the door ajar.

Joe, his hat in hand, nodded gently. "I just found out that Dudley had a heart attack yesterday. How is he doing? Is it alright if I visit with him for a while?"

"Yes, Joe. He can really use a couple of good friends right about now," she said very quietly and left the room.

Dudley sat inert, staring at his plate of food which was still untouched.

"How are you feeling, Mr. Dillon?" Joe asked very carefully.

"I'm alive, Mr. Dawson. I feel like I've been dragged through the streets of Paris, but I'm alive thanks to that good woman."

Joe nodded. "Grace is one of the good Immortals. She has saved a lot of lives throughout her history since the 1300s when they condemned her for witchcraft."

"I never thought I would be one of them," Dudley said and shook his head. "The Watcher's Academy teaches that many Immortals are thoughtless creatures—ignoring the lives of those mortals around them. But that does not describe Grace." He looked away and sighed.

"Sir, I failed my mission. I never expected anything like this would happen to me."

Joe shook his head. "No, you didn't fail. You had a heart attack—something that was outside of your control."

"That was kind of you to say it like that. Grace has a different view." He looked up into Joe's eyes—a sad helpless look. "I think maybe she was right. I've always really known what I've been doing is wrong—I guess it really never mattered—I guess no one ever really respected me as a professional Watcher—no one except you, Mr. Dawson. You had faith in me or you wouldn't have given me Grace. You expected I would be on top of this assignment," he shrugged. "I couldn't even get this right for you." He fell silent.

Joe could see the pain in this young man's eyes. Bearing the brunt of every small failure and screw-up assignment given to him, he had been given assignments that were only fill-ins with no future.

And isn't that how you used him too, Joe's subconscious prodded. *Didn't you request him because he was, in your estimation, easy to get around—a real no trouble Watcher?* Joe closed his eyes, ashamed of himself.

To everyone who looked at him, Dudley was the glorified image of a jolly fat man with a smile painted on his face. Inside he was really crying like Canio in the opera 'Pagliacci'.

La commedia è finita! (The comedy is over) Joe thought—the final words of that tragic play.

"Mr. Dillon," he finally said, "I'd like to hear, in your own words, what happened when you entered the Egyptian Oasis spa. Your colleagues didn't go in and you're the only one who can give me an accurate eye-witness report on at least two Immortals. The place is a total loss. You put your cover and your life on the line in this assignment and I intend to put you in for a commendation. You carried out your duty as a professional Watcher and you deserve it."

Joe pulled Dudley's small book out of his pocket. It had been taken off of him by one of the other hospital Watchers when he was brought in.

"Your notes stopped just after the Quickening exploded in the lobby. If you can recall anything further I would like to hear it." Joe pulled up a chair and sat down beside him.

The barge was lit up from stem to stern that evening though the celebration was very low key.

Duncan stood on the bridge at the bow. Leaning on the rail, he looked out onto the Seine. It was a lovely night. The full moon shone on the water creating sparkling diamonds with each gentle ripple.

Presently, Tessa joined him on the bridge. Leaning against the rail—with her shoulders nestled in his arms—he laid his head against hers as they both gazed out into the water. For a long time they didn't speak, they merely stood and held one another. The gentle and ever so slight swaying of the barge and the sound of that night complimented their mood. Duncan was the first to break the silence.

"I can't believe all that has happened to us in the last two months. We've been together a little over twelve years and in all that time it has mostly been a quiet existence. You've filled me with love, joy, and wonder watching and participating in your life." Duncan shook his head.

"I'm not a superstitious man, Tessa. I never really believed in the curse foretold by the gypsies. But as the years have passed—decades became centuries—I lost people I've loved at the most unusual times. I found myself looking back on it more and more lately. It seemed to me that the moment I asked you to marry me, something—some strange power in this universe has tried to prevent it. I nearly lost you three times in the space of sixty days. I can only assume that I am somehow cursed to be alone."

Tessa glanced back at him then pulled his arms closer around her.

"I'm still here, Duncan. Whatever forces in this universe are trying to keep us apart, they've failed. I'm not superstitious either and I don't believe in curses. I'm with you right now. I survived threats from both mortals and Immortals and I'm still alive. I'm real—and I believe it's by my effort that I'm here now. We each have choices in life, Duncan. When we first met, I was a lot younger and less experienced with life as a whole. You jumped into my life and took my breath away. I soon learned you were someone I could hold close and depend on and I did."

Leaning into him, her lips brushed then kissed the back of his hand.

"Times have changed. I've grown up in my experiences and desires. My brush with death in Seacouver taught me that I can't just sit back in life and be a simple passenger if I want to live. I have to be an active player myself if I'm going to make my way with you in our new life."

"Something has happened to me. The drawing, these visions – I'm going to take life by the horns and push the envelope as far as it goes." She looked to her arm. The streak was a dull pastel red now— a far cry from a few hours ago when it was swollen and angry red. She held it out for Duncan to see.

"I'm healing faster these days—care to speculate?"

Duncan let her comment die. In truth, he didn't have an explanation for what he saw now—no one did this evening. Not Grace, not even Coltec—someone who always seemed to find unusual events easy to justify in some spiritual sense.

Duncan exhaled and rubbed her cheek.

"I guess that's what scares me, Tessa. It's how fiercely you've been grabbing life by the horns lately. I'm just afraid that one day I'm going to wake up and lose you. Maybe that's naive and hopelessly chivalrous, but it's how I feel. This new Tessa is going to take a little bit of getting used to, but I'm ready for her." They were silent for a long time.

"The wedding is the day after tomorrow—do you want to go through with it after everything that just happened to you?" Duncan asked. "We can postpone it you know?"

Tessa turned around completely in his arms.

"Is that what you want? Another twelve years of just planning for that big event? Do you? I don't know how many more twelve-year periods I have to give you. I don't want to wait another moment." She searched his eyes for an answer.

He smiled and kissed her forehead. "I just meant that after all that's happened to you—"

"Out of the question," Tessa said, interrupting. Reaching to his shoulders, she straightened him up. "We've come this far and I've stared down the barrel of mortality already. I'm not going to let something like that put me off track. I know where I want to be with you in life—how about you?"

Duncan nodded. "I just wanted to hear it from you now. I know there are things to do yet and we do have friends here. We both know they're planning some other celebrations for us, but sweetheart, I would like to shut the world out for a day and be alone with you."

Tessa nodded. "If the arrangements haven't been finished by now it really doesn't matter."

Soft music was playing on the barge. She slowly wrapped her arms around his neck and pulled Duncan into an embrace as the music played on.

Sean and Fitz had opened one of Duncan's later years of wine and were swapping stories at least 300 years before his time. It was almost midnight and Duncan, questioning the wisdom of that third glass of wine, went up topside for a breath of fresh air.

"I thought I'd find you out here," Cassandra said as she approached him with a half-empty wine glass.

Duncan's eyes remained on the Seine and Cassandra could feel there was an ever so slight barrier between them. She leaned on the rail then edged closer to him.

"I hear you have a lovely service planned."

Duncan nodded. "Tessa has worked very hard to make what we want to see actually happen so the memories can be captured forever."

Cassandra nodded and gave Duncan a sideways glance. His eyes remained fixed on the Seine.

"Are you still upset about what happened at the Egyptian Oasis spa? I'm sorry, Duncan, I—"

"I don't want to talk about it, Cassandra. Tessa and I are getting married the day after tomorrow—it's a happy occasion. What happened is over and done with. Let's leave it that way."

Cassandra raised an eyebrow and thought, *OK – if that's the way you want it, that's the way it's going to be, but that's not what I'm feeling from you.* She rubbed the glass between her hands, warming the wine.

"It's always going to be this way, Duncan. I think you know that— these occasional, unexpected adventures—they are going to keep happening. You can't control them because you can't control Tessa."

"I'm not trying to control her. Tessa is her own woman. We complement each other."

"Are you so sure about that, Duncan Macleod of the Clan

MacLeod?" Cassandra said using her hypnotic voice. "There were times in the dark of night—long after I knew you were no longer a child—that I thought about you as you grew up, a pre-Immortal man—I sometimes thought on and off, it could be us together. We are, after all, Immortals now. Immortals have always, in many ways, been made for each other," she emphasized projecting her hypnotic words. Her hand reached to his back and began stroking his muscles, teasing him.

"And this Tessa is only temporary—she's mortal."

Duncan shook his head—his glass slipped from his hands into the Seine. He blinked several times and turned sharply to face her.

"Stop it, Cassandra. Stop your tricks," he said softly. "No more of this. We had our time together—it was fleeting but what we had was good—now it is over—now and tomorrow as well. You must accept that we were just not meant to be together—not in that way."

The face Cassandra made was not a happy one.

"Are you really so certain about that?" she asked, an eyebrow raised. "I'm not. Time will tell—it always does in the end."

"Time," Duncan repeated, "is the one universal constant—the thread that runs through everything in life—but not for our lives to be together."

Cassandra backed away and leaned against the rail. She finally nodded.

"OK, I get it. I think it would be better for everyone all around if I left right now and did not attend your wedding."

Duncan raised his eyebrows. Surprised by her reply, he was about to speak when she put a finger to his lips.

She shook her head.

"Please spare me any rhetoric about how you don't want to see me walk away offended from your moment of bliss. Tessa and I had a few words after she took Roland's head. That pretty much ended it for the two of us. I know when it's time to leave and where the door is." She looked out onto the Seine as she spoke.

"This party is getting old and so is my drink," she finished, dropping the glass into the water. "I will see you around, Duncan—all in good time."

Duncan watched as she walked away. He didn't make a move to stop her.

Chapter Forty-five

Duncan considered if drinking a third glass of champagne was honestly a good idea. It was still morning. On the positive side, it would help him tolerate all the fuss that Richie and Fitz were making in the hotel room they had rented to get dressed in for the wedding ceremony today. On the other hand, he hadn't eaten much yet and the alcohol was going to hit him sooner or later.

Duncan was smoothing his jacket over his traditional Highland formal colors when out of the corner of his eye he saw Richie having a minor meltdown once again about his tie. Richie was tugging at his tie in a manner suggesting he was either trying to escape it, or hang himself. *A futile exercise for any Immortal, to say the least*, Duncan mused.

Waving his hands in a frustrated manner, Richie looked to Duncan. "Mac, I just can't get this quite right no matter what I do."

"Here—it goes this way—no—push the tail through like this—oh, let me help you," he finally said, setting his glass down.

"Whoever invented ties should be hanged by one of them," Richie said as Duncan fussed with the knot.

"Come on, Richie, it's not that bad," Duncan said with a light-hearted grin. "You'll get the hang of it in a couple of centuries—by the time you're ready for your wedding, I guarantee."

"By that time, they will be outmoded, and retired to a clothing museum somewhere—right next to the chastity belt line," Richie finished in a smart-mouth tone.

Duncan was looping Richie's tie as Fitz walked by wearing his formal dress shirt but without any pants on.

"Hey, Fitz, you were dressed a moment ago. Where did your pants go?"

"Found a crease in my dress trousers—can't have that today. Will have it out in a spiff—don't mind me." He headed for the bathroom.

"Don't camp out in there," Duncan said casually. "We all need a quick turn by the mirror before we take off."

"I'll be out just as soon as this crease is."

"I thought you said your wardrobe was all wash-and-wear now."

"Not the formal stuff." He passed a hand down his jacket. "Now that you mentioned it, maybe I should press the entire suit," he finished and began stripping.

Oh God, thought Duncan. *I shouldn't have opened my big mouth. Once Fitz starts pressing, it will be hours before he gets his clothing back on.* Duncan reached for his half-drunk third glass of champagne. He swallowed the last drop and took a deep breath. *On a whole everything are moving along rather quickly,* he reassured himself.

"We'd all better move along a little faster," Sean said, "if we want to make it to the church before the girls get there. It is a tradition, after all, that the groom and his attendants are waiting for the bride-to-be and her attendants."

"I don't understand why we all couldn't have simply dressed in the barge and left for the church together," Richie said still pulling on his tie after Duncan had adjusted it.

Duncan shook his head. "It's some new wedding rite that Tessa concocted I'm afraid—and would you leave that tie alone, Richie. I just fixed it," he added. "It looks fine."

Duncan noted that Coltec and Sean were already seeing to the last of their grooming by using anything that reflected an image.

As far as he was concerned, Duncan told himself that he could leave at a moment's notice and so could Richie.

Something moist and 'salty' wafted by Duncan's nose, and he turned to find the source. The bathroom door was wide open—all the lights were on—a huge cloud of steam was billowing out of the doorway forming a fog in the room.

"Fitz, are you in there? Do I have to blow a foghorn to find you?" he finished comically. He blinked. *The wine is definitely hitting me. I actually find this funny.*

"Don't mind me, everybody. The mirror is all yours if you need it," Fitz's energetic voice replied. "I'm just steaming a tough wrinkle out. It's going down for the count right now."

"You mean if anyone can find the mirror in all of this, Fitz," Duncan said waving his hands to cut his way through the fog. "Maybe you should stop before it begins to rain in here."

Fitz put his head out of the fog. His naturally curly hair was curlier from the excess moisture.

"Fitz, I'm sure there isn't a wrinkle left. Put your clothes back on. We have to be ready to go very soon."

Duncan put a hand to his forehead. *How can Fitz take longer than a seventeenth-century women to get dressed? This can't be happening to me now.*

Duncan was more than happy to have his friends with him on this very special occasion, though he did appreciate a more quiet and solitary life. In times like these, he really wanted to turn down the volume of life around him, a bit.

OK, I'm ready, he thought. *I'll just step outside for a short walk and get some air until these kids are ready to go.*

"I'm going to step outside for a moment," he said to everyone. "We're going to have to leave in about ten minutes. Fitz, that means you get your pants on now. The wrinkle removing session is officially over."

"Who's driving?" Sean asked.

"Connor," Duncan replied. "That reminds me, he should have been getting ready with us." He shook his head.

You don't tell Connor he has to get ready in a specific place, Duncan reminded himself. *Connor didn't say where he was staying. I don't have to worry about Connor, he can take care of himself—it's these guys I better keep an eye on.*

"Hey guys, I think Duncan's got cold feet and is planning to escape," Richie joked as Duncan started for the door.

"Yeah sure, Richie," he replied.

"What, Duncan MacLeod of the Clan MacLeod evading a challenge? "Fitz said poking his head out of the bathroom. "Someone hand me a camera."

"Knock it off, guys," Duncan replied in mock gruffness. "The only challenge is getting all of you ready on time—and that means in the next few minutes. I figure if I step outside maybe you guys will be ready faster."

His hand was on the doorknob when everyone felt the arrival of another Immortal. When that familiar feeling hit, this time everyone ran for their swords and took up a defensive position. Duncan resisted that action, shaking his head. *Connor is the person I expect to be here now,* thought Duncan. This was the logical choice, but for some reason everyone had suddenly gone on high alert.

How much is this champagne really affecting me? I sense the presence, but it is just not as strong. Caution took hold of his numbed senses. He peered through the peephole in the door before opening it. Relaxing, he waved an all clear to the group before opening the door. A warm feeling flooded his senses.

"Connor, it is about time you showed up. I thought we were going to have to call out the cavalry to find you."

Connor smiled. "Are you kidding? I wouldn't be late for Duncan MacLeod's wedding for anything." Connor was wearing a formal tuxedo shirt, vest, and pants—under his usual tan trench coat. He returned a sly grin. "Something old, something new," he quoted the famous wedding saying.

"Well, that leaves, 'something borrowed and something blue'," Duncan filled in the rest of the line. "You just need to supply the last two and you are complete."

Connor motioned to through the door with a grand gesture. "Gentlemen, your chariot awaits."

Duncan and Tessa had arranged for a former novitiate, instructed by Darius, to perform the service. Duncan had wanted Darius to do the honor, but since his untimely death at the hands of Horton, Duncan had sought a way to honor the memory of his friend.

The service they had agreed upon was simple. Once the Roman Catholic Rites were fulfilled, Duncan had invited a Buddhist monk, in honor of Hideo Koto—his Japanese Samurai mentor, from whom he received the dragon katana many years ago; and, Coltec—to ask a blessing for their union, each according to the spirits they held sacred.

It would be a short ride to the church and afterward their friends had planned a surprise reception. Both he and Tessa secretly knew about it already.

"We better get going," Connor said again. "Let's get this troupe in the car, Duncan."

They started off down the familiar streets to St. Joseph's Chapel when suddenly Connor took a sharp left turn and headed in a completely different direction.

"Do you need a map?" Duncan asked as Connor wended his way away down to the Seine, near Notre Dame Cathedral. "Connor, where are you going? The church is back that way."

A sheepish grin formed on his face. "I'm taking you to get married, of course."

"But the only thing in this direction is the Seine," Duncan said gesturing out the window.

"Hey, I'm the driver. I know where I'm going."

Everyone looked to one another as Connor pulled the van into park in front of the Seine.

"We're here," Connor said and hopping out of the car, walked around and held the door open for Duncan. "Well, everybody out."

Slowly Duncan got out of the car and looked around. There was nothing here except the Seine and a deserted tour boat boardwalk. "I don't get it he said, what's this all about?"

Connor gestured to the boarding platform. Duncan looked from the platform to Connor as he walked slowly in the direction he was being herded. Reaching the end, he returned a gesture of '*I still don't get it.*'

It was a bright sunny day and a gentle breeze was blowing. Duncan could hear the quiet sound of leaves rustling and—a motor? He looked up the Seine to see a tour boat slowly approaching the boarding ramp. As he watched he heard the boat's engine die, and it began to drift slowly toward the platform.

Duncan blinked as it came closer. This tour boat was like none he had ever seen. The passenger seats were gone. The long deck resembled a float of flowers, ribbons, balloons, and white bells which hung from its lines high above the wheelhouse. A half wrought-iron trellis enclosed a modest open chapel. It was a floating wedding grotto.

In the rear of the boat stood his Tessa. She was wearing her lovely short, pink lace wedding dress, a brief and symbolic hair-veil, and the beautiful Celtic love knot necklace he had given her. She waved her bright bouquet of flowers at him.

"Tessa?" he called, astonished.

"Jump, Duncan! *Jump!*" she called as the boat continued to slowly drift alongside the dock. "You jumped into my boat before," she called louder. "If you want to marry me now, you'll have to jump into my life, like you did back then."

Duncan gestured with both hands as he followed the boat to the edge of the platform.

"In my formal Highland kilt, wrap, vest, and waistcoat?" He called. "You want me to jump wearing all of this—now?"

Tessa nodded vehemently.

"**Now**! Hurry, Duncan, I'm drifting away," she exclaimed.

A burst of adrenaline hit Duncan clearing the champagne cobwebs from his brain.

The Seine tour boat—almost thirteen years ago. I jumped into the boat to avoid a fight with someone whom I felt could have taken my head—I jumped into Tessa's life back then—I have to jump now!

He backed up a couple of steps then lunging forward ran the last few steps of the dock. His foot caught the very edge of the dock and he propelled himself over the few feet of water to the edge of the boat. This time, he almost didn't make it.

Tessa reached out, grabbing his Highland wrap, and was nearly hauled into the water herself as Duncan fought for a foothold and balance. Tessa—recovering, helped him onto the boat and into her arms.

"This is the very boat, Duncan. Connor helped me locate the exact boat and operator. I was standing right up there when I first saw you. You jumped into my life exactly the same way."

"Not exactly," he said straightening his vest and outer jacket. "I was a lot less formal back then," he finished with a big smile.

"I thought this would be very symbolic for us to remember," Tessa finished pulling her Highlander close.

The boat's operator fired up the engine and put it into reverse, returning to the dock to retrieve the rest of the party. Once everyone was on board, he started the motor once again to give the boat a good push, then cut the engine and let it drift silently and slowly with the current.

Connor stepped forward. "I'm doing the honors today with the lovely Tessa, Duncan," he said as he held out his arm for Tessa to join him.

Tessa looped her arm around his firmly, smiling. They took their positions at the rear of the boat and at the beginning of the long wedding carpet down the center to wait for their cue.

Tessa's dress had no train, so Ceirdwyn and Grace—each bearing a small basket of white rose petals, took up their positions before her, preparing to symbolically shower her path to Duncan with petals.

Duncan and his Best Man, Fitz, along with the rest of his groom-attendants, took up their positions at the front—in the small grotto by the chapel altar. One of the male flower attendants, from the florist shop, approached and pinned the ceremonial white carnation boutonniere on Duncan's Scottish lapel—briefly exposing a small segment of his Watcher's tattoo.

It figures, thought Duncan. He gave no hint of noticing as the young man pinned the companion carnations on the rest of his attendants then stepped to the side of the boat.

Duncan nodded, and the Master of Music started the song, 'Eres tú'.

Connor proudly looked to Tessa as if he were actually the father of the bride.

Before them, the flower-girls began spreading a living white carpet.

Each step brings her closer to me—to become a part of me, Duncan mused. Symbolism shaped his every thought and feeling as he watched her walk.

Tessa walked slowly to the front—to the chapel—to her new life.

Connor took her hand—removing it from his sleeve and entwining it around Duncan's arm—the symbolic act of *'giving'* and *'bonding'* with this new man, who would become a part of her in this new union.

Ceirdwyn and Grace sprinkled the last of the petals by their feet then moved to the bride's side of the alcove.

Tessa and Duncan faced each other for just an instant then turned to face the Father and the altar, which had been consecrated for their marriage ceremony in the Roman Catholic Rite.

"Do you, Duncan MacLeod of the Clan MacLeod, take Tessa to be your lawfully wedded wife, from this day forward?"

"I do," he said with the utmost conviction, and with absolute resolve. *My 400 years of life alone will be no more,* he thought. *Whatever curse has denied me a wife for so long has finally been broken.*

Turning to Tessa, the Father repeated the question. Tessa *felt* the words and their depth as he spoke—her answer, an eternal, "I do."

"Before I pronounce them husband and wife, Duncan and Tessa have each prepared words they would like to share before us all." The priest stepped back as Tessa and Duncan turned to one another once again.

A faint sparkle of light, high up on the footbridge near the Notre Dame cathedral went unnoticed in the clear, crisp morning.

Horton shifted his stance, the crosshair of his high-powered rifle scope moved across the guests on the boat. He blinked then leaned back into his rifle, steadying himself. His focus drifted—first on Grace, then slowly to Duncan MacLeod.

It would do little good to shoot an Immortal, he thought. *I would only make you angry by having you die in public—now how would you explain that to everyone? I would have just kicked a hornet's nest. If the time were right, then yes—but not yet.* A smile formed on his face. *But I know how to hurt you, Duncan—I know how to cut you to the quick.* Slowly he shifted his sight once again, this time to Tessa, framing her perfectly in the crosshair. His finger tightened on the trigger—*Tessa will die at the altar—her life snatched away from you before you could ever enjoy one sweet moment of marriage.*

An instant later, his scope suddenly and unexpectedly went dark.

Xavier Saint Cloud put his hand on the rifle scope pushing the gun aside.

"Oh, don't be such a spoilsport just because you didn't receive a wedding invitation," he said in a sarcastic tone.

Horton looked up sharply at him. *I don't need a sword,* he thought. *I could bite your head off right now.*

Xavier huffed as a dangerous expression spread across his face.

"A wedding is a happy occasion James—don't go and spoil it by killing the bride. You'll make MacLeod very unhappy if he were to lose his chance to consummate their wedding night."

"What do you care about MacLeod's happiness," he snapped back.

"Patience, my eager Watcher," he chided. He paused, considering Horton as one would an errant child. "Patience is something you learn with experience and time."

"Do you have a point to all this glib rambling, or do you just like to hear yourself speak?" Horton spat back, his tongue sharp.

Xavier chuckled then shrugged. "A first-year anniversary is very special for newlyweds, and I am planning a surprise—for both of them." Leaning against the rail, he settled in to watch the tour boat recede from sight. "Happy anniversary, Duncan MacLeod of the Clan MacLeod," he said with a knowing smile.

"What are you planning?"

Xavier glanced toward Horton only briefly, dismissing him and his question before returning his attention to the Seine. "I'll let you know when it matters—when it's time."

Tessa, placed her fingers gently in the palms of Duncan's hands, spoke.

"It's been twelve years since our souls and bodies met and we have learned along this way that nothing we face together can be worse than the emptiness we feel when we are not together. I believe in you, the person you will grow to be, the person I will learn to be by your side, and the couple we will learn to be together. You have been my best friend, mentor, playmate, confidant, and above all, my greatest challenge. So, I am truly blessed to be a part of your life, which as of today becomes our life together. Only forever can I say I love you."

Duncan nodded then spoke.

"I see these vows not as promises, but as privileges. I get to laugh with you and cry with you, care for you and share with you. I get to run with you and walk with you; build with you and live with you. These might seem as simple, normal daily life situations all mortals go through, but they become magical when you show me how to appreciate every minute of them. You know me better than anyone else in this world and somehow still you manage to love me. All the tears I have cried, and all the blows I have taken, all the nights I have spent alone and scared, surviving and living, determined not to give in, have shown me the way to you. I have been blessed."

Nodding to Coltec and the Buddhist monk to step forward, they each in their turn asked a blessing for this union.

In closing, the Father made the sign of the cross over Duncan and Tessa.

"And now, by the powers vested in me, I pronounce you Man and Wife. You may kiss the bride."

Tessa and Duncan embraced then faced their guests. This was a special moment—both felt it in their hearts. They felt the quiet excitement of their friends all around them. It was a joyous moment.

"I take great pleasure this day in introducing to you a new union and a new life—Duncan and Tessa MacLeod of the Clan MacLeod."

Epilogue

High up in a penthouse glass wedding bedroom suite—atop one of Paris' fashionable hotels—a sparse trail of party favors, a couple of champagne glasses and white rose petals littered the plush carpeted floor all the way from the front door to the bedroom. The smell of jasmine perfumed candles, flickering on the marble window ledge added an air of mystery as quiet music by Enya was played softly in the background.

"Duncan," she called in a provocative tone, "by the time you get rid of all those Highland clothes, I will have been asleep for hours," Tessa teased.

"Oh, I don't think so," came the eager reply. "Motivation works magic on me. Do you want to see how fast I can get out of a kilt?"

"Oh, not necessarily," she lazily called back. "Anticipation works near miracles on my libido too," Tessa replied as she licked her lips and fastened the front of her provocative honeymoon lingerie—a sheer, long lacy two-panel fly away, attached to an off the shoulders bra-strap top, with a matching string bikini bottom.

Strange, Tessa thought. *No matter what you may believe isn't important in your life, often times it is.* Getting married was one of those things. *After living and loving together for more than twelve years, I thought the ceremony would only be a formality—a confirmation of our love in front of our friends.* But once again her relationship with Duncan was teaching her to embrace new sensations each and every hour. Fortunately, this was one of the sweetest ones she could remember in a long time. *Strange, how the littlest things in life have the most lasting meaning. Nothing has really changed outwardly with us – or has it?*

Somehow she felt different than she had this morning. True, the champagne bubbles had tickled their noses and lips, mellowing their senses as the bright liquid slid willingly past their eager pallets. But there was a lot more meaning behind those words, "*I do*" then she ever realized there would be. *It's something I'm glad we finally did,* she mused. *I wonder why we waited so long. To see the look on Duncan's face today told me that this was an accomplishment for him as well. Even Richie—today Richie looked more like a man than he had the entire time I've known him.*

Crawling onto the bed, Tessa assumed a sexy cat like pose as her waving foot dropped the last shoe off the tip of her toe. She waited, watching the bathroom door. She didn't have to wait long.

Duncan was smiling as he slowly crossed the room wearing only his smoking-red pajama bottoms. His eyes scanned his lovely bride. *Yes, anticipation is just fine with me too.*

"Do you think we can accomplish anything more here than we could have on the deck of the barge," Duncan said sheepishly.

"I don't know," Tessa replied in a coy tone and patted the bed beside her. "I vote we find out. Shall we each take notes?"

Duncan stretched out next to her. "I don't think so. The Watchers do that enough as it is."

Tessa rolled toward him and drew her finger down the length of his muscular arm in foreplay. "We're seven stories up. If I so much as see a Watcher pasted to those glass walls over there, taking notes— I'm going to—"

"Then maybe we better turn out the lights fast so you don't kill anybody with my katana tonight," Duncan teased as he reached for the switch.

The moon rose full and bright, larger-than-life against its Parisian skyline backdrop. Its soft glow, a gentle caress to the ardent loving expressed below. Slowly as the night progressed, its white hue faded and was replaced with a dark ochre color, and eventually a brightly illuminated reddish hue—a *Blood Moon* night.

A satisfied smile formed on Tessa's sweat-beaded face. She casually wiped aside the moist strands of hair that were sticking to her rosy cheek aside.

Duncan finally exhaled and relaxed, returning the expression as Tessa rolled over and settled into the crook of his arm.

I actually think I tired him out, she thought as she lay beside him— each holding the other in quiet adoration. Casually they looked up and onto a perfect red moon hanging like an orb from the vault of the heavens. It was a long moment before Duncan broke the silence.

"You know this is a special night—not just because it's our wedding night, but because of that," he finished, pointing upwards.

"Do you think tonight's eclipse will influence our lives as husband and wife?" he asked metaphorically, and rhetorically.

Tessa considered what Duncan was saying. "OK, so it's rare— maybe it is a sign. How about this—when an Immortal and mortal marry, it's a rare occurrence anyway—so this is how the cosmos celebrates," she finished playfully. "What does it mean to others?" she asked.

Duncan considered what he had gleaned from the last 200 years of travel. "A Blood Moon is usually considered a significant omen of future events—immediate and distant."

"Good or bad?"

"Depends upon who you talk to. Both, in some cases," Duncan replied. "Some cultures were very fearful of such an eclipse. Some thought it was the preludes to the end of existence, the world, or life and times as they knew it. Some of the Christian groups—even today—refer to passages in the Bible –Joel and Acts—that talk about a series of Blood Moon eclipses before the end of the world."

"It is simply an eclipse," Tessa said.

"Some of the ancient cultures charted the movement of the stars and planets, Venus for example, for agriculture, ceremony, and passage of a year. They tended to interpret these planetary, lunar, and stellar motions as if they were living beings." He shrugged and pulled Tessa closer.

"What about that culture?" Tessa angled her gaze toward Solo. The small statue stood silently on a nightstand by the corner, illuminated in the soft reflection of the red moon.

Tessa's favorite little gold llama statue's feet were still sticky with wedding cake. Tessa had arranged for Solo to be on the top of the ceremonial wedding cake when it was brought out. Both she and Duncan had cut the first piece together, under Solo's watchful eye.

"The South American cultures—Mayans, Incas, and Aztecs—were generally fearful of the Blood Moon eclipse. This lunar event is so rare they must have thought it was being influenced by evil spirits."

"I know you told me once. Where did you get Solo from?"

Duncan shifted his position, pulling the silk sheet back over them squarely. "The statues were all unearthed at several dig sites. Solo came from an area near a volcano in Argentina. Some of the locals were working under Kawill at the time. I knew them."

"The Immortal I saw you talking to in the airport?"

Duncan nodded. "Kawill has been mining these cultural treasures away from its people for centuries and selling them to the highest bidder. Not all of it ended up in museums, though. Some he kept and some he destroyed."

Tessa propped up on an elbow. "Why destroy art? Especially art that is that old, Duncan. That's a loss to everyone. Is he mad?"

"Very superstitious. I have heard stories that he believes some of these artifacts are keys to a prophecy about his death. After he received word that this statue was found, I understood he practically tore the local depot apart. He was desperate to find it."

Duncan smiled. "Do you remember a ways back when you had your first exhibit at that small gallery opened? I was away for a couple of days, assisting in the arrangements to acquire your Solo. The statue was gone before Kawill got to the dig site. I doubt if Solo would exist today if he had gotten his hands on it first."

"What about the others?"

"I asked some of the locals to send me a message if any more were found. The others were unearthed from dig sites scattered up and down the area. Soon after they were found, they quietly left the area as well. I recently bought them through a third party. If the statues represent some mystical key to Kawill's superstitious puzzle, he is going to have a very hard time deciphering it now. Kawill knows I have at least one statue. He asked me in the airport."

"And you told him you did? Why did you do that?"

"He asked—why not? He doesn't know which one. Actually, I think I have the ones he is looking for," Duncan said with a very satisfied smile. "He thinks the others are still lost in some art dealer's hands. He'll probably spend the better part of his immortal life combing through every museum, antique shop, and garage sale on this planet trying to find them." Duncan chuckled. "Don't worry. He's not getting your Solo."

An unhappy expression formed on Tessa's face. "These statues are actually national art treasures. Solo is the property of the people of Argentina. I suppose you'll have to return Solo to them."

He kissed her forehead gently.

"Sweetheart, if I did that now, Kawill would just find Solo and take him, even if he had to destroy a museum and kill everyone in it to get him. He has no respect for that. Eventually I'll see to it that they all get back to the people they belong to, but not during your lifetime. You're having too much fun with Solo."

Tessa snuggled into Duncan's warm shoulder. "I am drawn to Solo for some reason—I always have been. I really can't explain it—I don't even care why. Solo is my little mascot. Somehow, I feel Solo is an adventure for me, just waiting to happen."

"I'm sure he'll lead you to it when the time is right," Duncan finished playfully then pulled the soft silk sheet over their heads for a little more loving.

*The End *
of this Story—and the beginning of a New Life for
Duncan and Tessa MacLeod of the Clan MacLeod.

Highlander *Imagine:*

Beyond Infinity

Slowly, Kawill Rockford's hand reached into the box on his desk once again—his other hand held the phone's receiver tightly against his ear. A rumble of thunder from a late fall storm building outside his Argentinian hotel room was making phone reception difficult. What he was hearing of the report from the other end displeased him greatly.

Kawill—an immortal Olmec descendent almost 1,200 years old—prided himself on his smooth self-control. But at the moment, all he wanted to do was crush the life out of something.

A crisp snapping sound from the box brought his attention back to it. His hand brought out a small, now broken, sculpture from a local dig site – a carved wooden llama. This ancient native artifact was more than 300 years old. Kawill knew the piece was authentic and its potential value to a collector. It had survived intact in the dry climate surrounding Llullaillaco, the slumbering stratovolcano, which lay in the distance from his hotel room. It had been carefully excavated, cleaned, and brought to him by one of his workers who knew better than to put so much as a scratch on anything he carried to his boss.

Now, slowly and meticulously, Kawill's fingers began breaking the remaining legs off the sculpture, one by one, destroying yet another irreplaceable piece of antiquity. In the next instant, he slammed the receiver on his desk effectively ending the call. His eyes focused only briefly on the small statue—slowly, he snapped its neck, then smiled. Dropping it back into the box he shoved it roughly to the end of the table then rose.

"The Highlander," he said quietly. "So this is your game. No doubt this is all just a big joke to you." Grabbing the small box, he threw it into the trash. A violent temper boiled under his businessman façade which he had carefully cultivated for centuries.

"You have absolutely no idea what you have trespassed upon and in whose face you are flaunting your little escapade."

A sudden gust of wind blew the first drops of the South American storm against the window as Kawill turned, piercing brown eyes gazing out into the rain.

"You haven't the slightest clue what you've held in your hands, or its connection to a power beyond any immortality we understand," he finished quietly grinding his teeth. Reaching for his phone, he dialed another number; his call connected after a long moment. Kawill's instructions were brief.

"Find Duncan MacLeod—and don't call me back until you do." Pressing the receiver, he ended the call and then traded the phone in his hand for his two-handed machete—his weapon of choice for taking the heads of those who stood in his way.

"You've meddled in my affairs for the last time, Highlander," he whispered.

Author's Notes

The authors wish to thank Ms. Gabriela Recagno, Directora del Museo de Arqueología de Alta Montaña (*Museum of High Altitude Archaeology*) in Salta, Argentina, for permission to use an image of the llama statue in this book. This statue was the inspiration for 'Solo' in this, and other, **Highlander** *Imagine* stories. It is part of a collection of llama statues, found with the mummies of three children offered as a sacrifice to the Inca gods on Mount Llullaillaco in Salta, Argentina approximately 500 years ago. Museum exhibit information can be found at their website: http://www.maam.gob.ar (May, 2015).

The stories of the child sacrifices mentioned in this book are fictionalized, but this practice was actually quite prevalent in the cultures mentioned herein. For more information about ancient South American cultures, search key words: Mayan, Incan, and Aztec.

The Olmec civilization is believed to have existed between about 1200 BC (BCE) until about 400 BC. These people were the forerunners of the subsequent Mesoamerican cultures (Mayans and Aztecs). For more information, search keywords: Olmec, Mesoamerican, and 'Ancients in Mesoamerica' and 'The Story of Chocolate'.

The volcanic eruption mentioned in this story occurred approximately 40,000 years ago west of Naples, Italy. This significant geological event is thought to have contributed to a severe cold spell or 'volcanic winter' in the Northern Hemisphere and possibly pushing the Neanderthals into extinction. Recent theories cast doubt on the volcanic extinction theory. For more information, search keywords: Neanderthals, Volcanic eruption, Naples, Italy

About the Authors
Wendy Lou Jones

Professional speaker, and actress, Wendy Jones has held professional positions in the USA, Canada, and Austria.

The author of numerous books, journal and trade magazine articles, the genera includes scientific and lay-magazines as well as books – fiction and non-fiction.

Works can be found in: Journal of Single Cell Biology, Medicinal Foods, Renal Nutrition, Bio-Techniques and Immunogenic; the former iSeries Weekly, and e-Business Quarterly, Midrange Computing, and Showcase Magazine; the pioneering renal demineralization book series: **Food Fuel Fitness** and **More Bio-fuel Less Bio-waste**; as well as fiction series – **Golden Downs**, and **Jerimy**. Wendy also holds patents in plant science, and scientific research devices in the USA.

Liliana Bordoni

Professor and Instructor of English as a Foreign Language in Argentina, Liliana Bordoni works with accomplished students – from the high school level through University. As a dynamic, self-starter in educational projects, and teacher trainer in the University, her work has been recognized by her students and colleagues in the educational profession. Her present passion is working with a group of self-funded trainee students - *The Pretenders* - crafting scripts and choreographing stage performances as a vehicle for youth English language instruction. Their past and current works have been acknowledged by educators as 'a breath of fresh creative air' for young students. Liliana is also the architect for the Highlander *Imagine* series.

CPSIA information can be obtained
at www.ICGtesting.com
Printed in the USA
FFOW02n1829170417
34607FF